SEAMSTRESS

NEW ORLEANS

Books by Diane C. McPhail

THE ABOLITIONIST'S DAUGHTER

THE SEAMSTRESS OF NEW ORLEANS

Published by Kensington Publishing Corp.

SEAMSTRESS

NEW ORLEANS

DIANE C. McPHAIL

JOHN SCOGNAMIGLIO BOOKS
KENSINGTON BOOKS
www.kensingtonbooks.com

JOHN SCOGNAMIGLIO BOOKS are published by

Kensington Publishing Corp.
119 West 40th Street
New York, NY 10018

All Kensington titles, imprints and distributed lines are available at special quantity discounts for bulk purchases for sales promotion, premiums, fund-raising, educational or institutional use.

Special book excerpts or customized printings can also be created to fit specific needs. For details, write or phone the office of the Kensington Special Sales Manager: Kensington Publishing Corp., 119 West 40th Street, New York, NY, 10018. Attn. Special Sales Department. Phone: 1-800-221-2647.

The JS and John Scognamiglio Books logo is a trademark of Kensington Publishing Corp.

Library of Congress Card Catalogue Number: 2021953423

ISBN: 978-1-4967-3815-8
First Kensington Hardcover Edition: June 2022

ISBN: 978-1-4967-4142-4 (trade)
ISBN: 978-1-4967-3817-2 (e-book)

10 9 8 7 6 5 4 3 2

Printed in the United States of America

SEAMSTRESS

NEW ORLEANS

CHAPTER 1

At the first thought of following him, fear so overwhelmed her that she had to remind herself it was only a thought. But that thought persisted, beyond and over her fear, luring her like a child provoking a dog with a snatched-away crust of bread. Now Constance was prepared. A menswear suit lay on her bed, waiting for her. Today she would follow him, would hopefully relieve her rising anxiety under the burden of Benton's penchant for secrecy and his persistent demands for money from her trust. She would not wait longer to expose his secrets. She had her suspicions, but she needed certainty.

Downstairs, the front door slammed as Benton left the house for the depot. Obsessed with punctuality, her husband was eternally early. Now she just had time to disguise herself, reach the station, and board the train before it pulled out. The difficulty would be to slip from her own home unnoticed. The unseasonable late autumn heat impeded her haste. Outside her open window, the birds chirped and fluttered as if nothing in the world were amiss. Constance retrieved the trim sack coat, designed for a young man, and slipped her arms into the sleeves, then tugged the lapels close in front. The suit fit her narrow body well, especially the slim trousers. Only the waist was too big. By an inch or two. She cinched the belt tighter and smoothed the fabric around her, leaving the gathered excess concealed in back, beneath her jacket. At the dressing table, she opened a small box and retrieved a bottle of spirit gum. Hands trembling now, she applied a line of it above her brows. While it grew tacky, she repeated the process with a thicker application above her lip. She tested the brow line with her finger and prayed the wide ash brows would adhere. A wave of relief washed through her when they stuck like her own, though her skin felt as if it would peel right off. She pressed again. Then the tapered mustache was over her lip. Could the image in the mirror be her? Could it not be her? That was the crucial point.

She slipped a gray fedora over the ash-brown wig. Ah, now. There he was. That young boy-man she needed to be, even if the mustache seemed a bit heavy for one as young as she appeared. Constance rose, then turned back to snatch up a bottle of alcohol, which she would need to remove the spirit gum, and dropped it into her satchel. Its buckles defied her. She stopped. Took a deep breath, buckled them more slowly. There. It was done. Upstairs she heard the girls waking and Analee bidding them a good morning. She picked up the satchel and slipped hastily from the house. No one saw her.

The air was clear; the day bright. Nothing in it seemed amiss. Ticket in hand, Constance stepped aboard the Illinois Central Chicago–New Orleans Limited just before it eased out of Union Station, its pulsing cadence gaining velocity, its momentum quieting into a settled tempo as the fleeting byways of the city gave way to the countryside.

Placid as the woods and intermittent farmland seemed, inside those sooty cars Constance noted a range of human emotion that vibrated in the closed air, a vibration like that in her own being. As she made her unsteady way from one car to the next, a harried mother under a thin shawl lifted her breast to soothe a fretful infant. One car back Constance cringed as a young wife, stylishly clad in a velvet-trimmed amber suit, lowered her head and wiped a gloved hand across her cheek at the hissed reproach of her husband that she had packed five shirts rather than six, in case one should get soiled. At the last seat an elderly man rested his half-bald head against the window, the waves of his white walrus mustache bouncing erratically in tempo with his intermittent snores. Across the aisle a man laid aside his book to gaze at his two children, who were giggling wildly as they pointed his Kodak box camera at the old man. A woman two seats away frowned at him as the children continued running up and down, snatching at the camera and arguing about whose turn it was.

At last, in the gentlemen's lounge, Constance spied her husband, seated with two other men at a card table. Trying to attract as little attention as possible, she settled herself in a leather armchair, opened the *Times-Picayune* to shield herself. She peered past the loose edge at the table of gamblers but was torn by the dire headlines of the paper: DIAMOND CITY, NORTH CAROLINA, DESTROYED BY HURRICANE: LOSS OF LIFE COUNTED IN THE THOUSANDS. Such ominous news, an unprecedented hurricane gathering strength across the Outer Banks, destroying an entire town, coffins and houses floating across the sound. Her stomach contracted at the death toll and the details of destruction. Perhaps the worst yet in history. And yet so far New Orleans had been spared from this year's storms.

In her peripheral vision she scanned the men hunched round the table, each focused on his hand of cards. Benton, his back to her, visibly intense, was thrumming the edges of his cards in silence. On the table in front of him, a meager little stack of chips. How much had he lost? In so little time? It couldn't have been more than half an hour. He fingered the pocket where she knew he kept a roll of money—when he had any. The other men waited, one with a strange mustache—she tried to remember the complicated term for it—that swept down and around his chin. A palpable tension vibrated in the air.

Beneath them, she felt more than heard the monotonous undertone of metal rumbling on metal. She heard the quiet dealing of cards, the muttered bets, the hard click of chips as she tried to concentrate on the hurricane. Suddenly, she jumped, the newspaper crackling, as Benton slammed his cards onto the table in furious resignation. The other men closed their hands, their cards unrevealed. No one spoke. After picking up his one remaining chip, Benton flipped it like a coin, slapped it on the table next to the burgeoning pile in the center.

"Might as well filch it all," he said. "Just for fucking luck. Yours, that is, goddamnit. Sure as hell ain't mine."

He rose, lobbed his money onto the table, stretched his back and neck to collect himself, and glanced around, disregarding the men's continued gaze on him. Constance ducked her head as he stared at her momentarily. He edged toward the far end of the car, then halted long enough to order a whiskey from the bar and pick up a folded newspaper. He dropped into a nail-head leather armchair, sipped at the whiskey, tapping the unopened paper against his knee, rage and despair rigid behind the flat line of his lips and the twitching of his closed eyelids. Then, slipping a pack of Picayune Extra Milds from his pocket, Benton watched the two men exit the car. He tossed the remaining whiskey down, slammed the glass on the table.

In no hurry, Benton, with a defeated air, rose and laid the still-folded paper on the chair. Again, he stretched his neck and back, then turned toward the opposite exit. Slipping an unlit cigarette between his lips, he stepped out the door to the open vestibule. Where was he going? Constance crumpled her paper, then tucked it carelessly between the seat and the arm of her chair. She rose, brushed at her suit, holding the hard edge of the seat back for stability before she made her way up the aisle, adjusting her gait to the rocking of the train. A blast of hot air and the sharp rumble of the wheels sheared into her as the door released onto the open vestibule, then clanged shut behind her.

Benton was just standing there. He flipped his wasted cigarette out into the wind, watched it fall, still glowing, onto the gravel. It disappeared, became invisible as the train passed on. Constance averted her face, focused on a high trestle coming into view up ahead. Her body taut, she clasped the vertical brass handrail. Benton eased closer, cleared his throat.

"You're very young for such a fine mustache," Benton murmured. "Still got that fine, soft boy skin. Mighty young to be traveling alone."

When she did not respond, he laid one hand on her shoulder, the other on her hip. Immobilized, she felt him rotate himself around her slight body, his back to the water now, obstructing her view. She turned her face as Benton touched the mustache.

She opened her eyes, stared into his. Benton froze, paralyzed by those eyes.

"You," he gasped. His hand gripped her arm.

She tore herself free, her hand pushing against him, as he stepped back, floundered on the edge of the step as he grasped at the handrail. The car door swung open. A man raced through the vestibule, arm outstretched. A flash of disorientation. A child's face at the window of the adjoining car. Off-balance, she threw up her hand. Benton's slipped from the brass handrail, and his body tilted backward, arms and feet floundering in the open air.

Constance pressed her back hard against the wall, gripping the handrail, as if the passing wind might lift her behind him. She stared at the passing terrain. The fields, the woods, a turnrow here and there, a fence, a barn—all tranquil. As if nothing had transpired.

CHAPTER 2

At the next stop Constance dismounted with her valise. Fear wrenched through her like a knife ripping through tangled yarn. What had she seen? What had she done? Was he dead? Was he injured or mangled and struggling even now for help? The terrible smack of his body hitting the water reverberated in her ears. She envisioned him below the surface, arms akimbo, eyes open, staring back at her.

Outside the depot on a hard wooden bench, Constance sat, struggling to quiet her breath, heaving in shock. The false eyebrows felt as if they might peel her flesh away. She could feel her skin ripped, blood flowing into her eyes like tears, her face a mask of horror. She raised her fingers to touch. The brows remained firmly in place and would until she deliberately removed them and the rest of this disguise. Finding a place to do that consumed her, to become herself again. Fear consumed her. She would never be herself again.

Hand trembling, Constance slid her money beneath the ticket window for a return to New Orleans. A washroom on the train would be less obvious than one in the station. She could shed these tainted clothes and change into her dress, but she must first find a corridor with no witnesses. Her steps mounting the train were unsteady. She tripped and instinctively reached for the hem of her nonexistent skirt. She glanced around in alarm, but no one seemed to have noticed. In fact, there were few other passengers boarding. As the train pulled out, the washroom in that car proved vacant; she entered, heart pounding, and locked the door. The space was cramped, making changing awkward. The floor was dirty where the now discarded trousers lay. The train lurched, and she banged her elbow on the sink, grimaced, grabbed its edge to hold her balance. She felt that her chest might cave in as she struggled into her petticoat, then the seven-gored green skirt. Her hands trembled almost to the point of impossibility as she strained to button her shirtwaist. A sudden horror overwhelmed her, pulsing like the rails below. Her mind saturated itself with the sight of his fall, the look of his eyes, the flailing arms. Constance lowered the wooden seat of the water closet and sat there, her face in her hands, until someone knocked at the door.

"Just a moment, please," she said as audibly as she could muster.

She rose, smoothed her skirt, buttoned three remaining buttons, and tied the bow at her neck. The remaining spirit gum lifted off with the alcohol, though her forehead was red where she had scrubbed. A bit of skin itched at the corner of her left eyebrow. Removing the man's wig mussed her hair, hard as she had tried to hold it tight to her scalp with a hairnet. In any event, she had to pull out the soft rolls of her own blond hair around her face and smooth it as best she could.

Another knock.

"I'm sorry. Please. Just one moment."

Straining to see her reflection in the cracked, heavily smudged mirror, Constance patted the fallen strands of hair into place, hairpins between her teeth, then anchored them in her high chignon.

The knock came again. In haste, Constance mounted her

small green feathered toque and rammed the hatpin through. She crammed the man's fedora atop the rumpled suit and closed the leather case, leaving one buckle half done. Her gloves now donned, Constance opened the washroom door. Clutching the half-secured valise, she murmured apologetically to the elderly woman waiting in the vestibule.

The sight of her corner house in the Marigny made Constance weak. How could she greet her children? Analee? She struggled up the steps with packages she had picked up from the church, grappled with the knob, and pressed her hip against the heavy leaded-glass door. A waft of damp heat rushed in before her. With the toe of her sealskin boot, she slammed the door shut, her chin atop her armload of packages in an effort to prevent them from falling. As several toppled onto the wide plank hardwood, Analee scurried out from the kitchen. Scooping up the fallen packages, she stacked them on the polished marble console in the hallway.

"Here now, Miss Constance," she said, "give me the rest of that load out your arms." Analee bustled to arrange them on the console. "Now, that's a good sight better. Want to hand me that satchel?"

Constance's heart pounded. "No," she said. "It's all right." She shoved the valise against the console, stricken now with panic as she glanced at the hall clock. "Oh, my. I am so behind. Is everything ready for the ladies?"

"Yes, ma'am. All gone be all right. Baking done and everything set on the dining room table with the pink Limoges, like you said."

"Oh, Analee, this heat is unbearable. I must freshen up. How did I ever allow myself to run this late?" Her mind felt incoherent.

"You be fine, Miss Constance. You just need to cool yourself down a notch." Analee rebalanced the packages in two separate stacks. "You looking a might peaked, Miss Constance. Mayhap you done tried to do too much. What you need is rest. Only so much time in life, you know. Can't do everything in one day by yourself."

Constance knew Analee was studying her. She tried to calm her breathing.

"Something got you upset." It wasn't a question. "I bet you run into that old Mrs. Duncan. One what always got something nasty to say, even when she ain't got nothing to say. She coming this afternoon?"

"No, Analee. I'm just rushed. And hot and tired. Mostly rushed. Or maybe mostly tired." Constance straightened the small valise beside the console. She needed to get it up the stairs. "And no, Mrs. Duncan can't be bothered with the orphanage. Too busy playing bridge."

Suddenly little hands and feet were all about them, dancing and tugging and pulling for attention.

"Mama, Mama," Delia's voice squealed up at Constance, "did you bring us chocolates?"

"Did you, Mama? Did you?" a second little voice chimed in. It was Maggie, tugging at her skirt.

Constance laid her hand on Maggie's soft blond curls, then bent down to kiss both girls. As she put her arms around their trusting shoulders and pulled them to her, she fought back her tears.

"No, angel. Mama didn't have time for the candy store today." No, she had killed their father. Trying to steel herself, Constance brushed a loose curl behind Delia's little ear, straightened her ever-crooked hair bow.

"Oh, Mama." Two voices at once, disappointment palpable.

"Can we have cookies, then?" said one from sudden inspiration.

"Analee made a lot," chimed in the other. "We helped. It's a whole big platter full."

"Yes, you may have a cookie. One each. If any are left from my orphanage auxiliary meeting, you may have another after supper." Constance kissed the top of Maggie's head, unlatched the tight little hands from her skirt. "Have you been good girls today for Analee?" She raised her questioning face to her housekeeper.

"Yes'm. They always good girls." Analee hesitated. "Had to stop Delia from shaking her doll, so she don't break it. She kept saying, 'You hush now. You just hush that crying.' She say that baby making too much racket and she had to make her stop crying. I scolded her some. That's about it."

Constance stiffened. Her heart was exploding. "You were shaking your doll, Delia?" Her voice came out edged and tight. "Why were you shaking your doll?"

"She wouldn't stop crying, Mama."

"Analee is right. You'll break her, honey." She managed words that would make sense. "Then it would be you crying. Shaking your doll is not the way to make her stop crying."

"Well, Daddy did it."

"Daddy shook your doll?"

"No, Mama. He shaketed baby David a lot, and he stopped crying. Maybe he breaked baby David?"

Constance gasped for breath, grasped the edge of the table, elbows locked. Her baby, her David. She had touched him, patted him, thinking him asleep. No response. No breath. No life. She knew babies sometimes died in their sleep, but who would anticipate such a thing? No one. Who would even think of such a thing? No one. She had returned home from errands for the orphanage, picking up hand-me-downs from a woman who had recently taken an interest in those children. The little dresses had been lovely, far fancier than those her own girls wore. She had greeted her girls then as she'd greeted them now, their excitement running through her, buoying her spirits. Hugging them tightly, yet eager to mount the stairs and peek in at David, her precious son, her boy after two girls. She had put no greater value on a son than her girls, but she had loved the balance of both in her life.

Her joy at his birth had overwhelmed her. More so than it had Benton. That had surprised her, puzzled her all those months. He had not been eager to hold this baby boy in his arms, as he had the girls. She had thought it a male characteristic to be prouder of sons than daughters. Yet somehow Benton had seemed less interested, more ill at ease with this precious boy than with the girls. So she had been surprised to find him standing there in the nursery, staring out the window, like a statue on guard. He had turned when she whispered to him, so as not to wake the baby. He had nodded and left the room, more quiet even than usual. She had glanced into the crib to be sure they had not disturbed the sleeping infant, then had followed him out and closed the door.

A bit later, her small bosom tight with milk, she had gone to wake him from his now too-long nap, touched the back of his silky fine hair, laid her hand on his back. He had not moved, even when she'd jostled him slightly. He had not opened his eyes. How many eternities had it taken her to absorb the absence of his breath?

Dr. Birdsong, her childhood friend, her doctor, her children's doctor, had held her and had simply said over and over, "It happens, Constance. Sometimes it happens." Had reassured her she was not to blame. The baby had not suffocated. "Thymic asthma, most probably," he had said, and he'd written it on the death certificate. "It happens. It just happens."

Now Delia's words struck her like a blow. "Daddy shaketed baby David a lot, and he stopped crying." Her infant son shaken till he stopped crying? By his father, now lying deep under some unknown water. Dead, like his son.

Analee shooed the girls from the room. Reluctantly, they backed away, their eyes bright with curiosity and fear.

"You ain't going down, now is you?" Analee took firm hold around the back of Constance's waist. "I got you, Miss Constance."

Constance shook her head but did not raise it. Her legs were failing her. Had Benton meant to do it? *Impossible.* He was not that kind of man. Benton had been broken by David's death. She had consoled him as best she could in her own grief, but he had been so distant. He had clung to her only once, his face buried against her waist, while she stroked his hair, where her own tears fell like slow rain. When he'd choked on his words, pleading, saying he should have known, she had repeated the doctor's words: "It happens. Sometimes it just happens."

"I got you now." Analee locked an arm around Constance's waist, holding tight. She stretched out her foot to scoot a side chair close and eased Constance into it.

Constance sat, hands limp in her lap, head rolled back, eyes locked above her, looking at nothing. Minutes passed before she spoke, and then, as if addressing no one, her eyes on the plaster above, she said, "They saw him?"

"I don't know, Miss Constance. I don't know."

"She couldn't just make that up, Analee."

"I don't know. Childrens is apt to make up most anything, do they get a mind to it."

Constance lowered her head and turned, her face blanched of color, the anger rising like a razor through her. "And just how would she get a mind to that, Analee? That's not a thing you just get a mind to."

Analee wiped at the sweat across Constance's brow, tugged at a fragment of something stuck to the skin at her eyebrow. "Them ladies gone be here right soon, Miss Constance. I'm taking you up. I'm gone put you down to rest. I'm gone tell them you took sick. Got a headache come on of a sudden. Them ladies can handle it all without you."

"No, Analee." Constance pulled herself upright. Testing her

balance, she glanced at the valise on the floor, then accepted Analee's hand for security. "Give me a moment to gather myself. I'll be all right momentarily."

"Miss Constance, you ain't gone be all right. But I know you ain't gone give up living . . ." Analee laid her hand on Constance's shoulder. "Mayhap they gone be times like this, long as you live."

Constance closed her eyes and shook her head. Her fingers clasped the water glass Analee slipped into her fingers. The water was cool and braced her some. She needed to get that valise out of the way. Out of sight. She needed to hide that disguise. But she could not lift it herself. Her small remainder of strength now failed her.

"Would you bring that valise up for me, after all, Analee? I'd as soon not climb the stairs by myself."

CHAPTER 3

A day's tardiness for Howard was not unusual; in fact, given her husband's erratic work schedule, it was far too frequent. An overextended meeting might easily cause him a missed train, resulting in a day's delay returning to Chicago. The occasional locomotive breakdown might result in almost as lengthy a holdup. Two days had once given her serious concern. Now three days with no word from him threw Alice into alarm.

The leftovers from the dinner Alice had splurged on for Howard's return, the dinner for which he had never appeared, lasted her two and a half days. The last of the roast chicken, squash, potatoes, and spinach were gone by the time she resigned herself to his disappearance and mustered the courage to go to the police.

The day was hot—no hint yet of fall weather—the heavy heat like wet clothing drooping on a line across the alley, like all those clotheslines across all those alleys dripping on the pedestrians hurrying to do whatever worrisome errand awaited them. Alice tugged the muslin sleeves of her lightest dress over her damp arms and buttoned the high collar. In reluctant surrender, she hesitated, touching the chifforobe where his few garments hung. After locking the apartment door, Alice descended the stairway and stepped out to the perpetually muddy street. The odors of horse dung, waste, rotting garbage, and offal assailed her. Raising her skirt, she looked both ways and balanced on the sagging planks of the boardwalk that pretended to give protection from the pervasive mud.

Two streets over she encountered a mounted policeman shouting instructions to a group of children racing along the street.

Alice called up to him. "Could you direct me to the nearest station, please, sir?"

The officer bent toward her, pointing, and spoke too quickly for her to clearly understand—but his extended hand at least gave her a sense of the direction in which she should head. She would ask again when she was nearer to the station, if need be. Holding her already mud-tinged skirt, Alice made her uncertain way to the station house.

Alice had never even seen a station house before. In spite of her uncertainty, this one could not be missed. Her apprehension rose as she neared the towering brick façade and stared up at the high arch rising half a story above the daunting reinforced doors. Her legs grew leaden as she mounted the imposing stairs. She put her foot on the last step and reached for the door just as a tired-looking uniformed policeman, hardly more than a boy, burst through it. Without changing his expression, he held it open and nodded before releasing it. Through the dirty cross-barred windows, she watched him race down to the street. When she turned, it was to face the intimidating height of the front desk, its dark, wide-rimmed wood scratched and worn. The officer on duty gave her no notice. He finished whatever he was writing before raising his unreadable face to stare down at her. Uncertain, she gazed first in one direction, then in the other, along the empty hallways. Somewhere far into the building, a hard slam reverberated.

The officer cleared his throat but said nothing, only waited. Alice realized he was expecting something from her.

"Good afternoon, Officer."

He nodded.

"Please, sir, I need to report someone missing."

"Someone?"

Alice assessed the hallways again. "My husband," she said.

The officer scratched something into his book, then waited.

"You see, he was due home three days ago." She felt the strength go out of her voice.

"Three?"

"Yes, sir. Three. And I have had no word from him."

"And you wish to file a missing person report?"

"Yes."

The policeman scratched something else, then said, "If you will wait, please." He disappeared. Another officer took his place and nodded, unsmiling. What were they doing?

Alice stood, with nothing better to do than examine the cool stone floors of the hallways and the high windows, which were covered with heavy metal screens. Anxiety flooded her. Perhaps she should not have come. After a bit, she began to walk back and forth, but soon she heard a heavy knocking at the high desktop. She looked up to see the second officer's scowling face. With one finger he motioned her back into place. She stood still, willing herself to breathe slowly. Minutes later, the original officer returned and motioned her to follow him. Alice turned and almost tripped on her skirt as she tried to keep up with his pace.

The office into which he led her was as sparse and bare as possible while still being functional. There was a scarred table-style desk; a straight-backed chair, to which he motioned her;

and a swivel wooden chair, occupied by a pleasant-faced man with unruly white hair, who glanced at her, then shuffled a set of papers and laid them in front of him.

"I have been given to understand that you wish to report a missing person," he said. "Would that be a child or an adult?"

"My husband, sir." She was puzzled at having to repeat this.

"Adult, then, I presume." He dipped his pen into the inkwell and scratched at the form. "Age, please?"

"Thirty-five, I believe."

"You believe? Don't you know your own husband's age?"

"Thirty-five, sir. It's thirty-five."

"Full name?" He dipped his pen into the inkwell again.

"Alice McGuire Butterworth, sir."

"No, Madame. His full name, if you please." He looked at her with somewhat undisguised disdain.

"I beg pardon, sir. Howard. His name is Howard McKee Butterworth."

"Do you happen to have any identification papers with that name?"

"No, sir, I do not," she said. She slipped her fingers up and down the drawstring of her handbag, feeling the nubbiness.

"Not your marriage certificate, Mrs. Butterworth?" There was an edge to his voice now that did not match his at first pleasant face.

"I did not think to bring it."

"The length of your marriage? Is that one you might know with certainty?"

"Two years this past July nineteen."

The officer lowered the papers and flipped two pages back on a desk calendar. "You were married on a Thursday? That seems an unusual day for a wedding."

"Because of his work and the train schedule." Alice struggled to describe his work as a cotton broker, traveling back and forth every few days between Chicago and Memphis. "Where the mill is. And the cotton brokerage. Also, where his mother lives," she added, her fingers twisting in her lap. She felt her forehead getting damp and pressed the back of her glove against the edge of her auburn hair.

The officer held up his pen, motioning her to slow down, silencing her while he scratched away at the form. Finally, she had given all the information she could, which in truth did not amount to much. A description: light brown hair; eyes the same hue; five feet, ten inches in height; medium frame; no distinctive identifying scars. He could be anyone, she thought, surprised at how ordinary he seemed in her description. Her depiction did not make him appealing. In truth, to her he wasn't. But her feelings about Howard had no bearing on his disappearance. There was little more she felt the need to tell the officer, other than verifying again that the last time she had seen him was when he'd left with his small leather suit- case one week prior. The officer stood, nodded, and motioned toward the door. He did not show her out.

Descending the hard steps to the street, she felt as invisible as she had while growing up on the plains with a father who es- sentially ignored her and two older brothers who mocked her in subtle ways—she was a girl, after all, and not much help to them on the farm. She had often felt invisible; sometimes she had wished she were. As she'd grown older, Alice had become so accustomed to her assumed lower status that she had failed to notice how it pained her. It pained her now. She stepped out into the street, where mud ruts sidled the planks laid in long rows to prevent carriage and wagon wheels from getting bogged down. At least if the driver were careful. She lifted her skirt and stepped around and over the pervasive puddles, with a renewed awareness of the oppressive odors of the streets—of manure and rotting garbage—as she made her way home. The Chicago heat was dogged. The early fall had brought no relief. Alice waded through it and up the narrow stairwell to her second-floor oven of an apartment. She was grateful, at least, it was no higher up. She slipped the key in the lock and was home.

CHAPTER 4

Or was it home? She lived with an ambivalence she could not escape, like the weight of the heat itself. In her mind, it was still Howard's flat, furnished with Howard's things, his silver in the drawer, his china in the cabinet, his heavy-lidded pots in the kitchen. His clothes in the chifforobe: one nice gabardine suit, three finely starched shirts, a long cotton nightshirt, one black wool bowler, and a pair of brown leather house shoes. Even the sheets and the slightly stained down comforter belonged to him. When they married, she had brought with her only the table linens she had embroidered for herself, three sets of them, and a wedding ring quilt and a crazy quilt, which she and her mother had made by the hearth from dress scraps on cold prairie nights, each seam line embroidered with complicated stitch designs she had practiced over and over.

She had one albumen print of the family, taken before she left the farm in 1896. She remembered the day they had made the trip into town for that photograph at the pleading of her mother. It had been her eighteenth birthday. In the photo, the boys stood behind their father, each with a hand on his shoulder. There was a space between her parents' chairs, and Alice stood, as if alone, on the far side, a hand on her mother's shoulder. She remembered that after the photo the menfolk had donned their hats and walked outside. Her mother had smiled at her, but Alice remembered seeing the light catch the tears in her eyes.

Her father had made it clear to Alice that the farm would be divided equally between her brothers, Gifford and Clancy. They were the men of the family, and they would farm it. Her mother by then had become right frail. Alice could remain there until she married. It was assumed she would marry. Her mother took her aside and confided, almost in whispers, that life would be difficult and lonely for her here on the plains. She wanted more for Alice and hoped Alice would think about trying life in the city, in Chicago, where, her mother fantasized, there would be ample opportunity for her to flourish, thanks to the trove of sewing skills her mother had given her, feeling this day would come. And so, with only a plain denim bag made from the legs of her youngest brother's worn-out overalls, embroidered with daisies on the outside, and featuring an inner pocket to hold the roll of bills her mother had secretly stashed away for years, Alice at last surrendered her home. On her first train ride she crossed those wide expanses with endless sky and abandoned the open prairie for her first glimpse of the unfamiliar, bustling, chaotic city life of Chicago just as the turn of a new century was approaching.

Her first days in Chicago were disorienting, to the point that she longed to take her remaining bills and buy a ticket back to the plains. By inquiring at the station, she learned of a rooming house for women and then ignored the terrible fear overwhelming her at both the cost and uncertainty of mounting a cab alone to reach it. The place was dire in appearance, but the matron was kind, the mattress clean at least, and the food adequate. Some other poor girl had discarded a newspaper, and in it, Alice found a wanted notice for an experienced seamstress at Carson Pirie Scott & Company. She was hired.

That chain of chance brought her to Howard, whose abandoned wife she now appeared to be, waiting uselessly on news from the police. As the days passed with no word, Alice rattled about the flat, scanning the street below, fanning her increasing anxiety with a day-old newspaper the boy at the corner had given her. She ate bread and cheese, not daring to spend more on food, since all household funds came from Howard. Afterward she tackled the housekeeping. With the broom, the mop, and the feather duster in hand . . . she was suddenly not sure how different this was from what life might have been like on the prairie—the life her mother had hoped to save her from—but she urgently needed everything to be perfect for Howard's return. Alice stepped into the small kitchen, but the sight of the enamel sink stopped her. Instead, she retrieved the vinegar from the cabinet and wiped the windows as high as she could reach, then lowered the upper panes, cleaned and closed them, grateful that the sashes slid easily, unlike in the cramped single room she had occupied before her marriage to Howard. Sweating profusely now, she opened the windows again. This gave her no relief, as the heat from the street below rose and mingled with the heat in the room.

Alice eased into Howard's armchair, unbuttoned her limp, wrinkled shirt at the neck. She fanned at herself, released three more buttons, then let her arms go limp on the dark leather of the chair. She laid her head back and closed her eyes. It was late in the season for such unrelenting heat. Once it eased, of course, there would quickly be the frigid Chicago winter to survive. And where was Howard?

Alice opened her eyes, gazed around her husband's flat. She had met Howard Butterworth at Carson Pirie Scott & Company two years ago, when he'd come into the store to purchase an expensive light green twill skirt for his mother in Memphis. It had needed to be shortened, as his mother had lost some height through the years, he said. The manager had summoned alterations. Alice had been the one available at the moment. When she arrived, Mr. Butterworth presented her with a set of carefully written measurements for the skirt, which she found both odd and endearing. What man had she ever encountered who knew his mother's skirt measurements? Let alone had them tidily written out and at hand in his pocket.

When Mr. Butterworth returned the following day to retrieve the skirt, he first examined her work, holding it close, as if he were a bit nearsighted. When he lowered the fabric, he smiled at her and complimented her handiwork. Smiled again and invited her to dinner at a fine restaurant, one she had never walked by, let alone entered. She demurred, however. How unsafe might she be with such a total stranger? A moment later, the floor manager bustled by and stopped to greet Mr. Butterworth, with exclamations of recognition and pleasure that he was once again shopping for his mother at the store. A brief conversation ensued regarding his mother's health and wellbeing in Memphis. When the manager departed after offering effusive thanks for his return business, Mr. Butterworth turned back to her and repeated his invitation to dinner. She accepted.

He was unfailingly decorous throughout the ensuing courtship, opening doors, assisting with chairs in restaurants, offering his elbow on the muddy streets, even urging her to wait while he readjusted street planks across a mud puddle. When first he delivered her back to her low-rent fourth-floor walkup, he remarked, "Well, we shall soon need to remedy this." He never pushed for feminine "favors," kissing her chastely on the cheek or forehead in farewell, sometimes the back of her hand. She was unused to such a man, so startling in his difference from her father and brothers, who were brusque, rowdy, rough farmers of the plains, men for whom women's function was to serve them, and that right quickly. In contrast, Alice was both puzzled and impressed that this gentlemanly stranger was interested in her at all. And always respectful.

Howard's profession as a cotton broker with the Memphis Cotton Exchange burdened him with an erratic work schedule involving frequent train trips between Chicago and Memphis. Alice was often surprised by his unexpected appearances, and equally frustrated with the disappointment of waiting an extra day, sometimes two, for his return.

The courtship was not extended. Though she hesitated, Howard stated somewhat bluntly that since marriage between them was inevitable, stretching it was a waste of valuable time. He considered an impulsive trip to the quick marriage mills of Crown Point, across the state line in Indiana, but he had no personal transportation in Chicago, and Alice insisted that they could manage the short waiting period required in the city, since he would be traveling with his work regardless. Finally, without fanfare, Alice became Mrs. Butterworth in a simple exchange of vows before a local justice of the peace.

There was no honeymoon. The travel demands of Howard's job with the cotton brokerage did not allow for extra days away. Nothing about this union aligned with Alice's fantasies of marriage or, she was sure, with her mother's hopes. She wore no white or lace, but a simple pale blue dress of summer chambray, cinched tightly over her corset, with wide lace standing tight around her thin neck. Neither was her wedding night what she might have hoped for. After a rather filling dinner at a small German restaurant, Howard hailed a cab to escort her to her new residence.

Her first glimpse of the Chicago gray stone building astonished her. Never had she imagined living in something so stately, with its long entrance stairway, recessed porch, high bay windows, and roofline rising like King Arthur's crown above. Howard laughed when she turned to him, her mouth still agape.

"It's not all mine, you know," he said. "Only a small one-bedroom on the second floor."

If the exterior had awed her, Alice was truly unprepared for the interior: the entrance hall with polished wainscot, the ornate spindle work and molding below the ceiling to create the impression of an open arbor, the dark turned balustrade and railing as Howard led her to the second floor and inserted his key into the second door. When he stood back for her to enter the apartment, she was pleased to find it less ornate, more simple and homelike. His leather armchair sat close by the window; a smaller, straighter lady's chair was on the other side of a spindled table, with an angled bookshelf beneath. *Hmm, like a trough for books*, she thought and tried not to laugh. She barely had a glimpse of the small kitchen before he took her hand and whisked her into the bedroom, where he deposited her small bag and said, "I will be with you shortly. Knock on the door when you are ready."

The bed was dark mahogany, with a simply carved rectangular back, and more elegant than any she had ever seen. The linens were smooth and very white. Alice ran her hand over them and touched her face. Then she took the tucked muslin nightdress from her bag, a new one with ruffles she had sat up late to stitch at its high neckline and on the edges of its billowing sleeves. She might have saved her work and her small splurge on the lace. When Howard responded to her quiet knock, the gown remained almost undisturbed, except that he raised it, not even to her waist in the back, gripped her buttocks, and took her hard and fast. She might as well have been one of the horses back on the plains of her upbringing.

Alice did not sleep, but Howard drifted off almost immediately, without a word. In the morning he dressed hurriedly, drank a cup of coffee, spoke briefly to her of his train schedule, and announced that he had arranged for a Negro porter to assist her in moving her things into his flat. She noticed that he did not use the word *our*. Before he closed the door, he kissed her on the cheek, looked into her eyes as if assessing that she was really there, kissed the other cheek, and left.

With the help of the porter—a kind, respectful man of middle age, heavily muscled and equipped with a medium-sized handcart—Alice moved her meager possessions into Howard's far more spacious flat on Kildare Street. She was now a resident of what had come to be known as K-Town, that plethora of streets running north and south, each street beginning with the letter *K*, the eleventh letter of the alphabet, as a location indicator. The Chicago streets were alphabetized by distance from Indiana. Alice could now always be sure she was eleven miles from the state border. The Kildare flat was a relatively spacious unit, far closer to the ground than she had become accustomed. Certainly, the heating here would be more reliable during Chicago's bitter winter than hers had been, but summer heat was summer heat, and simply to be endured wherever one lived in the city. Even as she endured it now.

CHAPTER 5

When the bedroom door closed behind Analee, Constance thrust the valise under the bed, but only barely, as the bed skirt caught on one of its corners. She hadn't time to deal with it.

At her dressing table, Constance inhaled and let the breath out slowly, counting the seconds as she patted her damp face and dusted it with powder. She would have to recover herself and that right quickly. She would manage to chair this committee for the orphanage. She would reassure her girls. She would behave as if she were not the only mother to have an infant son who had died. She would act as if she were not the only woman who had stood and watched her husband plunge backward from a moving train. She would act as if all might be well, though it never would.

And act she did, light and unconcerned about anything other than the list of needs for the orphanage and how to meet them: if and how additional committee members might be recruited, who would handle which items, how soon they might be procured and delivered. The donated parcels she had collected were divided among the group according to each member's interest in sorting and arranging.

"Lillian," Constance said to a woman across the room, "I wonder if you would be so kind as to take charge at this point of organizing a group visit to the children in the home, with treats and refreshments. We will need volunteers for the various tasks, ladies, so please don't be shy. Darlene, your tea cakes would be a certain delight."

Determined efficiency was her ally and her weapon against the weariness of shock that weighed her down. She must see this meeting finished before everything in her failed. At last, all decisions made, the ladies closed their fans and adjourned to the dining room, where they helped themselves, with appropriate compliments to Analee's unfailingly delicious cake and cookies. As expected, there were plenty left for the children, and then more to spare. Enough even to send to the orphanage.

As the ladies finally departed in pairs and threesomes, Glenda Rawlings tarried a moment. "Are you all right, my dear? You look quite pale."

"Oh, Glenda, I'm merely tired. And this unbearable heat will do me in, I do believe."

"Are you expecting Benton home tonight?"

Constance froze, unable to speak. His flailing arms seemed suddenly as if they might hit her in the face. She flinched but then found her voice. "No. I believe he said this trip would be at least a week, possibly more."

"Then you must join us for dinner. I don't believe you have yet made the acquaintance of Janette and Paul Leroux, who will be joining us. Welcoming the newcomers, you know. She well may be a valuable and generous supporter of the orphanage. Other endeavors, as well, but the orphanage first."

"That's very kind of you, Glenda, and of course, I look forward to meeting our newcomers." *Will I ever look forward to anything new again? Will I even survive?* "However, it has been a long day, and I truly am unusually tired." She could hardly imagine feeling anything normal again. "This stifling heat, perhaps. I believe I will even have Analee put the girls to bed. Indulge myself in a cool soak and retire early." She opened the door a bit wider. *Will she leave? Surely, she will leave.* "Give my best to the Lerouxes and convey my eagerness to meet them some other time in the near future, if you will."

Sensing her friend's concern, Constance leaned forward to give her a peck on the cheek before she closed the door and collapsed against it with her departure. Analee came down the wide staircase and took her by the hand.

"You best come sit, Miss Constance. I'll fetch you some supper. You need a mite more sustenance than tea cakes and sweets."

"No, Analee. Just take care of the girls, please. I have something of a raging headache. I'm going to put a cold cloth on my forehead and lie down. I will see you in the morning. Kiss the girls for me and tell them I love them."

Constance knew Analee watched from below as she pulled herself up the stairs by the handrail, one slow step at a time. She had to wonder if Analee was taken in by her ruse. No one else had ever known her so well.

In her room, Constance undressed and dropped her clothes across the carved mahogany footboard. Her green skirt slipped to the floor, where she left it. On the chaise by the open window, she lay back and listened to the emerging mix of crickets, tree frogs, and night sounds from nearby homes. In the deepening dark, she rolled her throbbing head from side to side against the high velvet back of the chaise and closed her eyes.

But though she might block out the world, she could not block out the events of the day. Nothing seemed real. Could Benton actually be dead? She had not ever wished him dead, no matter how grievous his failings. Everything had been just a blur: his face, his eyes on her, his arms beating at the air. That intruder flashing past. The thud of closing doors. Now she knew the truth of his gambling, his inordinate hammering her for money with excuses of investments, which she had known were lies. She had no way to gauge how deep his debts were, or to whom. Her thoughts jerked back to the man who ran past, the man she had taken for one of the gamblers. Was it his hand, not hers, that had sent Benton falling? Had Benton been murdered for debts, for money she had refused him, money from her grandfather's trust, which he could not touch.

He had taken her for a boy. And he had touched that boy, approached that boy, and the shock of it was beyond absorbing. Her head pulsated with bewildered fear and muffled grief until she fell into a stupored sleep.

Morning came. The girls burst into the room without knocking to find her still on the chaise in chemise and petticoat, skirt and corset strewn at the foot of the bed. Analee appeared close behind them, then stood in the door, taking it all in.

"Mama, what you sleeping in your chair for?" said Delia.

Analee took the girls by the hand and guided them back toward the door. "Mama don't feel so good now, girls. Let's give her a bit of peace this morning." She turned briefly as Constance stirred.

"Oh, Analee. What time is it? I—I don't know what I'm supposed to do."

"You supposed to have that luncheon . . ."

"Oh, Analee." Constance dragged herself to the edge of the chaise, but her legs refused to hold her as she tried to rise. "My mind is raw. I've forgotten everything."

Analee reached out to help Constance lie safely back against the chaise. "Miss Constance, you forget about that luncheon now. All that Mardi Gras planning gone get done just fine without you. You got to rest."

However, Constance could no more forget about that luncheon than she could have given up the meeting yesterday. She cared little for New Orleans social life, let alone the planning of the women's Mardi Gras krewe, Les Mysterieuses. But she could not afford a mistake. Life must go on as normal. Or it must appear to. For as long as it might. There would be more and worse to come. Until the inevitable, she must endeavor to maintain normality: plan ball themes, arrange menus, commission gowns, hire seamstresses.

Late in the morning, Constance rose, piled her hair in a loose bun atop her head, donned a lightweight linen dress and fresh white gloves. Her progress down the wide staircase was barely more energetic than her ascent the evening before. Yet at the sight of her children, her face brightened. She lifted her skirt to make her steps livelier as they rushed toward her, and then she held her arms wide and took them in. Her chest tightened. She kissed them each on the top of the head and released them. With kisses blown in the sunshine, Constance descended the outside steps to the sidewalk. To a life she longed to forgo.

CHAPTER 6

Clarice Dougan's house was a grand affair, a Gothic Revival of generous proportions, unlike Constance's narrow house in the Marigny. She felt diminished as she approached along Prytania Street in the Garden District. She stared up at the pointed arches and the steep gable roof, with its quatrefoil ornamentation and elaborate finials on the gable peaks. Constance caught herself and dropped her gaze to the double front doors, the windows, all crowned with arches and hoodmolds. Above the door gleamed a transom of diamond-shaped glass. Constance raised her hand to knock, but the door opened almost on its own. A pleasant-faced servant girl bade her in.

Constance was overwhelmed with greetings, not only from Clarice but also from half a dozen other women, whom she knew she was expected to recognize but didn't. There were introductions: Janine Musial, Alicia Constable, Maurine Thibodeaux, Beatrice Landry. Her mind began to whirl. *What am I doing here?* she thought. *I've no business here.* Constance felt her ribs imprisoned in her corset. She wrestled the urge to flee. Clarice guided her to a seat at the exquisitely appointed table, where her name was scrolled in fine calligraphy on the place card. Constance settled uneasily. The chatter in the room left her dizzy. She concentrated on her name, repeated it to herself in her head, as if she needed to memorize who she was.

"Well, now, isn't this exciting?"

Constance startled when her neighbor spoke to her.

The woman spoke without introduction, as if they knew one another. "They've done it once. And now again, the second time. And this year we'll be with them. You and I will be in Les Mysterieuses' krewe. But no one will know who we are, because of the veils or the masks or whatever we decide on today. Isn't that momentous? Women! A krewe of women. Turning the tide on men! We are making history here. Yes, this moment! Making history." The woman had barely taken a breath. She tapped Constance on the arm and picked up her fork to begin her hors d'oeuvre of boudin-stuffed mushrooms.

Constance leaned toward the woman as if wishing to speak more directly. In truth, she wanted to see the name on the place card. She had time to make out only the first name: Marianne. "Ah, yes, Marianne," she said. "It is history, isn't it? You are so very right."

"It is time that women spoke up for themselves, did for themselves, and we are part of that wave that will surely come to shore when we get the vote. But for now, having our own ball will have to suffice."

The woman turned to her neighbor on the other side.

"Indeed." Constance finished the last bit of mushroom, speaking to the air. Her fork clanged on the plate as the uniformed server whisked it away. It was replaced immediately with a sumptuous, but unpretentious luncheon plate of shrimp and asparagus, with a decorative sprig of green grapes.

On her left, a handsome older woman, uncorseted yet quite lovely, whom Constance vaguely remembered as Dorothea Richard, turned to her. Constance felt a sense of rescue.

"Indeed," Dorothea said. "Our first ball in 1896 did make history—the first ever all-female krewe of Mardi Gras. We managed that because it was a leap year, as is this one." She leaned forward and added in a conspiratorial whisper, "Well, technically not. It's been four years, but nineteen hundred can't be divided by four hundred, so February hasn't an extra day. But no one is paying attention to such mathematical complications. It's four years. So we are counting it as a leap year and taking charge regardless."

She leaned back and resumed her conversational tone. "Every convention turned on its head. Our ball was quite an affair, you know. You've probably heard." She was taking her time as she spoke. "All the fine gentlemen were astounded at our switching places, leaving them to undergo what we normally experience—waiting to be chosen, waiting to be invited to dance, waiting for permission our whole life through, from father to husband." She rested her fork across her half-finished plate. "Speaking of husbands, Constance, how is yours? I know Benton is away on his work so much. Does that seem to leave you free or abandoned?"

The questions came as a shock to Constance. Her stomach contracted. She had no answer for the first one. She had no idea if he were dead or alive, severely injured, nor what she would do if he returned. He had recognized her. Now this woman was speaking so boldly, throwing convention to the wind. Constance's only possibility was to answer as boldly.

"Actually, Mrs. Richard, I don't know how to answer your question." Constance toyed with a bit of asparagus before she laid her fork down. She put her hands in her lap and faced Dorothea Richard. "There are times when I feel quite free, and others when I fret and worry a great deal."

"You've never had anyone ask you such a question, have you, my dear?"

"No." Constance picked up her fork. "No, never."

"So, you are nonplussed that I am so straightforward?" Dorothea dabbed her napkin at her lips. "Well, after today, I assume you will become accustomed. In truth, I believe you will find it liberating. Much as I find it liberating not to wear a corset, especially these current ones with the pigeon breast, wasp waist, and heifer hips." She laughed at Constance's expression. "And you'll get used to my saying what I think."

Dessert finished, the women gathered in the simple but elegant parlor. They were here to be who they were, in place of who they were told they should be. An inventive, infectious group of women intent on determining who they might be if it pleased them, with a name to suit their purpose: Les Mysterieuses, the first ever female krewe for Mardi Gras four years ago. Everything had been turned on its head that previous leap year: women had asked men for a dance or a dinner date, and one woman had even asked a man to marry her. The whole endeavor had been not only outrageously unseemly, but in the end acceptably so, as well. Now another leap year—or ostensibly so—another ball, an expanded one, and Constance's invitation to participate had become part of her own expansion. Nothing depended on men except what these daring women deemed was theirs for the asking.

The discussion ran the gamut, from the location (all agreed upon the French Opera House), the committees, and the committee chairs, to the captain in charge and the choice of a queen, the foremost concern. Just as this female krewe had turned the table on men, now they turned the table on convention. Not one queen, they agreed. No. Why should there be only one? "Let us have four, one for each point of the compass, to include the whole of womanhood. One each of the various symbols of female identity—Semiramis, Pocahontas, Juliet, and Brunhilda. All womanhood included in royalty!" they declared.

Constance left the house with a tangled sense of uncertain despair and a slant of hope she had not known since her infant,

David, died. It was not until she reached the corner to board the streetcar that she realized the depth of that truth. How long it had been since she had felt anything other than grief. The loss of her boy had immobilized her, left her without energy, almost without purpose. But not entirely. She rose each day from dreams that left her depleted to a morning whose purpose belonged to her girls, who were more precious to her now than ever before. The grief snarled her with constant fear, but today something new had crept in, something small, the smallest bit of light, of newborn expectancy.

Riding in the falsely cooling gale of the streetcar's movement, Constance held one hand over her abdomen, which tightened in an alternate seesaw of shock and exuberance. How might she be seen by this new group? She lived on the lower boundary of the upper echelons of New Orleans society. Benton had been determined to rise to the top. She had despised his relentless ambition and all he demanded of her to assist him in achieving his aspirations. Constance was simple in her desires: family, comfort—both physical and emotional—children, friends, and a purpose to her life. Her children and the work at the orphanage provided her that purpose. She did not care to entertain or to be entertained. Fine clothing held little draw for her, though she loved creative surprises, not necessarily ones in vogue. Les Mysterieuses offered her that. Now she was opening herself to an experience she had no way of truly anticipating, while still carrying with her all the fear and uncertainty of yesterday, in the stranglehold of her gruesome experience.

Had Benton stumbled? *Yes, yes, of course.* Had he simply fallen? Had her hand knocked him from the train? Who was that man? Had he pushed Benton or startled him more, as he had her? Where was Benton now? At home, waiting, knowing? Would he shake her to death?

The fear, the uncertainty, the memories dazed her. Constance could not bear to return to her own house. Instead, at the next stop, she descended from the streetcar. A man on a bicycle came near to hitting her as she bolted across the tracks to the other side of the street. She barely missed a woman pushing a pram. She rounded the corner and was relieved to find a small coach, its driver flicking the reins slightly at his knee in boredom, apparently in need of a hire. She shook her head as the driver started to jump down and assist her. Gripping the handlebar of the carriage, she mounted and gave him the address of the orphanage.

CHAPTER 7

Day after day Alice paced about the flat, plying first one task and then another, only to abandon each unfinished. She went through Howard's clothing again, collecting a few dollars of loose change from his pockets. She was tempted to search his bureau drawers, of which she had opened only the top two to restack his ironed and folded handkerchiefs and underwear. After drawing his stilted wrath when she had once taken it upon herself to reorganize a few items in the other drawers, she had dared not violate his privacy by opening them again. Now she was desperate. She needed any odd dollars, quarters, dimes, and even pennies he was sometimes wont to drop beside his neatly organized accessories. She had even noticed him drop a roll of bills in a drawer now and then, and from these he would unroll and count out enough to cover their groceries and miscellaneous expenses, such as his endless cleaning bills. She was hungry, and the cool of autumn had commenced at last. She would soon need heat for the flat. Perhaps there was money there in the drawers even now, and his privacy be damned.

Alice had just reached for one of the lower knobs when she

was startled by a knock at the door. Her throat caught and would not let her breath pass. But then it did. It could not be Howard. Her mind raced. Unless somehow there had been an assault on him. He had been attacked and had been in some hospital, unable to communicate. Now he was recovered enough to return home, and he had no key. Rationality stepped in. The police would have found him. Her sudden imaginative hope sent her heart racing. She quelled the thought. She rushed toward the door but stopped short of throwing it wide. No one ever knocked at this door, not even the landlord. Alice slid her palms down her skirt and tried to ask who was there. Her voice emerged in a hoarse whisper.

Whoever was on the other side evidently heard something, for there was a second knock and a man's voice said, "It's Sergeant Ames, ma'am. I need to speak with you about Mr. Butterworth."

He is dead, she thought. *They have come to tell me he is dead.* Alice slid the latch and cracked open the door. Indeed, there was a policeman there. She opened the door wider.

"Mrs. Butterworth?"

She nodded, again slid her sweaty palms down her skirt.

"May I come in, please, ma'am?"

She nodded but failed to step back. He waited. When it struck her that she was blocking the way, she mumbled and retreated three steps. As he entered the flat, squeezing between her and the doorframe, the policeman peered around, taking in what details she could only guess.

"No need for alarm, Mrs. Butterworth. I've come to do some checking on your missing person report. Well, on your missing husband. Have you had any word of him?"

She shook her head. Her ears were ringing, as if there were an echo in his voice.

"No, of course not," he said. He twirled his cap nervously in his hands. "You would have notified the precinct, correct?

Well, I have no real news for you, Mrs. Butterworth. We have correlated your description to all homicides and injuries currently known in the city and surrounds. Nothing, unfortunately. Well, really, *fortunately* might be more to the point. What we have, ma'am, is basically nothing at the moment. I did speak with your landlord, and he apprised me of the fact that Mr. Butterworth pays twice yearly, always in full, by cash. So that would have been the last of June. You now have a bit under three months remaining until it is due again. I assume you knew all of this."

"No, sir. Actually, I did not. The flat was his, you see, and I just moved into it with him when we married."

"And are you on his bank account?"

Her stomach tightened. "No. No, I am not."

"Do you know the bank with which he is affiliated, Mrs. Butterworth?"

There was a long silence while she turned her head aside. "No, Officer. Actually, now that I think back on it, I find that I am not aware of his ever going to a bank here, or even mentioning a bank. Perhaps he handled his finances from Memphis, where much of his work was centered." Alice looked up at Sergeant Ames. "How odd that seems now . . . not to even know. We simply never discussed the financial side of—"

"So, you are not aware of how your rent and other finances were handled?"

"No." Again, she turned aside, feeling a surprising sense of shame. "No, you see Mr. Butterworth was . . . was reticent to discuss finances with me. He said . . . he said those things were a man's duty and I need not bother my head with such things." Another pause. "Well, he seemed to take any curiosity on my part as an affront to his ability to take care of things."

"I see. A matter of manhood, then. A common enough stance, I suppose. To be expected, in spite of the havoc it creates for women in crisis." Ames twirled his cap again and slipped it onto his smoothly oiled hair. "Well, I'll not bother you any further, Mrs. Butterworth. At least you may rest assured of a roof until the New Year." He tipped his cap and stepped away. "You'll notify us if you have any news." It was not even a question that trailed above the click of his boots, his retreating back in the stairwell.

The following morning Alice made no attempt at eating. She slipped on her pale gray walking skirt and a simple white shirtwaist. Nothing fancier. From the hall tree she took her shawl, her narrow-brimmed straw hat, her parasol, and pulled her gloves on at the same time she tried to close the door. The whole effort resulted in one glove and the parasol on the hall floor and a self-reprimand at her perpetual clumsiness. With the door finally locked, her belongings retrieved, Alice descended the stairs and set off for Carson Pirie Scott & Company, sure that she might return to her old job.

But such was not the case. The manager was new and had no positions unfilled. And no, he was not in need of extra hands for the holidays two months hence. She might inquire again at the time. And no, he would not keep her name and information for mailing in case of an opening. If such should happen, there were at least two to three inquiries for such jobs every week. And no, neither her past position there nor any reassurance of her advanced skills was of any import at this time. She was welcome to inquire again as often as she liked.

Though she had a roof, Alice knew she had little to cover food for more than perhaps two months, if she was exceptionally frugal and ate a small meal only twice a day. She had let herself become dependent on Howard for all finances, and now there was no Howard. She trudged home, dragging her abandonment with each step, her very eyes now fatigued.

Alice let herself into the empty flat and closed the door, then leaned her back against it. It was a way to feel something, the sturdy wooden frame supporting her. She was lost in the utter emptiness of it all. Had he, in truth, abandoned her, left her here alone with nothing? There had been no anger, no argument, no distance more than the ordinary. A simple goodbye of no great import, an ordinary goodbye, like all his other impersonal goodbyes. Was he injured? He had identification. Surely word spread through the official means—police, rail workers, company workers. But there was no more word than there was Howard. And Alice, with barely the means for subsistence.

In the hours that followed, Alice gathered herself with simple determination. With that sustenance, she gained strength. Her thoughts began to center. She had let six months pass by without purpose, nursing her grief, attending Howard's coming and going, using all her strength to maintain some glint of normalcy in his presence, weeping private tears when he was absent. Perhaps, she thought, she might inquire at the White Way Dry Cleaning five blocks from the flat if they might have occasional inquiries for alterations. She had to assume they did. All the staff were familiar with her there because of the unusual frequency with which she had delivered and fetched Howard's cleaning. Indeed, it proved they did have need and were all too happy to find an experienced seamstress in possession of her own private sewing machine, a useful gift from Howard—she choked at the memory—before baby Jonathan was born. Her fevered baby who had died in the desperate bath to save him.

Alice ran her fingers along the machine, the smooth surface of the metal, feeling its cold, its lifelessness. Yet if she put her foot on its pedal, rocked it as she had rocked her sweet son, it would whir to life, though her baby never would. She remembered her bulging belly, the alterations to her clothes, her anticipation and joy as she handled those soft fabrics, creating a layette, stitching the edges of soft infant gowns for the coming birth. She remembered the hours of that birth, the mess when her water broke, the absence of Howard, gone to fetch the midwife and failing to return in time, the last impelling pains, blood on the sheets—Howard's sheets—and the penetrating warmth of her infant boy slid from her as she held him, white and waxy. She had never felt such love, visceral and penetrating. Her thoughts ran back to his first bath in the sink to cleanse him, his soft skin emerging. And then to the last bath, only months later, the cold water in the sink to reduce his fever, her own fever, struggling into the kitchen with fresh towels, Howard's perfectly groomed hands holding him, Jonathan's beseeching eyes blank under the water.

She had not touched this sewing machine since the day her baby died. Now perhaps Howard was also dead. But she was not. She was alive. She had to face that being alive necessitated feeding herself, keeping a roof over her head. Her skills for doing so were finely honed, if limited. Now she had a way to use them to sustain herself.

CHAPTER 8

As Alice opened the door to the flat, something under her foot slipped with a slight crackle. Looking down past the dirty edge of her skirt, Alice saw the equally dirty edge of an envelope. As she reached down, she only just recognized the garbled handwriting: her brother Gifford's. He'd struggled through the fourth class at school before he gave it up to go work the farm with their Pa. The envelope was ragged and smeared, posted September 14, 1899, ten days ago, to her previous address, with markings of redirection, the first old flat marked out, the new one scratched almost illegibly up one vertical edge. It was her first news from the farm in two years. No one wrote to her from home. She swiveled side to side, flapping the envelope in the air. Then sat, held it in her lap, her hands gone numb. Alice did not want this letter now; this letter could only be dire news. She dreaded opening it more than receiving news of Howard. In time—she had no idea how much—she picked up a knife from the table and slipped it into the fold.

The letter was short but nonetheless difficult to make out.

*Sister, I will tell it straight out. Pa is dead. That
hurricane I herd was so bad down Texas way
come on all the way up hear acrost the plains and
acrost the farm. Trees was flung clean out the
ground, and one fell down on Pa. He's dead. Half
the roof flew off, but me and Clancy got it fixt.
Ma won't talk no more. Don't eat. Won't drink
neither. She can't get out the bed, just hold her
face 'gainst the wall. She don't cry none. I keep
thinking every breath she takes gone be the last
one. We got Pa buried by that field he liked and
fixt a place beside for Ma. It's ready for her. It
ain't no use you come home now, but I thought
you ought to know 'bout your folks.*

Signed your brother Gifford

Alice dropped the letter and laid her head on the table, one
hand under her cheek, the other hanging empty beside her. She
felt its emptiness and raised it to her breast. Her father dead.
Her strong, unwavering father dead, just like that. Right there
in his own field in a storm. She had loved him and loathed him.
Loved him for being good and steady, for carving a wooden
doll for her; loathed him for how he had made her loathe herself for being female, for not being a son who could plough and
help to bale the hay. But he had loved her in spite of himself.
That much she knew. She also knew what it meant when people
stopped eating and drinking. She had seen it when going with
her mother to help a neighbor. Once that happened, it didn't
take long. She envisioned her mother, frail and lying on the bed
alone, face to the wall.

Gifford was right. No doubt her mother had already taken
her last breath, likely days ago, while this letter was making its
erratic way to find her. This was her mother, the mother who
had loved her as a girl, dressed that wooden doll her father

carved. In her uneven breath, the tears that fell, untouched, Alice felt the weight of her own motherhood, of her infant son, Jonathan, his soft breath against her, the sensation of fullness in her breasts, the feeling of milk letting down, the heartbeat of life, what her mother had once felt for her.

I must live, she thought. *She carried me in her body, as I carried him in mine. She taught me to sew, and I made the gown in which to lay him in his coffin. I hold his memory. I alone. I must live.*

Alice sat beside the window, working on an extensive alteration for the White Way, taking in a waist for a young woman who had recently been quite ill. Who was this girl, she wondered. Had she sat with her mother, their hands touching now and then, an occasional smile of approval at a beautiful line of stitches? Alice sat back, her hands idle now, remembering her life with her mother back on the prairie. She recollected how unfailing the precision of her mother's stitches had been. Alice suddenly felt herself as the treasure she must have been to her mother . . . her mother, who had urged her to another life. Diminished as she had felt by the men in her family, Alice knew regardless that they had loved her. But she had been less than a boy would have been in their eyes—only a useful accessory to help with the cooking and laundry. Her mother had known the limitations of her choices for marriage out there. She had envisioned a different life for Alice, had encouraged her to come here to the city, with a gifted needle in her hand, to find a life of her own and a far wider range of possibilities for love.

Alice squinted at her stitches, pulling her long-threaded needle toward the light. The skirt was a fancy thing of Venetian broadcloth, fabricated in eight gores, with a small bustle, so that the alterations had to sit precisely to align with its support. A skirt that she could never hope to wear but that she took pleasure in perfecting for another. As she slipped the needle back into the next stitch, Alice felt it prick her in the dark beneath the fabric. She left the needle there, sucked at her finger, dropped her hand limp against the rustling fabric. Alice touched her finger to the needle again, then stopped and, almost unthinking, let the garment slide to the floor. She retrieved it and laid it across the bed, attentive not to loosen her carefully placed pins. The time had come to do something more about Howard's disappearance, however fruitless. Doing nothing had resulted in nothing. She rose, took up her plain wool shawl against the welcome chill, locked the door behind her, and dropped the key into her pocket. The uncertainty of waiting was dragging her down. She had to go back to the station house. Clearly, no one was coming to her.

Once there, Alice was relieved to see Sergeant Ames exiting one of the far office doors in the long hallway. He walked briskly to her.

"You have news?" he asked.

"No. No, sir. I came to find if you might have discovered anything. Anything at all."

He took her elbow and guided her back toward the entrance. "I'm afraid not, Mrs. Butterworth. We've had no leads whatsoever. And might I suggest that the absence of leads is possibly good news? I know the time is becoming extended now. Mr. Butterworth has been absent for quite a while, but we have no leads to indicate injury or death." He continued to guide her toward the entrance door. "I assure you, Mrs. Butterworth, there is no need to tax yourself by coming all this way to inquire. We will most assuredly notify you should we discover anything at all."

Since Ames now had the door open wide for her, there was little for her to do but go out. Yet she hesitated on the step. For what, she did not know. From inside the station, she heard the voice of another officer calling out, almost as if to ensure she would hear what he said. "That Butterworth woman back?

What kind of name is that, anyway? You'd think by now she'd have figured out for herself that he's left her."

Alice raised her eyes to the closed door. The tears were there before the thought that she had been abandoned could clarify itself in her head. All feeling drained from her body, as if her blood had ceased to flow. Dead? Yes. Injured somewhere, not remembering? Yes. Deliberately walked away? No. A plan to disappear, to leave her in this limbo, abandoned? No. But there it was. The shock of it filled her numbed body, like the prickling of blood returning to a foot that had fallen asleep. Had she let herself be asleep in this marriage? Asleep in her life? Alice closed her eyes and tilted her head to the open sky. The air on her face was suddenly chill. She lifted her skirt and stepped, without falling, into the insidious mud of the Chicago streets.

The way back blurred before her eyes. She kept them down, seeing only a haze of dull colors—black Balmorals, chestnut Chelseas, men's boots, women's boots—sidestepping puddles, balancing on the wooden boards that led her to nowhere. The way back. Not to her home. She had no home. Even if he were dead and it were not his fault, she had no home. With him gone, no matter the cause—accident, murder, an unexpected heart attack, deliberate abandonment—she had no home. She slugged her way back through a kaleidoscoping blur of boots to the empty flat. Home did not exist.

CHAPTER 9

Poydras Asylum for Girls had been established by a dedicated group of Protestant women to care for younger children, primarily girls, but it also accepted some smaller boys, especially siblings. At the age of eleven, the children were separated by gender, and the girls went to the upper levels of the Poydras Home, where they might learn a trade if they were not reunited with family members. The city was well supplied with asylums, as the orphanages were most often called; the need was unfortunately great. How Constance wished she had the power to give all of them the more fitting title Home for Children, regardless of the sponsor.

In truth, a large number of these children were not actually orphaned. A good number were half-orphans and stayed for a period of two to six years. But children in need were everywhere. Yellow fever was rampant and unmerciful in New Orleans in the summers, even when not at epidemic levels. That and cholera frequently left children with only one parent, who was often unable to care for them and also work. In spite of the times and the religious leanings of the city, families tended to be fairly small, which meant the orphanages were often able to keep brothers and sisters together, to be cared for and educated until their trade training began when they were older, enabling them to become self-sustaining. Constance rejoiced when a family could be reunited at that point, though she worried about all that had been missed, the effects of those long-term separations.

The wrought-iron gate opened quietly for Constance. She was impressed by how well oiled it seemed. She rang the bell at the door and greeted the matron, Mrs. Guidry. The staff had become accustomed to Constance's frequent visits. She nodded and smiled, made her way straight to the courtyard in back. Classes for the day were dismissed by the time Constance arrived, and a number of children were at play on the grounds. From the shadow of the doorway, she studied the groups. One troupe of girls ran in little circles, holding hands. At one point they twirled in a tight circle, erupting into giggles, until one girl tripped and fell. When her neighbor slapped away the hand she held up for assistance, she ran sobbing to the teacher in charge, who knelt, took her by the shoulders, spoke quietly, and sent her back to her playmates. At the far corner, a group of boys crouched on the ground with their marbles. A cluster of older children took turns pushing little ones in the two swings, while a handful of others jumped up and down impatiently, waving and pleading for their turn. Almost all were girls, and the few younger boys were probably siblings. Alone at the side of the building, one little boy sat digging his hands into the dirt, wiping at his face with his grubby fingers. Constance saw the tears when he turned his grimy face up to her. These were the ones she came for.

Constance pulled her long skirt aside—she had not been dressed for play—and settled beside him. She had already removed her gloves and laid them on the ground. The boy lowered his head and held his hands still against the earth. Without a word, Constance reached down, stuck her fingers in near his scratchings, and began to dig. The boy looked up at her in something of wonder. She continued to dig, carving a curved line in his direction. He watched, fascinated. She watched him watch. In a moment his fingers moved. Made a short, broken line in response to hers.

As she continued her line, Constance said without looking up, "What is your name?"

There was a long silence, in which his finger swirled, as if he might obliterate all the lines. "Walter," he said at last.

By now, Constance had brought her line full around, completing a circle that encompassed his jagged lines. As he leaned over to inspect it, she sat back and watched. The boy must have been about seven. His brown hair was washed and trimmed neatly. Hands and nails would have been clean except for his agonized scratching in the dirt.

"Are you new here, Walter?"

He nodded.

"Have you made any friends?"

He shook his head.

"Would you like to?"

Walter nodded again.

"Who would you like to be friends with? Do you know yet?"

Walter hesitated, looked around the courtyard, raised his hand and pointed toward the cluster of boys with their marbles.

"Johnny," he said. "He sleeps in the bed next to mine."

Constance picked up her gloves, brushed off her skirt as she stood, and took Walter's dirty little hand. She didn't bother to wipe it off. Together they walked toward the boys.

On her ride home, Constance tapped her gloves against her knee, then brushed at a bit of soil on her skirt. She lay against the seat of the carriage as if to nap, but her eyes were intent on the sky. *How blue*, she thought. *How constant.* And then, *No, never constant. Fickle, uncertain, unknowable—like life.* A life to which she must return. Uncertain. Acutely, piercingly uncertain. How could she ever know anything again? She might live on, not knowing if Benton was living or dead. Surely at some point she would know, but what would it mean? Would she be the wife who had tried to kill him or the wife who had reached out to save him? Would she be a widow by tragic accident or a criminal? And who was that man? What was he doing there? No innocent person would have then disappeared. She could not reconstruct the event. Too much was a blur of chaos. She could not see through the blur to find the blue sky. Perhaps she never would.

The steps to the house almost proved to be her undoing. Constance's breath came hard and fast, but her feet dragged with uncertainty up the front steps. Because she couldn't find the strength to lift her skirt, she tripped once. Constance ignored the sound of the ripping hem and pulled herself upward. She hesitated at the door, hand on the knob, listening. When she heard only silence, she entered and looked around. The house was the same, clearly. Yet not. Silence deadened the air as she walked from one empty room to the next until she reached the kitchen. From the backyard Constance heard the voices of her children, the quick laughter, the shrill little screams interrupted by giggles. One hand on the batiste curtain, she lifted the ruffle aside to view her girls playing chase as Analee folded dry laundry from the line and dropped it into her basket.

Constance exhaled. She had been conscious neither of holding her breath nor of the weakness with which her body sagged now that she could sit again. In her exhaustion, Constance dropped into one of the wooden chairs, knowing this respite would not endure. She laid her head on the kitchen table and closed her eyes, her ears ringing with the glad signs of her children's temporarily protected spirits.

CHAPTER 10

Chicago did not hesitate in getting cold. The winds whipped through the city. Shawls and hats went flying, unless held tight by gloved fingers, which would have fared much better in deep pockets. The mud began to freeze in treacherous strips along and between the planks, so that walking back from the White Way, arms loaded with clothes to be altered, became a challenge in diligent attention for Alice. In the flat, she would drop her load on the bed and warm her hands at the radiator, staring through the fogged window at the bleak city outside.

Once Alice had regained her sense of balance, she would slip into the bathroom, hold her hands under a stream of warm water, and examine her underclothing. For nothing. Day after day. Now week after week. How many weeks? She could not be sure. No, not true. She could be sure if she simply would. But she knew. She had known, despite some level of denial, for a while. Now the denial had to be put aside. She was with child.

There remained one month paid on her rent when she began to throw up, not just upon awakening but throughout the day. Her meager earnings from the White Way kept her fed—though now with the nausea she ate little—kept the heat going, but would not by any means pay the rent. Disoriented as she felt, Alice would have to find another place to live. Somewhere like the one-room flat she'd had before Howard. No, then she had been at Carson Pirie Scott & Company with a regular wage. Now she had perhaps half that much to cover everything, and the source of even that much was erratic and not to be counted on. What would she do? The only places she could afford would be far from the White Way, a far longer walk or the expense of a streetcar.

Without warning, she found herself yearning for home; for the wide expanses of the plains; for her hands touching her mother's, working some fancy stitch; even for her less than affectionate brothers. Suddenly she felt those brothers grab her, hold her hands behind her, felt one of them jerk her feet from under her, and down she went, with the splat of the mud and a hand on her head. She felt the sudden suffocation, heard the laughter as her mouth filled with mud. Then the sudden release when they let go and ran off in gales of laughter. And yet it had been home. With a wide horizon and the sky in all directions.

In the small windows of free time she could find while working on the alterations, Alice mounted the streetcar with a leftover newspaper the boy at the corner was always happy to slip to her. Her search for new housing felt futile. She returned to her previous building, with its one-room housing that she might afford, but nothing was available. She followed the landlord's suggestions, but to the same dead ends. Clutching the paper tightly, she pursued the notices with determination, but without success. A woman in one building pointed her finger in the general direction of a tenement settlement not far off.

Alice shook her head and walked away dejected. She knew already what was to be found there; she had naively ventured into one of the many scattered tenement areas of Chicago when she first arrived. It had been as dreadful as she might have envisioned: small wooden dwellings crowded against each other, with no foundations and an obvious lack of indoor sanitation. The air had been rank with the odor of human waste. Unwashed children eying her curiously, stray dogs barking and sniffing.

Not knowing where else to turn, Alice mounted the streetcar. Filled with defeat, a bout of nausea assailed her.

The days came and went. Alice sewed. Made her careful trips to and from the White Way. Read the seemingly useless housing notices in the day-old papers the sweet young newsboy continued to give her, though some bitterly cold days he was missing. One clear day Alice mounted the streetcar on another determined mission, not in search of housing, but in search of Howard himself. Why had she not thought of this before? Had she been too afraid of finding him? What limitations, what barriers had she imposed on herself out of the habits of womanhood? She would go to the cotton exchange. She would find Howard's brokerage extention. She would confront him.

Alice dismounted a block from the imposing building of the Chicago Board of Trade. The architecture appeared Gothic to her: the towering structure, the huge arched windows, which forced her to crane her neck as she approached along LaSalle Street. On her left rose the elegant Grand Pacific Hotel, which was appropriately named. Its size and grandeur stunned her. Thoroughly intimidated, Alice took a deep breath, raised her head, and continued toward her destination, now in view. On her right, the Royal Insurance Building rose to its also appropriately described skyscraping heights. In one window an ad promoted deposit vaults for silverware, papers, and jewelry. In another a large poster touted Revell's Furniture Store at Wabash and Adams. A sign on a Grand Pacific Hotel column promoted the Grand Pacific Café. Alice shook her head; none of those were of any use to her. She had envisioned nothing so grandiose.

The building where Howard worked dominated the corner

and had multiple entrances, which left her confused. The place was more intimidating by far for this simple plains woman than anything she had ever encountered. And this was her husband's familiar working environment. How much of him had she not known? Alice wandered around the corner. Her amazement was compounded as she approached the primary entrance, two stories high. At its apex were the extraordinary sculptures of the goddesses of industry and agriculture, who stood amid the draped folds of their gowns, each flanked by the symbols of her domain. Alice, unlike her uneducated brothers, had grown up with the luxury of reading with her mother. She recognized Ceres instantly, sheaves of grain on her left, her right hand atop an abundant cornucopia. This was the mother who had sacrificed all else to bring her missing daughter home. She thought about how her own mother had sacrificed to send Alice out into what she had envisioned as a better life.

At last, she lowered her gaze. Her anxiety rose with every step. She hesitated at the entrance, ready to turn back. But this was where her husband worked. For that reason, she had everything to do with just this place. The ornate door opened. Two gentlemen deep in discourse exited, but then one of them noticed her and stood back, holding the door open for her. She had no option but to enter.

"Thank you," she said with a slight curtsy and moved into the main hall.

It took her breath away. Nothing in her entire experience had been so grand: the soaring space, with its glass ceiling high above her; the walls alternately adorned with large windows and massive marble columns topped by ponderous capitals, cornices, and brackets; arched stained-glass windows interspersed with appropriate frescoes. How difficult it was to return her attention to the crowded interior, which buzzed with the voices of men stirring and gathered like a cluster of bees. Yet all of them seemed diminished by the scale of this structure! It was only with difficulty that she mustered the courage to ask one person, then another for directions to the office of the cotton exchange and the four huge elevators, one of which she had to take to find Howard. If he were to be found. She gave the elevator operator the floor number and stepped back, trying to make herself invisible among the men. The elevator was packed with them, all finely dressed and talking business among one another. How odd that she should notice the fabric and the cut of their jackets on a mission such as this! It was almost reflexive for her, given her expertise and experience. *A way to distract myself*, she thought. Her stomach lurched when the elevator stopped and started at each floor. *I can't throw up*, she told herself. *Don't do it, don't. Don't do it!* She swallowed the bitter bile as it rose in her throat.

Her relief at exiting the elevator, squeezing her way out from among the men, was short-lived. Now she had to open the door to the cotton exchange. She had to face some secretary there. She had to open her mouth and ask for Mr. Howard Butterworth, please.

"Howard Butterworth? I'm sorry, miss. We have no one by that name in this office. Could someone else be of assistance to you?"

"You have no one by that name. Are you certain? Look again, please. He works between here and the Memphis office. I'm sure he must be here."

"No, miss." The starched young woman ran her finger down a catalogued list of names. "There is no Howard Butterworth in our records. I am personally acquainted with all the gentlemen in this exchange, and I assure you, we have no one by that name in our employ."

"I know he is here," Alice insisted. "He is my husband."

"He may well be your husband, ma'am. But he is affiliated neither with the cotton exchange nor with this office in any capacity. Would you care to examine the list yourself? Or may I help you with anything else, before you leave?"

Alice stared at the woman's unrelenting face. After a moment reality entered her body, and shock numbed her. There would be no verification here. No more than with the police. The Howard Butterworth she knew as her husband did not exist.

In defeat, but with whatever remaining dignity she managed to find, she nodded to the secretary. "Thank you." Alice put her hand on the cold metal doorknob, then turned back to the young woman. "You have been quite helpful."

Somehow, Alice meant it. *Truth must always be of use.*

Near the corner of the corridor, Alice located the metal stairway and made her way down to the main hall, then slid along its ornate side walls, soaring, buzzing, and stirring with men, none of whom were her husband.

On the street she turned toward the concrete wall and vomited.

CHAPTER 11

Analee insisted Constance rest the next morning. Since no early knock came at her door, Constance managed to sleep until ten after nine. When she opened her eyes, she found her older daughter alone on the floor, coloring on a sheaf of papers, the childish images spread about her in the morning light. As Constance stirred, Delia clambered into the bed beside her. Outside Constance could hear Analee's quiet voice making up stories with the little one. The morning was quiet, restorative, and the bit of relief lasted past lunch.

Sometime in the afternoon a knock at the door seized Constance with panic. She rose from the davenport in an impulse to flee. But Analee opened the door to a young woman in a rose-colored day dress and a wide-brimmed feathered hat, who presented her card, gesturing quietly with an elegantly wrapped box in her hand. Analee bade her enter and took her into the drawing room.

"Good afternoon, Mrs. Halstead." The young woman held out her calling card. "I am Juliet Farleigh. I am here on behalf of Mrs. Dorothea Richard, whom I believe you met at the recent luncheon for the krewe of Les Mysterieuses."

"Oh, yes, Miss Farleigh. I had the pleasure of being seated beside Mrs. Richard. Would you have a seat? Analee, could you bring us a cup of tea, please?" Constance saw two little heads spying at the hallway door. They disappeared instantly upon her detection. Constance smiled, ostensibly at the attractive girl now standing in her drawing room.

Miss Farleigh remained standing. "I have the honor of delivering to you an important document from Mrs. Richard," she said, her voice taking on a tone of importance parallel to her words. "Perhaps you would like to be seated before I present it, Mrs. Halstead." She waved her hand toward the davenport, as if she, and not Constance, were in charge here. She set the red silk-covered container on the tea table and opened it with a bit of flourish. Inside lay a roll of parchment tied with a red silk ribbon.

Constance smiled again in a bit of amusement, both at the theatrics of the presentation and at the two play-tousled heads that continued to pop in and out of view at the hallway door. Constance gasped slightly, hand over her mouth, as the young woman untied the ribbon and let the roll of parchment fall in a flash of brilliant color and intricate forms.

"I am deeply honored to have been commissioned by Mrs. Dorothea Richard, Captain of the all-female Krewe of Les Mysterieuses, to present to you the following proclamation. That you, Mrs. Constance Halstead, shall be in attendance to Mrs. Marion Berger, Her Majesty, Semiramis, Queen of all compass points to the South, as Lady-in-Waiting for the Grand Ball on Friday evening, January tenth, following Twelfth Night, to be held at the Grand Opera House at eight o'clock in the evening."

At this point, Constance realized that her messenger was working hard to contain an outburst of glee. Constance herself found her ribs constricted. She felt caught in the unexpected blast of a door thrown open in a storm. She struggled to maintain her composure. As Analee set the tea tray on the table, Constance motioned Juliet to sit.

She could scarcely manage her panic. Constance leaned over the parchment and ostensibly studied in detail all the complex symbols worked into the design: the compass with four needles, each needle a scepter; the red poppies worked into the gold-embellished borders; the mythical figures, each veiled face a woman's. Regaining some sense of composure, Constance raised her eyes to those of Miss Juliet Farleigh, who burst into subdued laughter.

"Isn't it grand?" she said. "Yet again, we women take charge of ourselves! The men will have to wait on us, follow us, be called out by us. They will experience what we have to experience every day—waiting on the favor of some man." She set down her teacup, which she'd hardly touched. "Who knows, Mrs. Halstead? Perhaps next we shall have the vote!"

When the door closed behind Miss Farleigh, Constance stood watching her sprightly departing steps. *Only a few short years ago*, she thought, *I was that young. I am almost still that young. I shall never be young again. There is nothing left of me to be anything at all.*

"Take this, please, Analee," she said., pointing to the ornate parchment. "Don't let the children soil it. It may need to be returned. I am not feeling well. I shall be in my room."

Constance stood at her upstairs window, watching the girls chasing at tag, first one, then the other, back and forth between the two, until both fell down, laughing and tickling one another. Analee, in the yard with them, leaned over to tickle them both at once, at which they leapt to their feet. Across the alleyway, Constance noticed a man in a dark coat. He stared in the direction of the girls, separated from him by the high wrought-iron fence. She gasped with a chill of vague recognition. He walked on. Desperation filled her.

What have I done? Foolish, foolish! Why did I have to know what he was up to? I had this—these girls, this life, this home. This was mine. I was safe. Constance darted back to the window, her finger tracing its panes. The alley was vacant. *I will never be safe again. What if he walks in the door and stares at me with those eyes?* Her last vision of those eyes as they fell backward burned into her brain. They stared at her all the way into the black water. She tried to wipe them away. The blurred motion of that man as the train door slammed after him, the dull thwack of Benton hitting the water far below them. She could not escape. There was no escape. She would never be free from what had transpired.

Constance had lost track of time when Analee brought the girls to her bedroom for a good-night hug and a kiss. Constance was listless but roused herself from her chaise to embrace them. She held them as if she might never be able to hold them again. Somehow, they felt it, pulled back, and stared at her.

"Are you sick, Mama?" Maggie asked, a tiny lisp in her whisper.

Constance felt Delia's hand pressing on her cheek to turn her head. She studied the concern on that innocent face.

"Just a bit tired, my darlings," she said. "It's been a very busy week. Mama has had meeting after meeting, you know. Planning for Mardi Gras." Constance injected an upbeat of enthusiasm into those last words, trying to divert the girls' concern. "And lots of planning for the orphanage."

"Why are they there, Mama?"

"Why is who where, Maggie?"

"The orphanage, Mama. Why are they there? Why don't they go home? Don't they have a mama and a papa? Like us?"

Analee tried to steer the girls away. Constance held up her hand. But she took note, with trepidation. Why had Analee reacted to that question? Did she somehow know? How could she?

"It's all right, Analee." Constance took the girls' hands in her lap. "Sometimes things happen," she said. In the silence, leaves outside rustled against the window. A momentary distraction as Constance studied her daughters' curious faces. *Sometimes things happen . . . What will I say?* "Sometimes things happen," she repeated, pumping their little hands in her lap. "Things you don't know about yet. Now, let Analee take you to bed."

"But, Mama," cried Maggie. "We're not sleepy yet. Will you take us to the orphanage to play? Maybe we could play tag. Please, Mama."

"And you didn't finish what happens, Mama. Does their daddy get mad and send them there to think about minding him better next time? I hope Papa won't ever do that to us. Do you go there to help them learn to behave?"

The shock of Delia's questions constricted her throat. For a brief instant, Constance felt a gag reflex. She rose. Then sat back down and took their hands in hers again.

"All right," she said. "This is hard now. But I will tell you. Sometimes things happen."

"You said that, Mama. Three times now you said that," said Delia.

"But we don't know what happens, Mama," added Maggie.

Constance knew she had repeated herself. She had to find a way to the next sentence. "Sometimes people die. Sometimes they get very sick, and the doctor doesn't have the right medicine." A deep breath. "Sometimes there is an accident—"

Delia interrupted. "Like a horse could kick you or something?"

Maggie chimed in. "Or get runned over in the street if you didn't see a new motorcar?"

"Yes, yes, something like that." Constance felt the drain of every word.

"But what about the other one? The mama or daddy that

didn't get sick or runned over. If you have a mama or a daddy, you can't be an orphan, can you?" Delia was genuinely perplexed.

"You are absolutely right, sweetheart. Something happening to one parent doesn't make you an orphan. But many of these children are known as half-orphans. In other words, only one of their parents is alive and working."

"Then why are they there?"

"Their mama or daddy is away from home, working all day, Delia. Sometimes at night. No one is home to take care of them, so they go to live at the orphanage for a while, until they are old enough to learn a way to make money themselves. Then they might go back home and help out. Or they might go and live somewhere else while they work—like a grown-up."

The girls seemed to be waiting for more, as if somehow she had failed to explain life to them.

"There now, that's entirely enough for one night. Off to bed, little ones. Analee is waiting for you."

"But we're not tired, Mama," said Maggie.

"Well, your mama is. Exhausted. Now, off with you."

Constance watched them reach for Analee's hands, turn, and blow kisses. She blew one back.

As the door closed, Constance collapsed on the chaise, fingers clasped painfully around her shoulders, knees and elbows sharp but inadequate against her terror.

The following day, Constance sat at her desk and drew out a sheet of monogrammed stationery. One slow word at a time, then more rapidly, she penned her words, then folded the note and sealed the envelope. Downstairs, she bade goodbye to Analee and the children and hailed a carriage two blocks away. Her determination was the one necessity she now understood. At the stately Italianate Richard house on Prytania in the Garden District, Constance leaned forward and handed the driver her note. She counted each step he took, heard the sharp clang of the mailbox closing. There were no longer any other choices. Her options had disappeared beneath the high trestle of a moving train. She could no more reinstate them than restore the shock waves of dark water folding over Benton's eyes to their pastoral stillness.

CHAPTER 12

The day and night dragged past. Nothing interfered with her despair. Constance found herself repeatedly jarred, only to discover one or the other of her girls tugging at her, pulling her out of her fog for attention. Her mind was both void and entangled. Analee asked again and again if she was ill. To which she could only shake her head. Analee inquired also about Mr. Halstead's return. To which, again, Constance could only shake her head. She did not eat. She did not know if she slept or not; she had no sensation of either. She no longer even made an effort at pretense with Analee. Her very being had gone vacant.

On the second day of her stupor, she was aware of a knocking at the front door. A sharp rapping, like that of a man. It was the urgency, perhaps, of that sound that broke into her torpor. Constance blinked her eyes. *Here it is*, she thought. *Here he is. No, he wouldn't knock. He would break through the door. He would break me.* She rose and waited.

"They's a constable to see you, Miss Constance. Truth be, they's two. I stood them in the entry by the door to come fetch you."

They have come for me. It is over. I am undone.

Constance gripped the rail as she descended the stairs, one careful step after another, to her fate.

The sun was brilliant and burdensome through the leaded glass as Constance approached the heavy front door, which was slightly ajar. The backlit officers appeared as darkened silhouettes. She nodded. They did not, but stood directly in front of her, blocking her way, in case her impulse to flee overwhelmed her. The taller tipped his cap, staring at her directly, then turned his head to the other expectantly.

"Mrs. Halstead?"

"Yes."

"Mrs. Benton Halstead?"

She nodded. Whom had they expected?

The officer circled his cap nervously in his hands. "We need to speak with you, ma'am."

"Yes. Well, here I am. In person. Speak."

"Well, ma'am. Perhaps it may not be best to speak right here." A hinge creaked as he pushed the door behind him shut. "You might prefer to sit down. Might we come in, please, ma'am?"

"Am I in jeopardy, then? Do you wish to arrest me for taking hand-me-downs to the orphanage? Stolen goods, perhaps?" Constance astonished herself that her wit had somehow reappeared. But she had been inappropriately flip. She glanced from one to the other in what she hoped seemed like amusement. Then sobered when their faces remained unbrokenly solemn. "Very well, then. Follow me in, please."

Constance led them from the foyer to the salon but remained standing, in her head a lingering thought that she must remember to oil the hinges on the front door. In the drawing room, where she could see them, her awareness settled on the officers. Perspiration dampened her linen day dress. She bade the men wait a moment while she checked on her children. And tried to still her trembling. When she returned, Constance noted how the men were visually inspecting the house. *Finer than they had imagined*, she thought, *or not as fine as they had expected*?

"Now, gentlemen," she said, "what is it you wish to speak with me about?"

"My apologies, ma'am. Sorry to have to interrupt your schedule. We find ourselves in need of your assistance," said the shorter of the two.

"Assistance? Whatever for?"

The taller officer took the lead at last. "At the morgue, ma'am. We are in need of your assistance at the morgue, Mrs. Halstead."

"At the morgue?" She swung her head sharply. "That is what you said? At the morgue."

"Yes, ma'am." The taller one was in charge again. "I'm Officer Pulgrum, and this is Officer Dean. We are here to ask you to come with us to help identify a body, ma'am."

Constance released her hold on the back of the blue velvet chair, swiveled, then lowered herself at last into it, almost in slow motion. "A body?"

The officers had stepped in front of her as she sat. *Afraid I'll faint*, she thought.

"We believe it to possibly be that of your husband, ma'am." Officer Pulgrum's voice was steady.

Constance sat immobile, silent, choking on her breath.

"I'm sorry, Mrs. Halstead. There is no easy way to speak of things like this."

"No, no easy way," Constance whispered over her erratic breath.

"It's possible that it is not your husband. Which is why we need your help."

Constance jerked her head up toward them, then turned from one to the other. "You have come to have me identify my husband, whom you say is dead, and then you say perhaps it is not my husband and my husband may walk in the door this minute? What in God's name are you saying?"

The men looked at one another. Officer Dean took the lead. "A corpse was found in a body of water near the railroad trestle on a farm up near the Mississippi border. Apparently, fell from the train. There was a good bit of damage to the face and head."

Constance choked on her breath again.

"I'm sorry, ma'am. It may not be your husband. The man had multiple papers on him, all waterlogged, to be sure, and coming apart in soggy pieces. Our department has been drying and piecing them together as best we can. Some parts are missing. One appears to be an identification of a B. . . . something Hals . . . the rest illegible. There are other papers, as well, and it has been a bit difficult to reassemble everything. Part of one seems to indicate this address. Our investigation matches Benton Halstead with this address. Have you been in contact with your husband in the past few days?"

"No. Actually, I have not. He travels for a living. I assume, given your investigation, you know that already."

"Yes, ma'am. By what means and where does he travel?"

"By the Illinois Central. Between New Orleans and Chicago. He is in the timber business—a timber broker, actually. I guess that's the timber business, though he doesn't raise timber." She was stumbling on her thoughts.

"How long has he been gone this last time, Mrs. Halstead?"

"Something over a week., Officer Dean. I expected him home any day now."

"And has that concerned you?"

"No. Well, not much. Until yesterday, probably. His schedule is quite unpredictable. He's often overdue, though sometimes he's unexpectedly early. This has been a bit longer than usual. But I never count on his being home when he says he will. His work is far too unpredictable for that. I'd make myself crazy if I fretted over when he would and would not be home." She knew she sounded blasé, unconcerned that this might, indeed, be Benton.

"Well, ma'am, since there does seem to be a possibility this could be your husband, we must ask you to accompany us. Do you need to arrange for your children?" asked Officer Dean.

"No, they are in the care of my trusted housekeeper."

"Do you need someone to come to be with you, ma'am?" Officer Pulgrum asked. "This could be quite difficult on you."

"No. There is no one." There was that indifference again. How must she present herself? They had her. "But you will bring me home, I trust."

As Constance struggled to rise from the chair, both men extended a hand to help her. She ignored them, toed a packet of cast-off clothing for the orphanage away from the front door, and led the way out to the street.

"I'll bring the wagon around for you, Mrs. Halstead. Officer Dean will wait with you here in the shade."

"I assure you, sir, that I am utterly capable of walking around the corner. But tell me, exactly what do you mean by your 'wagon'? Are you putting me in a transport for prisoners?"

"No, ma'am. Not at all. We use a regular civilian carriage for such purposes. I apologize for alarming you."

"Thank you, Officer Pulgrum. Shall we go, sir?"

Constance set off at a brisk pace, clearly surprising the officers. She was aware how she often failed to meet the expectations for a lady of her social status. But a woman of any status might display anxiety in a wide range of manner when fetched by the police to help identify a body, one quite possibly her husband's.

Let them perceive me however they like, she thought as she mounted the carriage, again refusing their help. *In the long run, it is unlikely to matter.*

CHAPTER 13

The ride to the station house was silent, except for the resonance of ordinary life along the cobbled street and the steady clip-clop of the horses. Constance sat stiffly, clenching her handkerchief in her immaculate hands. *How many times have I ignored his absences? Now he is dead. I could tell them so and not have to see his damaged body.*

At the station house, the officers hitched the carriage beneath the shade of a low side portico. She hesitated before accepting the assistance of Pulgrum's outstretched hand. Officer Dean held open the heavy door with its barred windows. Again, Constance hesitated. Then looking straight ahead, she lifted her skirts, mounted the steps, and entered the gloom of the bureau entry. Only then did she look around, her determination flagging. From behind the massive oak desk, an intake officer nodded and raised his knobby hand to the two officers.

"This way, ma'am." Pulgrum stepped aside and motioned her through a second door into a small, poorly lit office. Dean followed and pulled back a starkly plain, rigidly constructed chair, indicating for her to sit. Sweat trickled from Constance's temples; whether it was from the enclosed heat or the tension of the moment was unclear. She dabbed at it with her handkerchief.

"Mrs. Halstead, we know this to be a terribly stressful moment. And we must prepare you that in this particular instance, it will be an exceptionally difficult one." Officer Pulgrum was grim. "Identification of the dead is one of the most unpleasant experiences a human being can be called upon to do, even at its least traumatic. Even if this man is not your husband, this will be a terrible drain upon you. I am hoping to steady you for what you are about to experience, even if this man is a complete stranger to you."

Constance knew this would be no stranger. Her head throbbed as if it might split.

"If, in truth, Mrs. Halstead, the body is that of your husband, I must warn you that the body in question has sustained a considerable amount of damage. It appears that death occurred some days ago in a plunge from a trestle on the Illinois Central. The impact with the water at some velocity, combined with the warming temperature, and some facial damage from . . . Well, ma'am, I regret the need to ask your assistance with this identification regardless of the actual identity."

Constance stared at Officer Pulgrum's rough hands as he tapped the eraser of a yellow pencil, its point still showing the knife strokes of its last sharpening. In the growing silence, she stared at the pristine order of the papers on the desktop.

Officer Dean eased toward the door, rested his hand on the doorknob.

"Do you feel ready, ma'am?" Officer Dean leaned toward her.

Constance nodded and stood but held a tight grip on the arm of the chair.

"Mrs. Halstead," said Pulgrum, "just one more moment, if you please." He motioned her to sit again. "Perhaps there might be another way. Not so difficult for you. Let me ask . . . Did your husband have any identifying marks? I'm thinking specific scars or marks, any old cuts or injuries that might help identify him? If there is one unique enough, there might be no need to put you through a viewing of the body. Or depending on where such a mark might be located, you might only have to see that one mark, if it's present. Are you aware of any such identifying anomaly?"

Constance dabbed at her damp brow and cheek. The close air of the office had become stifling to her. There were, of course, the old skinned knees that any boy would have had; the left thumbnail, which sat a bit crooked at the inside edge from a mishap with a saw blade early in his career. These would hardly be specific enough to serve as definitive identification. Nor would his one eyebrow that tended to rest lower than the other, but then she shuddered at the vague allusions to massive facial destruction. Constance rose again, as it seemed inevitable that she had to witness the ruins of Benton's handsome face, must have this forever branded into her memory.

As Dean held open the door for her, Constance had a sudden thought, a memory of a distinguishing mark that might identify her husband. She held up her hand.

"There is something," she said. "Something particular. I don't believe this could be confused." She looked from one to the other. "My husband has a birthmark, very small, a round deep red mark on the bottom of his right foot. As if he had just stepped on a lit cigarette."

The two officers looked at one another.

"Will you come with us, please?" Pulgrum gestured toward the hall.

Constance walked between them, one on each side as if ready to catch her should her knees or body fail her. At the door to the morgue, Pulgrum knocked and then entered, leaving her with Dean. He reemerged moments later and motioned them in. The odor assaulted her, gagged her. Someone held her elbow. Midway in the room, an attendant rolled a gurney into the aisle and pulled back the sheet covering the right foot.

On the bottom, just outside the arch, was what looked to all appearances to be a recent cigarette burn. The officers reached for her as Constance began to slip.

"Give her some time."

The sound of the officer's hoarse voice resonated in the depths of Constance's paralysis. She opened her eyes. Her vision filled with the ragged repair of a cracked ceiling. Where was she? Had they put her in a cell? Did anyone know she was there? Suddenly frantic, Constance scrambled with her hands, reaching, grasping for anything. Her fingers closed on the wooden edge of whatever held her. She gripped it tight, then tighter. Something to hold her.

"Ah, she's coming to. Fetch some water there, will you? Come now. Snap to."

At the sound of that heavy voice again, Constance turned her head to see the narrow shape of Pulgrum towering high above her. She reached out her hand, but he did not touch her.

"Just you hold on there a minute, Mrs. Halstead. Dean is gone to get you some water. Take your time, so you don't fall out on us again."

Constance closed her eyes. Turned her head from side to side. Tried to wipe away the thoughts of Benton's striking face destroyed. His eyes on hers. The look of sudden recognition. She felt the nausea rising. Swallowed hard and opened her eyes to the veined plaster of the ceiling.

"Take your time. You'll be all right." Pulgrum had not moved, his figure dark above her, his shadow over her face. "Ah, here's the water, when you're ready."

Constance nodded. Pulgrum leaned over, slid his hard arm beneath her shoulders, and lifted her to sitting. As he shifted her feet to the floor, she recognized that she was back in the office on a narrow wooden bench, her back against the wall. She blinked at the silhouette of Dean as he tentatively offered the water. She took it and sipped, then drank. Laid her head back against the wall.

What did they know? Everything? Nothing? What would they ask? And what could she say? A thousand thoughts swirled in her head before she opened her eyes again and nodded. Pulgrum took one elbow; Dean the other. Once on her feet, she felt her strength returning. They released their hold, and she stood on her own, but they hovered close, too close, in case. She stumbled to the chair on her own.

"We need to ask some questions, ma'am." The voice was Pulgrum's.

"Then ask," she said after a moment. There was nothing more to avoid.

"Mrs. Halstead, are you familiar with Storyville?" he asked.

She felt the shock of it, the unsuspected jolt of it.

"Of course," she said. "Who in New Orleans would not know a whole quarter legitimized for prostitution and crime?"

"And gambling?"

"Gambling? Oh, yes. Of course."

"Was your husband a gambler, Mrs. Halstead?"

She hesitated. "I'm sure he made his bets, Officer, like most men I know."

"Horses? Cards?"

"Cards." She looked up at him. "He liked to play."

"And did he win or lose, ma'am?"

"I'm sure some of both, Officer. Why?"

Pulgrum hitched himself onto the corner of the desk. Dean fidgeted.

"Are you familiar with the Black Hand, Mrs. Halstead?"

"I know it exists."

"You know it exists? Nothing more?"

"I know its reputation for evil. And violence."

"And murder?"

"Yes, and murder." She shook her head. The memory of Benton's rage as he left the table. The sudden blur of the man ramming past as Benton lost his footing.

"We found this on your husband's body, Mrs. Halstead. Water-soaked in his pocket. It took some time and some doing to try to separate the various papers and get them dried. We put them together as best we could, like some sort of jigsaw. Quite a challenge. All blurred and run together, or washed away completely. But this is what we've managed to assemble." He pointed to the desk. "Are you strong enough to rise?"

Constance nodded. Took her time, holding the arm of the chair to be sure. Then stepped toward she knew not what.

On a portable flat wooden tray on the desk lay some assembled pieces of smeared paper. There was little there to make sense of. But she stared. Then looked at Pulgrum for explanation.

"What do you see there, Mrs. Halstead? Anything familiar?"

She shook her head. She wanted to touch it, move those fragments of ruined paper, force them to make sense.

"We believe it to be a threat from the Black Hand. We believe your husband was heavy into the cards with them and owed them gambling debts he could not pay. We have reason to believe he was a frequenter of Storyville. Would you know anything about that, ma'am?"

"*Prostitutes?*" The word came out loud enough to shock Constance, even as she uttered it. She shook her head. "I can't imagine." She envisioned Benton and his almost wooden approach to sex. The idea of Benton with prostitutes almost made her laugh. His interest in making love had seemed about equal to his interest in tending a garden.

Early in their marriage she had blamed herself. Had bought the most beguiling nightgowns she could find. Had paraded herself before him with her wrapper off one shoulder and loose about her torso, only to have him walk from the room for some business detail he had forgotten. Hurt by his lack of response, she had blamed her lack of feminine beauty, her small breasts, her flat hips. It was a wonder she had ever had three babies— those infrequent, impromptu conjugal completions that had left her wanting and unsatisfied, but with child. Perhaps it was her body. Why had he chosen her and not some buxom girl? Yet though he was invariably polite and charming to such women, she had never sensed him flirting.

"*Prostitutes.*" She repeated the word almost in mockery.

"No, ma'am. We've no evidence of that, though a man might be a man regardless. No, that's not what gets a man in deep in Storyville. It's the gambling. And if a man can't pay, then—"

"Then what?"

"Then a note of threat, like this. If you examine the lower right, all pieced together there, it takes on the distorted outline of a hand. A *black hand*, we believe."

Constance thought of the odd man she had seen outside her fence. The set faces of those gamblers. Benton's urgent demands for money, the money from her trust, which she had refused to give him, which she had the right to refuse and which he could not take, because of Louisiana's Napoleonic law, which protected her. The papers she had seen him pull furtively from his pocket, stuff back in again in anger as he left that fateful morning.

"Would your husband have been susceptible to suicide, Mrs. Halstead?"

"*Suicide?*" The word stunned her, sent her cold. She shook her head.

"We wonder if he may have jumped from the train, Mrs. Halstead. He was over his head in debt to the Black Hand. It's in our list of possibilities."

Constance sank into the chair. In her mind the scene played in slow motion. She saw his eyes, his recognition, the blur of

motion, that man, and Benton in the air, the black water beneath him.

"Mrs. Halstead?" Pulgrum's voice wrenched her back into
the room. "It might have only been an accident, you know. It's
entirely possible that is all it is." He tapped his fingers on the
desk. "We are done for now, Mrs. Halstead."

Would he ever stop saying her name? This name that sent a
wave of horror through her.

"Officer Dean will see you home, ma'am. We will keep you
notified, of course, and will make arrangements for the release
of your husband's body when we close the investigation."

Constance was at the door when Pulgrum spoke again.

"Mrs. Halstead."

She stopped, turned back, one hand on the knob.

"The mob to whom your husband was in debt does not give
up easily, especially where money is concerned. I just wondered . . . Have they tried to make any contact with you?"

In an instant, the strange man at her fence leaped into her
mind. A jolt of fear ran through her. But there was nothing else.
Nothing she could name. No attempt to contact her. He could
be anyone—an unknown neighbor who took the alley as a random shortcut. She shook her head.

"You will let us know if there is any contact? Any hint of an
attempt at contact?"

She nodded and walked out with Officer Dean, aware of
Pulgrum's eyes still on her.

CHAPTER 14

The chill increased. Alice cracked the window during the night, then closed it tightly as soon as she rose, the remnants of bread she kept by the bed still in her hand. Alice pulled her heavy shawl around her, finished the bread, waited for the nausea to subside. But the absence of Howard would not subside. It was no longer the physical absence of the man she called husband. Now she faced a void in the nonexistence of that husband. Who was the man she had married? Whom she had lived with? With whom she'd had a son? A son who had died in his hands. A severely ill son who might well have died of his fever regardless, but who had died thrashing out of control in a sink of cold water, in the hands of a father who was not Howard. A man whom she had blamed, had struck, fighting him to try to save her child. A man she had never ceased to blame for her baby's death, whose stubborn, inexpressive grief she had not attempted to comfort. He could grieve alone and in shame, as she grieved alone. Now, in truth, she was utterly alone. And pregnant by a man who did not exist.

Chicago's early winter had fully arrived. The inescapable mud in the streets had become partial ice. Ice that she would need to negotiate back and forth to the White Way to pick up the alterations. She assumed that there would be plenty, as was usual with the change of seasons, but with bulky, heavier fabrics to deal with, a burden to carry in the freezing cold and on the ice. Ice that would be treacherous for her, on which she might break a limb. What then? She would be unable to work, to sew, to earn money, to get food. Treacherous ice on which she might lose another child.

The nights were her respite. The open window invited the chill into the room. Alice slid herself into bed, under the cover of the wedding ring quilt she had made with her mother long ago, one of those hope-chest items she had actually brought with her. Hope sounded so empty now. The sounds of the city at night soothed her: the soft clip-clop of the occasional horse and its creaking wagon, the indistinct rhythm of neighboring voices, the occasional running feet of someone on an errand in the dark, someone young and unafraid of ice. In the distant flicker of the gaslight on the street, Alice would fall into a deep and, for the most part, dreamless sleep. It was as if the seeming inexistence of a husband named Howard Butterworth, cotton broker, emptied her nights of disruption, though now she woke at daybreak, her morning tinged with Jonathan's death and her nausea, a new child in her womb. She consistently kept her bread within easy reach beside the bed to calm her stomach until she could rise.

The nausea passed, for which Alice was grateful beyond measure. This morning sickness had been only somewhat less than with baby Jonathan, but nausea was nausea. *It takes your body hostage*, Alice thought. *Yes, that was the word:* hostage. She dreaded waking, dreaded the movement of dressing herself, turning corners in the kitchen and down the stairs to the treacherous streets. With the holiday season approaching, she was correct about the abundance of alterations, but now she had to negotiate the streets in focus. She could manage that at least, but there was still the unrelenting fear of how to find housing, safe for herself and this baby to come.

When she took her single dish to the sink, there were tears and then sobs, which took her prisoner, *hostage*, there by that sink where Jonathan died. She gripped the cabinet edge to keep from falling. Her tears were as wet on her face as her hand had once been when trickling little streams of bathwater over her baby as she watched him laugh, his little arms waving in delight. Then the cold bathwater in which he died, the water meant to save him from his fever, in the wet hands of his father. His father, whose broken, guarded, silent grief she had scorned and ignored. She had adored her son. She still did, though he was not here. He would never be here. He would always be here in her memory, in her heart, in her very being. Her thoughts moved unexpectedly toward her own mother, in realization of how she had surely adored her own boys just this way, those boys who had lorded it over Alice, those boys whose right of inheritance had forced her into this life that now defied her, this apartment filled with memories that she could hardly bear. She held her breath until she could take it all in by force of will and walk away from the sink.

"Are you all right, Alice?" Mr. White held the pile of clothing to be altered over his arm. Leaning back, he studied her, his other hand on her shoulder.

"Yes. Yes, Mr. White. I am just a bit tired, but I am fine." She saw his disbelief clearly defined in the concern on his face.

"Are you sleeping well, Alice?"

She nodded her head and reached for the clothing, which he did not surrender. "Yes. Actually, sir, I sleep surprisingly well."

"Are you overloaded, then, Alice? Should I find an assistant to help you?"

"No, sir. I'm quite fine. The sewing helps me. It's more than just the money, sir." Alice hesitated, turned her head aside. "The sewing soothes my mind and gives me peace."

"It is always reassuring to have something of steady peace," he said, shifting the clothing. "So, nothing else?"

"No, sir. Let me take those now. I'll have them back as quickly as possible. Is there anything urgent among them?" This time when she reached for the clothing, he transferred the load to her. "Anything special I should know?"

"Actually, yes. Miss Caruthers—perhaps you know her— needs the beige twill skirt hemmed by next week for her honeymoon. Your work is always so quick. I told her I felt sure there would be no difficulty. Everything else is quite straightforward." White leaned toward her, then straightened, his face in a bit of a frown. "I almost forgot. Miss Caruthers had a friend, here from New Orleans for the wedding, I believe. At any rate, she has a hooded satin cape, falls below the shoulder, in need of some minor repair. I believe it's to do with the trim on the edges of the hood. Something she needs back home for Mardi Gras, I think she said. As to the trousers, I have pinned the lengths myself. There are several. Is there any difficulty in this?"

"Of course not, Mr. White. I should have the skirt to you well before that time, and the little cape as well. It all sounds quite simple. I'll bring the trousers one by one as I finish—or shall I wait and bring them all together?"

"All together will be just fine," he said. "You do not need to be trudging to and fro in this weather, and these two gentlemen did not express any urgency."

Alice saw the continued concern on his face. She felt a need to divert him. "I beg your pardon, Mr. White, but what is Mardi Gras?"

"Oh, Mardi Gras. It's quite a festival, I believe. In New Orleans each year to begin the season of Lent. Lots of fancy costumes and ball dresses. Apparently, the day before Ash Wednesday, before examining your sins and giving something up for forty days, you spend that 'Fat Tuesday'—that's the translation—to give yourself enough sins to examine." He chuckled, cleared his throat. "At least that's how I understand the tradition." White shifted his weight. "This is quite a load, Alice. Let me get a bag for you to carry these in."

"Thank you, sir. This will work just fine," she said, folding the clothing into the cotton bag he had fetched for her. "You have no need to worry." She tried a reassuring smile over her shoulder as she exited.

But Alice was wrong about there being no need to worry. The temperature had dropped. The icy wind hit her as she rounded the corner, and Alice pulled her dark woolen coat up around her neck. She should have worn a scarf. What had she been thinking? Or not thinking, in reality. She forged her way the few blocks back to the flat, holding herself as tight as possible to the sides of the buildings, hoping to shield herself from the wind. The never steady boards of the walk were in some places frozen to the ground, in others, sliding under the mud. Alice struggled to prevent her hat from flying away, to keep her coat around her neck, to keep the cloth bag steady and prevent the alterations from falling out. At the same time, eyes squinted against the wind, she tried to gauge the treacherous walkway and where to put her feet. It was like some childhood game, hopping from one point to another, avoiding the treacherous spots of mud and barely visible ice. Someone in the street yelled out from a wagon and lashed at the horse. Alice startled, turned to see the source of the commotion in mid-step. Her foot landed on a patch of ice; her face, her thinly gloved hands in the mud; her elbow on the edge of a plank. The pain shot through her. She tried to push herself upright, managed only to sink her hand deeper into the mud. Someone took hold of her arm to pull, and Alice cried out.

"I'm sorry," she said to whoever was trying to assist. "It's my elbow," she said, propping herself up on the other arm, dragging her knees beneath her in an attempt to gain her footing.

She heard a babble of voices as a small crowd gathered around her. Simultaneously, she could see the feet of others scurry past. She could feel their need to escape the scene. Finally, she found enough footing to reach out her uninjured hand for help. An older man, a workman from all appearances, and a young one, only a boy, reached out to hold her up, get her on her feet and onto the wooden plank. The boy stepped into the mud with one foot to retrieve the bag of clothes; one trouser leg and the hem of the twill skirt dragged in the wet mud as he tugged it onto the wood.

"Are you hurt, ma'am?" the boy asked.

"Only my elbow," Alice said, looking down, surveying the damage to herself. "Thank you," she said to the boy, again to the workman, with gratitude more sincere than she had experienced in a very long time.

Alice took the bag from the boy. "I will be fine," she said to them. "Yes, thank you. I am going to be fine."

CHAPTER 15

In the flat at last, Alice removed her muddy outer clothes. She spread them over Howard's chair and on the floor. Unlaced her corset and held her hands gently over her belly, where this new babe lay, becoming who it would be. She turned to the radiator, swiveled the knob to increase the heat, and warmed her hands against its ornamental metal. She unlaced her boots and slipped her toes onto the warm floor beneath it.

What am I doing? she thought. *I am having his child. And he is in Memphis, perhaps with his mother.* She remembered how touched she had been at his sheet of tidy notes with those measurements. She did not know now who he was or what he did. He was not the cotton broker he had presented himself to be. He clearly had legitimate work and a decent income. That she knew. Here was the flat, decently furnished, for which he had paid good rent. His clothing was that of a gentleman, and her own wardrobe had been well upgraded at his insistence. There had been the occasional dinners at various restaurants, not the finest, but fine enough. She remembered for a moment the dinner of their wedding night, the night itself, and an intense bitterness flooded through her. Where was he? How could he have abandoned her? Left her fearing him dead. Now Alice thought, *Who was—who is—this man who is my husband? I must leave this place, not just this flat. I must leave this city, this uncertainty. My child depends on me, is trusting me. I cannot lose another. I cannot lose this child.*

When Alice had regained herself somewhat, she bathed and washed her hair, donned her nightdress and a warm robe, actually one of Howard's robes, because it was heavier, taking possession of it now as hers. She had washed the bulk of the mud from her clothes, rinsed it down the sink, a kind of quiet determination taking hold of her. When she had tended to herself, a sense of resolution guiding her, she examined the bag of clothes from the White Way. Only the one trouser leg and one side of the skirt were truly soiled.

Alice put some water on to boil. She would have a cup of tea. She would eat the bread and cheese that remained. She would clean the mud from the skirt, iron it dry, and set about turning the hem. She would do the same with the trouser leg. Thank goodness the fragile satin cape had not been soiled. All that was needed for it would be a close re-stitching of its remarkable gold filigree trimming, loose in several spots, all minor. She knew it would take her the bulk of the night, but then she would be shed of all this. She would return them to Mr. White in the morning, along with all the rest untouched. Her apology for leaving with work unfinished would be sincere. It was hard to think of it. In her life she had never left a job unfinished. But this part of her life was over now. By afternoon she would be on the train to Memphis.

Central Station should not have surprised Alice after her recent exposure to the Board of Trade building and her glimpses of the other palatial buildings near it, yet the nine-story building with its thirteen-story clock tower overwhelmed her. Perhaps it was not so much the building as what she was doing that

overwhelmed her. Perhaps the scale of the building, its dwarfing of her, created an interior dwarfing of herself in relation to
this determination to find the truth. With her ticket in hand,
Alice sat on one of the long wooden double-sided benches to
wait. She marveled at the design of them, felt a sense of unease
sitting back-to-back with other passengers, whose conversations came into her ears as if directed right to her. Two women
whom she could not see, but could hear clearly, settled on the
bench behind her, laughing.

"I am so very eager to be home again in New Orleans,"
said one.

"Indeed," said the other. "This freezing weather will be the
death of me if I have to remain in this place another hour. How
can people actually live in such a clime?"

"Well, Mother, there are such people as Eskimos, who live in
houses made of ice. There really can't be a way to warm up
even the home. Yet they live like that. It must be some accus-
tomization in the blood. But not in mine. I will be so happy to
see home, in spite of our lovely shopping."

"Yes, dear, as will I. I'm not convinced the shopping, lovely
as it is, or the city, lovely as it is not, are worth the effort. I am
quite excited, though, to have plans in place well before next
Mardi Gras, don't you agree?"

"Indeed, I do, Mother. I am quite excited for this year's plans
and for the wonderfully unusual trims we have found. Now we
simply need the right seamstress. I wasn't altogether happy
with repeating last year's. Of course, so much of it is not in our
control, but surely the committee might find a better one."

"One would think, dear." The older woman stood. "Believe
I shall try to find a restroom before we board. Those on the
train seem rather cramped to me."

"I'll go with you. I agree."

Then they were gone. Some gentleman sat in their emptied
place and rattled open a newspaper.

Alice turned her gaze to the massive single arch that formed the ornate ceiling, its perfect pattern of decorative squares inviting her attention. They were perfectly aligned in each direction, each the perfect depth and dimension. It was not their decorative interiors that mesmerized her so much as their double precision: each one perfectly matched all the others, but a difference that did not call great attention to itself was evident in the manner in which each fit perfectly into the curve of the ceiling. *How is that humanly possible?* she wondered. *How are men able to fashion such precision?* She thought of the grandeur she had so recently been exposed to. Who were all those workmen who had realized some architect's vision? Where were they now? All those nameless craftsmen whose names would not be listed beside that of the architect.

She thought of herself, the endless garments she had created or altered or repaired. Who would know her name? It might be remembered for a week by some, but ultimately, the garments would be sent to charity. These ladies, returning now, did they know the name of the somewhat undesirable seamstress? The one who would sew on their trims and fit their fancy garments? Would the ball gown for this strange festivity ever be worn a second time? And what would become of the skill and talent of the nameless, forgotten seamstress who had created it?

Alice rose and fell into line behind the mother-daughter pair, now chattering about which men from which krewe—what was that?—were the most desirable of the available gentlemen and why. Alice wondered if any of them were capable of creating a square as complex as those overhead, let alone one that would fit in just one precise place in the curve of that arch.

On the overnight train from Chicago to Memphis, Alice had economized with only a standard seat instead of a berth. She had packed four sandwiches of ham on rye bread, which would not spoil and would last with care if she doled them out in small bits until past her arrival, since she had no idea how long it might take her to find a room she could afford. Or how long after that to find Howard or his mother. But the fall had shaken her into action. Another day in the Chicago cold, fighting the ice and the wind, was not in her. At least Memphis would be milder, and Howard had to know. His mother had to know. He would be a father again, and he would have to support her. His mother had never known baby Jonathan. She would surely want to know this only grandchild.

It seemed so long now, half her life, since Howard had disappeared, evaporated into thin air, as the landlord had said to her. The police had paid so little heed to her. They must have thought from the first that he had simply left her and covered his tracks, as that boorish one had pronounced at the station. Alice had believed, indeed with a degree of fear, they would find him. She had not given up until she had no other choice. She had gone back to the White Way one more time, returning the honeymoon skirt for Miss Caruthers, the satin cape, and the one pair of trousers she'd hemmed, along with the garments left untouched, and presenting Mr. White, who had been kind to her, with reasons of her mother's health as to why she must leave so suddenly.

No one would report her missing or make any attempt to trace her. Few neighbors in the building she trudged to every night even knew her name. They would scarcely realize they had not seen her in a while. If they did, it would be a passing thought. The landlord, of course, had his master key and would miss her eventually, when the rent came due.

CHAPTER 16

Though her feet pained her as they swelled in her boots and her bruised elbow throbbed, her back refused to relax against the hard seat of the train. Yet its steady rocking soothed her tired bones into sleep. When her head jerked, she saw a male passenger across the aisle eyeing her. Pulling her hat low on her cheek against his gaze, Alice averted her face and shifted away from him. With her back and shoulder to shield her from him, she rested her face against the hard green padding and closed her eyes.

When she woke again, it was dark. But she could see he was gone. She turned her shoulders and stretched out her hands one at a time, the throbbing elbow not coming straight, and sat up. Moonlight shone white across snow-covered fields. The rolling undulations of land sped past, the peak of a barn showing now and then, a window alight in a farmhouse. Someone with a sick child perhaps. She said a small prayer to the night.

Asleep once more, Alice felt herself lulled. In her dream, she was rocking a child, an infant boy, and crooning a lullaby. She lifted the edge of the soft blanket, one she knew. She had stitched it herself by hand. No machine had touched it. As the corner came away, the infant opened his eyes, blue as clear water. Indeed, the eyes were water and overflowed the banks of the tiny lids. Began to fill the space she occupied with the child, as if there were no boundaries or limits to it. The child's mouth opened in a silent wail, and water poured from it, rose, and covered the little face, openmouthed and struggling, the streaming eyes staring at Alice in terror. Alice's arms were paralyzed; she could not raise the child. She struggled to her feet, but they would not move against the pressure of the pouring water. The baby's mouth began to pucker like a fish, open and closed. The skin on his cheeks was turning to scales, and green algae enveloped them both. Alice struggled for breath.·

She woke to a firm touch on her shoulder. A bit of a shake. Alice opened her eyes and pulled herself upright. She shook her head, and her eyes roved the scene around her before she focused on the conductor, who stood before her, his uniform slightly dingy and a bit wrinkled. He bent toward her, his eyes searching and kind. She lifted her hand and nodded thanks. He hesitated only a moment, straightened, and moved off down the aisle.

In great gulps, Alice drank in her breath. Though she had slept soundly of late, could she ever again trust the oblivion of dreamless sleep? She lifted her painful elbow across her forehead, straightened her back against the seat. The outlines of the passing countryside, dark still but free of snow, emerged in the growing light. She sighed, dropped her arm, and watched as life pressed in on her, a life as unknown now as the passing barns and fences.

As the train neared Memphis, houses began to crowd out the barns, then streets with streetlamps still lit. As they passed, she noticed the moment some went from·lit to not lit, and she thought how unaware she had once been, how unaware most people lived, oblivious to that brief moment between life and death, just there, like that, then gone.

Larger buildings began to crowd out the houses, to rise high into the air, towering over the slowing train. Alice rose, stretched, reached up to the shelf overhead to retrieve her cumbersome bag. As she struggled to lift it and free it from the overhead shelf, the conductor reappeared. He touched her sleeve and waited for her to turn.

"That seems rather heavy for such a lady," he said. "Do you need something from it?"

"I was just taking it down."

"Sorry," he said. "Don't know why I was under the impression you were with us all the way to New Orleans. Let me help you here."

"You are very kind," she said.

Her swollen feet and ankles resisted the restrictions of her boots. Alice found the nearest bench in the crowded station. *Not ladylike*, she thought as she leaned forward and worked to loosen the laces on her boots. But who would pay any attention to her or what she was doing? She must have arrived at a busy time for the trains. Now the question was how to even begin to find her way or make a plan to locate this woman, ostensibly the mother of her phantom husband. She had little to go on. Not even a name. Only a vague street reference: at the corner of Fourth and Beale. Howard had described his mother as living in an area of fine old homes there.

At the edge of the station, she spied an information desk, occupied by a thin elderly woman in large horn-rimmed glasses. She seemed oblivious to the scurrying crowds, totally occupied in a book. Alice could just make out the title and smiled to see Walt Whitman's *Leaves of Grass*.

"Excuse me. I'm sorry to interrupt such a fine reading experience."

"No, no. Quite all right, my dear. I tend to have a lot of time for my reading. I'm not even sure why they maintain this desk at all. Very few seem to need my services, so you are a welcome interruption. How may I help you?"

"I'm looking for someone. I'm embarrassed to say I don't actually have a name or an exact address. However, it's important that I locate her. I have some serious news for her." Alice hesitated. "Both good and bad."

"Well, my dear, what do you have that we might begin with?"

"Only a fine old home near the corner of Fourth and Beale. Are you familiar with that area of town?"

The look Alice received from this woman shot through her in a flash of alarm. What had she said to elicit such a response?

"Are you sure of that information?"

"It's all I have."

"I wish I could offer you a seat, my dear. This may be disturbing to you."

"I have come all the way from Chicago," Alice said.

"Oh, dear. Well, let me be quick about this. There were, indeed, a number of fine homes at one end of Beale Street at one time. However, an epidemic of yellow fever wiped out almost the entire community there quite a number of years ago. Now in the particular area you have given and for several blocks in each direction, there are nothing but saloons, gambling, some rather loose women, and a good deal of crime. I could never recommend you go there, no matter who you need to find."

Alice felt the blow of this information. Nothing in her experience with this man, this father of the child she carried, had been true. Ever since he came so decorously into her life, nothing had been real. She steadied herself on the edge of the desk.

"Are you faint, my dear?"

Alice shook her head. "No. I am just waking myself to reality." She waved her fingers back and forth, a gesture at once of both acceptance and disbelief. "I will be all right. Yes. I will be." She raised her head and picked up her unwieldy bag. "Thank you."

* * *

Though the information had hit quickly, realization was slow to clarify itself. The weight of her life seemed unbearable to her. She had prayed to leave it behind with this trip. But she had placed her hope in Memphis on a phantom. A man who did not exist. Why would she believe him to be in Memphis at the cotton exchange, any more than in Chicago in an office at the Board of Trade? Why would she believe that the mother he had never taken her to see actually lived in Memphis, let alone even existed?

What now? Alice took a deep breath and stood in line at the ticket booth.

"I've made a mistake, sir," she said to the man behind the glass.

He smiled at her with a slightly quizzical look. And a warm smile. "At your service, ma'am."

"I accidentally purchased a Memphis ticket, when my destination is actually New Orleans. Could you help me to remedy that, sir?"

He gave her a puzzled, almost defeated look, then brightened. "Do you still have your original ticket, ma'am?"

"Yes, in my little handbag." She fished out the crumpled ticket.

"Another, separate ticket would cost a fair bit more," he said. "But if I add this on as a full one-way, it will be less. Now, there you go, ma'am." He handed the ticket under the window as she pushed the fare he had quoted back. "You have a nice trip now, ma'am."

In all this nightmare of lies and pain and uncertainty, there was still kindness.

And a way forward. In New Orleans she would find a safe rooming house. She would find work. She would provide a life for herself and her child.

Alice settled into her seat. With the first step toward hope.

CHAPTER 17

Alice shivered as she raised the heavy knocker on the big front door and let it fall. At least it was a shiver only from the evening chill and not from inches of snow on the ground. She stood wondering if she should knock again, when she heard footsteps approaching. With the click of an interior latch lifting, the door opened on the ruddy face of a breathless woman of uncertain age.

"Yes." That was all she said.

Alice shifted the cumbersome bag to the opposite hand and took a deep breath. "I've just arrived from Chicago, ma'am, and the clerk at the station offered me this address as a safe rooming house for women only."

"Oh, yes. Well, come right in, then. You're in luck, as fate would have it. I was just done cleaning the only room I have. If you had arrived yesterday, you'd have been clean out of luck. Vacated only this morning, yes. And now tidied up, as if awaiting your arrival. If you'd've tried to reserve it, you'd've been out of luck entirely. But here you are. Now, set your things down there, and we'll see about getting you fixed up. Right there, right there by the stairs. You'll have to carry it up, now, when we're done. It's on the upper floor. It used to be an attic, but we've done it up good. There's not plumbing up there, so you'll have to come down one floor for your private needs. You're not the frail type, are you?"

"No, no. I'm fully accustomed to walking up three floors. I'll take it till I find work." Alice pulled at the fingertips of her glove and slipped it into her left hand, ready to sign whatever was put before her. At least for the night. The long train ride had worn thin, and she was exhausted.

The room was, indeed, on the third floor. And Mrs. McLaren had spoken truly: the room was clean and orderly. It was also spacious for a third floor, though with the strangely tilted and erratic ceilings characteristic of attic space. Alice had just enough to pay the room and board for a good week and was able to negotiate a small reduction in exchange for helping in the kitchen while she searched for work.

Alice had a fair collection of copper pennies. She would need them for newspapers to search the help-wanted postings. The afternoon newspaper, the *New Orleans Item*, cost pennies. The *Picayune*, the same. She considered buying only one, but she dared not miss a possible opportunity. Her solution was to buy each one on alternate days, one the first day, the other the second. She operated on the assumption, which soon proved true, that most of the want ads would run for several days. She hoped her method would not put her at risk of losing out on the very one she needed.

The first day passed without result. There were openings for waitresses, but only in small, ill-paying cafés. Openings for help at laundries, for maids at hotels, and one for sewing alterations at a neighborhood dress shop. That was promising perhaps, though she had no concept of the various quarters of New Orleans. For two days, Alice made the rounds, only to find the position filled or to know she could not work in such a place. One turned out to be sewing for women at a house of legalized prostitution in what was known as Storyville. She had entered the house and was speaking with a woman in charge before she realized the extent of her mistake.

"You are here in reference to the advertisement for a seamstress?"

Alice nodded, aghast at the florid elegance of the woman's dress, then shocked beyond speech to see in her peripheral vision a laughing girl in bloomers and camisole tugging a well-dressed gentleman up the stairs.

"Perhaps you would be interested in a better-paying kind of work," the woman said, laying her hand over Alice's. "You have the face and body for it, you know?"

Alice fled. At the end of the block, breathless, she stopped. She would not give up; she made an oath to herself that she would not despair. Despair had brought her here. She would not allow it to bury her.

The following morning, Mrs. McLaren appeared from the kitchen just as Alice came down the stairs, yesterday's crumpled newspaper in hand.

"Hungry, dear?" she asked.

"No. No, ma'am. I, uh, I'm not so hungry in the mornings."

She felt the intensity of Mrs. McLaren's gaze. "Well, now. I'm enough of a busybody to insist on a bite or two to sustain you through the day, hungry or not. Come with me."

Alice followed her landlady into the oversized kitchen, where a rack of random pots and pans hung over the center chopping block, on which sat a baguette, partially sliced.

"Here," said Mrs. McLaren. "One slice of dry bread won't harm you none."

Alice took the bread, held it, took one bite.

"How's your luck with that newspaper now? Anything promising for you?"

"Not yet." She dared not talk about her appalling experience from the previous day. "Perhaps today."

"You don't know me, my dear, so perhaps you might not be

accustomed to my bold speech, but how many days have you money for?"

Alice choked on her bite of bread.

"Well, now. You needn't get that outdone about it, dear. But it's my guess you haven't much. You only have to nod."

Alice did.

"Well, now. I been thinking on this, and you may want to know. May be just the thing for you. No more wasted pennies on that useless paper." She cut another slice of bread and held it out. "Are you Catholic or Protestant, dear?"

Alice took the bread. "I am not Catholic."

"Well, no matter, dear, but at any rate, perhaps you know we have a rather large number of orphanages in New Orleans, both Catholic and Protestant. Yellow fever, even when it's not in epidemic, leaves a lot of orphans and half-orphans."

"I know I look a bit childish, but I'm not an orphan, Mrs. McLaren, and far too old to be taken in."

"Oh, that I know, dear. No, I'm thinking of the Poydras Asylum for Girls—it's Protestant, by the way—where the orphaned and destitute are taken in. And they have been known to assist widow women." Mrs. McLaren looked at her from the corners of her eyes. "The manager women who oversee it there bring in skilled women to teach the girls a trade, so they can make their way in life—not wind up in Storyville. You had a bit of a taste of that one yesterday." She emitted a gutsy laugh. "Sewing is prized there at the asylum. You'd likely be welcomed. I'm thinking you might have some luck in making an exchange of your skills for sanctuary there, if that doesn't sit too low for you."

"No, Mrs. McLaren. No, not in the least. I would welcome sharing my skills with . . . with motherless girls." She felt the tears close to escaping at the thought of her own mother's hands so close to her own, the gift those hands had bestowed on her. She imagined her hands holding fabric and needle next to the hands of some young girl. Her heart lifted in hope.

CHAPTER 18

When Alice descended the Magazine streetcar, her breath seemed to fail her. Nothing tall concrete like in Chicago, but awninged shops of all sorts crowded together under the trees along the street. She turned toward the Poydras Asylum for Girls, which was farther away. Her longing for home and her mother overcame her with an unexpected grief. She stood for a moment, pretending she had something in her eye, tilting her head back and pulling at the upper lid of her left eye. Feeling in some control of herself again, Alice readjusted her taupe woolen hat, smoothed her skirt, and approached the front entrance of the orphanage.

As she lifted her hand to the knocker, the door opened and a small blond woman halted her exit in surprise. Alice stepped back in equal surprise. It took both women a moment to regather themselves.

"Good morning. I beg your pardon," the woman said. "May I help you?"

"Yes, I'm sorry. I . . . Well, yes, I hope so." Alice tried not to stammer. "Yes. I have been made to understand that the orphanage might have need of a skilled seamstress."

The woman was silent, seeming to process this thought in her head.

"And you see, ma'am, I am one. That is, I am a very skilled seamstress. I understand you might need someone to help teach the girls my trade. So, I have come to inquire—"

"Oh, yes, indeed, Miss—"

"Mrs. Butterworth." Alice held out her hand.

"I'm so sorry. I was just on my way out."

Alice felt the dejection of a great mistake and dropped her hand.

"So, please, excuse my manners if you will. Come in. I'll take you to Mrs. Guidry before I leave. She will be delighted. This way please."

Indeed, Mrs. Guidry was more than pleased. The home had lost two seasoned sewing teachers in as many months. Alice's skills would be welcomed. So welcomed that Mrs. Guidry was not the least hesitant to provide a room and meals in exchange for them. The room was on the second floor, a boon to Alice now. After her days of deprivation in Chicago, she would welcome regular meals, even if simple and plain. The sewing room near the rear of the building, with windows onto Jefferson, was shaded by the gallery above, and had a view onto the lawn where the little girls played under supervision. Alice's face gladdened to hear their laughter as she toured the space.

She could move in the next day, Alice told Mrs. Guidry, but one last thing had to be settled.

"I am with child," she said. Straight and outright, as should be, though she knew it might cost her this sanctuary.

Mrs. Guidry was taken aback, as Alice expected. "We are not a home for unwed mothers."

"Nor am I one. I am a widow." Alice held out her hand for Mrs. Guidry to see her thin gold wedding band. Her fingers had swelled somewhat with the pregnancy, as had her ankles, which were thankfully covered. The imprint on her finger made it clear the band was no recent subterfuge. "I discovered my condition after Mr. Butterworth's—" She hesitated, turned her head aside. "After his recent death. I had an infant son, who died before him. I am bereaved and alone. Now I must make a life for myself and for this child. I pray you will not turn me away. I will earn my keep. You will see."

A fearful moment followed for Alice. Then Mrs. Guidry reached out and took both of Alice's hands in her own. Her touch was warm and kind, but firm.

"This place was founded by the Female Orphan Society, a group of determined Protestant women. Their purpose was to help not only orphans and destitute children but also widows. I believe that you and your coming child fit quite comfortably into our purpose here. We will welcome your services, Mrs. Butterworth."

CHAPTER 19

When Constance returned from her ordeal at the morgue, Analee put her straight to bed. "Mama didn't feel so good today," she told the children. The tray of gumbo and rice pudding she took up for supper, she carried away untouched. She made Constance comfortable for the night, put the girls to bed, then came and sat in the chair by the window, where she dozed until morning.

Constance was aware that Analee was there. She felt those strong hands lifting her hair from the pillow, braiding it slowly. Felt the covers Analee tucked in around her. Heard the small sounds of Analee's feet and her skirts as she shifted in the chair to get more comfortable. She must have slept. She had not heard Analee leave the room, and she awoke alone.

Suicide? Nothing like that had crossed her mind. An accident? It had to be. But the blur of the other man, the gambler. The Black Hand? She had suspected. Of course she had. Why else had she followed? She had only wanted to be sure, to be certain of her suspicions. To know why he kept demanding her money. He earned a good living. Yet he insisted she give him money from her inheritance for what she sensed to be nonexistent "investments." She had only needed to know. She had not meant for him to die.

In the days that followed, Constance went about the house as if by braille. Her hands were everywhere, on everything familiar: the children, the chaise, the davenport, the dishes, the door. She felt Analee's shadow near her, unobtrusive but there. In case.

By the end of the week, Constance had emerged from her lethargy. She found she could talk, even play with the girls, engage in their chatter. In the kitchen she helped Analee make shortbread for the girls, their favorite. When their little arms tangled around her in delight, she hugged them back and held them to her. She had to tell them now that their father was dead. She would hold them and wipe their tears away. She would answer their questions in whatever way she could manage. Life would go on.

When the police released Benton's body to Constance, with the cause of death entered as drowning, subsequent to a fall from the Illinois-Central Limited, cause unknown, she went to Benton's priest.

Though Benton had gone to Mass only rarely, Constance had occasionally accompanied him to the Saints Peter and Paul Catholic Church. As she approached along Burgundy—she had difficulty with directions due to the unusual New Orleans pronunciation, with an accent on the second syllable—she could hear the chatter of children's voices. Then the adult voice of one of the Marianite Sisters in charge of the school, their convent just adjacent. Constance entered the church, as she had entered with him, awed and comforted somehow by the quality of light as it filtered in through the high stained-glass windows that banked the sides of the church, beneath its towering arched ceiling. Her favorite window drew her, as always: Mary, alone, with a blue shawl hanging from one shoulder, her arms half folded to one side as if to hold a baby, but empty, and at her feet, two children playing. How had some unknown artist so faultlessly depicted her own plight? And as always, Constance's eyes were drawn upward into those arches, which pointed toward a mystery that she could barely conceive, but that she could feel in unexpected peace. She bowed and made her way along the side aisle. Father Joseph was somehow there, as if expecting her. They spoke briefly. He was so kind.

"He died without last rites, Father. You know I am not Catholic. I don't know what that means for him."

"Last rites are for the comfort and assurance of the dying, Mrs. Halstead. They are not a ticket required for Heaven, if you are concerned for your husband."

"No, Father. My concern is to know how to do this for him as it should be done. I need to do this right, Father. To make these arrangements properly and know he may have his service here, where he attended." She stopped. "Sometimes attended. And be interred in St. Louis Cemetery."

"You attended with him, yes? I've seen your face in the congregation from time to time."

She nodded.

Father Joseph remained silent for a moment, his face lowered. She wondered if he was praying. "I'd like to return to your statement that you are not Catholic, Mrs. Halstead. Au contraire to the stance of our recent Archbishop Janssens, whose mission to Catholicize New Orleans has tended instead to divide us, we all know and feel our city, our home together here on earth, to be catholic with a little *c*. To be universal. So, there we are." He laid a gentle hand on her shoulder. "Now, the death is ruled an accident? Not suicide?"

There it was again, that unexpected word. This time she was stunned with the realization that, yes, a man in the straits of huge debt to the Black Hand might, indeed, choose suicide. Perhaps this priest had known Benton better than she realized, had heard his confession.

"Yes, Father. The police have officially entered it as an accident."

"I will accompany you tomorrow, Mrs. Halstead, to make arrangements. It is not a thing I usually do, but then most of my bereaved are also Catholic. With a capital C. All interment is aboveground, because of the high water table. But you know that. I don't know why I'm even saying that. Just some sort of habit I have." He took her gently by the elbow. "Come. We will arrange a time for the vigil and the funeral Mass. Had Mr. Halstead much family here?"

"No," she said. "Only the children and me. And friends, of course."

"Are your children greatly bereaved at the loss of their father?" He had stopped, a rainbow of light falling on his shoulder.

"No. Well, yes, of course. They are quite sad, but they are very young and hardly understand." She could not stop looking at the colors of the light falling all around her.

"Perhaps they understand more than you may be aware of."

"Benton was rarely home, Father. His business required him to travel a great deal."

"Yes, I believe I knew that."

He seemed to be waiting for something more.

"And when he was home, well, he was hardly home." Constance stopped, listening to her words. There was an unexpected peace in her with this man, a bewildering trust in this near stranger. "Yes, hardly," she repeated, emphasizing the first syllable of the word. "He was not an easy man, Father. He was hard or he was distant. He might as well have been somewhere else. I sometimes wished he were." There, she had said it. For the first time ever, she had said it. Out loud. To a priest.

"Come with me, Mrs. Halstead. We will make sure that all is as it should be. At least as far as the service and burial are concerned." He took her gently by the arm and walked with her through the path of colored light falling across the stone floor.

* * *

Waiting outside was a tall, narrow-shouldered man, who turned at the sound of Father Joseph's farewell. Martin Birdsong, her family doctor, her dearest childhood friend. How had he known?

"Constance." He held out his hands to her. "I heard the terrible news. I went by the house, and Analee told me where I might find you. I peeked in through the door, but you were in such earnest conversation, I didn't want to interrupt." He clasped her hands firmly. "I'm so sorry, Constance. You must tell me whatever you need."

"Martin." She lay one hand on his chest. "If I only knew, you would be the one I would tell."

"Then let me walk you home." He offered his elbow, and she took it.

They walked in silence for a time. Above them, mockingbirds flitted among the leaves, pecking away at the blue-black fall berries.

"Is everything arranged to suit you, Constance? No difficulties?"

"Yes, all arranged."

"As Benton would want it?"

Constance stopped. "I have no idea what Benton would have wanted, Martin. My husband is not only dead, but also a complete mystery to me. I'm not sure I ever knew him at all."

"That may be true." Martin led her forward.

"So you knew things I did not?" She had stopped again.

"Perhaps. Perhaps I know only gossip, Constance. What have you learned?"

"That he was an inordinate gambler. That he lied to me about investments to try to get money from my trust."

"Ah, well, then, I expect there is no more for you to learn. There would be details, of course, but your two statements cover it. He was in debt to the Black Hand, I know. But given his tragic accident—I would bet he went outside for air and a smoke in a card game loss—I expect that is the end of that."

Constance tripped on her skirt at the remembrance of Benton's lit cigarette flying through the air. The feel of his hands on her, on the young man he believed her to be. His eyes. Then Benton in the open air.

"Constance?"

Martin clasped her upper arms, supporting her. She leaned against him, the tears released.

"It's grief, Constance."

"Not for him."

"Then for the loss of who he might have been. It's just as painful, Constance. Let it come."

Constance made it through the formalities, the technicalities of the modest coping grave of stone and plaster, topped with gravel. She comforted the children, who cried but were so used to their father's extended absences that they had hardly noticed a difference. She managed the friends from their New Orleans social milieu who came to offer condolences. She was grateful for Martin Birdsong's steady presence as business associates paid their respects. She accepted repeated remarks about the tragedy of such an accident, their comments on how the trains must be redesigned to have closed vestibules between the cars, their comments on the preciousness of her children. She prayed she did so with grace.

In a momentary pause in the flow of Benton's acquaintances, while Martin went to fetch some water, a small man darted into the line. His sudden appearance startled her, then terrified her. His bizarre A La Souvarov mustache froze her gaze above his thin lips as he whispered, "You shall hear from me soon, Madame. Count on it." Fear flooded her. He scurried away, disappearing into the crowd as quickly as he had come. She struggled to control herself, aghast, even as she reached out for the next hand extended to her in condolence. That was the man. The man she had seen near her fence. Perhaps the man on that train. Constance knew that sinister face.

The Mass was somber; the church half-filled. Constance sat with her veil, one arm around each child. *Too young for this*, she thought. Analee beside them, Martin just behind, lent her strength. The interment at St. Louis Cemetery was brief. Once done, Constance put her arms around the children to guide them toward the street. Their house in the Faubourg Marigny was near enough to walk. Martin and Analee were with them if one of the girls became too tired. Before she reached the cemetery's exit, Father Joseph stopped her.

"Be at peace, my dear," he said. "And do not be afraid. No harm will come to you."

Constance startled at those last words. Martin stepped discreetly aside. What did Father Joseph mean? He must have seen that man. In his face she saw that he understood more of who her husband had been than she would have imagined. She thought again of the confessional. *Ah, yes*, she thought. *Benton would do whatever took hold of him and then wash it away with words. Had he confessed his rage with his infant son? Would the infant son of Mary save him? This priest knows more of that man than I do.*

"You need not worry, my dear. You are wondering if he came to confession."

Eyes lowered, Constance nodded. Then raised her lids, her gaze direct. "Father, I am not so sure that I believe those confessions were sincere." Dared she speak like this to a priest?

"Ah, I see." He took her arm and guided her a few steps away. "The confessional is sacred, Mrs. Halstead. There is nothing I can share with you about your husband. But I can share with you my understanding of the God I serve."

Anger was rising in her. "That my husband could do anything and simply confess, and it's all wiped away."

"I was going to phrase it a bit differently, Mrs. Halstead. That would imply a God whose love must be sought after. You remember, I mentioned *catholic* with a small *c*—as in universal. Everywhere all the time. You see, my dear, if God's love is unconditional, then the purpose of confession is for us, not for God. I am quite partial to Psalm 139 which tells us that even if we make our bed in hell, even there his hand upholds us. It assures us that there is nowhere and no way we can turn, even away from him, to escape the love of God." He looked up at the sky for a moment. "That is difficult theology, I know. It goes against the human grain. And it may not be of comfort to you. I give it to you however you may take it."

She nodded her head again, thoroughly puzzled. She rejoined her two companions and guided the children onto the sidewalk. At a certain point, Analee reached down and lifted Maggie into her arms. As they neared home, they passed under the fringe trees that lined the street. The limbs were low enough to reach up and touch the golden leaves. Maggie stretched her hand up and pulled at them. Of course, Delia had to be lifted to them also, and only by Martin. The girls laughed as they batted branches back and forth, the leaves dancing. Between the golden tangle of branches and leaves, Constance could see blue fragments of sky.

CHAPTER 20

Through the following days, Constance negotiated life by habit: rising, putting up her hair, eating what little she could of the seductive meals Analee put before her—shrimp gumbo, hominy grits and molasses, and *îles flottantes*. She occupied herself from morning to night making lists for the orphanage; playing with the girls, tucking them in; taking down and brushing her hair, counting the obligatory hundred strokes; and, finally, lying in bed with her head and dreams in the treacherous vestibule of a moving train. Sometimes she was there alone; sometimes fully herself with Benton; sometimes cowering from a mustached man who said, "I will see you." Waking in terror and sitting the night through till morning, afraid to dream again.

On Wednesday Analee came to the back stoop where Constance was watching as the girls played tag, and handed her an envelope. She took it in puzzled surprise.

"Lady say give you this. Not a calling card. But she say give it. I sat her in the drawing room and said I'd fetch you. Now I'm gone go make y'all some tea. Then I'll come watch the girls.

It's about time they have a snack, anyway." Analee went back through the door.

Constance stood for a moment, examining the envelope. The address was in her own handwriting to Mrs. Albert Richard. The envelope had been opened, then resealed with red wax, stamped with an elegant capital *R*. This was the very note she had dropped at Mrs. Richard's house, here, back in her hand.

"Mrs. Richard." Constance nodded in greeting to her unexpected guest on the davenport.

"Dorothea, dear. I thought we had that settled at the luncheon."

In her elegant tight-waisted suit, but again uncorseted, Dorothea stood in greeting. Constance motioned for her to sit down. She herself sat perched on the edge of a small wing chair near her guest, wishing to be free herself of her own corset.

"I hope all is well," Constance said. "Tea is on its way."

"Oh, yes, my dear, quite well. Plans are going splendidly. Except one thing."

Constance looked down at the envelope in her hand.

Dorothea leaned toward her. "You see, my dear, I cannot accept this note of regret from you." She lifted her empty palm, laid her hand back in her lap. "Actually, of course, I can. More to the point is that I am simply not willing to. As captain of the krewe, I am here to insist that you accept the invitation to be an attendant for Marian Berger, Queen of all compass points to the South."

"Mrs. Ri . . . Dorothea, I deeply appreciate your visit—and the invitation—but I simply must still decline. For a number of reasons. Please, Dorothea, don't make me go into this now. I have only just buried my husband."

"Yes, I know that, Constance. It is a difficult time. You are a widow now." She took her time. "But are you grieving?"

"Am I grieving?" Constance's head shot up with a jolt. "I am a recently bereaved widow. From a terrible accident."

"Yes, I am quite aware, my dear," said Dorothea. "Yes. You are bereaved. But are you bereft? Is your heart forever broken? Will you never recover?"

"I'm sure that I shall recover at some point." Constance stared straight into Dorothea's eyes. "Most people do."

"Yes. Entirely true." Dorothea waited a moment. "I will be frank, Constance. I do not find you to be 'most people.' In fact, though I have not known you closely, my distinct impression over time has been one of admiration for your seeming independence, especially with regard to the frequent and extended absences of your husband. And his demeaner with you in public, I might add."

Constance stared. Was Benton's nature so evident, in spite of his cordiality in social settings, his burning desire to make himself accepted in New Orleans society? This woman was astute.

"I—I'm a bit taken aback, Dorothea. But thank you. I simply live my life in the only way I seem to know how."

"And as I said, I am being rather more frank than I ordinarily would be, though I am by nature rather untoward. You may have detected that at the luncheon. For some time now, I've been observing you from afar. Ah, I see by your expression that comes as a surprise. Well, good for my subtleties, then."

Analee entered with the tea tray, set it on the table between the two, and retreated. Dorothea accepted the cup Constance poured for her and sat back on the divan. Both were quiet.

"You see, Constance, I am a natural observer of people around me—a student of human nature. I am also a confidante of a number of gentlemen who do not ordinarily confide in women. But my dead husband's position in society and politics has left me with a certain power of persuasion that proves useful to some of them now and then. I keep my eyes and my ears open, you see. My point being that, as I have been in the company of you and your husband, I have noticed a certain distance between you. In addition to your own independence, I mean something else, less easy to define. I don't believe I am mistaken. Am I?"

Constance rested her cup in her lap. "No. Dorothea. No, you are not mistaken. Especially since the death of our son." She astonished herself to have confided so openly in this near stranger. Though she had no way to bare herself entirely: the long, welcome days of his absence due to traveling; the days she did not have to hide her grief from him, did not have to bear his hiding his own from her; their inability to comfort one another. When he was home, she sometimes heard him in the nursery, mumbling to himself. If she listened closely, sometimes cursing God, sometimes himself, and often times his father. But if she dared enter the room to touch him, he jerked away. Soon to be gone on the train.

Constance almost started when Dorothea spoke again. "I know. I am sorry for that. One never quite gets over the loss of a child."

"No, I believe that grief is what draws me to the orphans and the half-orphans—trying somehow to fill the void." The words slipped out, as if she had known this woman always.

"And now you have also lost a husband, but even in this brief conversation, I do not hear the same quality of grief or loss that I hear for your child. Am I right?"

"You are." Constance lowered her head, troubled to feel so transparent.

"It is for that reason—and also because I am aware that Benton had a propensity for gambling, gambling to extremes—that I am asking you genuinely if you grieve for him. You do not have to answer that, however."

"No, I will answer you, Dorothea." Constance set her half-empty cup on the tray and folded her hands in her lap. "You have somehow managed to see what no one else would even look for, all their *idées fixes* blinding them. Or if they see something outside their standards, they resort to gossip." Constance opened her hands in a gesture of helplessness. She saw by the bare shift of expression on Dorothea's face that there must be rumors.

"There is, indeed, a deep sadness in me for Benton's death, for the terrible circumstances of this accident—for many things— but you are correct in your observations. The relationship between us had its difficulties. And its distances. More than the physical ones of his work and travel. You are also correct that he had his propensity to gamble heavily and not always successfully. You seem to be offering me your trust, and so I will offer you mine and answer truthfully. No, though I am sorrowed and troubled by his death, and by its circumstances, it is not for Benton that I grieve."

Dorothea took Constance's empty hands in both of hers. "I thought as much." She sat back again, dropping her hands, and said, "Now, let us move on. Let us discuss Les Mysterieuses and the ball. I needed first to be certain you had not declined because you were in a state of genuine grief. Now that my mind is relieved of that concern, let us go to other considerations."

"Well, as I said, there is the issue of gossip and—"

"No one will know, Constance. Unless you wish them to. You will be costumed and veiled. We will all be veiled. Or not. As we wish. Unlike the traditional Mardi Gras festivities overseen by men, we are the *mysterious* ones. We will not have just one queen. We will have four, each enthroned, each with six maids. Our identities will not be revealed, except, of course, if a woman wishes to be known. It will be entirely up to her and no one else. You may participate yet remain virtually unnoticed, as you wish. I have a notion you are a woman who wishes to change things, even if it is only your own life. And Les Mysterieuses is doing just that—changing things. I am asking you to join us."

Constance rose and walked to the window. Outside a carriage passed by. Driving it was the threatening mustached man, who struck her with more fear than ever. She fought for composure and turned to Dorothea.

"There is one more difficulty. You were correct about Benton's gambling. And his losses. He was in debt when he died—"

"To the Black Hand?"

"I believe so. The police seem to have evidence."

"Have they approached you to pay?"

"No." She glanced back out the window. No one was there. "No. But I believe they may be watching me."

"They will want their money. They can be quite threatening. You will let me know? I have some political connections."

Constance looked at her in something close to disbelief. Dorothea nodded her head.

"I do, as does the Black Hand," she said. "So, you are left without finances? Is that the reason?"

"No. By good fortune, I have a trust from my grandfather. Sizeable enough for us to live. And fortunately protected by Napoleonic law. Benton attempted, but, as you know, he could not touch it."

Dorothea rose and took her hands again. "And you are afraid to waste it on something frivolous, like a ball gown? One not covered by your already paid membership?"

"You sense it exactly, Dorothea. I have two daughters to raise alone now."

"All the more reason to participate in changing the position of women. I have an idea. One that will help change the life of an actual woman as well as women in general. I want you to go with me to the orphanage. I know you have a passion already for the orphans. This will be a perfect fit for you. Well, now there is unintended wordplay! I will fetch you tomorrow at two." She leaned forward and kissed Constance on one cheek, then on the other. "You are not to worry yourself. I have the solution."

CHAPTER 21

Constance bid her children goodbye and opened the front gate. Anticipation had stirred her with a faint hope of possibility. Yet when the sleek royal blue horseless carriage drew to the curb with its quiet hum, Constance clasped her palm over her mouth at the sight of Dorothea managing the tiller. Constance laughed aloud at her new friend's exultant smile and threw her arms into the air. She clapped her hands as she rounded the vehicle, its gleaming carriage trimmed with scrolls of narrow brass, its patent leather fenders curving over wooden wheel spokes also trimmed with brass. Dorothea had the black landau top folded back, the carriage open to the bright air.

"Come now, Constance. No time for nonsense." Dorothea laughed. "We have an errand to tend to."

Mounting the horseless carriage was a novel experience for Constance. An exhilarating one. She settled herself on the gleaming black leather seat, tufted and finely crafted as any parlor divan, and as comfortable. A marvelous wine-red plush covered the floor and dash. Dorothea pulled the hand throttle. The engine hummed. She drew the tiller toward her, and they were on their way.

"I have had a lesson or two from my neighbor, Mr. Mont-morissey. Even before the car arrived," Dorothea said. "Now I am an efficient pilot, am I not?"

Constance nodded her head at Dorothea's glance.

"I'm dumbfounded, Dorothea. How on earth—"

"I am an independent woman, Constance. My husband left me with a more than reasonable inheritance. Why should I depend on a man to keep horses and hitch a carriage? Or need to wait by the street, trying to hail a carriage? Or even puzzle myself over the tangle of streetcar lines? Now I am free. I am able to go where I please when I please. At a handy speed, too, I might add. Fifteen miles an hour, if I've a mind to. But that's a bit reckless for New Orleans streets." As she talked, Dorothea managed the tiller and throttle through the tangle of horses, carriages, and streetcars. "We'll be there soon enough. And you, my dear, may find your life altered for the better."

Constance bit her lower lip. Not only was she unused to such a ride, but she also worried at the decision she would now be called upon to make once she met this young seamstress. Dorothea had described her as a bit lost but inventive in finding her way in the world. Her resourcefulness seemed to have impressed both Mrs. Guidry at the orphanage and Dorothea. Mrs. Guidry had presented Alice as gifted in her sewing skills and generous spirited with the girls at the asylum. She had observed not only the level of the young woman's skills but also her patience as she demonstrated beginning stitches again and again. Mrs. Guidry admired Alice's quiet urging of the older girls into imaginative techniques. The orphanage was fortunate indeed to have found a teacher like Alice, Dorothea had proclaimed. Without the orphanage, Alice would be homeless. The complication: Alice was with child.

Mrs. Guidry welcomed the two familiar visitors into the sitting room of the asylum. A young girl appeared with a tea tray and set it before them, curtsied, and disappeared. Mrs. Guidry declined to join them and stood as she poured the tea. Fidgeting, with little to say past welcome, she was clearly ill at ease. After stepping to an open door across the room, she brought a young woman into the light.

Constance stood, while Dorothea stirred her tea and smiled.

"This is Alice," Mrs. Guidry said. "Mrs. Alice Butterworth. And this is Mrs. Halstead. I believe you already know Mrs. Richard."

"Hello, Alice. I'm delighted to see you again. I hope you are well. Please, sit down. Let me pour you some tea." Dorothea was busy with her polite ministrations.

As they sat, Mrs. Guidry took her leave and disappeared. The three sat in silence. Constance could not think what to say.

"Well, now," said Dorothea, speaking in Alice's direction. "I desired to introduce the two of you because I believe you have needs that can be mutually satisfied. Constance is a recent widow, in need of a ball gown for Mardi Gras." She turned to Constance. "Alice is a skilled seamstress in need of shelter, board, and work." She stood between the two women, turning to first one, then the other. "Is this not a match, now?"

Alice watched as Dorothea rose to go to the tall window, where she studied the girls lining up in the courtyard. Her cup clinked as she set it in its saucer and placed both back on the tray.

"Ah, there is the very person I've been needing to speak with," Dorothea said. "I'll leave you two to yourselves for a moment. You will excuse me, won't you?"

As Constance nodded, Alice found herself in the silence of the room, and she was relieved when this elegant stranger spoke first.

"Where are you from, Alice?"

"The Midwest plains originally. Then Chicago. I came here from there." She omitted the useless detail of Memphis and her spontaneous decision to give up the pursuit of the unknown husband who had abandoned her, and his perhaps fictitious mother.

"Overnight?"

"Yes." Alice hesitated, unsure how much to reveal about herself. "Yes, sitting up. Not the most comfortable." There, she would be as open as she dared. After all, this woman must have a hint of her economic woes by the fact that she was living in the orphanage. She would test the waters with this young widow Dorothea had brought to her.

"You are comfortably installed here?"

"Yes, quite. Mrs. Guidry is a saint. Her sewing teacher left to be married, and she happened to have an empty room on the second. So, I have my own space, at least temporarily. And the girls to teach. The sewing room is quite well fitted out." Where was this conversation going? Alice wondered.

"Yes, I am familiar with it. I do a bit of volunteering for the orphanage. Perhaps Dorothea told you that." Constance seemed ill at ease now. "I hear there are new machines and arrangements for a new cutting table."

"Yes. We are rather well equipped. That's a great advantage."

"Dorothea praises your skills."

Alice glanced out the window. "I have some experience," she said.

"Yes, Dorothea has praised that, too."

An awkward silence ensued.

"I'm wondering . . . ," Constance said.

"I'm quite . . . ," Alice began at the same time. Then, embarrassed, added, "Excuse me. Please. Go on."

After another moment of uncomfortable silence, Constance said, "As you already know, I am a recent widow with two little girls to raise. Dorothea has invited me to participate in an all-women's Mardi Gras ball. I'm not sure, since you are recently arrived, if you know how unprecedented that possibility is."

Alice nodded and waited. No, she was not at all familiar with the customs of New Orleans society and certainly not Mardi Gras, which was an utterly unfamiliar concept to her. Yet her curiosity about its sewing opportunities was what had brought her here.

"Historic, in fact. This is a leap year, or purportedly so, and will be only the second time in our history that an all-female krewe will organize a ball. It simply flies in the face of convention." Constance glanced out the window. "Well," she said, "mine is very recent widowhood—but you know that—and widowhood has its own conventions." Constance hesitated. "I don't seem to know where to go with this conversation."

If this sophisticated woman had no idea, how was Alice possibly to conceive its course? Alice waited.

"Well, perhaps I should just get directly to the point. I'm learning such forthrightness from Dorothea. So here it is, Alice. Dorothea is in charge, the captain, and she is insistent that I participate in spite of my widowhood. She assures me I can be veiled in such a way that no one will know me. Mystery is, in fact, the very nature of the krewe Les Mysterieuses. So, if I follow her insistence, I will need a fairly simple ball gown made for this affair. One to disguise and not attract too much attention. Dorothea believes you are the one who can create it for me."

"I'd like to think my skills equal to such an endeavor."

"I—I'm a bit hesitant, but Dorothea seems so certain that this will do me good, help me find a new approach to life."

The phrase sent chills through Alice. Another woman here, one with a life that might be envied, struggling to create a new life for herself.

"Perhaps that is her purpose in bringing us together." Had she overstepped in her reply?

"Yes, well, here is my difficulty, Alice. I might as well be totally honest. My husband"—Constance struggled for words— "was killed in a terrible fall from a train."

Alice gasped, her hand clasped over her mouth. "I'm so sorry. So sorry."

"It was . . . it was unfortunate. And very grim." Constance stood abruptly. "At any rate, I have been left with unexpected financial difficulties. Yet Dorothea seems bent on my not declining the ball invitation."

"And Dorothea told you that I am also a widow in my own quite difficult circumstances?"

Constance nodded.

Now Alice stood. "And she believes that I am the answer to your problem. Perhaps I am. And you to mine. I have no other work. And I need work. I have taken on the responsibility of teaching the girls here at the orphanage, those old enough, the essentials of the sewing machines. And all ages hand stitching and embroidery. It means a great deal to me, and I will continue to do so even if I find another livelihood. It is such pleasure to me to be instructing them to sew. They are, for the most part, such lovely girls, and I feel deeply for their sad situations. But it does not occupy me completely, and my lodging here is temporary. I have ample time to work on your gown. My skills are fairly advanced, and I would welcome such a challenge."

"Alice, I realize that I am being vague—and slow—in speaking. I must learn from Dorothea to be more straightforward. Here is my situation. I am unable to pay for such a gown and your services at present. So here is what I can propose. I am prepared to offer you a sort of unpaid temporary exchange. A third-floor room—it is spacious and light—and good meals in exchange for your work on the gown."

"I would be happy to show you some small samples of my work. I have nothing else in my current circumstances."

"I trust Dorothea's assessment, though I would be delighted to see your work. I realize as I say all this, it isn't much of a bargain for you. I'm embarrassing myself here."

Alice took a deep breath. She felt a tinge of empathy for this young widow, so clearly ill at ease. "Don't be. I'm in somewhat embarrassing circumstances myself. I need work. My room here is only for as long as it is not needed for an orphan. I will soon need shelter, and should avail myself of both, sooner than later. I accept your temporary offer, then. Perhaps it will enable me to find a better place when I have finished your gown. It shouldn't take that long. When shall we begin?"

Dorothea reentered from the outside terrace. Alice saw instantly the self-assured smile on her face. *A woman who is accustomed to having charge over life*, thought Alice.

CHAPTER 22

Dorothea made quiet arrangements to transport Alice to the Marigny house two days hence and ushered Constance back to her waiting vehicle.

"I thought this would be advantageous," she said, pulling the tiller toward her to make her turn from the curved driveway onto the street. "For both of you."

The car hummed along past little shops of various sorts on Magazine. Constance held her anxiety. As they passed through the Garden District, fine houses to the left, the Irish Channel to the right, only blocks off the river, she thought with some trepidation of the commitment she had just made. Such a quick decision. She was a bit uneasy now at the thought of a stranger living in her house, at the thought that she would truly be participating in a major Mardi Gras event, against all convention. Glancing up at the emerging balconies where families lived above their stores in the Lower Garden District, Constance silently questioned her hasty decision. There was more to it than bowing to Dorothea's insistence—Dorothea, who now steered them through the growing business district toward

Canal. Constance liked Alice, another widow, more than she had anticipated. Her skills were evident. But Constance had no extra funds for fabrics and trims. She was not intimidated by participating in an all-women's krewe—she would have been greatly tempted by such a venture before. But now the utter unknown of Benton's death, of her own chilling sense of guilt, made this secret break with convention distressing. It was herself more than her engrained way of life that she must now overcome.

"I have a thought, Constance," Dorothea said as she deftly turned the tiller left, then right, left again, steering the car proficiently through the tangle of streetcars, carriages, wagons, and other motorcars on Canal.

"Yes?" Constance felt not only unnerved by the traffic but also uneasy that Dorothea might perceive her hidden fears.

"I am constantly aware of the waste of things. So much. In this city. Extravagances that go unheeded, the unused discards of excess. It is one of the reasons I think both of us are invested in the orphanage. And willing to make these journeys to the other side of the city to be of use there."

The kinship of the orphanage relieved Constance's nervousness. "Perhaps," she said. "It makes me glad to donate my girls' outgrown things."

"In that case, would you be amenable to my donating some things to you?"

They had entered the Vieux Carré, the river close beside them as they bumped over the cobblestones of Decatur Street. Whistles and horns from steamers and barges, melodic cries of street vendors, calls from one ornate balcony to the other charged the air with distracting noise.

"To me? Whatever for, Dorothea?" Constance was embarrassed that her surprise was evident. She couldn't imagine wearing Dorothea's discards, elegant as they might be.

"To ease my conscience about my own excess." Dorothea jerked the tiller as a young boy darted across the way.

"I'm afraid I don't understand." Dorothea was about to give Constance her hand-me-downs? No, she couldn't accept such a thing. Everyone would know. And Dorothea would know that everyone would know.

"I have a number of gowns from years past in more than one attic trunk. Worn once and discarded. Things should be of more use than that. It's sinful, actually. If you would take a few of those for Alice to dismantle and use the bits and pieces as she can, it would ease my conscience considerably. There are also things like laces and trims, buttons, perhaps even appliqués that would be of benefit to the girls at the orphanage in refining their skills for a trade. Better than the simple cottons they have. If they are to find placement other than at the mills, they will need those refined skills. How would you feel about that idea, my dear?"

It took Constance a moment to get her breath. Not only had she found a skilled seamstress, but now the treasure of fine fabrics and trims had fallen unexpectedly into her lap, as well. She found it difficult to let the amplitude sink in. She was unused to such generosity.

"They are all in good condition, if that worries you."

"Oh, no, not at all, Dorothea." Constance felt the flush in her cheeks.

On past Jackson Square, the car rolled over the rough cobblestones until they reached the farmers market. The melee of sounds now combined with an assault of smells on the senses: the enticing aroma of fresh baguettes and croissants, followed instantly by the terrible reek of the fish market, then the bloody odors of the butchers' market, and finally, at the end, the soothing, enticing chocolaty scent of ground chicory. And a hint of pralines, all sugary, with a waft of pecans.

Dorothea slowed the car. "I think we should have a praline to celebrate. And take some home to your children. Do you need more time to think?"

Constance had not realized that there had been a pause. "It's just—it's just that I am so deeply touched at your generosity. Not only with me, but with Alice, too, and with the girls. I don't quite know what to say."

"Thank you would be an adequate response." Dorothea pulled to a stop, set the brake, and jumped down. "You're not turning down a praline, now are you?"

The children, who had been waiting on the steps with Analee, ran to the gate and jumped up and down with glee. Constance cherished their excitement at seeing their mother in this gleaming vehicle and then at the surprise of a praline each.

As Constance greeted them, her joy at her daughters caught in her throat. A block up the street a man stopped in his footsteps and fingered his distinctive A La Souvarov mustache, thin and growing round his face, where the top of a beard should be, connecting to narrow sideburns. Named for the great Russian general who never lost a battle. When he touched the brim of his hat at her recognition, fear blazed through her excitement. She whirled her body to block the girls from his line of sight, gathered Maggie in her arms, and motioned Analee to pick up Delia, their sticky fingers regardless. Constance saw in her expression that Dorothea had recognized the grim shift in the mood of things. Constance uttered a hurried farewell and mumbled her thanks before she and Analee bustled the children into the house, the girls whining for a ride in the car. When she set Maggie on her feet and pulled back the edge of the curtain, the man was gone.

Dorothea still stood by the footboard, staring off in that direction. Constance saw that somehow Dorothea knew more about this incident than she did herself.

Constance sat by the children's beds long after they had fallen sleep. She could not still her fear for them. And for herself. Clearly, the Black Hand was at her door. Not only at her door, but shadowing her wherever she went. She had heard the tales of their cruelty and their power. However unsure she remained about precisely what had transpired in that train vestibule, there was no doubt that Benton's life had been at risk from the Black Hand. They might stop at nothing to obtain the money he owed them. Would they come after her for what little inheritance she had? What of her girls? The depravity of Storyville—its bordellos, saloons, gambling, heroin and cocaine—might be legally contained, certainly was politically connected. A prominent legislator owned one bordello. The houses drew patrons at the top of society; some at Miss Josie's said they went only for the music and conversation. But Storyville had few limits and no bottom to its depths. The thought took her straight to Benton and his terrible death, the desperate flailing of his limbs as he plummeted into the black water. For the first time since his death, Constance shed tears for her husband. And for herself.

CHAPTER 23

By morning, Constance had gathered herself. After breakfast she and Analee climbed to the third floor to prepare for Alice's arrival. Constance could not remember how long since the room had been occupied. The air was close and sultry. She could have written her name in the dust on the furniture. In fact, she did. Then wiped it away with the side of her fist. The bare mattress required linens; the rag rug, a thorough airing; the curtains, laundering.

"Come with me. We got plenty of stuff we can use to fix this place up homey."

Before she could resist, Constance felt Analee tug at her hand, pull her toward the adjacent attic storage. The hinges creaked as Analee opened the door. The dim-lit space loomed in Constance's vision, and she jerked her hand free, stopping on the threshold. No, she could not have Analee searching about. Not now. Not until she could dispose of that suit, that wig, and the fake facial hair she had managed to conceal up here. She had not found the time or the means to rid herself of that incriminating disguise. She could not take the risk.

"Stop, Analee. There is nothing we need in there." Constance took a deep breath to calm herself. "We just need to get that room clean and ready. We don't have time to go poking around in here for odds and ends to make it more homey. The girl will not be staying that long. She's here only long enough to make a ball gown for me. Now, come on out of there, and let's get back to cleaning this room."

Constance was aware of the look Analee threw her, askance, surprised, but Analee closed the door. She hurried past Constance, who stood for one blank moment in the empty hallway, wondering how Analee would see her if she knew the truth. Constance followed Analee into the dusty room. She snatched the feather duster from the basket of supplies they had hauled up the steps and swiped the surface of the dresser, where she had written and erased her name.

"Hold on, Miss Constance. You got to put that thing down. You gone stir up a dust storm. Got to have a damp rag to get this much dust. More than one, for sure." Analee took the duster from Constance's hands and dropped it in the hall. "Here. Help me roll up this rug. We got to get all this stuff downstairs before we go cleaning this place."

By the time the room was ready to receive Alice, Constance had exhausted herself, and Analee, too. They sat in the kitchen, drinking tea, saying little. The children played at their feet, tired out from running after the two women, up and down the stairways, into the yard, back and forth under the wet curtains in the bright sunshine. A new sewing machine, on loan from Dorothea, had arrived that morning, to be installed in an extra room on the second floor. It was a marvel—its sleek body decorated with a fine scrolled design in gold and red, the surface edged with the same, as if inlaid, and set in a beautifully finished oak cabinet. The children could hardly keep their hands off its magnificent surface and had to be forcibly pulled away from sitting on its rocking treadle.

Both rooms were ready for Alice's arrival. Constance was still uneasy at having an unaccustomed person in the house. But she liked this young woman, liked her courage in coming south as a widow to make a new life. Alice would be too busy with her sewing for much exchange between them, except for fittings and design decisions. Constance might otherwise even be unaware of her presence, except for meals. She could make do there. Although she hated superficial conversation, she was accomplished at it. She had grown up with it at meals. And in the rest of life. She couldn't remember one conversation with her family of any authentic significance. Every mouthful watched for perfect balance and to see that her lips opened only so much. Every word that she could remember balanced on how to sit, hold her shoulders straight, not to speak or laugh so loud and, for goodness' sake, not to slurp.

It was for that very reason Constance was drawn to this krewe of Les Mysterieuses, women who were of a mind to break old expectations, if only for one night. Actually, their second time in four years. Veiled and anonymous, preempting priorities men took for granted as theirs. Perhaps it was this bold, unfamiliar shift in the balance of power that both excited and frightened Constance. But Alice would be installed here tomorrow and would play her own role in that alteration—Constance smiled at the unintended pun of her thought.

From the front window, the children watched for Dorothea's magical vehicle. When it pulled to the curb, they flew, chattering and squealing with excitement, into the kitchen, where Constance and Analee were discussing small final details of the new living arrangements, primarily about a cutting table and wall hooks for the sewing room.

Dorothea arrived not only with Alice and her embroidered denim bag but also with three magnificent gowns, which, given their pristine condition, might have never been worn, though

Dorothea described each ball with accompanying anecdotes, as she laid out the gowns.

"See this one," she said, spreading a cream silk charmeuse gown with immense mutton-leg sleeves, exquisite lace in an exaggerated V, gold braid trim that circled the skirt, except for about ten inches where it was torn loose from one side of the pleated train. "My late husband had imbibed a bit too much before the Grand March, bumbled himself over my train, and tore the trim off with the heel of his shoe while I tried to help him regain his balance." She laughed as she gestured with her hands. "So, I simply reached down, scooped up the trim, and slipped it over my wrist, as if that were a loop planned to hold up my train. He heard lots of train jokes after that, you can be sure."

The very word *train* pierced Constance to the core. Nothing would ever again be ordinary. Not even a simple word.

CHAPTER 24

"Now, these are to be treated as raw material, dress fabric and trim straight from the supplier—no timidity or hesitation to cut them up as you see fit." Dorothea regarded both women, as if to assess their willingness to destroy such exquisitely made gowns.

Constance knew well that Dorothea could see her reluctance. She glanced at Alice, who was unreadable.

"These are to be nothing but fabric and trim now. They are yours to use in any way your imaginations can dream up. These have been living in a storage chest for several years, doing not one soul any good. Nothing about them will be recognized. Especially in an unexpected new design." Dorothea clapped her hands together and turned to go. "And whatever you don't use for the gown, use to teach the girls at the orphanage. It will give them practice for higher employment. They could use some beauty themselves. I can hardly wait to see what the two of you dream up. I hope you have sharp scissors."

Dorothea smiled as Analee opened the door for her. She turned back with a slight chuckle. "If she doesn't have sharp scissors, would you be certain she gets some?"

Constance felt an unfamiliar lightness at the two women's laughter and watched Dorothea depart. She turned her attention to Alice and ushered her up the stairs, every step both of anticipation and a mild anxiety at what she was doing. Was any of this wise, given her circumstances?

The previously dust-covered third-floor room was now gleaming, the furniture polished, the glass knobs on the drawers sparkling, the mirror over the chest clean and spotless. The white wrought-iron bedstead rose against the wall opposite the windows, which welcomed the sun through their squeaky-clean panes. A slight breeze ruffled the white dotted Swiss curtains. On the polished floor, the crocheted rag rug, well beaten outside on the clothesline, now actually showed its bright colors. In one corner sat a small slipper chair and footstool. A blue corded coverlet lay over the bed.

Alice set down her luggage and stared around her, almost in disbelief. Never in her life had she lived in a room so light and fresh. The rooms of her flat with Howard had been furnished for a man: dark, with a heaviness characteristic of the period. Even this house, on its lower floors, echoed the darker wood, heavy patterned wallpaper, excessive ornamentation, and the rich, vivid hues of the Victorian era, though perhaps with a somewhat lighter touch than most.

But here—here was a space to lift her spirit, to give freedom to her hope for a new life. Alice walked to the window and pulled back the curtain. She felt as if she were in a tree house. Below her were branches, both bare and leaved, through which she could see down to the well-kept yard, where Analee was hanging wash as the girls ran beneath the dripping clothes. From her windows in Howard's Chicago flat, there had been only brick and stone around her. Here she felt she belonged to the world.

"Thank you," she said to Constance, who smiled. "Thank you."

*   *   *

As the days passed, Constance became more at ease with a stranger in the house—a stranger who came and went quietly, whom the children took to as their initial shyness evaporated into teases for attention. Constance found her first consults with Alice informative and creatively open over possible transformations of the gowns Dorothea had so generously donated. Here was a young woman who knew her trade. These elegant gowns in no way intimidated her. Alice spoke in knowing terms of the qualities of the different fabrics: how this satin might lie if cut on the bias; how the silk might be folded for cording and applied in designs with the grace of well-wrought script or pulled into narrow ruffles that widened for floral petals from center to edge; how the beading might be removed from this train, combined with ruching from that sleeve, and applied in an unrelated composition across a bodice. Constance marveled at Alice's quiet confidence in her suggestions, the surety with which she proposed a seemingly endless list of design ideas. Nothing about these exquisite garments, which so intimidated Constance, seemed to bring Alice the least hesitation. While Constance saw them as finished jewels of design work, Alice seemed to view them as only so much raw material.

"How have you come by this extraordinary talent for seeing things as something different altogether?" Constance asked one afternoon, as they laid out Dorothea's garments for scrutiny.

"Oh, experience at Carson Pirie Scott. But primarily, perhaps, a gift from my mother." Alice lifted the beaded sleeve of one gown and examined it inside and out, in much the way Constance might have examined the girls' ears for cleanliness.

"She was a seamstress herself?" Constance tried to see the sleeve as Alice did.

"No. Oh, no. She was simply a wife and mother of the Midwest plains." Alice took the new scissors and began to clip at some stitches on the back side of the silk. "We hadn't much out there, and most of what there was focused on the farm and on my father and brothers, who ran it. She and I kept the garden, long rows of vegetables, flowers where we could fit them in. Milked the cows and slopped the hogs. Fed the chickens and chased them down for Sunday dinners. But she always made time for me. And for herself, I know, in making time for me. Her grandmother had come from France and had taught her the finest stitches as a girl. And Mama taught them to me."

Constance was struck by the intimacy she discerned between a mother and child, something she had yearned for all her life, something she wanted to give to her own girls. She could never offer them the rich gift of skill with a needle or with anything, for that matter. Her mother had given her nothing but things, fine things to be sure, and rigid instructions on how to keep them as fine as they were on the day they were given. They were all over this house: pieces of Haviland Limoges, a tiny gold Swiss clock under a glass dome, a sterling vanity set, a beautiful china doll, which was only to be admired and never to be taken from its stand and played with.

"Did you make all your own clothes?"

"Well, yes, of course. There was no other way to have them. Not for the women. We ordered the men's heavy overalls from the mercantile in town, but Mama made their shirts. Then so did I. But for us, all we had was what we made. Simple shapes to wear for work. But then Mama would show me how to do the bias for a sash or make a little rosebud for the neck of my dress from the scraps. And a rose for her own, if there was enough left over. On those long evenings after supper, when my pa and the boys were in bed, so tired, we would sit in front of the quilting frame, by the hearth for light, and stitch up scraps to cover the beds in winter. Oh, I can't begin to tell you how cold those prairie winters were. Chicago too. Ah, but now I'm here, about as far south as I can get, and I'm hoping it won't be cold like that."

"No, not very. True cold is quite rare here."

"Anyway, Mama taught me how to see the colors—we didn't have all that much choice, but enough that if you didn't see it right, you'd wind up with an ugly quilt on your bed come winter." Alice had been pulling steadily at the thread she had snipped. Each stitch had been pulled out separately and whipped around her finger until now she had a neat little ball of continuous silk thread. She pulled it from the tip of her finger and handed it to Constance. "There, now, that will serve us well for beading. Or for some satin stitch embroidery. Mama taught me a right good number of fancy stitches. Made those leftover fabrics beautiful, in spite of themselves." She stood and stretched her back.

"Just you and your mother, Alice? No sisters?"

"Just the two of us. So, I got all the sewing time. And Mama to myself."

"Will you teach me, Alice? Am I too old to learn? Do you have to begin as a girl?"

"I will teach you. Of course, I will. And we can teach these young girls together."

Constance felt an unbearable longing to see something beautiful emerge from her fingers. Suddenly it was no longer enough to provide for the girls at the orphanage. She wanted to receive what they were receiving in their lessons with Alice. And she wanted the ability to give—not so much give, but share, something not physical. She wanted a hint of the sister she had never had, the sisterhood she saw in her girls.

The new scissors proved, indeed, to be razor sharp. Hesitant as she was to slice into these beautiful gowns, Constance took a deep breath and cut into the fine silks, tracking the seam lines, as Alice instructed. As each section became its own piece of separate beauty, rather than hidden in the wholeness of a gown, Constance watched Alice move the pieces, laying them out, different weights and textures beside each other, overlaying one another. As Constance became excited with seeing the variations, she, too, began to play—yes, play, imagine that—with various possibilities. She felt like the child she had never been allowed to be.

Between dismantling Dorothea's magnificent gowns, repositioning elements into all sorts of possibilities, rearranging again, Constance and Alice took time out to mount the streetcar and return to the orphanage, Constance with her regular haul of donations and Alice with her skills.

Constance was always delighted with the excitement over new donations, but now she was even more enamored with watching the older girls hover around Alice to observe this or that new technique of cutting, pinning, basting, adjusting, and finally sewing. The girls were not just learning a trade to support themselves in life; they were enjoying the process. Alice made every step an adventure, every adventure a pleasure, whether it be measuring and pinning a hem, or deciding which stitch to use for a button or, even more alluring, which for the buttonhole. The girls fairly competed for her attention, but Alice had a quiet manner of assembling them so that all could see, remembering their names and addressing even the shyest to bring them into the discussion. She handled confusion in such a way that none hesitated to ask again, and soon the girls were sharing skills with one another, asking for one another's help unhesitatingly. And all the while, Constance was learning from her, as well—not only the stitches, but also a way of being a woman in the world.

"You have such a way with these girls, Alice. I'm envious not just of your skills, but of your ability to share them and make even tedious steps enjoyable. I hope perhaps, as my girls get older, you will still be available to teach them. No one ever showed me so much as how to reattach a loose button."

"I would love to teach you whatever I can. Perhaps in the evenings, after dinner. I have noticed your attention when I am showing the girls. I expect you have absorbed more than you realize." Alice was picking up loose threads and poking pins back into the green felted pincushions. "As to your girls, well, of course! It would be a delight to work with them—if I am still in New Orleans, which I fervently hope to be. I must take some time in the next few days to begin looking for a permanent position. Your gown won't take a great deal longer, now that we have a basic design in mind. Well, I say that, but it's not entirely true. We know how much flare for the sleeves, the rounded neck, filled with lace above and a high-fitting collar. And we know the length of the train and only a very small bustle. It is the fine details that actually take the time."

Alice replaced the pincushions on the shelf and organized the various spools of thread according to color, from white to black, then pastels from warm to cool, then vibrant to dark in the same system of order. Constance was always mesmerized to see the orderliness with which Alice realigned all that she did. When she had finished and surveyed the result to her satisfaction, Alice nodded.

Outside the tall windows, Constance and Alice could see the girls playing stickball, tag, blindman's bluff. A few of the younger ones sat drawing in the dirt with twigs, pretending at school. Constance smiled. As did Alice, who turned to close the door behind them. There were days when the sadness of one or another of these girls brought tears of their own to Alice or Constance. On one such day, Constance had fetched an embroidered handkerchief from her pocket, instinctively wiped the tears from Alice's cheek, and handed her the handkerchief. When Alice had tried to hand it back, Constance had shaken her head.

"No, that belongs to you now."

CHAPTER 25

Today, as they mounted the streetcar, setting out on what seemed like endless forays for needed supplies, Constance returned to their previous conversation.

"What is it that you have in mind, Alice, once we are done with this extravagant gown?"

They both laughed, each a bit embarrassed.

"I'm not at all sure. Truly, I don't believe myself familiar enough yet with the city to have anything in mind. I very nearly got myself in quite a jam from not knowing when I first arrived." Alice settled into the seat, smoothed her skirt beneath her. "I found a position advertised in the newspaper that looked promising. When I went to inquire, I unexpectedly found myself in a . . . well, in a house of ill repute. Women in very fancy dress and women in pantaloons and camisoles, right there in the parlor and hallway. When I said I was there about the position that was open, the woman laughed—a raucous laugh, to be blunt. 'Perhaps you'd be interested in a better paying job than sewing. You have the face and body for it,' she said and poked me with her fan."

Constance's chest felt hollow. She clenched her hands, then released them. The image in her brain was of Benton, not Benton with a prostitute, but Benton hunched over a gambling table, that man with the sinister mustache eyeing him, expressionless. Then, just as suddenly, her mind leaped back to the startling situation Alice had unknowingly put herself in.

"So, you inadvertently discovered Storyville?" She struggled to keep her voice even.

"It appears that I did. I couldn't get back out the door near quick enough."

Constance was aware of Alice's look.

"Are you all right, Constance?"

It took a few moments for Constance to get breath enough to respond. No, she would never be all right again in her life. When she was an old woman rocking on the porch, watching grandchildren, she would still carry Benton's death within her.

"Yes. I'm fine," she said. "It's just that . . . Well, it's just that the area has such a reputation. Not only the prostitution, but also a sinister reputation for violence of all sorts. And for all sorts of reasons."

"What could be worse than prostitution, except, of course, murder? But why would anyone murder a customer? Then there would be no customer. Are you sure you are all right?"

"Yes, I'm fine now." Constance stood, a full block before their dismount. She would be telling that lie always. "There is gambling," she said, not turning her face back to Alice, grabbing for balance as the streetcar came to a stop. "It can destroy a man. More than prostitution."

As the front gate clanged shut behind Constance and Alice, Analee came spinning out the door, her dark face ashen. Maggie was in her arms, crying, her face tucked into Analee's shoulder, little fists twisted hard under her chin.

"Whatever is the matter?" Constance ran up the steps, rested her hand on Maggie's blond curls, and gently turned the child around into her own arms. "What is it, baby?"

She looked to Analee for an answer, expecting it to be a bug bite or a broken toy, perhaps a cookie dropped in the mud. Analee's expression warned her differently. Constance took the little girl inside and sat with her in her lap.

"Shhhh, now. Shhhhh, honey. Mama's here. You're all right. It's going to be all right now. What's happened, baby?"

Maggie's sobs quieted as she twined her arms around her mother's neck.

"What is it, baby? Did you get scared?" Constance's own level of anxiety was rising. Her breath felt tight under her collar.

Maggie nodded her head against her mother's neck, right where her breath seemed imprisoned.

"What scared you so, baby girl?"

"She ain't been able to say just yet," Analee said. "I went to bring the clothes off the line, and there she was by the hedge, crying just like that."

"Where is Delia?" Constance asked.

"She in the kitchen, making a mess with her little set of water-colors."

"Are you sick, honey? Does your tummy hurt?"

Another shake of the head.

The three women exchanged puzzled glances.

"Here, now." Constance resettled Maggie in her lap. The child was sucking her thumb. She had not done that in perhaps a year. Constance began to examine the little fingers to see if one had been smashed somehow. "Did you hurt yourself?"

"Uh-uh. That man make me scared, Mama."

"A man? What man?" Constance had difficulty controlling her voice, keeping it calm when she wanted to scream. She knew without hearing the answer.

"That man out there." She pointed a small finger in the direction of the kitchen.

Analee was already gone. Constance heard the back screen slam in her wake.

"Out back where, Maggie? Where was he?"

"By the fence." Maggie's sobs had ceased, but her breath was ragged. Constance continued to pat her back, relieved at least that she could talk now. "I was playing in the bushes, and I seed him over there."

"Over where?"

"Outside."

"Outside the fence?"

The back screen slammed again, and Constance heard Analee's tense voice trying to reassure Delia, who had abandoned her paints and run to see what was going on now.

Maggie looked up at her mother, nodded again. "I thinked he was playing hide-and-go-seek, but he got my arm and pulled me. Scared me so bad, Mama."

"Of course it did. Of course. And then?" Constance could barely speak, but she had to conceal her own terror from Maggie. She knew this man, these evil men, would not only ruin a man's life but would also terrify a child. But how far they would go, she had no inkling. As far as to harm a child?

"He letted me go. Just let go, and I felled down. He said, 'You go tell your mama now. Tell her I be back.' And he runned away." She threw both of her little arms in the air in a sweeping motion toward the end of the alley behind the house.

Not safe. Not safe even here in her own home. Her very children not safe.

Constance stood and hitched Maggie onto her hip, carried her into the kitchen. Assured by Analee, Delia sat again with watercolors not only on the multiple pages of paper, but also on her hands, her face, and her pink checked pinafore.

"Well, Analee, I do believe we will need to clean these girls up a bit before they have their supper." Constance shifted Maggie into Analee's arms. For the sake of her children, she must retain her fragile equilibrium. "All right, girls. Run upstairs with Analee and get yourselves presentable."

Analee took Delia by the hand, shifted Maggie onto her hip, but before she stepped away with the girls, Constance felt her fixed gaze assessing Constance's steadiness. She turned to Analee, holding the edge of the table. She knew the color was likely drained from her face. She raised her chin and assured Analee she would be just fine. Analee remained reluctant.

"Go on, now. Get these girls cleaned up. I'll take care of this mess in the kitchen."

"Don't throw away my paintings, Mama."

"I won't, darling. We'll pin them up on the side porch when they are dry tomorrow, all right now?" Would even the porch be safe?

"Okay, Mama."

Analee headed for the steps. Constance knew she had managed a convincing act. When she heard their steps and girlish chatter as they went up the stairs, she turned to Alice, who had been silently watching. The questioning gaze that met hers told Constance all she needed to know about Alice's own alarm at what had occurred. She motioned for Alice to sit down with her at the kitchen table and laid her folded hands on the tabletop.

What would she tell this stranger? What could she possibly say? In the end, she decided on an authentic piece of the truth.

"My husband was a gambler," she said.

Neither woman spoke for a moment. Their silence filled the room.

"I see," Alice said at last. "This is what you meant about Storyville."

Alice rose and began organizing the watercolors, piling the dried pages one on top of the other, lining the still damp ones along the edge of the table to make room for the two girls to eat their supper.

Constance also rose, wet a cloth at the sink, and began wiping away the spills of paint. As she rinsed the cloth and wrung it to hang it on the bar by the window, Alice spoke.

"You have never mentioned just how he died."

Constance felt the nausea rising. She held the edge of the cabinet and leaned over the sink, her elbows rigid. She was grateful that Alice gave her time.

"He drowned." She turned to look at Alice, but only for a moment. "He fell from the train."

"The train? And drowned?"

"Yes, as the train traversed a trestle over some water, a lake, a pond, a river—I don't really know—somewhere up the line, he fell."

"How do you know, then?"

"His body was found by a farmer. The police deciphered his wet papers and came to tell me." *No, not to tell me. To ask me to identify a dead body.* But she could not say that. Could not talk about the ordeal at the station and the damaged body and the smell of the morgue and . . . No, she could tell none of that. Not ever.

"I'm so terribly sorry, Constance." Alice hesitated. "But I'm having difficulty putting the puzzle of today together with any of what you have told me."

"He was a gambler, Alice. It is my belief that he may have died owing money to the mob in Storyville. They are not above trying to frighten me into handing some or all of it over to them."

"Would these people really harm a child?"

Would a man shake his infant son to death? Why had Benton been in the nursery just before she found the baby dead? Had he gone in to see about the baby crying as he walked down the hallway? She knew his sudden, unexpected blasts of anger over trivia. She had seen his irritated intolerance of a crying baby anywhere—his own or some stranger's on the streetcar. It had occasionally been apparent with the girls, but it had been much more so with David—like the intolerance she had seen toward Benton by his own father, so dismissive and full of disdain. She had abhorred that man. How like him Benton had seemed to become after he confided in her once, only once, how his father had caught him with his friend Joey, just adolescents, in a pissing contest, comparing their "equipment." His father had lashed him bloody with a belt buckle. And had forbidden him to see Joey again. She knew the physical scars. Now she knew how truly deep those scars had been.

Her brain was meandering. Not in appropriate ways. She tried to bring herself into the room again, to be present, polite. This was a conversation unlike any she normally had.

"Yes. There are those capable of such things, Alice. I do not know what they may be capable of."

"But you are frightened of them?"

Frightened? Of them, of myself, of life. Constance's breath caught like the edge of a sob.

"Yes," she said. "Yes, I am very frightened."

She had come close to saying, "Terrified." But she was cognizant of Alice's alarm. Would this incident frighten Alice into leaving? It might.

CHAPTER 26

The sounds of feet and chattering stopped the women's voices. Simultaneously they turned toward the door. As Analee entered with Maggie again on her hip, the little girl pulled at Analee's lower lip, and both dissolved into a hoot of laughter.

"Do it again, Analee," Maggie begged.

Analee pursed her lips and blew a noisy breath onto the child's cheeks, evoking another howl of laughter. Analee pulled the thick Sears Roebuck catalog from the cabinet and set it in the chair with one hand, then settled Maggie on it with the other. Delia climbed into her own chair and surveyed the meticulous organization of her paint supplies.

"Who fixed my stuff so good? You do that, Mama?"

"No." Constance nodded at Alice.

Delia jumped back down from her chair and threw her arms around Alice. "Aren't they so pretty?" she asked. "I'm going to paint one for your room tomorrow."

Constance studied Alice's face, searching for some indication to reassure her that Alice would even be here tomorrow. What she saw was a smile of acceptance at her older daughter.

"You can help me paint it, if you want to."

*   *   *

Though the tension never left her now, the following days of sketching ideas, rearranging pieces of cut fabric and trim, pinning and basting, and scrutinizing in the standing mirror at least diverted Constance's attention from her anxieties. Together, she and Analee kept a close eye on the children, the guardian role passing wordlessly between them in a carefully choreographed dance, where a mere glance, hand motion, or lift of the chin elicited a response. Alice watched and in subtle, unobtrusive ways joined in the guardianship. The girls took to her, especially Delia, who was entranced at having an admirer and assistant for her artistic endeavors. She stood beside Alice for hours, watching her sketch or match the subtle shades of one fabric to another, this thread to that fabric. Here was a curious and interested child to whom Alice could show her own talents and in whom she could nurture inherent young talents.

The gown became a collaborative work, involving both women and, unexpectedly, Analee, whose innate artistic bent emerged from some hiding place she had maintained for years. Analee's secreted talents enhanced a design that would be meaningful to Constance, realized through Alice's knowledge of what might and might not be done with the materials they had and the limits of her skills.

Constance set up repeated trips to the library for the two of them, and took the girls along, in search of information regarding the symbolism of the queen she would attend, symbols that could inspire her own ideas for the nascent design. With stacks of books in hand, Constance and Alice would settle in the children's area, with much shushing. The assortment of picture books would entertain the girls while they conducted their research.

Constance was interested only in the actual history of the real woman Semiramis. The wild mythologies and legends that had grown up around her over the centuries bit too deeply into

Constance's own uncertainty and guilty fear. She could not bear the legendary, magical figure featured in multiple, sometimes conflicting embellishments, certainly not the damned creature of Dante—consigned to Hell in the Circle of Lust—or the tragic figure of Voltaire or Rossini's opera. But the real woman Semiramis, who had taken the throne at her husband's death and remained there until her son came of age, who had ruled, expanded, and stabilized the Assyrian Empire, here was a woman who could lend her hope. Aside from history, the only myth of Semiramis that touched her was that of an abandoned girl raised by doves.

Whatever ideas she and Alice came up with must be toned down, simplified. Though there were four queens, rather than one, the gown of an attendant should be modest in design. Any number of ideas excited Constance, and her excitement passed to Alice, and vice versa, but only by working backward from that excitement to something simpler could they find an appropriate balance. Underneath it all, there was for Constance the consideration that she was a recent widow and that she must be unrecognizable.

In truth, Constance felt unrecognizable, even to herself. Who was she now? Who had she ever been? Someone who was no one, other than to her children. And Analee. Her father had been essentially absent, much like Benton, except that his absence had not been physical. Her father's absence had been of the heart and mind. He'd been present only as a keen observer of her manners or lack thereof, of her social graces or lack thereof. He had been repetitiously fond of the old English saw that children, specifically girls, should be seen and not heard. Apparently, that had applied also to girls who had grown into women, like her mother. As a child, Constance had simply observed, with unnamable feelings, absorbing lessons as children did, how he silenced her mother with a look or a dismissive, derogatory umph. One barely audible.

As Constance had grown older—old enough to visit other homes in the neighborhood with her mother—the differences she experienced in those homes had brought into question the set dynamic of her own. Children were both heard and seen in those houses in a manner denied to her at home. They sometimes ran right through the house, to her alarm. When nothing bad happened, when no one called them down, she joined the play, at first hesitantly, as they called to her to come on. Their raucous running and jumping on their galloping stick horses frightened her as she stood at the side of the room, watching. It was a sweet girl named Suzanne who pulled her from the sidelines and handed her a little whisk broom from the fireplace to join the stampede. And she did. Her anxiety made her clumsy, and she tripped. Suzanne's mother picked her up, laughing. "You just need a better horse," she said, brushing the ashes from Constance's skirt and fetching her an unused broom with wide bristles from a kitchen closet. Yes, it was so much more stable, and fun. But a fun tinged by anxiety about her father's response to the dark smudge of ashes that clung to her gingham skirt.

Her mother was a different person during those outings. She came alive, laughed, and chattered away with her friends. Constance listened in rapt attention when conversations settled on serious business. She was amazed at her mother's emphatic opinions about riding horses, women's subjugation, the vote, even politics, all punctuated by the dance of her lively hands and the engaged responses of the women, rapt in deep conversation while the children scampered about. Who was this inspired woman who, once they crossed their own threshold, became so grimly silent; who rushed her to her nanny for a bath and clean clothes before her father returned from his office; who sat with her hands in her lap and murmured amen to her father's tedious blessings; who never lifted her own fork until he did; and who scolded Constance in a quiet voice if her eager hand touched her own fork before her father lifted his to the plate?

Who was this mother—not the lively woman she had watched all afternoon—this silent woman of no opinion? But Constance learned from her how to be not just two women but as many as it took to please, to play the part, depending on whom she was with and what was expected of her. As she grew, Constance learned to measure the cues from whatever company she was with as to who she was expected to be. Without being aware, except by a pervasive anxiety, she read the responses of those around her: the slightest opening or squint of an eye, the most minute raising of an eyebrow, the invisible tapping of a toe under a long skirt, a throat clearing, or a face turned aside. Though she worked hard, harder than even she knew, to be acceptable to others, she was haunted by her perceived failures, especially with her father. She avoided him if she could. She stood or sat quietly if she could not, head down, trying to think ahead what he might ask next. Her truncated answers to his rare questions left her unfulfilled. Sometimes she blurted out withheld bits of herself, only to be shushed by her mother.

Constance's one consistent time alone with her father was while reading, he with his newspaper, she with whatever book might be her current assignment. Sitting at an angle from him, with her sharp farsighted eyes, she could read the front page and the less interesting back one as he held the opened paper in front of his face. She especially loved his subscriptions to the New York newspapers. Now and then, a headline would be such that she could not contain herself.

Such were the headlines—and especially the images—for the opening of the Brooklyn Bridge. She was less than ten when she put aside her book and tiptoed close to his open paper. She stood transfixed at the sight of what she could only decipher as the towers of a castle and the hypnotic symmetry of line after line running to and from those magical turrets. It proved impossible not to put her finger on those lines, trace them to the looming towers of a nonexistent castle, fireworks blossoming from them, all the while murmuring, "A bridge, a bridge."

The paper snapped as her father whipped the page sideways and into his lap. Her stomach lurched as they stared at one another, the moment frozen.

"Sit down and open your book, Constance," he said. Then, after a moment, he looked again at the mesmerizing image on the front page. "I'll give it to you when I am finished."

Constance gulped in the next breath. For once, her father would actually give her the news. It was not until he rose and took the one sheet from the paper, handed it to her, and folded the rest under his arm that she actually believed he had meant it. She devoured the words, the curving symmetries of those lines, marveled at this feat of human ingenuity. Days later Constance would read the headlines, in much smaller print and without images, of the deaths of twenty-five in a panic on that bridge when a woman fell on the steps. There was no need to touch those words. She hardly needed to read past the subtitle. Something in her deflated, like a balloon punctured and gone flat. When she tried to speak to him as he lowered the paper to turn the page, he simply said, "You are too young for such things." And that was that.

Until, of course, to prove the reliability and strength of the structure, an entire troupe of elephants was marched in a grand parade across the bridge. Such a show! And her own resilience rose. Her father let her keep that page, as well. The whole endeavor transformed into a great fairy tale for her. She kept the papers from her father carefully folded in a dress box from Maison Blanche that her mother gladly provided.

In the years that followed, she added another page to the box, one that announced the dedication of the Statue of Liberty. Another page or two about the much-anticipated World Cotton Centennial in New Orleans, but she discarded them after her father took the family for a thrilling, but ultimately tiring, visit to the exposition, which was emblazoned with hundreds of newfangled electric lights, almost bright as day. The strings of neoteric bulbs left nothing hidden, including her excited exuberance, which her father immediately squelched with admonitions to "Calm down and behave like a lady."

Constance's reminiscences shifted to her marriage. Realization dawned on her that she had simply traded her father for Benton. She had been a lady, and it was a lady Benton had wanted. Perhaps any lady would have done. Constance had been convenient and available. And as her father's daughter, she was Benton's stepping-stone through his own magical gate into New Orleans society. She had not been the bridge he needed, transporting him into social acceptability, but she'd been good enough, and likely as close to that social entrée as he might hope to come regardless. From there she was simply an accoutrement to his ambitions. She would do, as long as she didn't laugh too loud or talk too much, didn't express her opinions or start to tell an anecdote he considered his own, and didn't ever contradict him. Most of all, she had to keep her hands in her lap or folded and still, in spite their being as unconsciously necessary to speech as her tongue, just like it was for her silent mother. In that sense she had married her overbearing father and become her silenced mother. Both in one package.

To her great surprise, the world around her found her beautiful. She could never understand why. Regardless, she became Benton's primary improvement project: Would she please pull down her skirt? Was she aware the toe of her boot was scuffed? Her hair was too flat against her head. Did she not understand how to fluff it? Why was she wearing that open-necked dress to dinner? These were business partners, and she needed to be covered with a jacket. Would she stop talking with her hands? She must learn to speak without pausing—her hesitancies were such an irritant. The list was endless. Yet she devoted herself to trying. She put her life's energy into every detail: herself, the girls, the house, the household management, her failure to be alluring to him. That last item was the one that pained her, emotionally and physically. If she opened herself to him, tried to make herself tempting with a new gown, an open robe that revealed a bit of flesh, he rebuffed her. If not, he took her silently and only for his own gratification, often in ways that repelled her. If she addressed the issue in any way, he reminded her that this aspect of marriage was meant for the indulgence of men. She was a lady, after all, not a whore. If he needed to remind her of that, he would. And did. She wept her secret tears alone in the attic, longing for something different, for the romantic affection encountered in novels, hinted at by twittering friends at intimate luncheons, or at soirees where she might witness a husband whispering in his wife's receptive ear if he thought no one was looking. No, she was not a whore, though his manner toward her sometimes made her feel like one.

CHAPTER 27

Alice's question broke through the spell of the past. "What would you think of using this beading to enhance the bodice in some way?"

Constance felt disoriented as her awareness returned to the present, the bright sunshine casting an oblique slant of light across the sewing room floor. "I'm sorry. Could you repeat that? My mind was elsewhere."

"I was looking at all the beading on this wide sleeve here and thinking how you need to be a bit understated, because you're still in mourning. So, I'm seeing these beads on the bodice, but in a much simpler design. Something linear, perhaps."

Linear. Instantly, Constance saw lines, the curving convergence of cable lines on the Brooklyn Bridge. "Wait!" she said, running from the room. "Wait right here." As if Alice might disappear somehow.

Constance knew exactly where to find the box with her handful of newspaper clippings. It was on a shelf just inside the attic door. She ran up the stairs and was back minutes later, her excitement palpable. She rummaged through the few clippings to one at the bottom and lifted the page out with a flourish.

"This," she said, pointing. "This! Right here. Can you do this?"

Constance saw the perplexity on Alice's brow as she studied the image of the famous bridge. She tried to look with Alice's eyes and saw the towering architecture, the Gothic arches, the lines of the streets running through.

"Oh, no," she said. "I meant these." Her finger traced the lines of the cables, the mysterious almost parallels that somehow curved and converged with one another, coming visually to a single point. Her finger traced those hypnotic lines, just as she had as a child, standing mesmerized on the outside of her father's newsprint barricade.

"I see it," Alice said. "Yes, I can see it. Of course." She raised a delighted face to Constance's questioning gaze.

"Of course we can do this." Alice sat down, holding the old clipping in her hands. "Now talk to me about how this fits into your theme."

"Oh." The word emerged slowly, as if that thought was an obstacle she had not considered. She sat down opposite Alice, disappointment dropping into the chair with her. Her mind went back to Semiramis, that queen of the Assyrian Empire, that woman who took unprecedented control at her husband's death and not only ruled but also expanded, conquered, annexed, succeeded. There was a word for that: *success*. She accomplished so much, more than her husband had, before her young son came of age.

Constance's spirits sank at the thought of her lost son. His absence seemed to be with her always, a part of her very anatomy. She was a different person now, never to be free of her baby's death but obligated to fulfill her role as Benton's wife in New Orleans polite society, from which he had craved validation. She worked hard to engage again in life, especially with her girls, for her girls. They brought her such joy alongside the emptiness of her son, balancing her emotions like children on a seesaw.

Now she moved into the swirl of ideas filling her mind. Semiramis, a woman who truly succeeded. She looked down at the box and saw the clipping of the Statue of Liberty. She remembered a poem from an old auction catalog her father had saved as a memento of the fundraising efforts for the pedestal of the statue. It had been written for the auction by a Jewish woman, not only a poet and writer of renown, but an ardent activist as well. Constance had tried to memorize it as a girl. *Give me your tired, your poor, your . . . your . . . masses, yearning to breathe free. . . .* Her brain would not retrieve all the words for her, but she could feel their kinship. Even the poet's name—Lazarus—spoke to her now.

That's who I am, Constance thought. *I'm not poor, but I'm tired and struggling to be free—of my fear and these terrifying threats over Benton's debt. Struggling to know so many things. Can I keep my children safe? Oh God. Can I raise them on my own?* The thought assailed her that at any time, Pulgrum could arrive to arrest her. *Oh my God, the yearning, yearning to be free. To simply be at rest, at peace, at home.*

You're homeless. Ah, and here was Alice, whom she hardly knew, but with whom she felt a strange connection. This homeless young widow now, with nothing but her skill, seeking to find her way.

Constance's mind came back to the envisioned design. Her mind tangled with various bits of information she had acquired in her voracious reading of her father's library. She had devoured those books. Not that her father had approved her reading—perhaps he had believed she would understand and assimilate only the barest thread of it. That would certainly have been his assumption. He tolerated her reading because she was not adept with a needle and her concentration on books at least kept her quiet and out of trouble. Constance attempted once or twice to engage him in discourse on some topic of history or philosophy she'd encountered, only to be met with dismissal, generally an implication that young women were expected only to skim the surface of topics, while their depths were intended for men. But Constance secretly plunged into those depths, immersed herself, swam in them freely. Books were her anchor to life when everything around her, other than outings with her mother, was tamped down into the most boring of bland.

In truth, it was Dorothea's avid retelling of the story of Semiramis, far more than social ambitions, that had ignited Constance's desire to participate in this ball. That and the whole enterprise of women turning the tables to organize a krewe, to take advantage of a turn-of-the-century leap year to upend the rules of social intercourse. At the first Les Mysterieuses ball there had been one queen, Arthemise Baldwin, whom she had met once or twice but did not really know. Now there were four, and Dorothea had put her in attendance with one whose story resonated with Constance and magnetized her. Her mind was everywhere.

All this in response to a simple question from Alice.

"I'm sorry, Alice. What was your question again?"

"I want to understand how the Brooklyn Bridge relates to this costume we are designing." Alice handed the yellowed piece of newspaper back to her.

Constance took it, thinking how her father had first handed it to her, just something to humor a little girl, but a whole troupe of elephants had stamped across that bridge, and it had held. So would she. How little her father had suspected the woman she would become under whatever disguise.

"You were talking about lines, lines of beads, I think, were you not?" Constance tried to focus.

"Yes, something simple. Something linear. I must have triggered something profound. You raced upstairs and returned with the cables of the Brooklyn Bridge!" Alice looked up from her seat and laughed. "That's quite a connection."

She laughed again, and Constance joined her, rattling the old newspaper as she lifted her hand to cover her mouth, then threw both hands out toward Alice.

"This woman, Semiramis, did things," Constance said. "In just a very short time—five years, I think—she stabilized the Assyrian Empire after a terrible civil war."

"I'm looking for the connection."

"It was unheard of that a woman should rule, any more than a woman should be president, but she achieved what her husband had not. She—" Constance stopped, a hard knot rising in her chest and tears sudden in her eyes.

Alice rose and touched her arm. "What is it? Here, come sit." Alice stepped aside for Constance.

Alice guided Constance to the empty chair and pulled a second near, then sat beside her. Constance felt the urge to give in to her desperation, to her grief, to the unexpected relief of someone offering her comfort. She had held herself together now for such a long time, ever since she had found her baby unbreathing. She had come home with a glow of satisfaction at the trove of clothing for the orphanage, however overly fancy. She had imagined those girls' delight at such lavish trims, their excitement with their sewing teacher there, with remaking the dresses to fit. She had left her parcel at the door and removed her gloves, laid them on the console as on any ordinary day. Her girls had bounded in with hugs and kisses before they ran out the back door with Analee. Constance had mounted the steps to the sound of their laughter. Walked down the hall, half expecting to hear the soft cooing and bubbly sounds of a waking baby. There was Benton, stock still at the nursery window. All was quiet, the baby still asleep. So she thought. She motioned Benton out, closed the door quietly on her dead son. Why had she failed to check? It had all been so ordinary.

Constance took a deep breath. She held it as she raised her chin and held her head back until she could speak again.

"Well, you see, Semiramis had a son. She held that empire together and accomplished all she did for that son." She took another deep breath, looked Alice in the face. "I had a son, you know. A son who died. Just a baby. I'm sorry. The thought just overwhelmed me for a moment."

Alice dropped her head and rose. She went to the window. Outside, the bare branches of the sycamore tree rustled in a small wind. All was quiet in the room.

When Alice turned, she said, "I also had a baby son who died."

"Oh, Alice, I'm so sorry. I had no idea. I didn't mean—"

"No, don't be sorry, Constance." Alice looked back and raised her hand. "Here is something we share, you and I. This grief. I know how it can take you unaware. There are moments I cannot hold it at bay."

As Alice turned her face to the window again, Constance took a ragged breath and rose. She laid the fragment of newsprint, still in her hand, on the sewing table and stared at it, looking at those curving lines, their simple symmetry and beauty holding up what? A bridge? Connection? Life?

"We can do this," she said to Alice. "We can."

Alice turned. "Yes," she said. "We can."

Constance left the paper where she had laid it, carried those lines in her mind. She picked up the wide sleeve and studied the beading: imitation pearls and small rhinestones interspersed with a few of glistening colors: watery blue and aqua, palest rose and coral.

"You were suggesting we use these beads. In a simple design, you said. Something understated, so as not to take attention from my Queen Semiramis."

"Exactly. But remember, even as an attendant, the mission of this group is to give all the women power, so think about that as we work on your gown and what it represents."

Constance noted the glance Alice threw her to be sure she had recovered. She nodded ever so slightly and drew her fingers across the beading.

"Well, then. Lines. Curved lines. Strong lines."

"Ah, what about this, Constance?" Alice reached for the pencil and a scrap of paper on the sewing table. Her hands moved quickly. The drawing was not expert, but it was legible.

"Yes," Constance exclaimed. "Yes, I see it. Perfect."

The sketch showed a bodice only, the simple lines of beads beginning together at the center of the bosom and sweeping down and out in widening curves above the waist around the bodice to meet in the center back—a virtual echo of the lines of the Brooklyn Bridge cables.

"That's it exactly," said Constance. "That's it. It's perfect." She wanted to hug Alice in her excitement but contained herself. "You have it, Alice."

"Now, what else? I need to have the whole design in mind before I start cutting. Or sewing fabric that winds up having the wrong lines for the beading and the embroidery."

"What else?" Constance wandered the room. "I'm thinking." She stopped and turned. "I wish I had my father's books. I believe there were legends around Semiramis—you know how stories get mythologized as they are retold down the ages. Yes, a legend that she came from a fish goddess and was raised by doves." Constance laughed. "How mythical can things be! At any rate, she rose from the water and into the sky." She waved her hands above her, still laughing.

"Ah, now it's coming. And it can be done with such subtlety," Alice said. "Absolutely no competition with the queen. You can be anonymous and mysterious as you choose. Here. Let me show you."

Constance watched Alice's hand flick the pencil over the paper again. She took up the finished sketch. The drawing, awkward as it was, nonetheless was clear: the sketchy lines indicated a womanly figure, and tight doodles represented the beading, great puffs of sleeves, a narrow skirt flaring at the bottom, falling to a slight train over a small bustle in the back. Constance squinted at the lines of beading, trying to decipher their shapes. She turned to Alice, questioning. Alice's finger began tracing the lines, as Constance's had traced the lines on the back of her father's newspaper so long ago.

"Here," Alice said, pointing to the converging lines at the center of the bosom. "Here we put a dove, its beak releasing the curving beaded lines around the bodice, its wings open across the bosom, and the edges of its wings repeating the narrowing curved lines. Then, you see, the tip of your veil can repeat those same curving lines. In fact, we could put beading across the top of the veil, with a second line under your eyes. We have enough beads for that, I feel sure, between all three of these gowns."

"I see it, yes. This will work, Alice. It's wonderful. How ever did you think of this so quickly?"

"I believe we did it together, Constance. You brought the stories and the Brooklyn Bridge! Who on earth would have thought of that?"

"And down here at the hem and the train? Those lines look wavy."

"They are. Smaller curves than on the bodice, but curves that repeat the lines and represent the waves of the water. On the train, the lines move apart, making room for a fish on each side, swimming toward the center. We could even anchor that design at the middle of the train with an outline like those Gothic arches on the bridge, just one narrow, simple geometric shape to hold the center."

"You are utterly brilliant, Alice. Oh my! Where on earth did you come from?"

"The Midwest plains—a simple farm girl with a mother who knew how to stitch."

Both women laughed, and Constance was aware of how long it had been since she had felt this light, how long it had been since she had laughed, since she'd felt like herself.

CHAPTER 28

However, the feeling of being herself, the self she was never allowed to be by her parents or her husband, was not to last. Not long at all.

As the afternoon progressed, the children came and went, staying longer each time, entranced at the process they were seeing. Their mother sat at a small table with six glass bowls in a line. With a tiny pair of embroidery scissors, she snipped away at the threads holding the intricate beading to the scraps of a once elegant gown. There was one bowl for creamy imitation pearls, another for sparkling rhinestones, and one for each of the muted colors in the design: the mixed beads of pale almond, hushed blue, silvery aqua, soft coral, and pink.

Constance grabbed for the bowl of rhinestones as Maggie pulled it from the tabletop.

"Oh, honey. Mama has to keep these very safe, or they will spill all over the floor. You mustn't tip them like that. You must help me keep them safe. All right?"

Maggie turned a puzzled face up to her mother and released the edge of the bowl, but her face showed a cloud coming on. "I want to see the magic."

"Of course you can see the magic. But you must ask first, and I will hold it down where you can see."

"But I want to touch them. Will they make me twinkle like they do?"

Constance laughed. "No, angel. But you know what? You have a twinkle all your own."

"I do?" A face of disbelief.

"You have a twinkle in your eyes that makes your mama so happy."

"Can I see it, Mama? Pick me up to the mirror?"

Constance lifted her into her lap. "Well, now. I'm sorry to tell you that won't work." Maggie pulled at her mother's chin in curiosity. Constance ran her fingers through the tangled hair and caressed her cheek. "No, you can't see your own twinkle. Not even when you are grown up." *Isn't that the truth*? she thought. "Only someone who loves you can see it. That's the real magic." She joggled Maggie on her knee, then set her down beside Delia, who sat on the floor, watching. "Look into my eyes. Oh, you both are twinkling so brightly. Someone must love you so much!"

The two looked into each other's eyes, pointing little fingers, giggling. "You got twinkles, you got twinkles," came out in a singsong harmony as they ran off down the hall, passing Analee in the doorway.

Constance took note of Analee's ashen face as the girls disappeared. She leapt to her feet and took Analee by the arm, then guided her into the room.

"What is it, Analee? Here, sit down."

Analee shook her head and held out a folded sheet of paper that was wrinkled and soiled. Constance reached out to take it, eyes still on Analee. The paper felt brittle in her hand. She fought off an irrational impulse to throw it.

"What is this?"

"I don't know, Miss Constance. Maybe don't want to know."

"Where did you get this?" Constance began to unfold it.

"Man come up to the front gate. I was sweeping. He handed it over the gate. He say, 'Come here, nigger. You give this to that woman in there.' And he walk off, whistling. I seen him before. Got one of those real thin mustaches make a line right up to his ears."

Constance jerked the paper open. There on the dirty paper was the imprint of the Black Hand. Her eyes focused. She fought the scream. It released itself as a tangled, part sob. She grasped her arms around her torso and folded over. She struggled for breath, felt the world disappearing, absence enveloping her.

"Grab her now. She gone faint." Analee had gone into action, Alice already at her side.

Together they managed to get Constance into the chair before she collapsed. Analee positioned her head low as Alice picked up the fallen paper, examined it.

"What is this?"

"That the Black Hand, Miss Alice. They bad. They'll kill you fore they think about it."

Constance, lifting her torso, had the impulse to stop Alice as she examined the soiled paper, the ragged script.

> *Dead or not, Benton Halstead owes $3500. You*
> *will pay it. Or lose again.*

Or lose again? The children?

Beneath the words was an imprint of the Black Hand.

Sergeant Pulgrum took the note and studied it. Flipped it over, then back, and laid it on the desk

"You received this when? And how?"

Constance glanced from Pulgrum to Alice, then back. She repeated the fragments of her story, pulling the words together like the torn, waterlogged bits of the note found on Benton's body.

"They will take my children. I must pay them. I will have to. You said the police were on this, but nothing has happened. You know they kidnap children. They bomb people. They kill—"

"Now, now, Mrs. Halstead. Slowly. Please."

"You know it. They do. I have to pay them so they will leave me alone, leave my children alone!"

"Mrs. Halstead." Pulgrum propped himself on the edge of his desk, facing her, elbow on his knee, his hands clasped in front, one index finger extended. "Mrs. Halstead, if you pay, they will be back for more. I believe this is already more than your husband's gambling debt. I can't be sure. But I think it likely. We have information, you know."

"No, I don't know." Constance felt anger rising. She could not afford to lose her temper with this man. He was her only thread to safety, however fragile. "My children are in danger, Sergeant Pulgrum. I know you know more than you are telling me. I know that nothing has been done. I know my husband has been—" She stopped herself. What was she about to say? She took a breath and shook her lowered head.

"Yes, I know, Mrs. Halstead."

He knew what? She wanted to scream. Kick the desk. Smash his blue paperweight through the window. She wanted to rip apart that married name that was not her, not now, not ever. Trembling, she waved her hand, palm down, with a sense of utter uselessness and felt the clasp of Alice's steady grip.

"Mrs. Halstead."

Constance braced herself.

"We are going to put a guard on your house round the clock,

beginning now, until we have this situation under control. I am asking you not to pay these criminals. They will only come back for more." Pulgrum sat upright. "We've seen them in action before. If they believe they can make you pay, they up the ante. It's a given." Pulgrum leaned toward her again.

Constance sensed his shift and raised herself to face him.

"The men they send on their errands are penny ante, Mrs. Halstead, expendable. The higher-ups don't give a fig if their errand boys get caught. Or killed. They just chalk that up as the price of business. You are not the one who owed them. But if you pay them, then they will know they have you hooked, and they will come again. We know the pattern."

Constance saw that he was studying her. He wanted to see that she was hearing. She wanted to trust him but could not override her fear. She wanted reassurance.

"We have seen this repeatedly, Mrs. Halstead."

She sat straighter, Alice's hand on her shoulder.

"Yes, they kill people, they bomb, they kidnap children, but there is a pattern. Men who owe them and will not, do not pay quite often die. The bombs are a whole other thing, more for politics and threats. They don't usually kidnap children, unless they are trying to extort money from a man of wealth. I will be frank, Mrs. Halstead. You do not fit their pattern. You are simply convenient. Your husband owed them, and—I'm sorry—he is dead. They know you have a trust of your own that Mr. Halstead could never touch. They are trying to terrify you into paying them. If they find they can, you become their mark for more."

Constance took a deep breath. She studied his face for a moment, hiccupped, and gave a faint nod.

"You understand me now?"

"Yes."

"You will not give them any payment?"

"No."

"They gave you directions in this note. We are going to follow these directions exactly. Except that we will have plainclothes police deliver. Then we will have their errand boy, and
they will go to something else. Is that clear to you?"

Constance glanced at Alice, felt the squeeze of her hand. She
nodded.

Unable to sleep, Constance rose and laid her hand on the
window sash, her head on her hand, and rocked her forehead
back and forth. With a heavy sigh, she sat down on the edge of
the chaise and faced the darkness. *How can this possibly be
true?* she thought. *What did I do to find myself in this nightmare?*

After falling back onto the chaise, toes still touching the
floor, Constance ran her fingers over the layered texture of the
upholstery. She had wanted such a simple life, what she envisioned as typical, without drama: husband, children, a garden,
some friends, suitable spouses for her children, more children,
walks in the evening, holding hands and laughing. She knew
such things were not, in fact, typical. She had grown up with
her own parents, for heaven's sake. She had witnessed hints of
the various dramas in friends' households, though no one had
alluded to them. Yet somehow she had absorbed that fairy-tale
ending of "happily ever after" as the beginning of actual adult
life.

She had grown, developed a meagre bosom, and gotten her
first blood early. Though she had never been able to see it in her
own mirror, she had known that others considered her fair, if
not actually pretty. Neither parent had commented on her appearance, except to tell her to stand up straight or tuck in a
loose hair; to call attention to a scuff on her shoe and instruct
her to leave the pair at the foot of the stairs to be polished; to

drill her to get up from the table and wash her hands before dinner. And why did they have to remind her every time? Her mother might make an observation or two to the seamstress when clothing was fitted: "Can we do a bit extra here to enhance the bosom? And I know the bustles are smaller now, but perhaps just a tad of unobtrusive padding here about the hips? There, that will help." And to her: "You simply need another year or two—and a baby or two—and you will round out nicely. Don't you worry." And she didn't. It wasn't she who worried, though she was almost as straight up and down as a boy. She was keenly aware of the hourglass figures of young women around her, but she was far too lost in her books to care much, except when keenly aware of her mother's concern in public.

Constance arrived at womanhood well read, skilled in reciting certain poems, adequate on the piano, as long as the piece was one she had memorized. And quiet. Responding with a certain light wit, but with care not to focus attention on herself, while the gentlemen conversed on politics or the weather. She was adequate with the steps of the quadrille and knew how to bake an excellent hen, with just the right mix of seasonings, none too heavy handed.

Into the complexity of her simplified life had stepped Benton Halstead. She remembered her first glimpse of him. Someone— she had no memory who—had been playing the harmonica while she fingered her way through "Auld Lang Syne" on the eve of the New Year, 1895. When she played the last chord and the lingering trill of the harmonica died, she scooted to the end of the piano bench to find him leaning toward her, his hand out to assist her rising. The smile on his face almost alarmed her; she couldn't for the life of her have said why. Yes, alarmed her and disarmed her. No other gentleman had yet been quite so forward. When she did not take his hand, he tucked it into his waist and offered his elbow. That she felt a chaste enough gesture to accept, and she did, then walked to the punch table as he sang the words from one of the verses, just loud enough for her to hear:

> *And there's a hand my trusty friend!*
> *And give me a hand o' thine!*
> *And we'll take a right good-will draught,*
> *for auld lang syne.*

So unexpectedly, Constance stood at the refreshment table, fascinated at how this man held the silver ladle just so. It registered that he poured a small stream rather than dumping the punch all at once into a cup and overfilling it, so that the punch spilled down the sides, the way men often did. In this he was like her fastidious father. Within a few months of quite proper courtship, perhaps seven or so, he spoke to her father for her hand. As if it belonged to her father and not to her. Then afterward Benton asked her to marry him, a mere formality, it seemed. So, lacking other suitors on the horizon, at some level believing still in her marriage fantasy, she accepted.

Now, as she lay here on this chaise, Constance's fingers roved the textured surface of the upholstery. At the edge, where the braid touched the carved wood, the sharp tip of a splinter brought her back into the dark room. She was cold. She rose and slipped under the bedcovers. Wrapping her arms around herself, she rolled onto her side, adjusted her pillow to support her neck, and fell into a fitful sleep.

She fought for balance on the moving train, shadowing Benton, who tossed cards into the passing void at each open-air juncture between cars. On and on they walked. On and on the cards flew out into the sky. She could see the leering faces: kings, queens, jacks, more kings, more queens, nothing but royalty sailing on the high wind of the train's progress. She feared he would turn and see her, yet she wanted him to. Nothing changed. She followed on. At the next open vestibule between cars, Benton glanced at the last queen before he flung it into the void and turned. He grabbed her hand and pulled, forced his mouth on hers. As they stared into each other's eyes, her back to the open, she lifted her feet and rose into the air, away from the train into silence, flying, holding him aloft as she rose. But he struggled, fought his way loose. He plunged into the black water below. She rose, weightless, with nothing to hold her to the earth, the speeding train and the black water far beneath her.

Somewhere between panic and the freedom of weightlessness, Constance woke, her eyes blinking fiercely against the morning light, hands grasping at the sheets and the mattress, fighting to hold herself steady against a continued sense of motion from the train. *I killed him*, she thought. No, he killed himself. She scooted over the edge of the bed, slid her buttocks down to the floor. *I touched him. He's dead.* The thought became a silent cry inside her head. *He's dead.*

Constance heard the competing giggles of her girls and their vying feet pattering on the hall floor. She turned to pull herself up and had her face barely above the edge of the bed when they burst in, their surprised voices in a jumble.

"What you doing, Mama?"

"Did you fall out of bed? I didn't fall out of bed for a long time."

"You hurted yourself, Mama?"

"No, no," Constance said as she pulled herself upright. "You know, I heard some little girls running and laughing in my hall, and I thought I'd surprise them. A little hide-and-seek, but you found me before I could hide."

"We can go back out. Maggie can count to ten now." Delia,

pushing at her sister, had already begun to pull the door shut again.

"No, no. It's all right, girls. So much more fun to have you with me. Come in here and give me a kiss. Both of you." She marveled at their upturned faces.

What have I done? she thought as she pulled her fingers through their loose curls. *What in God's name have I done?*

CHAPTER 29

The front bell rang. Constance was ready. She waved a concerned Analee away and opened the door to Sergeant Pulgrum standing there in street clothes, at least the street clothes of a day workman, two unknown men beside him, one in similar clothing, unwashed, one in a rumpled suit. Each gave her a solemn nod. These men would accompany her. Keep her safe. Though she had kept her anxiety at bay with the children, now it ascended, spread through her chest like an oil slick without rainbows, and caught in her throat.

"Morning, Mrs. Halstead."

He was fastidiously polite, but Benton's name rammed through her.

"Good morning, sir." *No, not good. Not in any context. The many things we say from habit*, she thought.

"I would introduce you, but there is no need. It will be better on the scene if they are just strangers, but I wanted you to see them, so you would be assured they are with you at the time." Pulgrum pulled at the front bill of his workman's cap. "Of course, I will be there, as well. I want you to be at ease that you are protected."

Constance studied the men again. *At ease? An impossibility, perhaps forever.*

"Do you have the packet?"

Constance nodded, going weak. She trusted these men, especially Pulgrum. But could she trust herself? She should tell them how inadequate she felt.

"I have a tendency to faint," she blurted.

"We will be close by, Mrs. Halstead."

The name sent some fierce energy coursing through her. Her weakness diminished. She left the men at the door, turned to retrieve the packet Pulgrum had delivered to her yesterday, a thick envelope filled with papers cut to size, to which she had added a few required twenty-dollar bills. The thickness of it confounded her as she struggled to force it into the narrow neck of her tooled leather handbag.

Pulgrum realized the problem and stepped inside. "Here, it won't hurt to remove a few of these." He opened the envelope, pulled out several cut papers, and laid them on the table. "Try that now."

The envelope slipped in. She clasped the bag shut.

"I am ready," she said.

The men sauntered to the street corner as workmen might. As instructed, she waited until they reached the corner before descending the steps. Constance turned the opposite direction, took parallel streets as she made her way alone to the wharves. The way was not far. It had been a convenience to Benton to be located near enough that he could oversee the operations of the transports to and from the boats that brought the lumber from Mississippi and Tennessee to be milled, then reloaded and carried back up the river to Memphis, St. Louis, and other expanding cities. She had walked these wharves with Benton, their strolls beginning with her hand on his arm but ending with her standing alone, abandoned, as he rushed off, shouting both to and at men at work. *Like a bevy of ants*, she had thought once.

Constance had cringed at his gruff treatment of these men, as if their sole function was to serve his will. But had he treated her differently? Perhaps in tone, if not in manner.

Constance brought her attention back to the overcast light and her turn onto Chartres. She was almost there when the Black Hand's reputation for deadly, unthinking violence hit her. She hesitated. Then focused on her instructions. One mistake would give her away. The results too dire to think of.

Constance's hands trembled as she stumbled on a cobblestone at the end of the street, then onto the uneven planks of the wharf. She must steady herself. On the periphery she noted one of the plainclothes walking at an angle in the general direction of the designated drop at the juncture of Spain Street and the wharf. At the edge of the wharf, she spied with relief Pulgrum's tall back. The third man was not in her sight.

Constance took a deep breath, lifted her skirt, and stepped forward. As she made her way past a group of men lifting lumber onto carts, she heard someone call out.

"Mrs. Halstead. Mrs. Halstead."

Constance turned in alarm to see a suited man, vaguely familiar, sprinting toward her. Her heart pulsed against her chest as she fought the urge to run. The man halted in front of her, a bit breathless. She backed away.

"Didn't mean to startle you, ma'am," he said. "Name's Marchand. I worked with your husband. You won't likely remember me, but I've seen you down here with Mr. Halstead once or twice. I wanted to say how sorry I am. You must be here walking, remembering him. I'm so terribly sorry. Such tragedy." The man backed away and raised his hand as if to wave himself away.

Constance nodded and looked beyond him. She could no longer see Pulgrum or the man to her right. She could see no one except this impulsive fellow with his misguided comfort and his terrifying interruption of the plan she must follow.

Constance nodded to him, muttered a barely audible acknowledgment of his concern and kindness as she again lifted her skirt and stepped away. Let him take her response as grief. Her eyes were on the bench at the edge of the wharf, where she was to hand over the packet. She fingered the tooled leather of her bag as she walked forward, clicking and unclicking the clasp with each step.

Out of the trees at the side of the wharf, she caught sight of that face that beleaguered her well being, the thin dark man with his sinister mustache, barely covering his leering grin. He might have been the devil standing there. The cells of her body blazed within her. She gave one last click to the clasp of her handbag.

The man took a threatening step toward her. From behind, Constance heard the crash of falling lumber. The man spun and disappeared into the trees from which he had emerged. Constance froze, her head whirling in confusion, as Pulgrum, then the other two raced past her in pursuit. They were gone. She was paralyzed in panic on the wharf, not knowing what to do. She turned a full circle. Men were scurrying, working, reloading and hauling the spilled lumber, shouting instructions above the din.

Constance was fearfully lost. She turned back toward the street from which she had come. Suddenly the supervisor, Marchand, was at her side again.

"It's like this, you know," he said. "Always organized chaos. Accidents all the time. Don't know what that melee was, but sorry it disturbed your reverie for your husband."

Constance stared at him, everything in her empty now.

"You'll be all right walking home, will you?" he asked. "I could accompany you."

Constance shook her head and began her way back to Chartres. She had gone only three blocks when Pulgrum stepped out of the side street in front of her.

"We lost him." He was breathing hard.

Constance was paralyzed by the terror that hit her. That man was loose. Nothing had gone as planned.

"Moreau had to make his way around a dray of lumber. Fellows were rearranging some loose planks that fell. Something about the confusion attracted attention, and our quarry recognized Moreau, even in disguise. Don't know how. He must have seen him in Storyville sometime, maybe. At any rate, he's gone." Pulgrum pulled himself up straight. "The men've gone to the precinct. I'll walk you home." They set off in the direction of her house.

Constance was numb with disbelief and confusion. And monumental fear.

"Will he harm us?" Even her voice trembled.

"I don't believe so, no. What they want is the money. You are a secondary mark, as I explained before. Now they know we are on it, and I expect they will go on to something else."

Constance knew he was studying her. She worked to hold herself steady. Suddenly she was fighting to hold back an unexpected well of tears. She concentrated on feeling the back of her head, the point where the crown of her hat touched her hair, a spot she used to still herself. If only she could hold her focus.

"We will have an extra guard near your house for a while. You will be safe."

For a moment Constance could not find a voice with which to respond. She quickened her steps. She unclasped her leather bag, drew out the packet, and handed it to him. He took it and returned her twenties in a seemingly absentminded way.

"You won't know the guard is there, Mrs. Halstead. I will have a man in plain clothes round the clock for at least a week. If they contact you again, they will do so quickly. We know their patterns. We've watched the Black Hand a long time now. Their patterns are fairly consistent."

"And what if this time they are not?" She had found her voice, had got the words out, however bitter.

"That is why I will have your home under guard," he said. "Just in case, but mainly for your peace of mind."

"You think I have any peace of mind?" Her voice came out bitter and forceful. She had not intended that, but she meant it. "My husband is dead, my children are threatened, and your plan was disaster. I should have just paid them. What will they do now?"

They had reached her gate. Pulgrum released the latch and pushed the gate open.

"In our experience, nothing. But we will keep you safe, Mrs. Halstead. You and your children." Pulgrum pulled the gate shut between them. "I will have the extra guard here within the hour. You will not notice him, but he will be here. You can be assured of that."

"I can be assured of nothing at this point, Sergeant Pulgrum. Perhaps I shall never be assured of anything again."

Constance turned and moved rapidly up the steps into her house, then slammed the door behind her. She stood leaning against it, struggling to quiet her raging fear and anger. Nothing, nothing assured her. Her life was upended. She had heard the gruesome tales, perhaps diluted in respect of her womanhood, but she knew the vile things these people could do. What if Pulgrum discovered she had been on that train, might be responsible for Benton's fall? She stared at her fingers. At their tips she could sense the roughness of Benton's gray serge jacket. No one could have seen her. She had been so careful. Well, plenty had seen the young man she was not, though possibly not manly enough: the conductor; the bartender; the random passengers from car to car, some child running about wild and an angry father, the dealer at the table, the man running through the vestibule, an old woman at the restroom. Her soft skin and lack of a beard, in spite of the mustache, could have given her away. The way she had walked or used her hands—she wasn't a man, and in spite of the nearly flat chest her mother had fretted about, there was a way of manliness, which she did not possess.

Yet Benton had approached her on that train vestibule, not her, but a boy he did not know, until she had opened her eyes. The thought made her sick. Made her remember how, in their marriage, he had handled her sexually, often without actual intercourse, in strange positions with unusual appetites. Her mind struggled to block out these thoughts, but they would not release her.

Alice was waiting, Analee beside her. *They will be eager to know what happened*, Constance thought. Then she took note of their faces: Alice's color drained, Analee ashen.

"What's wrong?" Constance flew to them, grabbed their hands. "Where are my children? What have they done to my children?"

"The girls are safe in the playroom, Constance. They will be fine. But you must sit down."

"Did the police get that man?" Analee's voice carried a sharp edge of distress as she drew Constance to the chair at the end of the settee.

"No."

Alice and Analee looked at one another. Constance could see fear etched in every feature of their two faces.

"What happened?" Alice said. "Tell us what happened."

"You are certain my girls are all right? You would tell me the truth . . . Are you telling the truth?"

"Yes, Miss Constance, the girls is upstairs playing house with their dolls. I promise you that."

"They are safe. You can believe it," said Alice. "Truly, you can. Now, tell us what transpired. They were so sure they could nab him."

"I know. There was some commotion on the dock, some planks falling, and it attracted attention. That man must have recognized one of the plainclothes. Must have seen him before somehow. And he bolted. They went after him, all three, but he was too fast, and he had a fair lead, I suppose. Or knew all the alleys. Or . . . I don't know. Pulgrum says they will leave me alone. It's their pattern, he says. But I'm terrified. Pulgrum is putting an extra guard on the house immediately, Twenty-four hours for the next week, at least." She refused to sit down, gripping their hands as she spoke. "Now, what has disturbed you two so? And you're sure about the girls?"

Both nodded their heads and looked again at one another. As Constance waited, they both began to speak at once.

"We was in the backyard . . ."

"We had the girls out back . . ."

"We was both blindfolded . . ."

"Playing blindman's bluff . . ."

"Delia screamed, then stopped . . ."

"Then she was screaming again and running to Alice. We's jerking off blindfolds."

"Yes, running to me and I'm holding her, looking to see if she's cut . . ."

"Or fell down . . ."

"Wait! Stop!" Constance intervened. "Now, stop. Alice, is Delia injured?"

"No. She is not. Not at all, Constance. I promise. Just terribly frightened." Alice looked at Analee.

For reassurance to continue, Constance thought. *What is so terrible?*

"There was a man, Miss Constance. I don't know. Didn't get a good look for the bushes and the time, but . . ."

"We believe it was that same man, Constance, the one with the strange mustache. I only had a glimpse as he ran. But I would swear it was him."

"Oh God!" Constance did sit down at this. "He ran straight here. No one could have guessed!" She gripped their hands again. "What did he do? Why did she scream? Where was the guard?"

"He grabbed her arm, Constance. And covered her mouth—the space between the screams. He whispered in her ear to tell her mama he'd be back. And he let her go and ran."

"She must be terrified. I have to go to her."

Alice and Analee jointly constrained her, advising her not to go now, assuring her that Delia was calm and the girls were playing, insisting that Constance herself must be calm, so as not to alarm them again. Constance nodded, but tears sprang from her eyes. Alice half sat on the arm of the chair, and Constance felt strong arms holding her, steadying her. Analee stood before her, holding her limp hands. As Analee reached out to wipe away the tears, Constance laid her cheek in that warm, familiar hand. All her grief and fear poured out in tears.

CHAPTER 30

Alice and Analee, one on each side, enfolded Constance as her anguish subsided. A calm settled into her. She was steadied by their presence. Alice knew this grief, or something like it. Grief of any kind was always grief. She had so far survived her own: her infant son's death, her husband's abandonment, her frantic search for a man who ultimately did not exist and never had. But she had not felt this debilitating fear that overwhelmed Constance.

Alice slipped from the arm of the chair as Constance calmed and stabilized herself. She knelt on the floor beside Analee, who had dropped Constance's hands into her lap and was smoothing back her hair.

"You say Pulgrum will have the guard here soon? Will we see him?" Alice said, shifting her weight on the floor.

"Yes. And no. Within an hour and in disguise. He says we may not even notice him. No more than the first one."

"Then we must organize ourselves. Dorothea Richard is due to call in an hour to go over the design for the gown."

Constance seemed to have forgotten. "I can't do this. No. I

can't do any more!" Alice and Analee heard her voice rise an octave as she protested.

"Yes we can," Alice said, now on her feet beside Constance.

She took Constance by the hand, led her up the stairs, Analee following, past the playroom, where she paused half a second so Constance could see and hear the girls at play, and on down the hall to the sewing room. Across the tables lay the various major pieces Alice had cut and begun to organize into something that could become a whole. Alice stepped into the room, looking back to study Constance's reactions to the morning's work, the reenvisioning and assembling of what promised to be an exquisite design. She waited in silence as Constance took a deep breath and walked between the tables, her fingers touching the fabric here and there.

When Constance stopped, Alice spoke. "Can you begin to see it?"

"Yes. Not entirely, but yes. How have you done this?"

How indeed? Alice asked herself. "I've spent a lifetime— well, a short one, to be sure—using scraps of things to create something new. My mother taught me how to see new things in the old."

"How did she do that? How can anyone do that?"

"First, with only simple shapes, for crazy quilts. From scraps of fabric and old clothing we cut apart. Sometimes we had to work around a rip or a tear. But we'd get what could be salvaged, cut it in every imaginable shape, and play with them. Like working a jigsaw puzzle. When the design made our eyes happy, we would quilt it, then do fancy embroidered borders at every seam. Later she showed me how to design flowers and leaves in the middle of various shapes with satin stitch, fishbone, and French knots. They were beautiful, those quilts. And warm for the prairie winter nights." Alice thought of her mother's hands, those beautiful designs created by flickering firelight at the hearth. She had a sudden nostalgia for home, an unexpected wishing that she had brought more than one of those quilts with her to Chicago, from Chicago here. She felt how long had been this unforeseen journey, its arduous demands, its debilitating sorrow.

Alice bent to the woven basket where she had stored the various trims she imagined useful to Constance's proposed design. When she felt she might do so with composure, she lifted the basket to the free end of one of the tables and began to draw a few small treasures from its depth: some strips of satin bias she could cord and work into the various lines, should they find themselves short on pearls; fragments of wide and narrow grosgrain that might prove advantageous for the wings of the dove or could be rolled into a cone for its beak; a rectangle of denser fabric, contrasting in weight and texture to the gown, from which the Gothic tower of the bridge might be constructed at the center of the train. Finally, three scraps of a shiny fabric, almost silvered, which to her eye simply begged to be converted into fish.

As she laid out these bits, Alice knew that, as vividly as Constance had translated the image of the Brooklyn Bridge and the symbols of Semiramis into a vision of the overall design, she would not know how to transform these bits of scrap into that idea. The realization struck her that the two of them had converged these ideas, playing off one another's imagination. The developing elegance and simplicity of this gown could be attributed to neither of them individually. She felt her body lighten as she sensed the gift they were to each other. *We can do this*, she thought. *Not I, but we can do this*.

As quickly as one thought followed another, Alice felt the coming void of the end of this project. For now, this gown was her shelter, her food, her safety. Once it was done, her time here was done.

The days of nausea had long ceased. Mostly, she was aware of being constantly hungry, but fortunately, Analee was almost always cooking away at the stove and eager for someone to taste and give approval. She had loosened the seams of her two dresses enough to hide the expansion of her middle, and it could perhaps go unnoticed until the gown was done and she was gone. But gone where? She had allowed herself to be absorbed so fully into this household that she had failed in her awareness of how short term her time here was. As she leaned over the basket, filled now with the dull ache of her dread, she felt a small flutter in her belly. Then another. She gasped and rubbed her hand on the right side, below her waist. Her baby. Her baby was alive and moving.

"Are you all right?" Constance asked.

Alice heard the concern and turned her face directly to Constance.

"Yes," she said. "Yes, I am fine. I am truly fine. I am with child."

She saw the incredulity on Constance's face.

"With child?"

"Yes. I have known it since soon after . . . since after I lost my husband, but I dared not dwell on it." She dared not continue, dared not speak too much of loss to Constance, whose loss was equal, if not greater. The death of her husband at least was confirmed. Alice was left in limbo; perhaps she might never know where Howard, whoever Howard was, had disappeared to. Or she might as easily bump into him on the street one day, some other woman on his arm and a look of assured astonishment on his face. Yet Constance had these girls. She had a home. She had an income, if not a great one. Alice had nothing to lend her security. She had nothing at all except her skill. But now she would have this child. Her child, who was alive in her body.

"The baby is kicking. Right here." She touched the spot again in wonder and smiled at her companions.

CHAPTER 31

Dorothea Richard arrived punctually at two, presenting her card to Analee.

"Good afternoon, Analee. Are you well?" She drew the gloves from her hands finger by finger and dropped them into her bag, needlepointed with extravagant scrollwork. "The weather is favoring us, don't you think?"

Constance was already down the last step and rushing a bit toward her guest. The turmoil in her head had moved to her abdomen. Her mind had numbed itself, and she hoped that lifelong habit would serve her now for appropriate manners. It was as if a heavy stone had been laid on her chest and she had to hold it there with her breath, her posture, with words that did not simply spill from her mouth unchecked. For a fleeting second, she pictured the embroidered, beaded dove there at the center of her chest, holding up the cables of the Brooklyn Bridge. *I am strong enough*, she thought and held out her hand to Dorothea.

"Please come in, Mrs. Ri—" She stopped herself. "Dorothea."

As Constance chatted for a moment observing the formalities of good manners, she noted the clear disinterest on the face of her guest.

"We are not here to practice good manners, my dear. Shall we have a look at the design for your gown?" Dorothea walked toward the stairs.

Constance raised her head. The weight in her breast had evaporated. She took the lead and ushered her guest to the sewing room, where Alice waited. Constance's attention whipped instantly to the preceding moments, to news of the coming baby, to the safety of her girls, to . . . to . . . She stopped herself and turned to observe Dorothea's reactions.

Her imperious guest stood at the door, surveying the room. When she nodded, Constance took another step forward and opened her mouth to speak. Dorothea held up a hand, and Constance stood silent, watching, holding herself still despite an overload of emotion.

"How lovely." Dorothea stepped into the room. She walked along the tables, as Constance had earlier, touching the fabrics here and there. "I can see the full layout, the gown itself." Beside the sewing machine, she smiled as she traced her fingers over the red and gold ornamentation. She looked up at Alice. "You have done an admirable job here, Alice. I am entirely familiar with your raw materials." Dorothea laughed. "This is an impressive transformation."

Constance realized how from the laid-out pieces of fabric, Dorothea could envision the whole. She was impressed and suddenly aware of how many gowns and costumes this woman had overseen through the years.

"Actually, the design is a collaboration between us," Alice said. She directed Dorothea's gaze back to Constance. "It is Constance who had the vision. I am lucky to have the experience to translate her vision. There is a great deal yet to do, of course."

How generous she is, thought Constance. She felt a mixture of sadness and gratitude for this young stranger who had entered her life.

"Yes, I believe I told you from the beginning I perceived that you two would be a fine match for each other's immediate needs."

Constance was struck with the awareness now that Alice's needs extended far beyond the immediate. As did her own if the Black Hand at her fence could not be apprehended.

Dorothea examined the bowls of separated pearls, beads, rhinestones, and crystals. She lifted various scraps from the basket. Constance watched as Alice described the plan for ornamentation, Dorothea nodding in agreement.

"Ingenious," she proclaimed. "And not overdone. That is of extreme importance."

Constance met Dorothea's gaze.

"You must be as lovely as you are without being recognized or standing out above the four queens. Oh, I know we are working for equality, but there is still a certain amount of decorum and Mardi Gras tradition to be observed. We are breaking so many rules already. We can only go so far at a time without resistance and chaos. You two have devised an understated symbolism, clear to yourselves—which is all that truly matters. You must be certain now that your veil obscures recognition."

"Yes, we have a plan for that. I cannot afford to be recognized. As a recent widow, I truly do not belong at this ball."

"You are a recent widow, and you are a woman. Those are the very reasons you do belong at this ball."

Constance backed away to let Dorothea exit and followed her down the stairs. Alice came last and closed the door. As they entered the drawing room, Dorothea turned to Constance.

"I believe there was some difficulty with the Black Hand and your husband's debts. Have they left you alone?"

Stunned, Constance gripped the arm of a chair. From the corner of her eye, she could see Analee rushing toward her from the kitchen and turned to raise a hand to stop her. She might sit, but she would not faint. She knew that both Dorothea and Alice were watching.

"Please sit." Constance waved her hand in a semicircle that included Alice and Dorothea. She turned her head. "You, too, Analee. We are all in this together."

The women waited as Constance collected herself. Once she began to speak, she did not stop. She found herself as forthright as Dorothea. No detail of what she knew of the Black Hand remained untold: Benton's gambling debts, the ruined papers on his body, the connections Pulgrum had made, the sinister man with the bizarre A La Souvarov mustache, the sinister note, Pulgrum's plea not to pay the extortion money, his plan gone so horribly awry, the terrifying threat to her children only hours ago.

Silence enveloped the room when Constance ceased speaking. Her eyes never left Dorothea. Constance awaited Dorothea's reaction. Only Dorothea's. The others had lived this alongside her.

Finally, Dorothea stirred, stood, and said, "I will handle this. I wish you had come to me sooner. I told you early on that you must let me know if they continue to threaten or hound you. I will take care of this now."

"How can you possibly—" Constance began. She stopped when Dorothea held up a hand.

"I have my ways," she said. "Storyville exists because the powers that be sanctified that defined section of New Orleans as a protected enclave of sin. And so it is. The gambling is quite as vile as the prostitution. And as destructive. Perhaps more so. The place is filled with criminals of every ilk. And by men of every social standing, from the lowest to the top. Some with power and influence—even over the Black Hand. Some whose power and influence I am well acquainted with." Dorothea paused. "I have some pull—for a woman. There are those who are indebted to me in one way or another." Dorothea opened the needlepoint bag and drew out her driving gloves. "I regret that you have had to endure this terror, and your children, as well, but it will end immediately. Of that, you can be assured."

Constance walked her to the door, where Dorothea leaned forward and kissed her on the cheek. "Do you think your girls would like a quick ride around the block in my car before I head to city hall? Have they ever been in a motorcar? I know how excited they have seemed when I arrive in it. Bring them down. We have time yet to lighten their day."

CHAPTER 32

Alone in the sewing room, Alice paused as sounds of laughter and high glee floated in from the playroom down the hall. Constance's own laughter anchored that of the little ones. A certain calm had maintained itself in the house since Dorothea's visit, though no one had played outdoors or put on a blindfold. None of the adults had left the house; no errand was more important than their mutual safety. Danger still lurked, unknown and menacing. It could be anywhere. Alice grasped its hovering gravity. For this moment, however, they were in this house, in these rooms, playing, laughing, mother and children. And Alice was threading a needle.

She held her needle still as she gazed at this beautiful beadwork, the elaborate stitches, this exquisite project that offered fulfillment to her creative spirit. Soon it would be done, she thought, each draw of that needle bringing her closer and closer to the end of her employment, to the end of this sheltered place, even with its present harrowing moment of insecurity. It was not her personal insecurity, though, that hovered around and within her, but a shared uncertainty, one in which she was included. Her inclusion would soon be done with. What would she do then?

There was the orphanage, of course. She would be safe. But there would be no sense of inclusion. She would be little more than a stranger offered temporary shelter in exchange for her service, a much-needed teacher for the girls, but not one who belonged either with them or with those who kept the orphanage going at all levels. She was not one with any of them. No one there would truly know her. No one there had any need to know her except as a woman who could instruct the girls so that they might become skilled workers in the mills for ready-made clothing, which had begun to flourish. So that they might work long hours with little pay, but enough at least to keep them alive. The rising demand for ready-made clothing offered a steady demand for girls with these straightforward skills. Alice might hope for a few whose skills exceeded the basics, for whom there might be employment in the higher design workshops.

Alice could provide such competence for them, for the orphans and the half-orphans, who might then contribute to any remaining family. But she herself could not depend long on the orphanage. The infant turning now in her abdomen would be born in a matter of months. The orphanage was no place for her once the pregnancy became more advanced, and certainly not when the birth was imminent. What would she do? There was no refuge for orphaned adults.

Alice had no doubt that she could find work. If nothing else, she could go to the mills herself. How hard that would be now. Already she found herself tiring more easily. The long hours of the mills, without breaks, the pressure for speed—she was fully aware how grueling the work was. She had heard about it in Chicago. And she had heard about it in New Orleans, at the orphanage, before this temporary rescue. Here in this house she had everything she needed: privacy, respect, challenging work, and admiration for it. Alice picked up a pearl with the tip of the needle, shook it down and, holding the needle high, watched it slide down the length of thread to its designated place. She tucked the needle into the silk and anchored the pearl in its place. If only she could be that pearl, that or any other of these pearls, anchored, belonging.

Alice rose and walked to the playroom. At the door, she stood observing Constance and her girls. Her heart was pierced with longing for her own mother.

Maggie held a wooden toy vehicle in her hand, acquired days ago from a street peddler hawking his wares. On hands and knees, she raced it in circles around her mother, who watched intently, lunging at unanticipated moments to tickle the child, who fell over giggling and kicking before resuming her race as fast as she could, watching her mother, teasing out another tickle, falling in laughter again. In the corner, Delia imitated her mother, tickling her china baby doll, flipping it so its eyes opened and closed, impersonating her sister's shrill giggles.

Constance looked up, smiled, started to rise, but Alice shook her head.

"I came only to tell you I'm at a point you might want to see. Nothing urgent. Take your time with the girls."

"Come and join us."

Alice's pregnancy was beginning to make such easy maneuvers difficult now. "Hmmm. Maybe not on the floor. I'll sit in the chair."

Constance pushed herself to standing. "We've already had quite a good time this morning. Girls, can you give Miss Alice a hug? How about one for your mama?"

There ensued a rush of tangled arms around first one, then the other.

"Mama needs to go look at her wonderful new dress. You girls can play till lunch. I'll call you then, all right?" Constance leaned down to kiss each of them.

Straight back to their play, Maggie commenced running her

wooden car up Delia's back, and both of them tickled one another and the doll in a wild scramble. In the midst of the giggles, Alice heard Constance turn back with a warning to Delia to be gentle with her doll.

"I be careful, Mama. I take good care of my baby."

In a deep flash, Alice could feel the moment of bitter shock as Jonathan's empty face, eyes wide, emerged from the cold water in that porcelain sink. Her own fever weakening her as she struggled with Howard to retrieve her baby from his hands, pounded his arms. His voice, desperate, protesting, "I couldn't save him, Alice. I had to get his fever down. I couldn't, couldn't . . ." He finally surrendered Jonathan's bare little body, that sweet, empty face dripping cold water onto her own fevered arms.

Unable to walk now, she put her hand on the wall for balance, near to gagging. When she felt Constance's hand supporting her, Alice took a deep breath, but she could not yet straighten her body, Jonathan's unbreathing face in her vision, Howard's mumbled "Don't, Daddy. Please, please, Daddy, don't," echoing in her ears, the slam of the door at Howard's departure, her dead baby in her arms.

"Are you still having nausea?"

Constance's concern dispelled her distress.

"No. I'm all right." Alice knew she would never again be all right. Nor trust herself not to be seized by unanticipated shock. "Just a bit dizzy. It's gone."

Alice straightened and led the way into the sewing room, her hand touching the wall as she went. Once at the cutting table, she lifted the skirt with its short train, shook out the folds though her hands trembled. The silk emitted a whispering rustle as she turned it for Constance to see the progress. Her eyes bonded to Constance's face to detect her reaction. Alice nodded her head as Constance's face registered astonishment. Alice had counted on that. And on the somewhat awed wonder as Constance lifted her gaze to Alice's face.

Everything they had conceived was now in place, with the addition of one last thing. Two glistening fish appeared on each side of the beaded rectangle, symbolic of the Gothic arched tower of the Brooklyn Bridge, just as they had mutually planned the design. But above that rectangle there was now a third shimmering, pointed oval, shaped the same as the fish but minus the tail. This pointed oval glimmered with delicate iridescence as the fabric moved. Visually, the shape was a subtle repetition of the Gothic arch and finished off the rectangular shape so that the impression became that of a lighted flame at the center of the design, a light reminiscent of Liberty's torch. At a deeper, hidden level in Alice's mind, the shape completed an allusion to Constance's three children. This she had done for both of them, for their dead sons, regardless of whether Constance ever fathomed that aspect of Alice's addition to the design. Every stitch in that simple shape had given Alice comfort.

CHAPTER 33

Alice descended from her room after her rest, a habit she had adopted as her pregnancy progressed, to find Constance and the girls in the sewing room. Entranced at the pearls and iridescent crystals in Constance's palm, they did not notice Alice at the door. Alice could not quite make out the girls' awed whispers, but she watched their tentative hands coming close but not quite daring to touch. *I must make a beaded pouch for each of them*, she thought, *or, better, a collar to wear on simple dresses.* Had she seen them with such dresses? she wondered. Always in ruffled pinafores. What was she thinking? She would need to work quickly if she intended to make anything, even something simple, for these girls. Her time here was limited.

"You be so pretty, Mama," Delia said. After turning to see Alice there, "Miss Alice!"

Alice found herself enveloped in an ardent, if diminutive, hug.

"You making Mama beautiful!"

"Well, Delia, Mama is beautiful without my doing one thing. You know that?"

Delia tilted her face up to Alice. "I know."

"I am hoping to make something for her that is as beautiful as she is." How she would miss these girls. But at least for a while, she would be in the company of the older girls at the orphanage. It would not be the same. Far from it. But it would be something, for the time being.

"Alice and I are going down for some tea, girls," Constance said. "I will send Analee up to play with you and help you straighten your playroom."

"Can't we go outside, Mama? I promise I won't go near the fence," Delia demanded, tugging at her mother's skirt.

As Constance's face blanched, Alice took her by the elbow.

"Not today, young ladies," Alice said, stepping in. "There's a bit too much breeze for your doll babies. And besides, I'll bet it's time they had some tea of their own. One whispered to me that they would love a tea party. Now, don't tell them I gave away their secret. Oh, you have a tea set right here." Not releasing Constance, Alice leaned over the play table and picked up a blue flowered teapot. "So lovely. I'll ask Analee to bring up a bit of tea—or maybe juice, if you prefer—and some cookies for you. How would that be?" She set the teapot between the girls.

"Cookies? Oh, yes. We don't have to have the tea," said Delia.

Constance laughed. Laughing herself, Alice released her, but nothing could release the acute sense of the cost of fear.

Downstairs, installed in her room, Constance breathed deep, laid her head back on the upholstered padding of her chair. Alice watched her rock her head from side to side.

"Will this ever be done with?" Constance said. "Will this ever go away?"

Alice sat quietly, giving Constance time. She saw the strain on her face, the tension in her arms, even with her hands listless in her lap. There was nothing to say. No answers to such questions existed.

Analee entered with a tea tray, set it on the table between them. When Constance failed to open her eyes, Analee looked at Alice in silent questioning. Alice shook her head.

"I think the girls are waiting for cookies for a tea party." That was all she could say.

Analee nodded and left the room as Alice poured a cup of tea. She studied Constance's unresponsive demeanor. After setting the cup quietly on the table, Alice shifted in her chair and leaned toward Constance.

"Do you miss him?" she asked.

Without moving, Constance said, "No." Then sat up in her chair and held out her hand for the cup of tea. "No, not in the least." Alice felt Constance's direct gaze. "Do you, Alice? Miss your husband?"

Alice was unprepared for such a question. She remained silent for a moment. Then, "No," she said. "Not in the least."

Constance dropped a cube of sugar into her tea, stirred it, then sat back and took a sip. "Are you looking for him still?"

Again, Alice was taken by surprise. She looked away, then answered candidly. "I sometimes see someone from a distance who I think might be Howard." She also sat back. "It never is, of course. But it gives me a jolt. Then I wonder if I saw him, happened to bump into him on the street, what would I do? What would I say? I've no idea."

"And you've no idea what happened to him, Alice? None. The police . . . ?"

"The police did nothing much. One officer was kind and seemed concerned. The others were blatantly convinced he had abandoned me."

"They didn't search at all?"

"I don't know, really. Perhaps at a minimum. Only one seemed to offer any help or consolation. Nothing led to anything."

"So, you decided to come south?"

How much would she be willing to divulge? She hardly

knew this woman, yet here she was, living under the same roof, cared for and respected, as if she belonged. Yet shortly she would be gone. She would be back at the orphanage, and then what? She felt hopeless to anticipate what future she might have with her newborn child. She envisioned, with a clutch of fear, the very real possibility of poverty, of squalor, the fetid odors of the tenements. What would it be to confide in this kind woman? She'd never confided in anyone, unhappily, not even in her mother. Her mother's love, her closeness was Alice's treasure. It was what had held her in life. So she had held her hurts with her brothers, her distant father, deep within her. Her mother had loved them, too. Of that the evidence was clear. If Alice had felt shunned, unimportant in the family, she had kept it to herself. She had stitched it into every piercing of the needle as she sat with her mother, quilting scraps of her out-grown clothes, working in daises and ivy with the power of colored thread.

"Not right away. I thought he might come back. I found work doing alterations."

"What was his occupation?"

"He works . . . worked . . . I don't know . . . in the cotton brokerage. Travels a great deal back and forth to Memphis." Alice went quiet.

"Did the police inquire at his office? Surely, they would. I can't imagine . . ."

"I've no idea, Constance. They never said." Alice paused. "However, I did."

Constance's cup clattered as she set it down. "You? Alone? You went to his office? And what did you find? Surely, he was working, or else his office would have been frantic to find him. Somebody had to pay attention. What did they say?"

Alice took a deep breath, let it out. "They had no idea who Howard Butterworth was. As far as they knew, he didn't exist. Never had."

Alice's fingernails bit into her palm as she clenched her left hand. She did not divert her eyes from Constance's face, watched the information refuse to register, then break in with all its incredulity. Constance leaned forward, no sound coming from her open mouth. Alice watched her sit back, close her lips, blink. From upstairs the sound of children's laughter broke the silence. No one spoke.

Constance rose and paced about the room, then stopped, as if to speak, shaking her head. "I thought I knew what some men could do, what they are capable of. Alice, I can't imagine."

Alice waited, her mind lost in her wanderings around the Chicago Board of Trade, the confusion of seeking directions, the clanking of that elevator, the slight grind of the hinges on the door to the cotton exchange, the dry feeling of her tongue as she asked that efficient woman if she might see Howard Butterworth. Howard, who did not exist.

"Would you want him back, Alice?"

The question brought Alice back into the room. For a second, she sat remembering where she was and why. Would she want him? Whoever that man was had failed her from the day she married him.

"No." There it was. From her own lips.

"But he is the father of your child. He may not be Howard Butterworth, but he is someone. He should be accountable. To this child. To you."

Alice had struggled with just such a conviction. And she had released it.

"I will make a life for us, Constance. I have the skills to do that."

"Your skills do not set him free of his responsibility. You have searched for him?"

"Yes. In Chicago, at the board of trade." Alice felt the finality, the shock and hopelessness, the disbelief with which she had closed the heavy glass door to the cotton exchange behind her; felt the disorientation with which she had made her way to the elevators, an empty space beyond recall until she sank into the chair by the window after she locked the door of the flat behind her, the flat where she had lived with an unknown man. "I also searched in Memphis. His travels took him back and forth along that route."

Alice felt the bulge of her pregnancy as her hands tightened over her abdomen, over the hardness of the corset she loosened more day by day.

"And nothing?"

"Nothing at all. He said his mother lived there, but it wasn't true. He was buying a skirt for his mother in Memphis when I met him, but he never took me there. When I arrived, I discovered the vague address he had given me was on a street of saloons and gambling establishments. So I got back on the train and came to New Orleans."

"He didn't come here to New Orleans?"

"Not that I ever knew. Not that he ever said. Only Memphis and Chicago."

"That seems odd. New Orleans is the very hub of the cotton trade. Why wouldn't he have come here?"

Indeed, why wouldn't he? "He didn't talk much about his work. Actually, he didn't talk much about anything. But no, only the Memphis-Chicago connection."

"If he was hiding his identity, why wouldn't he also hide where else he might be? New Orleans is crucial to the cotton industry. It's at the very center of things. And New York. I know New York is vying also. Have you considered New York?"

Alice shook her head. No, he had ridden the train to Memphis. Of that one thing she had no doubt. He had mentioned it too often. Complained about the train schedule, the Memphis station, the heat, the mosquitoes. Never had he mentioned New York.

"Why, he could be right here. Right now. It's possible, Alice.

Out there on the wharves. Right now, as we are talking! Have you considered that? Or at the cotton exchange downtown!" Constance's excitement was clearly rising. "Yes, at the cotton exchange. Why not?"

Alice could not follow Constance's rising excitement. Unclear what she would do if she should find the man who was not Howard, Alice sat quite still, waiting for Constance to return to this room. To reality. Was this energy somehow more about her own widowhood than about Alice's abandonment? Alice leaned back and closed her eyes.

"Yes, yes! The cotton exchange. Oh, my, it is a magnificent building!"

The image of the Chicago Board of Trade flashed through Alice's mind, all these magnificent buildings, all erected to honor the enterprises of men. With well-dressed women on their arms at their social engagements, events where women's importance depended on finery and a man offering an elbow or pulling out a chair at the dinner table, all the rituals of etiquette that elevated women who belonged beside those men—or to them. Alice opened her eyes, gazed up at the ceiling, that high ceiling designed to keep the heat away. But the heat of the moment was entrapping her.

"Do you have a photo, Alice?"

How did Constance keep hitting her with the unexpected?

"Yes," she said, her voice faint. Why was she reluctant? Because Constance had not one photo of her dead husband anywhere? An unfaded rectangle on the drawing room wallpaper was the only evidence Alice had noticed of where such a photo might have been. Was its absence grief? She pondered Benton's invisibility in the house. She had imagined it to be grief.

"What sort of photo?"

"A wedding photo." Alice felt a slice of apprehension. She had answered the question with as clear a description as she could muster. Why on earth had she kept that photo? Why had it not gone into the trash when she moved? "We eloped," she said. "Went to a justice of the peace. No wedding. And now, the truth of it, no marriage."

"And the photo?"

"Some poor-quality print from a fellow on the street trying to eke out a living from photos of marriage-mill couples."

There. She had told the truth. To a woman she hardly knew, but with whom she felt such kinship Alice could begin to imagine what her life might have been had she had a sister along with those overly valued brothers.

"Well," Alice said, rising. "I have pearls to sew." She left the room, went up the stairs to her work, each step taking her a bit closer to the day she would need to leave this place of respite.

As she twisted the fine cording, her fingertips satisfied with its smooth stitching, Alice snugged it beneath the beaded bridge, transformed now into a torch, a symbolic way across impossibility and a light for the way. She dropped the sewing into her lap and stared out the window, comforted by the presence of leaves and the absence of concrete. What if Constance were right? What if Howard had concealed more than his identity? Alice was relatively certain he had not concealed his line of work. He knew too much about the cotton business and had never indicated a hint of expertise in anything else. His travel schedule seemed a verification of that. How many other lines of work had that sort of schedule? Of course, Constance had seemed to suggest something similar in Benton's line of work, so perhaps Howard might have been engaged in something different. She dismissed that almost without hesitation. However, the information that New Orleans was a major center of the cotton trade, coupled with the fact that it was just a few hours more on the train, did strike her as at least interesting. Intriguing, in fact.

Alice picked up her handwork again. Perhaps she would inquire. She had a few months yet to stabilize her life. In truth, she would as soon never see Howard's face again or hear his voice, but he made a fair living. Of that much she was certain. Wherever he might be, he was the father of this child she carried. If she could find him, he could be made financially accountable.

CHAPTER 34

The gown for the Les Mysterieuses ball progressed daily toward what Alice and Constance had envisioned. Alice had Constance in the sewing room constantly for fine adjustments in the fit. Though Alice never mentioned it, Constance's fairly straight figure, narrow hips, and small bustline presented a challenge, much like her own. Not to their design vision, but to the current demands of popular fashion, to which the gown must adhere. The swan neck S shape was de rigueur. Constance's natural shape was definitely not that of the Gibson girl rage. The gown would need ruching for augmentation at the bosom, but the small bustle would serve at the hips. Though this contorted image was touted to represent a "new" woman, supposedly a freer one, the unnatural corseting required was hardly synchronistic with the ideals of suffragist-oriented women like Dorothea Richard. In fact, such corsets had the potential to do actual damage to the ribs and body. However, beauty trends tended to be dictated by reasons that, at the natural level, had little to do with actual beauty. And women tended to follow them.

Alice had arrived at a resilient recognition of this truth. She had spent the bulk of her life on a Midwestern prairie farm. Along with her mother, she had worn clothing that fit her body and not the reverse. Clothing that had not interfered with milking or churning, chasing the hens or gathering eggs. Her skirts had been wide enough that when she mounted a horse, she could throw one leg over, remain modestly covered, but ride like the boys. No corsets or lacing had interfered with her freedom. No one had cared the size of her waist as long as she could help plant the corn and hoe weeds. Beauty had emerged from her mother's fingertips, her nimble use of needle and bright-colored thread. Beauty had lain in what sort of stitch could marry two scraps on a quilt and what other stitch mirrored a rose or a thorn or the seeded center of a sunflower.

It was only with the shock of her arrival in Chicago, her work at Carson Pirie Scott & Company, her initiation into the fine details of women's fashion that she had grasped the stringent burden on women of adherence to whatever stereotype might be considered beauty at the moment. Carson's had presented her a mandate that as their employee, even though she generally worked out of sight, she had to adhere to the current vogue. To uphold the fine image of the enterprise. She was not to betray their image.

Alice remembered her first corset fitting, the corsetiere she had visited at the store's insistence. She had grown up working with measurements. Alice and her mother had worn nothing they did not make. She knew how to do this. Yet apparently not. Alice's humiliation at disrobing for this woman only increased as the session continued. The corsetiere measured not only around her at every imaginable circumference but also every vertical curve from shoulders to knees. Knees? How could that possibly apply? Yet it did. Something to do with adjusting the posture. Now, of course, she comprehended how that step worked, but at the time she simply had difficulty standing still. The corset interested her not in the least, but she was immensely curious as to its construction: fifty empty channels through which slender bands of whalebone would be fed, all these intricate dimensions not just to rearrange her shape but designed specifically for her shape. The precision of the process fascinated her, though she felt no inclination to ever make such a thing herself. The perfection of the process intrigued her: the planning, the measuring, the challenge of assembling all these pieces, and then the ornamentation—ruffles, rosettes, ribbons—all to disguise what was deemed a necessity. This was like her crazy quilts, hers and her mother's, all those fragments of fabric coming together into something practical, then decorated in such a manner that its practicality took second place. Only the corset was to confine her, make her acceptable to a world where she was a stranger. Those quilts had been to warm her, comfort her with the sense of home and belonging.

The thought of belonging brought her back to the work at hand. She took a deep breath. Everything necessary to enhance Constance's shape would be accomplished. The corset would diminish her waist, but not to that of a maiden. Constance had borne three children, after all. However, it would make a considerable difference. They had adjusted each fragment of fabric and trim. The gown would fall perfectly from that corseted waist. Extravagant Juliet sleeves augmented the illusion of a small waist even more. Additional rows of compact ruffles added generosity to the bosom of the corset, and Alice had cut the bosom of the gown generously, with almost undetectable gathers along each side to amplify the volume. Analee had beaded the dove at the center, from which flowed the expanding lines of pearls around the bodice. That embellished open-winged bird would further draw the eye, adding to the illusions of ample bosom and tiny waist. The mysterious court attendant at this historic ball would be of no boyish shape, but as womanly as the next. Then would come her mask and the challenge to make her visibly invisible.

Constance and Alice had not discussed a design for the veil and headpiece, but Alice had her ideas, and Analee conspired with her to bring them to fruition. The veil must conceal Constance's identity without appearing to do so overtly. It must simply enhance the beauty of this gown.

Constance slept poorly. Dreams she had no memory of woke her more than once. Unable to find a comfortable position, she took the extra pillow and wrapped her arms around it in something akin to an embrace. She nestled her face against it as she had once nestled her babies in her arms, inhaling their soft, clean milky scent. David was gone. Her grieving would never end. Now her girls were in danger. All because of Benton. Was the Black Hand simply using these messengers to frighten her? Or was their threat against her children meant to leave her no choice but to submit to their extortion? At some point she dozed off again.

"Mama, Mama." Maggie was shaking her. "Mama, I have a bad dream."

Constance came alert, awake, on guard.

"A bad dream? What did you dream, Maggie?" Constance rolled over and lifted the child into bed, a warm, beloved child in lieu of that pillow. But a child with nightmares, a child who was afraid.

"I don't know, Mama. Just make me scared."

"You can stay with me, baby." Constance ran her fingers through the tousled curls and shifted her weight to embrace Maggie fully. "Shh. Now, you go to sleep."

Sleep evaded Constance. Pulgrum's failure to capture this threatening man had shaken her. Who could have predicted that crash of falling lumber on the dock? At precisely the wrong moment. The fleeing of that man. And to return and find he had seized one of her girls, touched her, terrified her. Now here was Maggie in her bed, fearful of bad dreams. And she beside her daughter, horrified of much worse things than dreams.

Constance's fear had drained from her any trust of Pulgrum and his detectives. And had dampened her faith in Dorothea. She would raid her trust and pay off these thugs. Would the trustees allow her to withdraw such a sum? Whatever it took to protect her girls, she would do. She had lost one child to Benton. Money was nothing more than money. She could not lose another child. She could not let her girls be injured. Or terrified. She must take care to protect herself in the bargain. Her girls could not lose their mother. Though they might regardless. Though Pulgrum might arrive at her door any day with a warrant for Benton's murder.

CHAPTER 35

Alice woke knowing with all her resolve that Constance was right. Alice would have to go to the cotton exchange to inquire about Howard. If she failed to do so, she would be haunted by the possibility that he could be nearby, that she had failed to do her utmost for this child she carried. If he were to be found, she would find him. She would file for divorce for abandonment and hold him financially responsible to his child. She could do this. Constance had lent her the energy and the commitment. The gown was well enough along that she might take a morning off to visit the cotton exchange.

As she lay in bed, her gaze traveled to the window. Her eyes rested on the bare treetops, the limbs holding fragments of sunlight like bits of fabric in a quilt under construction, like comfort pieced together from throwaways. *There is hope*, she thought. *There is something to life that we fail to understand. Life is a great puzzle*, she thought. *All these pieces of me forming something I cannot see, may never see whole. The pieces will come together somehow. It is a matter of trust. It is a matter of seeing life with new eyes.*

Rising from the comfort of her temporary bed, Alice donned her shirtwaist, her simple gabardine gored walking skirt, and her only warm tailored jacket. None quite fit her now, in spite of the alterations she had performed on them. The shirtwaist was becoming tight, not only at the waist but around her bosom, as well. She tugged at it to relieve her discomfort beneath her arms. The skirt would do for now. Each of the six gores had wide seams, which she had been able to let out sufficiently. There was still a bit of fabric remaining for more. A relief, since she had only one other skirt, the one she wore every day to do her work on the gown. There were only four seams in the jacket to let out, and she had taken them to their limit. She pulled the front as near closed as possible, tugged again, then let go with a sigh. It would have to do. There was no alternative.

Luckily, she never spilled on herself and found it easy to remove any spots on her work skirt, left by enthusiastic little dirty hands, with a bit of soap and water on a rag, the touch of a hot iron. *Well,* she thought unhappily, *dirty hands will not be a worry for the time being.* The children were kept safely in the house with incessant adult supervision. For how long no one could predict. She knew the children were restless and pining to run free outside. Their short daily walks at least got them in the open air—three women on guard around them, absolutely no running, adult hands refusing to let go of theirs, and the instinctive childhood need for freedom and play thoroughly squelched. Alice donned the small wool hat she had fashioned for herself in Chicago, narrow brimmed with a side bow knot, soft enough to pack. Even though it was technically still winter, New Orleans weather was far warmer than that of either Chicago or the plains. A winter without months of snow and ice and wind would have been beyond her imagination. This was a place of perpetual spring, she thought, until summer arrived, of course.

From her bag in the corner, Alice retrieved the wedding photo. She had not looked at it since Howard disappeared. Not even when she had packed it in the bag. Now it was thoroughly wrinkled. Why had she even brought it? It was out of focus, a bit blurred—had Howard shifted as the shutter opened?—and now it was faded. The photo struck her vision as if she had never seen it before. Perhaps she had seen it only as she wished it to be. What had once seemed to be warmth in its tones now took on a yellowish hue that made them both appear sickly. Alice shook her head. She tucked the photo into the pocket of her skirt, counted her change, and closed her little cloth bag. Was this an act of insanity? She took a deep breath, picked up her gloves, and made her way down the stairs.

Constance was in the hall, on her way to join Analee and the girls for their breakfast. Alice could hear Analee making up stories with them.

"Once upon a time . . ."

"There were two little girls . . ."

"Who loved to . . ."

"Tickle Analee!"

Alice and Constance both laughed upon hearing the girls jump from their chairs and run giggling to Analee, whose deep, warm laugh rang out above them all. A momentary chorus of laughter, its harmony immediately halted. Alice studied Constance's face, her lips pressed together, her eyes moist. Constance's fingers rested on Alice's arm with a calm pressure.

"You've decided?"

Alice nodded.

"I hate for you to do this alone. I just can't—"

"No, you can't. I would need to go alone regardless, Constance."

Constance dropped her hand. "You have streetcar money?" She turned, as if to find her bag.

"I do. I have plenty. For both ways." Alice lifted her skirt. "It will not take me long. I should be back by noon, I think." She turned as if to go. Then said, "That was foolishness. If I do not find him, I will be back. If I do, I haven't any way of knowing what might ensue."

Constance seemed ready to speak, pulled back, hesitated. Then, all at once, she said, "If nothing else, Alice, you will have sight of one of the grandest buildings in the city, one of the grandest ever built, in fact. That florid thing cost three hundred eighty thousand dollars to erect! It is as ornate as a cathedral. But, oh so mixed up. A bit of everything thrown in—Second Empire, Renaissance, Italian, with Corinthian columns, no less. Gold ceiling medallions, frescoes, murals, sculptures— even a fountain, where the futures are sold. Well, not *in* the fountain." Constance laughed uncertainly. "And an ornate steam elevator . . . Well, just don't bid on the cotton futures." Constance stopped then.

Alice took her hand and smiled. The idea of buying a future gave her a brief chuckle. Her recognition was sudden—here was a friend, doing what she could to lighten this endeavor, which might alter Alice's life and psyche in unpredictable ways. Here was friendship, which Alice had never experienced. Not once. She felt the support of it, and simultaneously, she bore its lifelong absence deep within her, the ever-present loneliness she had never named. Alice nodded goodbye, opened the front door, and made her way to the street.

The cotton exchange, at the corner of Carondelet and Gravier, was fully as fine as Constance had described it, equal in various ways to the grandeur of the Chicago Board of Trade. Alice registered once more the magnificence of such palaces of commerce, these bastions of trade. The streets were packed: fine-suited men; fewer women by far, but visible in heavily plumed hats; noisy carts; and the occasional children running, shrieking madly through the crowd. Women might be magnets of attention in their fine outfits, might put on their own balls in leap years, vie for suffrage, but the world belonged to men. It seemed it always had. For the most part, only in governments with a succession of power based on primogeniture, such as hereditary monarchies, had power belonged to a woman, *one* woman, not women of equal standing—like that of Semiramis. The struggle for the vote had not yet made much progress. There was nothing but courage and determination to indicate it ever would. But there was progress: divorce, for example. If this day led her to him, Alice would, indeed, divorce Howard. She dodged the various modes of traffic—pedestrian, steam powered, electric powered, pushcarts—threading her way through the crowded street toward the majestic entrance.

As she hesitated at the entrance, the thought of taking out the photo hovering in her mind, a passing gentleman, smartly dressed, stood back to hold the door for her. What choice had she but to enter? She noticed his somewhat quizzical look as he continued to wait. She realized just how apparently lost she had to appear here among these grand echelons of cotton commerce.

"May I help you find something?" he said, shifting his briefcase to his other hand.

"Thank you. That's very kind of you." Alice entered the heavy door he held open.

"Are you looking for a particular office? Perhaps I can direct you."

"No. I . . . Actually I am looking for a particular person. I hadn't expected such a vast place or quite such crowds of people." In Chicago she had only to enter the board of trade and ascend the elevator to the cotton exchange. This place was a packed flurry of people and activity in every direction. This venture had been a mistake. She turned back toward the door, nodding to the man briefly. "Thank you, anyway. I'll come back another day. I believe I will need more information."

"Just a moment, ma'am. Let me see if I may be of some assistance."

Alice could feel her mettle going soft, a paralyzing hesitation taking hold of her.

"It might be far simpler than this chaotic activity indicates. Here, ma'am. Just follow me. I know exactly where to take you."

He apparently took for granted that she would follow. And Alice did. Through the agitating crowd, past the fountain, of which she could only see glimpses for the men thronged around it, bargaining and bidding in loud, occasionally strident and quarrelsome voices. Across the crowd, she could see the steam elevator. Then, unexpectedly, an area of relative quiet, where a handful of women, all dressed in dark indigo, sat at a line of desks.

"Miss Drake," the gentleman said, "this lady is attempting to find someone but has little information. Perhaps one of you may be of assistance to her?" He turned to Alice, bowed slightly, and disappeared into the crowd.

"Yes, and how may I help you, please, ma'am?" said the plumpish woman.

Alice pulled in her abdomen and straightened her shoulders. Cleared her throat. "I am looking for a particular cotton broker who I believe may do business here."

"His name?"

"Howard Butterworth."

"Let me check our directories. Just one moment, please."

Alice watched Miss Drake's pudgy fingers run down the lines of names, turn pages as she studied the directory closely. Some minutes passed.

"I'm afraid I do not find that name, ma'am, at least not in any official capacity, among the offices here. That does not mean, of course, that he does not do business here. Only that he does not have an office in the building. Do you have any other pertinent information that might be helpful?"

"I have a photo." It crinkled slightly as Alice pulled it from her pocket and showed it to Miss Drake.

"Hmm. A bit out of focus, but the face seems familiar somehow." She turned to her neighbor. "Does this man look familiar to you?"

"No, not at all."

"I'm sorry. It's just not coming clear to me, but I do believe I've seen him somewhere. Possibly not even here. Sometimes I'm sent with messages to the wharves. It may have been there. That's the association I seem to have. Perhaps it might be useful to inquire there. I'm sorry not to be of better help."

Miss Drake was craning her stout neck to see around Alice, motioning to the next person to come forward. Alice murmured her thanks and backed away. Holding the crinkled photo in her fingers, she turned and, almost running, pushed her way through to escape the crowded building. The noise of the men's voices quoting prices, calling out bids swirled around her as she searched for the door. Two heavyset men, back-to-back, turned as she slid sideways between them, her hand holding the photo stretched behind her. The space between the men narrowed and she found herself trapped as they turned to identify the disruption she had caused. She pulled herself through the viselike space. Caught between the elbows of the men, the photo ripped. Alice jerked herself free, holding only the lower corner of the photo. Around her, dozens of feet shifted. A man's boot in spats covered the remainder of the photo. Light from the door led her to the street. Outside Alice halted, her breath coming fast and shallow. After a moment, she raised her hand to examine the fragment of photo still gripped in her fingers. There were her feet, her own feet, in the crisscrossed, buttoned strap shoes she had bought for the day she would begin a new life. That fragment of photographic history slid through her fingers and dropped to the pavement, where it was trodden beneath the hurried feet of businessmen on their way to somewhere, anywhere that was not where they were.

CHAPTER 36

The day was unusually chilly. Analee had brought in a load of wood. Constance was seated in her rose upholstered rocker by the hearth, the children on the floor at her feet as she read to them, when a knock came at the door. As always with any unannounced arrival now, her heart began to race and her breath caught in her throat.

Her hands froze on the arms of the chair, the book open in her lap. Even the most peaceful of moments was tinged with fear. Fear of the Black Hand. Fear that Pulgrum had found her out and come to arrest her. Fear of things she could not name.

Both girls jumped to their feet and scampered to see who had come. That in itself terrified Constance, and she cried out for them to stop. Which they did. In surprise and confusion. Then Constance could hear the authoritative voice of Dorothea Richard exchanging pleasantries with Analee. Her arms relaxed as she rose to greet her guest.

"Dorothea." Constance leaned forward to receive a friendly kiss on her cheek. "I didn't expect you. Please, come in. Have a seat. Analee will make us some tea."

"Don't bother, Analee. I'm stopping by only to bring some news."

Constance felt the reassurance of Dorothea's firm grasp on her hand.

"Good news. You will want to hear this, too, Analee. Girls, I've been thinking about your dolls. Could you go put them in their very best dresses and bring them down from your play-room for me to see?" Dorothea tousled Maggie's curls, leaning sideways to half hug Delia.

As the girls scampered up the stairs, Dorothea motioned for Constance and Analee to sit, as if she were the hostess, rather than the reverse. "I came as quickly as I could to tell you. Your worries with the Black Hand are done."

Analee clapped her long fingers over her mouth.

"Done," said Constance. "How can you know that? Did they arrest that man? How can you be sure?"

"Slowly now, my dear. I will tell you as much as I can, though I cannot tell you the whole of it. I have certain confidences to keep." She perched on the edge of the sofa to continue. "I told you previously that I have a bit of pull with some of the 'powers that be' in the city? Yes, well, it's true. I do. And I have successfully exerted that pull to your advantage. They will not bother you or your children again. Of that you may be assured."

"I don't understand, Dorothea. How can you have sway over the Black Hand?"

"Not over the Black Hand, my dear. No, I have sway with some of the political powers who do have sway over the syndicate."

"But how is that—"

"Possible? Quite possible, dear Constance. Storyville operates only under the auspices of the political powers of the city. My late husband was one of those powers. As you may have surmised, Constance, I was not simply an ornament at his elbow. With time and a sharp eye and wit, I have come to know a great deal about some of the men who run this city, a number of whom I greet at social functions and at Mass."

"I still don't understand!"

"Those men hold the power over Storyville. Some are its patrons. Some, like your Benton, frequent it for their need to make a bet. But ultimately that place of instituted sin remains viable at the behest of those who run the city, and every thug there knows it. If one of those in power communicates to the syndicate to withdraw their 'persuasions' in any given direction, that will be the end of it. Their livelihood, if you can call it that, depends on cooperation with political power."

"And you—"

"I do not use my pull lightly or frequently. But those ruffians have crossed a line this time. This has not been their usual pattern, I have to say. Normally, if they see no way to success, they . . ." Dorothea hesitated. "I'm sorry, Constance. I'm so sorry . . . They find a way to finalize the problem. And that is the end of it. They move on to the next poor dupe."

The jolt of the train, the other gambler darting past flashed across Constance's mind. She raised her hand and rubbed at her forehead.

"I truly am sorry, Constance. I simply have no other way of telling you all this. I do not mean to distress you. What I have to tell you is to reassure you of your safety."

She mistakes me as grieving, Constance thought. She brushed back the hair her hand had inadvertently loosened and raised her head, took a deep breath, and nodded to her guest. "Why has our situation, my situation, been different? Do you know?"

"We can't be certain, of course. But likely that man with the sinister mustache is a bit of a rogue. Which will most certainly be his ruination. The Black Hand is not known to tolerate disloyalty, especially involving money. Either he will be found dead quite soon or he will be set up to fall into the hands of the authorities for a major offense, murder, likely. But he will not come near you or your children again. Of that, I can assure you, Constance. Word has gone out, and the reins are pulled in. This ordeal is over now."

Both women rose, and Analee with them. As she allowed herself to fall into Dorothea's surprisingly strong embrace, Constance noticed in her peripheral vision the tears on Analee's cheeks. She held out her hand to Analee's strong grasp.

"Now, where are those girls?" Dorothea said, stepping back. "They were supposed to come show me their dressed-up dolls."

"They have probably changed those dolls three times by now," Analee said. "They get to changing those clothes, and they can't quit coming up with another idea. Fore you know it, they changing each other. I'm going to fetch them for you right now."

Upon returning home, Alice was surprised to see Dorothea Richard's motorcar pull away. She was out of breath when she stepped into the house, simultaneously overcome with her own experience and curious to know the reason for Dorothea's visit. Had she been there to examine the progress on the gown? What if she had disapproved of something?

As she entered the house, Alice was immediately startled. Constance had her by the shoulders, laughing and crying at once. Curiosity conquered Alice's fatigue and anxiety.

"It's over, Alice." Constance's voice was dense, and the assuredness of it penetrated Alice's agitated spirit.

"What's over?"

"The Black Hand threat. Dorothea has pulled some strings, and it's over."

"How can she do that? A woman with—"

"With the right connections to powerful men. I vow I believe she is using some sort of blackmail."

"Blackmail!"

"Well, not really, but she seems to know some scuttlebutt on some of our city politicians who are connected to the legal status of Storyville. And to be using it on our behalf. It's too complicated to explain quickly. Perhaps over dinner." Constance grabbed for her hand and pulled Alice into the drawing room. "Now, what did you find? You look so pale. Did you find him?"

Did I find him? Alice thought. *No.* She shook her head.

"No. Did you find anything? A clue? Someone who knew him?"

Again, Alice shook her head. *How to tell all this?*

"Then what?"

"The place was a madhouse. So many people. So many men. And loud." Alice stepped to the window and glanced out, almost a habit now since the threats and with the detective on guard.

"Come now. Sit. Let yourself calm down. You're home now."

Home? Was that what she had heard? It was only a figure of speech, but it penetrated Alice's awareness. She would never be home. That she could foresee. She lowered herself into a chair.

"Now, that's better. Would you like the footstool?"

Constance bent to move it, but Alice shook her head. She was glad of Constance's silence while she collected herself. Under her fingers she was aware of the layers of the cut velvet upholstery—the fingers that had held that photo. Her last proof of her marriage, should she need it in a divorce. Alice raised her eyes to Constance's face.

"A woman at the information desk thought she recognized him."

"Recognized him? From your photo? Was his name in the directory?"

"No. Not his name."

"But she knew him?"

"No, she only thought he might have looked familiar. From some other place. She sometimes carries documents to the wharves. It might have been there, she thought. But she wasn't even sure. The photo was blurred. And Howard is not a distinctive-looking man—handsome, yes, but nothing unusual about him, so . . ."

"The wharves? I've been there a few times with Benton. Let me see the photo. Perhaps I might know him."

"I don't have it." Alice stared out the window. "I panicked in that place. I had to get out. So crowded." She absentmindedly pulled at the seams of her skirt. "It tore."

"Tore? Do you have the pieces?"

Alice wondered if she would ever have anything other than pieces. Pieces of fabric she could rearrange into something of use and beauty. But pieces of life? Would they ever become a whole?

"There was only a small corner left in my fingers. The rest was gone. So, I let it go."

An effervescent trilling pulled her gaze to the window again. A wren flew from one of the bare lower tree branches. Alice found herself envying its freedom.

"We must make an outing to the wharves," Constance said.

Alice took in the *we*. For a second time, she absorbed the unfamiliar, assuring sense of friendship. Again, she suffered a momentary sense of loss at what she had never had, had never even known she was missing. The realization transported her to her mother, the mother who had been her friend, who had sent her away to what she envisioned as a more promising life. Alice was glad her mother would never know.

"Yes, we must do that tomorrow." Constance's voice broke into Alice's reverie. "I can leave Analee and the children now without fear of the Black Hand. We are so near. We have only to stroll down there after breakfast."

Alice nodded, but she found herself stopped short at the idea of a stroll. This search for the man who had deserted her was no stroll. She was not on some pleasure walk. Dared she speak to her employer about her feelings? Her benefactor? What was this woman to her? A friend? Alice had no pattern within her for friendship. But then, she had no pattern for that gown that now hung upstairs, with only stitches remaining to completion.

"This is hardly a stroll for me, Constance."

"No. This is no stroll. Forgive me, Alice. That was un-thoughtful of me."

Alice felt as much as saw Constance's outstretched hand. She took it.

"I'm so relieved, elated really, at Dorothea's news that—I'm sorry—I am not fully present yet. I'm afraid I'm distracted from your news by my relief for my girls."

"As is natural, Constance. Of course." Alice stood and brushed at her skirt. "We must have this gown finished before we distract ourselves further," she said. "We will go when it is done. There is nothing more in that woman's response than I knew before. Anyone could seem vaguely familiar to anyone in a poor-quality photo. But you will be wearing that gown the day after tomorrow. We have the headpiece and veil to finish before then."

"You are gracious, Alice. And kind. Thank you. Luckily, it is warm this year, and I will need only my cape for a wrap. Imagine if this were last year. It was near to freezing!"

"Was it?" Alice felt again the bitter cold of Chicago, the un-expected terror of her boots out of control on the ice, the pain of her fall—all that had led her to this place and this moment. She excused herself and left the drawing room, turned to the stairway and the work remaining.

CHAPTER 37

"Thank goodness I do not have to wear a mask," Constance said. "Not only would that be so stiff and uncomfortable, but it limits your vision terribly, as well."

Alice was wrapping the finished veil over the bridge of Constance's nose, which made her want to scratch it. The pins with which Alice had secured it momentarily at her hairline made her want to scratch there, too. Constance could tell how carefully Alice was trying not to disturb the rolled fluff of her hair, as if a bit more hair hanging loose would matter. At least not now. But it would matter for the ball tomorrow night. For her anonymity, not one hair must show. *Like that squashed men's wig upstairs in the attic*, Constance thought. How she had worked to conceal her own hair, thick and unwieldy, under it in order to rush from this house unnoticed that early morning. A slight shudder passed through her.

"Are you chilly?"

"I'm all right. Just anticipation of seeing how well you have managed to hide me, I suppose."

"Just a bit more, then. Hold very still now."

Constance felt the tug on her hair as Alice pinned the forehead portion of the veil across and down her hairline. At one point she flinched.

"I'm so sorry. Almost done." Alice touched her arm. Constance felt her tucking something in at the bridge of her nose. One more tiny adjustment at her hairline. "There now."

Alice passed Constance the hand mirror. Hardly daring to move her head, Constance took the silver-handled mirror and gasped. The veil was Alice's surprise for her, and pure surprise it was.

Across her forehead a fitted sheath of silk pongee, bordered above her eyes with a line of small white goose feathers. The effect was that of winged eyebrows. For a second time, Constance reverted to that fatal morning, to the glued pull of those ashy eyebrows. Why must she continue associating this beauty with that tragic moment of her life? Why must everything regenerate her merciless guilt? And the unrelenting uncertainty that she had caused his death.

At the bridge of her nose, a beaded dove spread its wings in a beautiful curve lining her lower lid, an almost exact replica of the dove embellishing the center bodice of her gown. From its beak across the top layer of tulle tiny pearls flowed in curved lines that echoed those on the dress. Alice had doubled the layers of tulle, the bottom layer slightly longer with a finished edge of the tiny pearls. The effect was one of incredible lightness, yet the veil thoroughly concealed her lower face, its weighted drapes falling to her collarbone. Constance's face had disappeared. Only her eyes remained visible. Those eyes that had given her away.

Alice began to wrap the headpiece over Constance's hair, a length of silk charmeuse in a simple fashion reminiscent of that on the dance card that lay on Constance's vanity, the dance card she would hold on her wrist by its cord but never use. Constance turned her head and leaned toward the vanity mirror. *Oh, the cleverness of Alice*, she thought. No, the headpiece on the dance card simply wrapped around and under the chin, with only a black mask for the eyes and no real concealment of the face. This wrapping mimicked her own Gibson Girl hair, fluffed out around the hairline, pulled back and twisted into a knot in the back, much like a bun. A far cry from that wig now concealed. Constance turned from side to side, holding her looking glass at various angles to see her reflection in the larger mirror. She would not have known herself.

"I can't believe this, Alice. How on earth . . . ?"

"You are pleased?"

"Pleased? I'm ecstatic!" Constance laid down the glass and put her hands out to Alice, who took them. Constance held those talented hands in hers for a moment. Then stood and enfolded Alice in a grateful hug.

"We are not quite done, you know," said Alice. "You'll need to sit back down."

From the vanity stool, Constance watched and listened.

"The veil will be sewn to the headpiece across the forehead and the temples. There will be tiny buttons from there down and around the sides."

Constance fingered the smooth, tiny pearls edging her veil.

"Now, do you want a poppy?"

"A poppy? Whatever for?"

"I've noticed it on your cards. Is it important?"

"Oh, the poppy. It's quite a mixed symbol—a symbol of silence, you see. How strange. And yes, it is the symbol for the ball motif. It seems that women have grown tired of the silent, subservient role. So, they have taken that very symbol to flaunt the reversal of roles for this event."

"Would you like to flaunt it?"

Constance froze for a moment. "I think not, Alice. I am choosing to remain silent, incognito. I don't wish to call attention to myself." She waited while Alice seemed to puzzle over her answer.

"Perhaps all the more reason," Alice said. "Your silence is chosen, not imposed."

"But it would draw such attention. A bright red poppy?"

"Perhaps not. What if it were not bright red?"

"Not red?"

"There is a white poppy, with an almost black center. I noticed some once in the window of a florist in Chicago. I was mesmerized. I turned around and went in to see them. The florist was a bit outdone with me that I did not buy even one." Alice laughed. "But it could have all sorts of meanings for you."

"Yes, and what would those be?"

"You've already explained why the ladies chose it for their motif. But the white poppy with the black center would be even more meaningful. All the things you've said—I believe I remember this correctly—plus peace."

"Peace?"

"Yes, I can't remember now if it was the Egyptians or the Greeks, but someone ancient used the white poppy as a symbol of peace, perhaps because it might put you to sleep." Alice laughed again. "We can tuck it in right here over the ear."

"I love the thought of peace. I need it so badly." Constance pulled at a strand of loose hair. "The black center—a token of widowhood." *And guilt*, she thought. "Will it be difficult to make?"

"Not at all. Not if the girls will lend me a bit of watercolor for the black." Alice laughed again.

Her laughter made Constance happy. Such a while since she had felt this way. "How on earth did you know that about the poppy, Alice?"

"My mother had a book on mythology. I loved to read. We had only a handful of books out there while I was growing up. I must have read that book a hundred times."

"This outfit is getting more and more complicated. It will take a great deal to get me ready. You and Analee have the strength to lace me into that corset?"

"Of course."

Constance felt the slightest weight lift as Alice took the swirled headpiece, securely pinned for stitching, from her head and set it on the side of the vanity. It was magical, of course, as it should be. Yet somehow more than that to her, almost miraculous.

"The girls must help us, too." Alice drew the pins from the veil. "I will find an assignment for them. They must have the last exciting touch. Then you will be quite ready."

Would she be ready? For an evening of watching as an outsider? An observer of women taking the lead while she herself remained on the edges. She would be there, however. She would be present, one of Les Mysterieuses, a woman known only to herself.

In the night Alice woke and rolled over in her narrow bed. The room was cold. In spite of her warm blankets, when she stretched out, her feet hit a section of chilly sheet that had not been warmed by her body heat. The baby was moving, a foot perhaps pressing against the skin on her right side. Alice laid her palm over the little bulge and held it there until the baby moved again. She curled onto her side, reached out her hand to touch the slanted ceiling where it angled down to the floor. As her fingers pressed against the boarding, Alice was seized by a powerful sense that she could identify only as belonging. Like the realization of never experienced friendship, this sudden sense of belonging revealed some deep void within her that had not so much lost something, as had never held anything of hers to lose, so foreign to her that she had no way to give it an identity. Something akin to what was missing had been hers with her mother, both friendship and belonging. Yet because of the masculine rule of the farm, neither had truly been hers. Her mother's first allegiance had been to her father. To her father, though he loved them both in his way, she and her mother had hardly been more than trappings to fulfill his needs. Alice's belonging there had been to her father, and not with him.

When the morning came, Alice rose, feeling still the mystery of her sensations in the night. She washed her face and hands, pulled her hair into its customary bun and pinned it. She donned her gored skirt and her too-tight shirtwaist, tied her boots. She wished to look as decent as possible. This afternoon she and Analee would begin the transformation of Constance into a mysterious and unknown goddess. This was a day such as Alice had never imagined. Never had she dreamed of creating anything so fine as this gown and headpiece. Never had she conceived of the chance to plumb the depths of her creative hunger and produce something as glorious as this gown and veil. Nor had she imagined the generosity of spirit in such women as Constance, to say nothing of Analee and Dorothea.

She found Constance and Analee at the kitchen table, sharing chickory coffee and the fresh beignets Analee had fetched early from the market. They ceased their conversation when she entered, the wood floor creaking slightly as she crossed the ample space. Sunlight from the window silhouetted their heads.

"Ah, there she is," said Constance. "We were just discussing you, Alice."

Analee scuffed back her chair and rose to retrieve another cup of coffee. Alice sat, wondering. Constance reached for her hand.

"Alice, if you should find Howard, would you be with him again?"

So unexpected was this question, Alice could not answer. She shook her head.

"For the baby, perhaps? If he asked you?"

Alice thought for a moment. Shook her head again. "No."

"But you went looking because of the baby, am I wrong?"

"Yes, for the baby. But only for Howard's financial responsibility. Wherever he is, this is his child. He may abandon me, but not the child."

"The gown is complete. Magnificently so. Tonight is the ball. What are your plans after this?"

Alice took a deep breath. "I will go back to the orphanage to work with the girls for a time. They will need to learn everything I have to teach them so that they can find work, not in the mills—no, not in the mills. But with designers and skilled seamstresses who make the Mardi Gras ball gowns and the opera gowns and . . ."

Analee set a china cup beside her, with a plated beignet.

Constance squeezed her hand. "Yes, the girls there do indeed need your mentoring. But there is no need for you to live in the orphanage, especially not with the baby coming."

"But . . ."

"So Analee and I have been talking. I have a proposal for you."

"But my work here for you is done, Constance."

"Perhaps I might not say that, Alice. Hear me out. I am also deeply invested in the orphanage and those girls, as is Dorothea. So yes, I am very much interested in how the girls may fully benefit from your expertise. But that does not mean you need to live there."

Alice opened her mouth to speak, but Constance shushed her. Where could Constance possibly imagine she might go? Perhaps she was aware of some small rental, in which case Alice would need to move only once. Alice's brain flew through possibilities, probable or not. She sat back and waited.

"Especially not with your baby coming." Constance also sat back. "The gown is done, it's true. But the girls and I will have other needs now, especially with spring coming on. The girls will need Easter dresses, I am sure. They are growing so rapidly."

"If you are asking if I might be available for that, the answer is certainly yes. With immense enthusiasm. Your girls are an immense joy to me." It relieved Alice to think she would have at least a minimum of work assured.

"Yes, I am asking that. And more. We have all become very fond of you, Alice. I believe you feel that here among us."

"You have made me extraordinarily welcome, Constance. As have you, Analee." Alice smiled at one, then the other.

"So here is my proposal. As you already know, we have an extra bedroom on the second floor. Ultimately, it would be for one of the girls as they begin to grow up and want separate rooms, but that time is still years away. The room is large enough to accommodate both you and the baby furniture—crib, changing table, small chest—that I have stored in the attic. You would have both comfort and a degree of privacy."

Alice's heart was racing. She knew the room. Of course. It was lovely, but she could not impose herself on this family. She would not.

"You are so kind, Constance, but I cannot take advantage of your kind generosity. You cannot take me and this baby on as an act of charity. You are so passionately kind, but just making Easter dresses for your girls hardly covers—"

"Alice." Constance held up her hand to silence Alice's protests. "You are not and never will be my charity case. Please. You must never think such thoughts again. You are my friend. And I need a friend."

As do I, thought Alice, aware suddenly of the tears she blinked back.

"Don't protest now," Constance said. "Hear me out to the end. You are such a talented seamstress. Perhaps I should actually use the term *couturier*. After this ball tonight, once it is over and done, everyone attending will be wondering about that gown and veil. We will return it all to Dorothea. My secret attendance will be secure. Well, perhaps. Who knows?" Constance glanced out the window, brushed back her hair. "At any rate, I've considered this carefully. Dorothea will have the costume. Women all over New Orleans will be wanting gowns for weddings, dinners, balls—there is always something. Dorothea will guide them to you. You will have more demand than you can accommodate, with ample income to contribute to the household, and plenty left over to save for yourself and your child."

Alice felt Constance take her hand. "The only other condition, dear Alice, is that you save time to teach the girls at the orphanage to sew. In fact, that is primary. They need to be able to find work when they leave."

"Constance, I want to give them greater proficiencies than just those basics for the mills. I want to give them the opportunity to make real lives for themselves. They need more than survival."

"As do you, Alice." Constance released her hand. "Now tell me you will stay, so that I can enjoy this event tonight."

Alice breathed in the possibilities, the sense of belonging, the peace of it.

"Yes. I will stay." Only then did she let the tears come free.

CHAPTER 38

"Now, about your Howard Butterworth—we still have time to make a foray to the wharves for a few inquiries. I am planning to go with you, since I have nothing to do between now and getting myself into my exquisite costume."

Alice felt Constance's gentle fingers wipe away the tears on her cheek. Everything in her felt settled. The search for Howard remained essential but had lost its frantic urgency. Alice nodded.

"I would welcome your company, Constance. And your familiarity with the wharves."

"Then we are on our way. Analee, you have the girls. Perhaps they might find it exciting to help set that bedroom straight for Alice."

Alice donned her new boater, a gift from Constance's collection, and followed Constance out the door.

Outside the world seemed peculiarly hushed, the air still and silent, the half-light of a clouded sky blurred like her lost photograph. How, without it, would she begin to inquire? How, in fact, would they manage this regardless? And with only the remainder of the morning to begin their search.

Alice grasped Constance's elbow. "Let's don't do this. We haven't time today. We've more important things to do."

"More important than finding Howard? We have at least two hours, Alice. We shouldn't waste any time we have now that the dress is done. Who knows what demand you will be in once this gown is seen? You are likely to become the couturier of the day." Constance opened her parasol. "And then there's the baby. You will not be wanting to haunt the wharves before very long."

The wharves covered miles of waterfront. Every changing section of wharf was another shift in a kaleidoscopic whirl: stacked rows of huge trunks of cypress and pine; stacks of milled lumber separated by grade; five-hundred-pound bales of cotton from compresses upriver; stevedores bent under 132-pound bags of green coffee from Cuba; high on wooden carts, massive mounds of green bananas tied with red ropes; grain disgorged from barges and loaded straightaway onto ships bound for Liverpool; sheaves of sugarcane bound for one or another of hundreds of mills, to return again as sugar to be loaded into cargo holds.

Alice felt as if she had fallen into a bed of ants, felt overwhelmed and claustrophobic even in the open air. But she followed Constance, who had taken her by the hand and was pulling her along through a labyrinth of cotton bales, was sliding through and past the scurry of stevedores toward a more open sliver of wharf over which a steamship towered. She could never have done this alone. Without Constance's perceived assurance, she would have no idea even which way to turn next or what part of these vast wharves to seek. Even with Constance's guidance, she found herself fearful, wanting nothing more than to turn back. Eyes and head turning in a swirl, Alice nearly tripped when Constance abruptly halted.

"Excuse me, sir." Constance reached out to get the attention of a fellow standing atop a bale of cotton, calling out instructions to some workers struggling with a cart.

"Yes? May I assist you, ma'am?" The chap was clearly annoyed at the interruption.

"Could you by any chance direct me to a Mr. Marchand? I believe he works in this area of the wharf."

The man waved his hand dismissively. "No, ma'am. Marchand will be a good bit farther that way, near where the lumber gets stacked." He turned and shouted again at the workers and jumped down from his perch on the cotton bale.

Alice felt Constance nudge her as she watched the flurry.

"Well, on we go."

"Someone you know?" Alice caught her breath as she hurried behind Constance.

"He's the man I met down here when I came for the Black Hand fiasco. He was very kind and seemed to be knowledgeable. At least he's a beginning. I'm thinking he might be able to give us leads to follow when we have more time after this ball is done. I'm hoping this will give you some clues to follow on your own."

Ahead of them the bales of cotton gave way to piles of planed lumber, stacked high in varying lengths, and those gave way to lower stacks where rows of half-loaded barges rocked in the water at the dock's edge. The sounds mixed with the lapping waves and with the sharper crack of wood as men hefted the lumber onto carts and off again as they slid it onto the barges—sounds utterly different from the thudding weight of the cotton bales. Above them, from a pulley of sorts, a man jumped down, waved his hand to another supervisor, and jogged toward them.

"Mrs. Halstead." He removed his hat and brushed back his hair. "I'm surprised to see you here."

Constance nodded. "Mr. Marchand. My friend and I are here on an errand." She glanced at Alice, who blanched. Surely, she would not have Alice explain the situation of her lost husband.

But then Constance continued. "This is Mrs. Butterworth, my friend from Chicago. She is visiting me, and we realized in conversation that a relative of her husband may now be in New Orleans. It's possible he's in the cotton industry and working the wharves. You came to mind—and again, I cannot thank you enough for coming to my aid in that terrible incident with the Black Hand."

His embarrassment was evident to Alice; she hoped her relief at Constance's performance was not equally detectable.

"At any rate, I thought we might inquire if perhaps you know of him or could help us in some way. It's a distant possibility, I know, but I wanted to acquaint her with our city's bustling waterfront industry, and today is so nice and lovely. You never know in this late winter, early spring season. This time last year it was just above freezing."

Marchand seemed not to know what to say and glanced over his shoulder at the workers, then turned to Alice. "Yes, ma'am. Happy to oblige if I can. The relative's name?"

For a brief moment Alice was frozen. "Butterworth," she said. "The same as my husband's. His name is Howard Butterworth."

Marchand appeared blank for a moment, scratched his balding head awkwardly with the hat between his fingers, then looked out across the river. "Butterworth. Hmm. Howard Butterworth?" He glanced down at the wide dock planking; then his face brightened, and Alice reached for her friend's arm. "You know, it sounds a bit familiar, that name, but I just can't place it. Won't come to me. Seems like I came across that name in the past few months. I try to remember folks, but it's awfully hard when there's so many about all the time. Try to make some kind of association to the name. When I try to call that one up, seems like I met some fellow that I associated with bread so I'd remember."

"Bread?" Alice was thoroughly puzzled.

"Yes, ma'am. You know, bread and butter. Butterworth. See how that works?"

Before Alice could speak, Constance intervened. "Would you happen to know where you met, Mr. Marchand?"

"Um, no, ma'am. I'm surprised I came up with that association. They don't always work for me. I could have come up with the same for you, Mrs. Halstead, telling myself to remember it rhymed. Bread-Halstead. See how that works?"

"Well, thank you, anyway, Mr. Marchand." Alice squeezed Constance's elbow. "I'm having quite the adventure here in New Orleans and looking forward to a delicious luncheon. You have a nice afternoon, now."

Both of them curtsied slightly and turned back the way they had come.

CHAPTER 39

The day passed, though Constance's sense of time seemed warped, as if she had slipped into a dream in which small events tumbled over themselves, going nowhere. There seemed nothing to do and everything to do. Her mind leaped unceasingly to that fateful morning she had transformed herself into a young man, a boy really, though heavily mustached and wigged, everything accomplished in a rapid sequence to make the train. To follow Benton to an unintended death. A death for which she sustained responsibility and after which she was now defying the conventions of widowhood. She, the sweet innocent her parents had raised, the ornamental wife who had succumbed to a husband's invectives, the woman who had refused to surrender the money her husband demanded; she who had grown to distrust him, suspect him of what she knew not—womanizing, gambling, illicit business dealings? Whatever her vague suspicions, they had been fierce enough for her to disguise herself and follow him. Ah, yes, she the handsome lad on the train, watching him squander yet more to the Black Hand; she the handsome lad to whom he had turned in desperation; she with her hand extended, watching him fall to his death, knowing at last who he was, what he was, this husband of hers. But had she accepted now who she was? No innocent girl, naive and believing, now she lived with her life in disguise, with the feel of his worsted serge jacket yet on her fingers, watching in horror his flailing arms, the look on his face midair as he plummeted.

Constance covered her face in her hands and sobbed.

When Analee entered the sewing room, Constance choked on her breath as she attempted to wall up the tears, but with Analee's arms now warmly around her, she heaved in grief, not for Benton, but for the wilderness of uncertainty she had entered, from which she feared she might never emerge. Who was this woman named Constance, this stranger she could no longer label, this person she no longer knew? A widow without grief? A mother unable to protect her children? A friend who must hide who she was? A murderer who had no idea if she was responsible for her husband's violent death? One of Les Mysterieuses, a mysterious woman unable to shed her disguise. And now she must put it on, wrap herself in it, and go out into the world.

As Constance dried her tears, Analee released her. But clasped her still at arm's length, holding her steady.

"You gone be all right now. You gone be all right."

Constance studied Analee's face, this resilient, familiar face, those dark eyes holding her. The cells of her body began to calm. *She knows*, Constance thought. The sudden realization penetrated with reassurance. *She knows what I am. She knows me.*

Analee released her then and said, "I'm gone fetch Miss Alice. And the childrens. Make them little girls happy to help dress they mama up."

"Just give me a moment, Analee. I need a few minutes." Constance's breath was ragged still.

Analee nodded. "Yes, ma'am. I bet those girls might need to gather up some fancies for they dolls and bring them in to dress up same time you getting fixed up. Then they be busy making those dolls fine as Mama, instead of hanging on to Mama. I be back in a minute or two."

At the sound of Analee closing the door, Constance stood still for a moment, then went to stand before the gown where it hung. She gazed not so much at it as into it, as if into a mirror, seeing herself in the gown. Its simplicity of line reassured her. The graceful lines of pearl on the bodice transported her to her father's study, to the newspaper photo of the Brooklyn Bridge. Today, tonight, she was crossing a bridge into another sense of self, an unknown, unexplored woman, a woman incognito, even to herself. And holding those lines of strength was the dove, Analee's handiwork, the strength of peace holding every-thing, there on the gown, there at her heart, again on her face, beneath her eyes, allowing her a new vision, though she herself would not be seen. Constance fingered the smooth finish of the silk, this fine fabric given to her by someone who believed in her, who mentored and cared for her, whoever she was as a woman, without the constraints of convention. She turned the gown and gazed at its train, centered with the Gothic arch of the bridge, now converted into a torch of liberty. Everything in this gown spoke of strength and transformation, nothing left behind. There were her children, the girls as shimmering fish swimming freely, even her dead son transformed into light, the light of the bridge into the unknown.

As she gazed at the pearls, the iridescent pastel crystals, it struck her how these simple objects, little more than fragments of tantalizing brightness in themselves, meant nothing. Only in combination, in coming together with purpose, did they hold such meaning. *This is how we are meant to be*, Constance thought. *Our meaning in mutual purpose.*

Constance turned at the click of the doorknob, and her smile as Alice entered was one of pure warmth and gratitude. She held out her arms to embrace this exceptional woman.

*   *   *

The gown was transferred from the sewing room to Constance's bedroom, where it hung on a hook beside her window in what now became the official dressing room. As Alice and Analee performed their ministrations, the atmosphere was tranquil, and their quiet confidence filled Constance with a sense of peace. Even the girls were in a state of concentrated focus with the adornment of their dolls. Constance could not imagine in what spare moments Alice and Analee had managed to create two simple silk gowns from scraps and leftovers of fabric and trim for those two lucky dolls, along with veils from remnants of tulle for their faces. The girls sat on the floor beneath the corner shelf that held the small domed clock Constance had received as a child herself, a gift from her parents. She glanced now at these two beautiful children, so resembling their father as to be uncanny, except for the blond curls, which they had inherited from her and which were a gift from her own mother's lineage.

Constance thought of her mother now. What would she think of Constance's life as it had come to be? Her mother, the lady who became an animated magnet when away from her father. The lady who loved to ride horses, loved even to groom them and brush them, plait their manes and tails, adding ribbon and bows to prevent them unraveling. Her mother's mother—Constance barely remembered *Grandmère*, and only with a bit of leftover dread at her sternness—had not approved, but *Grandpère* had colluded with *Maman* to allow for freedom in and out of the stables. *Maman* had ridden sidesaddle with assurance and grace. People had commented on her accomplished ladylike riding style, which had placated *Grandmère*, but alone with *Grandpère*, she had thrown up her skirts, straddled those horses, and raced with him to the ends of the trails. He had died before Constance was born, but she had grown up aware how her mother loved and missed her father.

It was to him Constance owed her financial security. It was

he who had left his estate to her mother in trust and thereafter to her children, of which Constance was the only one. Thank goodness for the protection of Louisiana's Napoleonic Code. Constance was aware that in no other state did comparable protection of a woman's right to property and assets exist. Thanks to that, Benton had been unable to access her trust. Constance shook her head in mild amusement at the double entendre of that thought: no, he had not been able to access her trust, not only financially but in every other aspect of their marriage, including—no, especially—in his role with their infant son.

She shook her head to throw off the thought of David's death, the sight of Benton shaking her innocent baby, and, in doing so, knocked the hairpins from Alice's hands. Analee bent to retrieve them.

"All right now," she heard Alice say as she took back the handful of pins. "We're almost done here. We just have to get this head full of hair pinned as flat as we can for your headpiece."

Constance remembered the challenge of donning that man's wig in such a way that when she wrenched it off in the confines of a dirty railcar restroom, her hair would somehow resume its fashionable fullness. She had been grateful for a hat pliable enough to fit in that leather satchel and wide enough to cover her tangled hair. Why was her mind spinning in all directions today? She had only to focus on the moment and the exquisite disguise Alice had created for her. This ball, this gown constituted a new endeavor for women, and she was one of them, wearing these symbols that marked a new life: these pearlized lines of strength, this dove of peace, this poppy in all its complexity, this flame, this bridge. The impossible bridge across impossible obstacles. She would be wearing that bridge. *No*, she thought, *I am my own bridge*.

As the swirled headpiece, with its fantastical veil now fully attached, descended over her head, Constance had the distinct sensation of disappearing, even from herself. Not even she knew how she really looked, who she really was. Alice's guiding hands on her arms, Analee holding the train aside so as not to trip her, Constance turned to gaze at herself in the oval cheval glass. As Analee dropped the hem of the gown and tilted the mirror slightly, the girls looked up in hushed silence from the intensity of beautifying their dolls.

In the glass, Constance saw not herself but a resonant symbol of who she might be. Indeed, of who she authentically was, if only she allowed herself. *I am the dove*, she thought, *holding all the converging lines of my strength and possibility. I am the light for my children, as they are the light for me. I am the one beckoning to the one in myself yearning to be free.* Constance took a step toward the glass and looked into her own eyes, seeing into herself through and with her own eyes. This was what Benton had seen, she realized. It was not solely his recognition of her that had thrown him off balance and off that train, but also a deep and startling recognition of her absolute reality. It was at that moment, she had reached out. And Benton had fallen. She closed her eyes, hearing the terrible blow of his body hitting the water.

CHAPTER 40

The carriage Dorothea had sent to fetch her was festooned in garlands of colorful flowers, the peaks punctuated with red poppies. Plumes waving high in the slight breeze bobbed as the horse tossed its head against the reins. This was only one of the eight carriages, one for each of the ladies-in-waiting, that would form a small procession on Toulouse and would arrive simultaneously at the entrance to the French Opera House at precisely eight o'clock. The uniformed driver assisted her into the fairy-tale carriage as Analee and Alice made last touches and blew kisses, and the girls called out their good nights and "Love you, beautiful Mama. Come home before midnight!" The ride was luxurious, a respite of quiet in which to absorb the weight of her feelings, the thoughts that had overwhelmed her as she prepared for this ball, for being one of Les Mysterieuses. In truth, she had recognized and faced the mystery she was to herself, to the emerging complexity of her own internal contra-dictions.

As the procession of garlanded carriages drew to a halt be-fore the grand edifice of the French Opera House, spectators gathered at a slight distance, greeting them with catcalls and whistles and then an outbreak of applause. A man's voice yelled out a snide insult as the women alighted from the carriages. Some of the masked women turned, but Constance walked straight ahead and into the foyer of the opera house, where she caught sight of Dorothea waiting. *She might well be the queen herself*, thought Constance. But the captain Dorothea was, and she very much in charge, pointing and directing, lining up the ladies with specific attention to the exact distance between them. Her elaborate bodice was a deep shade of teal and had long side trains dangling near to the floor over an aqua tulle skirt and train, its wide golden lace trim swishing to and fro as she issued commands in an audible stage whisper. Around her neck hung a bejeweled whistle, which she blew loudly three times. A hush ensued from the crowded ballroom, and Dorothea led them in pairs to the four sets of waiting seats, two ladies for each of the queens. They stood together, facing the curtained stage, and when Dorothea gave her signal, they sat as she turned away and moved to the stage.

I'm here? Is this real? thought Constance. But there she was, in her seat, her two eyes uncovered, watching in wonder as Dorothea blew her whistle again. The blue velvet curtains began their ascent, revealing a tableau like nothing seen in any Mardi Gras previous: four massive arches, held aloft by wreathed Corinthian columns, framed the four queens, each in a setting perfected for her representation of four types of fair women. There was Brunhilde, a star shining high above the hillside behind her, dark, rippling hair hanging below her waist, standing in full command, spear in hand. Constance could not help thinking the star so large and bright might have shone over Bethlehem. She was momentarily grateful for her veil, not only for the concealment of her identity but also of her amused response to the scene before her.

She struggled to contain herself as her eyes moved to the second vignette: here was fair Juliet, standing beneath rather than on her balcony, garbed in simple lines, her head wreathed in flowers, a cross of stars high above her. *Ah, those star-crossed lovers*, thought Constance. Again, she was glad that she could hide her amusement. *How clever these women*, she thought. The third was Semiramis, a quarter moon low above the exotic turrets behind her crowned head, a long-handled fan in her hand, like the fan of a servant. How should Constance interpret this? At once she noticed the replication of the shape of Brunhilde's spear, but it was enlarged. Semiramis, the queen who had served for her son yet had conquered her foes and enlarged her kingdom. And was this moon waxing or waning? Rising or setting? Or perhaps the enigma of a waxing moon rising. Ah, somehow that was comfort. Last, before a rising sun, framed by trees that reached out to touch one another, stood Pocahontas, her costume appearing authentic, a feather in her headdress, the emblematizing dawn of a new age, a new woman in a new world. *May it be so*, thought Constance.

Dorothea's gleaming brass whistle was at her lips again, its jewels twinkling as if they, and not she, were commanding the signals. One by one she led each queen in a grand march of presentation, announced in the rich tones of the celebrated actor Arlington Joseph. The processions were trailed by cheers and applause. Then together, all four queens in procession, and finally the attendants in sequence behind them to the swelling orchestral strains of *Aida*. The four fair queens mounted their respective thrones; the ladies-in-waiting resumed their seats. Elaborately masked and costumed members of the krewe Les Mysterieuses glanced at their dance cards to commence their callout of the waiting men. Constance knew from conversation at their luncheons and meetings just how these women relished the leap year turnabout of men having to await the sound of their name before taking a lady's hand for the quadrille, of the women leading the men to the floor, the women ostensibly in charge. Now she was grateful to Dorothea for her role as a lady-in-waiting. Without it, she would be compelled to call out three different men in their white-tie finery for three different rounds of dancing before the second grand march. Dorothea had known Constance could not do that. She might break the conventions of widowhood by her presence, but she could never venture that far beyond them without breaking herself. Now, at the end of the final grand march, before the general dancing began, she could slip away amid the revelry and find her way quietly home. Like Cinderella, her carriage awaited. She would not be lingering till midnight. She would mind her daughters' injunction.

The parquet floor swirled with dancers. At the edges of the crowd, avidly conversing and drinking, Constance skirted her way, head lowered, hoping not to be noticed. Masked faces nodded to her; gentlemen stepped aside to give her passage. As she searched for Dorothea, her restricted vision frustrated her. The veiled mask, which made her truly a mystery, hampered her. Swiveling to avoid catching her train on a chair, Constance found herself face-to-face with an ominous figure. A man staring directly into her eyes. A man dressed appropriately in white tie, a small brass-tipped wand in his gloved hand, with which he tapped her shoulder as if casting a spell. A man with eyes that gleamed with malice through his black mask, a malevolent grin beneath his thin A La Souvarov mustache. Constance froze in terror.

"You will pay," he uttered. "One way or another."

And then he was gone. Constance twisted her head one side to the other to see. What was he doing here? How had he found her? She had to get home.

In her frantic search, she caught sight of Dorothea surrounded by a group of krewe members. As she struggled toward them, Constance caught sight of Martin Birdsong. He seemed to be studying her. She gave no sign of recognition, though she desperately wanted to run to him, to find safety. Dorothea was much engaged in the excited conversation of first one woman, then another, before her attention turned to Constance. Her face lit in quiet recognition, then concern, but she gave no hint to those around her as to who this might be. What did she see?

"There you are, my dear," Dorothea said. "I hope this has proved a pleasant evening for you." She reached out and took Constance by both hands. "You ladies go and enjoy your privileged time now," she said, politely dismissing the other women. She led Constance a few steps toward the outer edge of the crowd. "You are magnificent, my dear. If I didn't already know, I would have no inkling who you might be. Is everything all right with you now?"

Constance shook her head, squeezed Dorothea's hand. "That man is here . . . was here."

"Did he threaten you?"

"Yes." Constance's voice was hardly more than a whisper, and Dorothea leaned close to hear her above the music and laughter. "I will never be free."

She felt Dorothea's grasp as an ornately costumed woman approached, pulling a tall gentleman behind her. Constance turned toward the door, only to see Martin standing before her. She stood impatiently, thinking he would move aside. Instead, he spoke.

"I beg your pardon, Madame. I am indeed aware it is a night for the gentlemen to step into the background and allow the ladies to take the lead, but I wanted to say that your costume this evening is magnificent."

Constance nodded her head at him, panic overwhelming her. She moved to go around him. He leaned to the side, blocking her escape. She tipped her veiled face up in consternation.

"It is a night for the queens to be honored, to be sure, but I must say I believe you have outshone them." Martin still did not budge.

Did he recognize her, or was he simply being forward?

"It's the simplicity with which you have adorned yourself, I believe. Adorned by being so unadorned, I might say." He smiled.

She had seen that smile all her life. So difficult now to behave as if she did not know this old friend, a friend of her childhood, a friend she desperately needed at this moment. Yet she must not give herself away. She tried to move past again, but he moved with her.

"You are the epitome of Les Mysterieuses. And you have yet to dance even once. I perceive that you are possibly trying to escape. I wonder if you would do me the honor of one dance before you go?"

Constance pulled back.

"I beg your pardon. It's so difficult to change old habits," he said. "I am not supposed to be the one asking for dances tonight. Let me see. Ah, perhaps I might ask you if you would like to ask me for one dance before you disappear entirely."

How like him, Constance thought. She wanted to run but stifled her impulse. There was nothing that evil man could do at this minute. The children were safely in bed; the house was locked; Analee and Alice were awaiting her return. They would be on guard for anything amiss. She held out her hand.

Martin was adept on the floor, but she knew that already. He had been her friend forever. He had been her friend when she had no women friends. He had been her friend in knowing she was not cut out for society's conventions. He had saved her multiple times before at various balls where she had no interest in flirtations, at dinner parties when she had no interest in the conversation, at society gatherings where she had no interest in the cause at hand. He had saved her children from various fevers and itches. It was he, in fact, who had delivered them both, who had put them in her arms for her first glimpse of their dear little wrinkled faces and misshapen heads. It was he who had come to pronounce David dead and had put him into her arms for the last time. At the thought, she dropped Martin's hand and made her way hastily from the floor.

As she reached the entrance, Martin's hand was on her arm.

"I'm sorry," he said. "I shouldn't have broken your convention here tonight."

She looked at him, sure that her eyes must convey her distress. How well he knew her.

"I am terrified, Martin. The Black Hand rogue was here. He threatened me again."

"Come with me," he said.

He took her arm and steered her through the spinning crowd. Like the turning and swirling she sought to escape in the ballroom, her emotions were whirling inside her. Would life never be simple again, forever taking her unaware into grief? Once they were outside the opera house, she took the hand Martin offered to help her mount the carriage. She settled her gown around her and gripped his hand.

"I should go with you," he said.

"No, I must do this alone."

It was only after the driver had flicked the reins and the carriage had rolled away from the curb that she realized, with an unexpected sense of both relief and concern, that Martin had given her address almost automatically. Beyond the sound of the horse's clopping hooves and the creaking wheels, she was aware without turning of the similar sounds of a carriage following close behind. Her sudden terror diminished when reason told her that the sinister rogue was always on foot. She knew without turning that Martin was riding behind her, guarding her safely home. She calmed in the light of passing windows along familiar streets, streets along which she had grown up, where she and Martin had grown up. If she halted now to give him thanks for protecting her, she knew he would deny this and say he was simply going home.

CHAPTER 41

February gave way to March, with its bursting colors of a too-early spring. Such warm weather was a welcome contrast to the near freezes of the previous year, as if this newborn century was impatient to exhibit its glory and all the unforeseen changes it would bring. Alice's heart expanded at the sight of white snowdrops in lieu of absent snow; the vivid purples of wild petunias, pincushion flowers, and irises laced with the varying hues of tulips; and the glorious flowering shrubs—azaleas and camellias—lighting up the shade, covered entirely in blossoms as if they nurtured blooms but no leaves. She had seen the prairie carpeted in wildflowers, but this display was unlike that wild one of nature, somehow singularly intimate and welcoming, whereas the prairie engulfed and dwarfed her. *There is not one thing that humankind has done on earth that is equal to one square inch of this*, she thought.

With the gown finished, the ball concluded, the air warm and inviting—though Constance seemed perpetually on guard—Alice had time for other things, which spooled out before her as she would spool out silk thread. Things of pleasure and leisure, which had never been part of her life; the closest thing to leisure having been her sewing time with her mother, sewing not for utility's sake, like patching shirts and overalls, but sewing to create beauty, to feel her mother's hands and breath close to her. Now she and Constance and Analee walked the children to the park, guarding them closely. In spite of her concern for Constance's tension, she luxuriated in the feeling of the open air, the feel and sound of the great river nearby, the patchwork of light and shade on the ground as they walked. *Could I sew something with that much wonder to it?* she thought.

On other days she and Constance took themselves purposefully to the orphanage, where they met with the older girls on a side porch, its high ceiling and fretwork giving it a lovely sense of coziness for all its being outdoors. These "almost women" crowded close around them to see the examples of finery Alice had brought with her. They knew, better than she, the frightful fatigue and workload of the ready-made factories and mills, the tedium of long hours, the crowded rows of women unable to acquaint themselves with each other for the requisite demanding quotas of the workload. The skills Alice offered seemed an almost magical key to a life different from the one they had expected and dreaded. Mrs. Guidry, the widowed matron of the orphanage, welcomed Alice and her skills and was well acquainted with Constance, so recently bereft yet never failing in her commitment to the well-being of the girls here. Though Alice had resided there only briefly, Mrs. Guidry had been loath to have her snatched away so soon. Alice relished the warmth of this reception and Constance's steady support.

In short order, Dorothea had obtained generous contributions, with help from Constance and acquaintances of both genders, to fund a full sewing room supplied with machines from Sears, Roebuck and Company, which were lower priced than the pricey Singer but sturdy and durable. Members of the women's auxiliary group had begun collecting and contributing unused fabrics and thread, as well as embroidery needles and floss, trim odds and ends of an immense variety, buttons, laces, and ribbons of all sorts to supply Alice and her eager students. Boxes and baskets had begun lining the walls of the revamped sewing room, as if someone were moving into a new house. Indeed, for Constance and Alice this represented their vision that these girls might avail themselves of means to move on to a new life.

As the provisions expanded, so did Alice's body, which was moving toward a new life, as well. She was slower these days and easily fatigued, yet her spirit energized the work in a way that seemed to compensate for the diminishing energy of her body. There were months yet to go, and she prayed that by the time she would need to prepare to deliver, the older girls would be equipped to come forward and supervise the younger girls, who were beginning the basics in this treasury of possibility. Two or three of the older girls already exhibited an innate finesse in handling the machines and understanding the potential and limitations of various kinds of fabrics and trimmings. The girls loved those trims. Their imaginations, for the most part, raced, unlimited. But they learned from their failures, not only what not to do but also how new possibilities might be achieved. Alice watched them with pleasure and contentment. She was beginning to relish this new life of her own.

On a Thursday afternoon in late March, Alice went to the orphanage alone, leaving an anxious Constance at home. Constance had thrown herself into this project untiringly and at the same time was devoting even more time to her own girls, consumed with anxiety for their safety. She would keep them occupied for hours in the kitchen with Analee, with cooking and baking projects suited for such little hands. Played games with them indoors and out, read to them, teaching them words and names for things. Today she had simply been tired, and Alice had suggested—more than suggested—that Constance remain home, prop her feet on the footstool, have a nap, and renew herself so that she could take the lead at the home while Alice was out for her birthing. Alice had prepared Constance to do the basics: operate the treadle and perform the threading, fill the bobbin, manage the presser foot, and complete the turns of a seam.

This afternoon, in fine weather, Alice would descend the streetcar, enjoy a lovely walk, and be home in time for a nice tea. They could all be outside, and the girls could bring their tea set down. Analee could set their little play table out on the lawn. The spring weather was so entirely inviting, so why not?

But as Alice stepped into the house, she was struck by the unusual quiet. She laid her hat and gloves on the front hallway chest and went to find Analee in the kitchen, watching the children inside as they enjoyed their cookies and juice, their make-believe tea party.

"At it early, are they, Analee? Just couldn't wait for us grown-ups?"

"Yes'm. They right eager." Analee turned from the window over the sink, drying her hands on her white cotton apron. "Let me fix you up some tea right quick now. We got good little tea cakes left from the girls' baking yesterday. You want me to bring it all outside?"

"Well, that would be lovely. Where is Constance?"

"She don't feel so good, Miss Alice. I done put her to bed. She be more tired than she bargained, I reckon."

"Hold off on the tea a bit, then. I'll just go up and check on her now. Do you think she's asleep?"

"Don't rightly know. I pulled down the shades on the windows so she could sleep, but she's been a mite restless, it seems. I keep hearing movement up there."

CHAPTER 42

After tapping very lightly on Constance's door and hearing nothing, Alice opened it barely a crack to peek in. Constance lay on the bed in her clothes, her boots unlaced but still on her feet. Her hand was over her eyes, but she turned toward the door as the crack of light streamed in from the bright hallway. Alice heard the slight moan of pain as Constance turned her head.

"You're awake, then. I don't want to disturb you. You're more tired than we knew. You go back to sleep." Alice moved to reclose the door as quietly as she could, but another slight moan stopped her. She opened the door and went in. "What's amiss, Constance? You have a headache?"

Constance held out a limp hand. When Alice took it, an immediate alarm surged through her. This was the heat she had felt when baby Jonathan died. She could not go there. Her attention focused on Constance with instant clarity. All her energies sharpened. She placed her hand on Constance's forehead and flinched. This fever was high.

"Constance." Alice kept her voice low. "Tell me what you are feeling. Are you nauseous?"

Constance shook her head. Another slight groan of pain. "My head. It's my head." She tried to adjust herself slightly, but her movement elicited another whimper. "And my neck."

"Your neck?" Alice laid the back of her hand on Constance's cheek.

"Everything hurts. All over me hurts."

"Oh dear, Constance, not the flu. It's late in the season for that. I am so sorry." Alice loosened the unlaced boots and slipped them off, then tucked them under the end of the bed. "We need to get you undressed. Oh, my heavens, you are lying here in your corset! All these clothes on that aching body of yours. I'm going to fetch Analee. I'll be right back."

Constance groaned, but this time seemingly in protest.

Alice patted her outstretched hand and laid it back over her chest. "Promise. Quick as we can get the girls organized, we'll be right back."

Alice warned herself to take care as she hurried down the stairs to notify Analee. Together the two women gathered up the girls, who fortunately, having finished their cookies and poured the last drop of their apple juice "tea," were eager to go back to the playroom and play dress-up with the new silk gowns for their dolls. They were sure their dollies were eager to be getting all fixed up for the ball, and they chattered of Cinderella and their mother's mysterious Mardi Gras ball. One even turned on the stairway to ask why Mama hadn't had glass slippers or how Prince Charming was to find her. As they crossed the threshold of their playroom, they instantly entered another realm, a land of enchantment, where they were content to stay for quite a spell. For that Alice was grateful.

Constance shifted and moaned as before when Alice opened the door and the two women entered. Alice noted how swiftly

Analee took charge, how she knew just what to do and how to do it. Speaking softly but firmly, she issued instructions on when and which way to turn. Within minutes, Constance's skirt and shirtwaist were in Alice's hands, and Analee was at work on the corset, which thankfully was lightweight and not one of those heavily boned pigeon-breasted ones. After that, too, had come from Analee's into Alice's hands, she rolled it and laid it on the seat beneath the outer clothing, which she had folded neatly over the chairback. She was overwhelmed at a sudden loss of knowing what to do.

As Alice turned back to the bed, she realized that Constance was shivering now. With assistance from Analee, she pulled the covers from beneath Constance, then back over her before tucking the blankets around and under her shoulders. Memories flooded her of her own mother wrapping her thus as a child. She couldn't remember what illness she might have had, but she remembered her mother's face, full of both love and visible fear. From the corner of her eye, Alice spotted Maggie standing backlit in the doorway, her doll hanging limply over one arm, the thumb of her other hand in her mouth. Alice slipped quietly to her and led her out into the hall.

"What is it, angel?"

Now Delia crept toward her from their playroom, put her arm around her little sister, reached out to stop the forbidden sucking of her thumb.

"Don't do that. You're a big girl now," she said to Maggie. "We heard Mama crying."

"Mama sick?" Maggie shifted her doll to her chest.

"Mama is a bit sick, girls." Alice knelt beside them. She was at a loss what to tell them. "Analee and I are taking good care of Mama."

"Like Mama cared for us when we got sick?" said Maggie.

"Just like Mama would take care of you, pumpkin."

"Can we help do it?" asked Delia.

"Take care of Mama? I'm not sure what you could do, sweet girls."

"We can get the cloths wet and . . . ," Delia said.

"And twist them, so they don't leak on the bed." Maggie completed the sentence.

"And fold them to put on her head and make her cool. Is she hot?"

"Well, at the moment, I think she's shivering cold. That's why we are wrapping her up in her blanket."

"But she can be shivery cold, and her head can be hot. Maggie was when she got sick, and Mama put the wet cloths on her head, and her head got cool and the rest of her got warm again."

Analee's gentle hand touched Alice's back. The girls looked up, and Alice twisted her head to see the concern in that kind face.

"Still got the chills," Analee said.

The girls were tugging on Analee's apron now, and she leaned her tall figure down to them.

"Can we wet the cloths and twist them for Mama's head, Analee?"

"Why, I do believe you can. That's a good way for you to help your mama." She raised herself up, then held out a hand to each of the children. "Let's just go get us a clean bowl of water and some dry cloths. We'll be right back, Miss Alice. Come on now, childrens."

Alice watched the threesome head down the stairs before she turned and went back into the bedroom. She would be hard pressed to put a name to all that flooded her now: her uncertain fear for Constance; her unfamiliarity with sickness in grownups; a memory of herself sick as a child, her mother holding her hand and humming old hymns; the memory of her fevered infant son, of Howard holding him in the sink to cool him down, of Jonathan's face under water, his infant eyes growing wide, her scream, Jonathan's breathless body in her arms, the look of terror on Howard's face, his voice as he muttered, "Don't, Daddy. Please, please, Daddy, don't." Alice grew weak. She felt her way to the chair, where she sat on the rolled corset and collapsed against the folded clothes, uncaring now if they wrinkled or not.

Alice sat, waiting to gather herself. With a deep breath, she rose, holding the back of the chair for support. After a moment, she edged her way to the bed where Constance lay quietly now, the shivering ceased. She laid her hand on Constance's smooth forehead. So hot, so very hot.

Before Alice could think what to do, the door opened. Analee entered, balancing a large bowl of water, which she placed carefully on the floor a little way from the bed. Each of the girls had a stack of three bath cloths balanced in front of them, carried like icons in a sacred procession, though Alice doubted they had much experience of church ritual at this age. The girls sat cross-legged on each side of the bowl, still holding the cloths in their arms. *Oh, to still be so agile*, Alice thought. She felt a twinge of envy then, not for that young agility, but for the girls themselves, for Constance's motherhood in spite of the loss of her son. Then the baby kicked or turned, whatever it was that babies did in that secret place of the womb. Alice laid her hand over the bump protruding at her side, a little foot stuck out perhaps. *There is nothing to envy*, she thought, scolding herself, feeling shame. Soon enough, her own motherhood would be there again. In truth, even in bereavement, her sense of motherhood had never forsaken her.

She studied the children, so concentrated on their task, wetting a cloth, wringing it out, or twisting it, as they said in their quiet whispers, then handing one at a time up to Analee, who folded and laid the first on Constance's burning forehead, the next one under her chin, the third one against her flushed cheeks, one, then another, and another, and then handed the cloths back to the girls. *Like a well-organized assembly line in the recently established garment industry*, thought Alice, her mind immediately leaping to the young girls at the orphanage and their own project to keep the older girls from such work. But first, there was Constance to think about. Alice was aware that her thoughts were scattered and swirling, while Constance lay here, so ill.

"Why do I hurt so bad, Analee? Every inch of me hurts." Constance's voice was muffled.

"I expect you got the influenza, Miss Constance. I don't rightly know, not being your doctor. But right now, I'm working on getting that fever down you got." Analee changed out the cloths in another round, removing the ones that had warmed, replacing them with cool ones.

"Where are the children?" Constance's query was almost a moan.

"They right here. Right here beside you, handing me up these cool cloths."

Alice stood at the head of the bed, feeling somewhat useless, holding the cloths in place so they would not slip, trying to keep the pillow dry around Constance's disordered hair.

"Should we send for the doctor?" Alice looked to Analee for guidance.

"I don't know just yet. Let's see do this fever come down. If it don't, one of us can go for Dr. Birdsong."

"Dr. Birdsong?"

"Yes'm. That's her doctor. The children's doctor, too. Mine, too, do I need him. The whole family, but he's been her friend forever. They go so far back, they might've been in diapers together." Analee chuckled as she changed out yet another round of cloths. "He don't live too far. Office is in the house. I can tell you how to go, if we see we need him. He'd be here in the pitch-dark night, should we send for him."

Alice had grown accustomed to feeling a bit confident. Her skills had given her a foundation here, but now she felt only her inexperience. She glanced at Analee and saw compassion in her expression.

"Why don't you fetch some fresh cold water, Miss Alice? I got this."

CHAPTER 43

Constance's face remained flushed. Her body shivered in what Analee called a fever-frost, no matter the blankets and quilts the two women laid over her. In those shivers, Constance moaned, seemingly unwilling to move her head because of the pain that extended through her neck and down her back. It seemed to Alice and Analee that the pain was all over Constance's body. Just the readjustment of the covers or an adjustment to arrange the pillow under her neck for a bit more support elicited groans, at times an outcry, which made Alice cringe. The girls were still asleep, so Alice was the one who wet the cloths and wrung them out for Analee as she applied them to Constance's face and neck.

Alice had seen influenza in her father once. She remembered her mother's gentle, unceasing ministrations. Her mother had sat beside the bed all day, leaving only for brief trips to the outhouse, then again all night, sleeping in that straight-backed chair to wake at her husband's slightest movement, to swaddle his burning head in cold cloths. It had been Alice's job, then, like it was now, to keep fresh cold water available for the change out of the cloths. She had stayed by her mother except for her own trips to the outhouse, when she had breathed in the clean fresh air of the outdoors before opening the creaking wooden door to the fetid air inside, and then had primed the pump and hauled the pail of fresh water to her father's bedside. She could hear the clang of it hitting the planks of the flooring, her mother shushing her as the water sloshed over the edge. Now she was in the sophisticated city of New Orleans, an adult, a skilled and talented woman, but she felt just as helpless now as she had out there on the prairie as a child.

"What do you suppose is the matter, Analee? You think this is the flu?"

Alice tucked the blankets a bit tighter around Constance's shivering form. She touched her flushed cheeks again. So hot, so hot. People weren't supposed to get that hot. Yet Constance shivered with cold. Analee lifted the folded cloth from Constance's forehead, replaced it with a fresh one from Alice.

"Don't rightly know, Miss Alice. Looks to be, but if it is, it's fierce." Analee changed another warm, damp cloth.

Alice made up her mind. This could not continue. "I'm going for Dr. Birdsong, Analee. It's time."

Analee touched her arm reassuringly.

"Thank you, Analee." Alice turned away from the bed. "Should I get the girls up and fed before I go? You won't be able to go downstairs to feed them if they wake and come in."

"They'll be all right, Miss Alice. I'll just put them to work fetching water. They ain't generally too hungry right away. You won't be long, and best to get him fore he got a office full of folks."

Alice nodded. She was disconcerted at having to leave, having to negotiate the streets of the Marigny, though they were not difficult, but she always became uneasy when she needed to remember the number of blocks before turning right, and which names of which streets came in what order. The same had been true in Chicago; she had always been on edge that she would wind up in some unfamiliar, possibly dangerous, neighborhood. The closed, organized blocks of that city seemed so systematic and easy, since they were in numerical order or followed the alphabet, so one always knew the distance and direction to the state line, for example. Why that had been important eluded her. She had learned the system yet had never quite trusted herself in a place where all you could see was the next building, next corner, and never the wide horizons far from you, the wide sky, which could orient you, make you sure of the direction you were headed. In the city she felt closed in, as one street followed the next, every turn determined by how the street was laid out, how tall the buildings were, how wide the lots. But it was the sky she missed most of all, that immense sky, which somehow grounded her, made her feel that she belonged to the earth.

For that reason, she had welcomed her few trips to the wharves here. In spite of their crowded clutter and incessant noise—the cries and commands of the longshoremen and supervisors, the bone-clenching slam of lumber and uncut sections of tree trunk, the repeating heavy thud of cotton bales, the banging of chains and boats—yes, in spite of the din, there was the sky, the sky opening out above and past that great river, past its prison of buildings and trees. The sky, no matter what color it was, no matter if it was clear or cloudy, that same sky gave her a sense of belonging to the earth.

Constance gave a small cry as Analee adjusted the damp pillow again, and Alice pulled herself back into the enclosed air of the room.

"All right. Just tell me clearly how to go."

"You just take a right out the front gate. Go three blocks and then left. Two more blocks and it'll be on the left. You don't need no number. Sign at the gate say Martin D. Birdsong, Doctor of Medicine. Plain as day. You got that?"

Alice nodded and backed away from the bed. She handed Analee one last cool cloth as she repeated in her head, *Right three blocks, left two blocks*, like a child memorizing a nursery rhyme.

In truth, Alice had no difficulty finding Dr. Birdsong. At her knock, he answered the door himself, it being early and there being no patients yet. Before she had time to explain, this dark-haired, clean-shaven man had his bag in hand and was leading her down the front steps, then holding the gate for her. His pace was such that Alice had difficulty keeping up and answered his quickly appraising questions somewhat out of breath, but he did not slow his steps to accommodate her. By the time they had reached the house, he had pulled every detail she knew from her and had left the ones she did not tucked carefully beside the ones she did. At the gate he waited only momentarily for Alice to come through. Then Alice watched in astonishment as he simply opened the front door as if the house were his own, and mounted the stairs two at a time. *As if he simply belongs here*, she thought.

Alice followed more slowly, lifting her skirt with one hand to assure a firm footing, gripping the rail with the other. She could not afford another fall. She would not chance it. This child she carried was all in life that was truly hers. She had experienced the dire unpredictability of a life broken and unspooling.

Marriage held no appeal for her. Why was she even thinking such a thing? As far as she knew, she was at this moment still a married woman. There was some indication that Howard might be in New Orleans. If not presently here, at least known here. Known because he was now and then here. She would find him if she could. But for the moment she had to safely mount these stairs. And she must do what she could to care for Constance.

The children were at their stations at Analee's feet, twisting and handing up the cool wet cloths. They jumped up at the appearance of the doctor and threw their arms around his legs, greeting him as they might an uncle. He had been their doctor all their lives and their mother's much-loved friend. He bent to hug each of them and whispered enthusiastic praise for their help in caring for their mother. Analee and Dr. Birdsong began speaking quietly, while Alice stood aside. The doctor turned his head and made room for her in the conversation. Analee was telling him the details of Constance's fatigue in the days leading up to the alarming onset of her fever.

The thermometer from his bag registered 104.7 degrees of fever. Alice cringed at the number, so nearly the same as her dead baby son had suffered. When she had reached out to his cradle to soothe his fretting in the middle of the night, she had cried out at the touch of his skin, so hot it had been. Now her hands went instinctively to her abdomen in a gesture of innate protection.

"You all right, Miss Alice?" said Analee.

Unaware she had inadvertently gasped aloud, Alice looked up at the two faces turned to her in surprise.

"I—I'm fine," she said. "I just . . . Well, the degree of fever alarmed me, is all. I'm fine."

She wanted them to turn their attention back to Constance and away from her. She had to, at some point in her life, find a way not to respond so reflexively, so intensely to reminders of Jonathan's death. It did not serve her well. Not, at least, until she found Howard.

"That fever mighty high, Doc." Analee changed out another cloth with Delia. "You think she got the influenza?"

"Hard to know exactly, Analee. There isn't anything much going around these days except head colds and hay fever, a few upset stomachs. The usual, you know. Haven't encountered any cases of influenza."

"The yellow fever?"

"Too early in the year for that, Analee, and not hot enough, though it's been unusually warm this winter. February felt like May, but even then, it's not so hot as when we usually have the summer outbreaks."

Alice reached down and took another cool cloth from Delia, handed it to Analee.

"She seems to be in a good bit of pain, Doctor," Alice said. She was trying to hold herself together and move her thoughts away from the fever.

Dr. Birdsong leaned over and spoke. "Are you in pain, Constance? Can you tell me what hurts?"

Alice saw the empty look as Constance opened her eyes. Dr. Birdsong repeated his question. Alice smoothed the damp hair away from Constance's burning forehead as she nodded, then wrenched in pain at the movement.

"Constance, what's hurting?"

"Head." Her voice was barely audible. "Neck."

"Anything else?"

"Mm-hmm. Hurts. So bad . . ."

Dr. Birdsong lifted Constance's wrist and counted silently. He leaned over with his stethoscope, pressed it gently, then moved it, pressed again.

"Constance, I'm going to have Analee and Alice give you something for your pain. You won't like it, I'm afraid. It's quite bitter and hard on the stomach. Does your stomach hurt?"

Constance nodded, then winced at the pain of moving her neck.

"Powdered salicylic acid, ladies. You will need to dissolve it in tolerably hot water. May be difficult to get down her." He leaned toward his patient and patted her limp hand. "I'll be back, Constance." He stood observing her for a moment.

"Let's step outside," the doctor mouthed, then ushered the women out the door. "We'll be right back, girls. I think I see a nursing career in your futures."

In the hallway, Alice stopped between Dr. Birdsong and Analee. She felt a conflicting sense of both belonging right here and being a total outsider. They seemed to assume her presence simply as one of them, but Alice was intimidated by their familiarity with one another. They had known each other at the most basic level for years, while she felt herself a stranger to everyone, even those little girls in there.

"How many days past the Mysterieuses ball did you notice her fatigue?"

The Mysterieuses ball! How could the doctor know that? He knew she was there, in spite of the careful disguise. Alice glanced at Analee in consternation, only to see her face as stoic as ever.

"You needn't act as if she wasn't there, ladies. You know I was there myself. I had a dance with her, helped her into her carriage home."

Still, Analee stood unmoved, and Alice followed her cue.

"Come now. Would you actually believe I wouldn't know my friend since we were as young as those two little girls in there?" Birdsong shifted on his feet, appearing a bit outdone. "All right, all right. You win. I beg your pardon, ladies. Or should I beg the pardon of that young widow in there, now so ill? A widow who should be in mourning and not out at fancy balls, is that it? Especially the ball of an all-female krewe—a ground-breaking precedent, I might add, festivities making history."

Alice stepped a bit closer to Analee. The nearby warmth of her tall body was a comfort.

"Well, then, let me rephrase my question. Let's see, now. All right, how many days back did you begin to notice any fatigue or weakness?"

"Now that ain't hard to answer, Dr. Birdsong. She start seeming a bit peaked maybe a week or so ago. Six, seven days before she came straight out sick and fevered."

"Thank you, Analee. I think we can rule out influenza, then. Has she eaten any unwashed fruit or had anything to eat or drink that might have been unclean that you know of?"

When Analee shook her head, Alice felt his eyes on her.

"No, Doctor Birdsong. I've been with her virtually every time she's left the house. She's had nothing that I have not had myself."

"And you are feeling fit?"

Alice's hand went to her abdomen. She couldn't help but sense he noticed. She felt herself examined under his keen medical eye.

"Yes, quite."

"You're sure, then?"

Alice found his insistent questioning annoying. Apparently, she had given herself away.

"I beg your pardon, Alice. I wasn't making myself clear. The reason I'm asking these questions is that it's possible to contract typhoid from eating anything unwashed or possibly washed in unclean water. I'm thinking there might be a strong possibility of typhoid indicated in these early symptoms. If so, all of you caring for her, plus the children, could also be in danger of catching it."

The fear that took hold of Alice left her numb. Here, at last somewhat safe, assured of care in her pregnancy—and now this. She knew the devastations of typhoid fever from tales she had heard since she was old enough to comprehend them, tales of inordinate internal bleeding, of an old man whose bowels had torn open inside him, of a pregnant woman who had lost her baby. Alice held her hands to her belly, held herself still through an impulse to flee, stood rigidly silent. She could not stay here if Constance had typhoid fever. She could not eat in this house, play with the children. She would have to leave, seek refuge in the orphanage, after all. Was it too late already? Alice's fingers tightened over her abdomen.

Alice could see a mirror to her alarm on Analee's face: her rich brown color had drained to an ashen hue, her dark eyes had widened. Her hands were frozen in midair, one damp cloth hanging loosely across her palm.

"Now, don't be alarmed quite yet, ladies," the doctor said. "I am only asking for information. I need to rule out all possibilities." He turned toward Analee. "Has she exhibited any stomach distress? Nausea? Vomiting? Any—" He hesitated.

Alice felt his hesitancy in a brief glance in her direction. He would likely feel comfortable with Analee, but it was doubtful that he would say more in her presence. Perhaps he hadn't a sense of what it meant to be a prairie girl.

"Any bowel problems?" He raised his head to Analee as he said it.

Analee shook her head.

Alice sensed Analee's discomfort, however competent she might be, and spoke up.

"No, Dr. Birdsong. There is so far only this inordinate fever and her bodily discomfort, the aching all over, but especially the terrible pain she complains of in her back and head and neck. As you can see, she's also suffering from weakness and immense fatigue. She has pain, quite bad, in her stomach, but it doesn't seem related to any nausea or intestinal difficulties."

As Birdsong turned toward her, Alice detected a bit of relief on his face, both at her speaking up without embarrassment and at the absence of these symptoms of typhoid. She watched him shake his head slightly, as if in puzzlement.

"Good," he said. "We may yet see them, and if so, Alice, I would advise you to confine yourself, with the children also, and let Analee take charge of our patient." Birdsong shook his head, perhaps at himself. "As a matter of fact, out of an abundance of caution, Alice, let's call the girls out now and implement this plan immediately."

Birdsong opened the door behind them and motioned to the

girls, a finger to his lips. Alice watched their concerned backward glances at their mother as they tiptoed out.

"You girls are quite the good nurses," he said. "You must grow up quickly so I can hire you in my office. Now, for the moment, I'm worried about those dollies I know you love so much. I'm just hoping they have not fallen ill also. I wonder if you could run to your room and check on them. I'm sure they have been missing you and wondering where on earth you are and why you don't come back to take care of them."

"Will you make our mama well now?" Maggie asked.

"Will you, please?" Delia chimed in.

"I'll do my very best, girls. Just like you will for your dolls. And Mama is going to need lots of rest, so we must keep the house very quiet. Can you help do that? That means your dollies can't be crying now, so you'll have to stay close by and keep them happy, sing to them, and tell them stories. Miss Alice is going to help you. She will be fixing meals for you, so Analee can take good care of Mama. Do you have little strollers for them?" When the girls nodded, he continued. "Maybe Miss Alice would help you take them to the park for a stroll now and then. How does that sound?"

When they all turned to Alice, she looked from one to the other and nodded, though her heart sped up at the thought of guarding them outdoors alone. The girls' faces broke into smiles, and they headed for their playroom.

"As to treatment," Birdsong said to the women, "for the moment, we will simply do what we can. Which, unhappily, is not much."

CHAPTER 44

Alice studied Analee, trying to assess the effect of all this on her. Some of her color had returned, and now she held the cloth loosely in front of her with both hands. She nodded first at Alice and then at the doctor.

"Well, now," Analee said, "just what would the 'not much' be, Doctor? Sides what we doing already? Well, sides what I'm gone be doing now?"

The doctor shuffled his feet, his stance taking a more assured tone.

"What you are doing now for the fever is quite adequate, Analee. And, of course, you, too, Alice. What you have done already, and now your supervision of the girls. I know you are both worried and want to care for Constance and help her. But I do want you as safe from any possibility of contagion as possible. Analee, you can handle the wet cloths to cool her by yourself?"

Analee nodded. Alice imagined her alone there in that darkened room, swapping out over-warmed cloths for fresh ones from the large bowl, wringing and replacing them over and over. Alice imagined the dull, insistent pain in Analee's back from stooping and standing with no assistance. But Analee stood stoically and nodded.

"What do you believe this to be, Dr. Birdsong?" Alice asked.

"I'm not at all sure. Hardly seems to be influenza. It could be any number of things, from typhoid fever to, less likely, typhus."

He seemed to be talking to himself, Alice thought. Even the good doctor didn't really know. It struck her how little any of them really knew.

"If her pain continues, you can give her the salicylic acid powder. It's terribly bitter, truly unpleasant, and very hard on the stomach. You say she has pain in her stomach now?"

Analee nodded.

Alice pondered his repeated verification of information. He seemed almost to be repeating it to himself. And so, she asked, "What purpose can be served by waiting when Constance is in such pain?"

Dr. Birdsong regarded her with what she felt was a respectful gaze.

"The salicylic acid doesn't work quickly, but once it does, it offers fairly long-lasting relief. However, it is prone to induce nausea and stomach pain in a fair number of users, so I'm just hesitant to try it yet. It doesn't heal anything, or I would be giving it to her this minute, I assure you. Are you by any chance familiar with its use, Alice?"

Alice thought on what she knew of "doctoring" out on the prairie.

"Is it by chance derived from willow bark, Doctor?"

"Why, yes, actually it is. May I ask how you know this?"

"Willow bark tea was a fairly common remedy for aches and pains, especially bad ones, when I was a child. I'm trying to think how I made that connection. I'm not entirely sure. Something about the bitter taste of it." A hazy memory flashed through her mind of an old man her mother had helped nurse through some ailment. It was the shock of him spitting the tea straight back out that she most envisioned.

"I'm impressed that you would remember it at all."

Alice chuckled. "It's nothing to be impressed about, Doctor. Just one of those fuzzy tidbits that stays in your head somewhere. I would likely not remember it at all had you not emphasized the bitterness of it. And its slowness to take effect, yet then be quite effective. Those are properties I do remember my father talking on about quite vehemently when my mother would serve him up a cup of willow bark tea for his aching joints on the farm."

At the thought of her parents together in the kitchen, beside the woodstove, Alice was hit with sudden nostalgia. She rarely thought of them together, was more prone to remember her mother as simply her own, her father and brothers as outsiders. But, of course, there had been a marriage between her parents. Her mother had tended to both her father and her brothers, just as she had to Alice. The realization hit her that, of course, her mother had not belonged to her alone. and she almost gasped in disbelief. She wondered if her father and brothers, like her, had thought of her mother as uniquely theirs.

"Yes, the tea from the willow bark has long been known as an effective remedy. Hundreds of years, actually, maybe thousands. The more recent salicylic acid powder is a concentrated form derived from it, far more bitter, but also more effective. Also, far harder on the stomach. So, advances also have their drawbacks." After picking up his bag, the doctor turned to the stairs. "For now, Alice, I want you and the children to keep yourselves distanced from the sickroom and from any cleaning that may be necessary. Do you by chance also cook?"

"Yes, of course." She had a flash of loading the woodstove with her mother. Alice wondered what woman did not cook. Well, perhaps those who were privileged to be waited upon, she mused. She found herself wondering what sort of home this man had grown up in.

"Then I will ask you to care for the children and cook, if you will, while Analee cares for Constance. Analee, will you be able to sleep in the armchair? As you have moments to do so . . . catnaps. And still keep the cloths as cool as possible on Constance's face and neck?"

"You ain't even got to ask that, Dr. Birdsong. You know better than that. How long I been knowing you now?" Analee flicked the corner of her apron at him.

Once again, Alice felt herself the outsider in this house.

"More days than I can number, Analee. Keep her as cool as possible." He was already on his way down the stairs. "No need to see me out. Take care of each other. I know my way. I'll return in the morning."

Analee and Alice exchanged glances when they heard the front door close below them. Alice nodded to Analee, who disappeared back into Constance's room. Alice stood looking at the closed door for minutes before turning to seek out the children, who would now be in her charge. The baby stirred within her as she entered their playroom to the sounds of their anxious greeting and questions.

Day and night ran together for Constance in an indistinguishable timelessness, in which time had no meaning—time or anything else. What was there other than this utter fatigue, this pain, this utter deathless death? Death would at least be an ending. Her suffering could be over. She moaned. Where were her children? Where was anything of the familiar in her life? Where was Analee? Ah, she must have whispered or croaked her name, for there were those strong hands brushing, soothing. There was the wet cloth. Ah, the cool. And Analee's voice, soft and assuring. Singing. A lullaby. To put her to sleep. A hymn? To wake her? Would she ever wake? She wanted her children. She needed to tell the children good night.

"My girls—"

"They with Miss Alice. They be fine, Miss Constance. Now, don't you worry 'bout them. They be fine."

Constance heard the soothing voice, the soothing words beside her ear, and the low humming, the lullaby. She felt herself slipping, floating, rocking.

Click. Click. Click. The train was clicking, rocking, clicking, clicking, rocking along. Floating somehow, the train, floating over the river, fish swarming in pools below. Gold and silver glimmering in the morning light as the train rocked above them. She clung for balance in the open vestibule. Benton stared at her, his mouth open. His lips moving, saying something to her. A man's wig tossing in his hands and a hat. Were those hands his? There were too many hands. Her own hands were reaching to catch his words.

The train was loud, and the wind, the wind blew the words away. She watched as they emerged from his mouth, like fish from the water, and slid away, pulled by the wind out over the river, the fish jumping to catch them, splashing, up and back, leaping into the air to catch the words. She watched them fall as the wig fell, the weight of the wig falling down on her head, hurting her neck, her back, her very legs pushed down, down, down. So heavy. Her hands flying to catch the words, to tear off the wig, her hands and the fish. So many hands. Not hers. Hers and not hers. Benton floating away from the train, falling over the water, following the words, lost in the fish, in the splash and the light of their glimmer, the shining rays of their light blinding her. Only her mouth alive now, her lips moving, his unknown words floating free in the light.

"Benton. Benton. I didn't mean it. I needed to know. Only to know. Please, Benton, bring back the words. Forgive me. I didn't mean for you to die. Don't die, Benton. Don't die. I didn't mean it. Please."

"Miss Constance. Miss Constance. Wake up. Wake up now."

Why was Analee on the train? Her voice floating out there in the light with the words.

Constance felt the gentle rocking, ah, gentle now, the rocking, rocking, the clicking gone. Just the rocking of the train. She inhaled. Started to stretch, but no, it hurt too much. Everything hurt. Her whole self was nothing, nothing but overarching pain. Had she fallen with him from the train? Ah, no, there was something soft, something solid underneath the pain. A bed. Her bed? Was she in her bed? Was that Analee's face, Analee rocking her like a baby, rocking her awake? She breathed. And breathed again.

"Analee?" Constance struggled to get the name out, to get the name right, but it came out slurred.

"I'm right here, honey. Right here."

"Analee?"

"I'm here."

Constance tried to find her, tried to find her hand. She was pulling at the covers, picking at them like picking lint from clothes. She sensed Analee's reassuring clasp, holding her hand to still it.

"You gone be all right, honey. It's all gone be all right."

Constance held on to that hand. There was nothing else to hold.

"Analee?"

"Yes'm?"

"I think I killed him, Analee." There. She had said it. "I did."

"I know, Miss Constance."

Analee's fingers stroked her brow. So gentle, that touch. As gentle as forgiveness.

"It don't make no never mind. That man was killing himself. I expect you done him a favor, saved him the trouble of doing it himself."

Constance stirred, her mind still wandering in the dream of things, her body plagued by pain. "I killed him," she insisted.

"I ain't so sure, Miss Constance. Don't make no never mind. That man was needing to get free of himself, needing to get free of his own killing, free of his own sinful self."

"You didn't hear me," Constance mumbled, trying to turn her head, but the pain was too intense.

"I hear you. But I don't need to hear you to know, Miss Constance. I done known for a long time now. I put away that suit and that wig. Won't nobody but me ever know, and I ain't telling. I ain't even told you, now, have I? You gone be all right, Miss Constance. You just rest and get yourself well."

Analee's cool fingers felt soothing on Constance's hand and arm. She no longer felt any urge to move her aching body.

"I killed him, Analee." Within her an unexpected sense of calm and peace settled the painful urge to move.

"He didn't have no peace in him, Miss Constance. Life didn't hold no promise for that man. No meaning, neither. I seen it in him the first time you brought him home. He never was gone hold to life too long." Analee shifted in the chair and let out her breath. "He might have just got you to save him the trouble."

CHAPTER 45

Alice was already at the door before Dr. Birdsong could knock. She opened it and stepped aside. He closed and propped his umbrella against the wall before he stepped in.

"She's been delirious in the night, Doctor. Or incoherent. I don't know the difference. It is not easy for Analee and me to communicate clearly from one end of the hall to the other."

"I've been expecting this."

Birdsong took a stride toward the wide staircase, but Alice stopped him with a firm grasp on his arm.

"What do you mean, you've been expecting this?" She studied Birdsong's face as he turned back to her. There was something in it both grim and somehow assured.

"Symptoms often present in such comparable ways, Alice, that it is almost impossible to tell one disease from another. But I believe we are looking at typhus." He grew quiet.

Suddenly he began talking to her in earnest.

"It didn't take us long to rule out influenza, because of the preliminary length of fatigue. We've had no epidemics of yellow fever in recent years, but cases do still occur randomly.

However, even though it has been unseasonably warm, as I said before, it is far too early in the year for yellow fever. Which left me with a probable differentiation of typhoid fever and typhus. The two are sometimes difficult to distinguish. And we've had outbreaks of neither, though isolated cases do appear."

He seemed to Alice to be quite invested in helping her to understand the steps involved in his diagnostic process. Perhaps, she thought, having her as an audience was helping him to clarify things to himself. She felt the baby kick and shifted her weight.

"It seems," Birdsong continued, "that since the city improved the water and sewage systems, culverted and paved over some of those open drains through the streets, thanks, by the way, to female property owners having the inordinate means to vote on that . . . Did you know that, Alice? The women voted! Yes, it happened! Isn't that extraordinary! The more I think about the prospect of female suffrage, the more committed I become to the cause. Well, I digress. At any rate, thanks to the vote of the women, we have a much cleaner city and far, far fewer instances of typhoid fever. I sound as if I'm giving you a lesson in medicine, Alice."

Alice nodded, fascinated at this man, who spoke to her as an equal. Howard had never deigned to speak to her in such a way. In fact, he had not spoken much to her at all, and his silence had sometimes been stifling.

"Or history. Or the social sciences. Well, enough now."

But he did not stop. Alice tried to take in both the critical information he was conveying with regard to Constance's condition and the fact that this man was treating her as an intelligent equal. The baby was quite active now, and Alice massaged her upper abdomen.

"That's why you were asking about the water. And washing the food."

"Yes. And isolating you and the children from Constance.

Even Analee from you three, since she will remain exposed while taking care of Constance. You are expecting, and the girls are so young. We can't have any of you ill, if we can avoid it."

Alice followed him as he stepped to the stairway. Neither she nor the children could risk being endangered with exposure, yet she was loath to think of Analee coping alone at such a critical time. And deeply indebted to Constance after all she had done for her.

"Has she been able to take the salicylic acid?"

"I believe so. But you must ask Analee to be sure."

"And tolerating it?"

"Again, Doctor, I believe so. But only Analee has been with her. She and I speak to one another from opposite ends of the hallway, but it is not always the most efficient means of exchanging information."

"Yes, of course. Has she developed a rash?"

"I'm sorry, Doctor, I—"

"No, Alice." He scratched at the part in his hair and ran his fingers back through it. "It is I who am sorry. I've been unduly anxious, as you can imagine. Constance is one of the dearest friends I have. We go back to our early childhood, you know? I remember the first time we met. We were playing with a group of children in the park. A game of tag. I tagged her, and she turned and tagged me right back before I could get away. She was fast, that girl."

"Yes, I know about your lifelong friendship. Of course, you are preoccupied with her recovery, Doctor. I understand." She thought how brief her own time with Constance had been in comparison to his. *A lifelong friendship.* The very thought was foreign to her.

He stood with his foot on the first step, holding the rail with one hand, his bag in the other. "Forgive me, Alice. I should be asking after you. Are you well?"

"Quite well."

"The girls?"

"Indeed. We have set up an efficient little hospital for the dolls. Their nursing staff is superior. You would be quite impressed."

Birdsong chuckled. "Perhaps I'll step in to inspect the facilities before I leave. Thank you for understanding my preoccupation. I will make every attempt to be more aware of your own situation, Alice."

Alice watched him mount the steps and turn the corner at the landing. His footsteps echoed in the stairwell.

The typhus lasted another ten days. No one else in the house became ill, but Martin Birdsong insisted on maintaining the semi-isolation of his patient and Analee. Slowly, Constance regained her strength, sitting up, taking a few steps, then a few more, until finally she was able to walk down the hallway and, with the doctor's permission, greet her girls.

Delia and Maggie were constantly anxious to see their mother. Though Alice kept them thoroughly entertained—playing dolls, taking walks, teaching them rudimentary embroidery stitches, and reading bedtime and naptime stories—they missed their mother sorely. When Alice had told them to be ready for a surprise that afternoon, the girls had jumped up and down and guessed everything from cookies to paper dolls to a new puppy. Their excitement was palpable when Alice announced it was time for them to face the window and close their eyes. They expected that on the count of three, they would open their eyes to some wonderful new thing below them in the yard, like that new puppy they had set their hearts on. Instead, they heard their mother's voice at the door behind them, where Analee supported her. When she called their names, they turned in wild joy, dashed to her, grabbed her around the legs in exuberant hugs. It was all Constance could do to stay on her feet: she clutched the doorjamb for balance while Analee supported her from behind. Alice ran over to warn the children to be careful with Mama.

"You well now, Mama?"

"You tired, Mama. You been working so hard to get well."

"Maybe you need to come play."

"Can we have a picnic now, Mama?"

With warnings from Alice and Analee, the girls began to calm themselves. Constance held on to Analee's arm for support while entering the playroom and for stabilization while sitting in the low rose rocker. The girls busied themselves for a good quarter hour regaling her with enthusiastic stories of their adventures since she had disappeared into the sickroom. They rattled out their sentences in tandem, interrupting one another, finishing each other's thoughts, their heads bobbing back and forth for verification and agreement. Constance's strength began to flag, and the girls vacillated between concern that their mama was too tired, playing nurse to her the way they had to their dolls, and disappointment that she needed to leave again so soon, but they were comforted by the promise that they would get to see her every day now.

As the days passed and the buds of spring burst into full bloom, so, too, did Constance seem to flourish. Her cheeks regained their normal blush. Her steps grew steadier and more assured. She ventured down the stairs and ultimately out of doors, to sit in a wrought-iron lawn chair and watch the girls at play. Martin Birdsong still came daily, often late in the day now. Late enough to stay for supper when invited, which was often. With his presence, the little group of women and the two girls began to settle in with one another, almost as a sort of family, comfortable and secure with one another.

CHAPTER 46

Late on a Monday afternoon, Officer Pulgrum knocked at the door. Analee answered and showed him into the backyard, where the adults were watching the girls at play.

At the sight of him, Constance felt light in her head. Her pulse raced, and her breath seemed to break in her chest. One hand clutched the hand Analee extended to her; the other clasped the collar of her shirtwaist.

He has come for me at last. Constance perceived, but only barely, the firm grip of Analee's hand on hers. She attempted to rise but found her legs too weak beneath her. She felt Alice's hand on her shoulder, pressing her gently down. She collapsed back into the chair, unable to speak. But her breath had returned of its own accord.

"Afternoon, Pulgrum. Beautiful day." Martin Birdsong was taking control of the situation for her. "Mrs. Halstead is just recovering from a serious bout with typhus. Still doesn't have much strength, I'm afraid. Can we be of assistance here?"

"Afternoon, Doctor. Typhus? Haven't heard much about such of late. Have I missed news of an outbreak somehow?" Pulgrum doffed his cap and scratched his lank brown hair.

"No, Pulgrum. No outbreak." Martin reached out to shake hands. "Our patient here seems to have contracted the only case I am aware of at the moment. Such random instances are hardly rare."

Constance felt, more than saw, the sweep of the doctor's hand away from her toward the wharves and the port. A chill swept through her. She took a ragged breath, as if she were trying to stop weeping. She turned her head, searching for her children. Alice had gone to them to distract their attention. Constance took in the scene. They must not witness their mother being arrested. They must not see this. She was acutely aware of the two men's eyes on her now.

"Constance? You're not having chills again?"

Martin was instantly at her side, the back of his hand against her cheek. She was aware enough to know that her mind had gone empty. She glanced up at Martin in helplessness.

"Perhaps we've had you out too long."

She heard his words as if from a distance and felt him lifting her to standing.

"Pulgrum, will you excuse us, please?"

Martin guided her toward the back door. She could feel his bracing support. She was utterly dependent on it. Without it, she would collapse. She could hear Alice and Analee urging the children to pick up the hobbyhorse and the ball and come inside.

"I have something important to speak to Mrs. Halstead about, Doctor."

Constance's head was thrumming; her pulse pounding against her temples.

"As you can see, Pulgrum. Mrs. Halstead is hardly in good health at the moment."

Constance heard, rather than saw, the latch on the opening door, the clack of Martin's shoe against it to hold it as he guided her inside. The children's chattering voices reached her from a distance.

"It's of the most crucial importance, Doctor." Pulgrum's dogged steps followed them onto the porch. His voice sounded as if it had come from somewhere far away, and echoed in her ears. "I beg pardon, Doctor." Pulgrum was not backing off. "This is of the utmost importance. Perhaps if you assist Mrs. Halstead to a seat and stabilize her for a few minutes, I can deliver this news regarding her husband's death."

"Is this really the time?" Martin turned on Pulgrum in a flare of anger.

"I can wait." Pulgrum took a step back.

Constance could feel an opening of the space around her as he did so. She wanted to weep. Would he have mercy on her, after all?

Alice and Analee passed by with the children, who had gone quiet now. Constance heard their footsteps going up the stairs, heard the two women's muffled instructions about dolls and toys, and the closing of a door, the quiet steps of the women's return.

Martin guided Constance into the drawing room. When she was safely seated, she felt his hand again on her forehead, then firmly encircling her wrist to count her pulse. She could feel it pumping hard against his fingers. And in her ribs, her head, her neck. Her fear had taken hold of every cell. She opened her mouth. With everything that was in her, she wanted to scream. But that would terrify her girls. She would not leave them in an even greater panic than her simple surrender, her walking handcuffed out the door, would induce. She had a sense her body might suddenly explode.

"I'll see if I can't get rid of that man," Martin said as he touched the crocheted afghan Alice had tucked around her. "Whatever he wants can wait."

"I assure you, Doctor, unless Mrs. Halstead is still truly ill, my errand here is not one to wait."

Constance startled. She had not been aware that Pulgrum had followed them in from the porch. Martin stood up straight and made himself an obstacle between his patient and the police officer. Alice and Analee backed away but stood firmly behind her, each with a hand on her shoulder.

Pulgrum sidestepped Martin and extended his hand toward Constance, something small and flat in his fingers. A photograph. "We have the evidence we have been seeking to confirm Mr. Halstead's murder." He came closer, waving the photograph for her to take.

Martin was behind him and grabbed the extended photograph.

Constance, now still and numb inside herself, held out her hand. "Let me have it, Martin." Her voice had gone quiet, resigned.

She could see the reluctance with which he relinquished it to her. She examined the faces of the two men before her, one stoic, one afraid. Why should Martin be afraid? Did he suspect the truth? Had the words of her delirium reached his ears as well as Analee's? She felt Analee's grip on her shoulder. Analee knew.

Constance raised the small bit of photographic paper, tilted it in the light. There she was. Not herself, but some bushy-faced young man, turned marginally away from the camera, one imprecise hand raised. There was Benton, off balance, blurred, unrecognizable, his distorted body akimbo, taking flight. And there was the man of her nightmares: the man who had threatened her children, who had tried to extort her money, the wiry, strangely mustached rogue of the Black Hand who had twisted her with fear for her children, for herself. The man who had darted across that train vestibule as Benton fell. There he was, arm extended, his hand against Benton's chest, an expression akin to glee on that threateningly mustached face.

"We have him, Mrs. Halstead. We have your husband's murderer. We apprehended him last night, or rather this morning. Well after midnight. Over in the Quarter. He is in the precinct jail and will remain there until we believe we have everything he has to give us."

Constance sat in bewildered relief, her terror melting only slowly, her fear and guilt transforming little by little as the certainty that had eluded her solidified within her. She stared at the photo, the clear image of another's hand shoving Benton from the train, a hand that had tortured her children. A hand that did not belong to her. Here, finally, it began to sink into her body, her heart, her spirit at last that she was not to blame. Yes, he had been shocked to recognize her eyes, but it had not been the surprise of her eyes that had caused him to lose his balance, to fall to a horrid death. *I did not murder him*, she thought. *I did not kill him with the surprise of my just being there. I did not kill my husband.*

"Where did you get this photograph, Officer? How?" Martin quizzed him.

Analee's hand relaxed on Constance's shoulder. Constance felt the steady warmth of it coursing through her and breathed. Things were slowly making sense to her.

"Well, quite a story there, Doctor. Quite a story. Young photographer came to the precinct last week to give it to us. Seems he was on that train with his family. Had one of those portable box cameras Kodak came up with. Man was letting his little boy experiment with it, taking photos to keep the child entertained. Boy got all excited and ran off to the vestibule door before the father managed to settle him down and give him a book to read."

Pulgrum shifted his weight and twisted his cap in his now free hands. "Anyway, seems those box cameras . . . They really are just a box with some sort of lens . . . So the whole thing has to be shipped back to Kodak up in Rochester to be developed and reloaded. Takes a while. Father got it all back in the mail, flipped through the shots. Nothing but blur, for the most part, and he started to just toss the whole stack. But there was one of an old man with a walrus mustache, which the kids had thought was funny and wanted to keep. And at the bottom of the stash was this. He'd read about Mr. Halstead's death in the papers. Blurred, for sure, but clear enough to see this man pushing him from the train. Clear enough for an arrest, though it's taken us some time to find the devil. Clear enough for a conviction."

Pulgrum reached out for the photo. Constance could not let go of it and stared at the blurred images frozen in space, unmoving, Benton still alive, not dead, looking at that young man he had not known to be her but then suddenly had. The last moments of life, here in black and white, before her. Here in her hand, his last inhalation. She saw the look in his eyes, not on this scrap of photo paper, but in her memory, her being, her deepest self. She saw how he saw her eyes.

Analee leaned over and gently pried the photo from her grasp, then handed it to Pulgrum with only a glance. This was not something she wished to see. Constance looked up then, looked around at all of them, these people around her, this room, this crocheted afghan beneath her other hand. She felt herself pulled out of memory into the moment and into this place from somewhere else, somewhere that did not exist except in that photo. When she became fully present, she took a deep breath, straightened herself in the chair, handed the afghan to Analee.

"What now, Officer Pulgrum?" Constance rose of her own accord.

"We are holding him, of course. He is charged with the murder of your husband. The evidence is clear. He has given his confession. We are trying to take advantage of his guilt to pry important information from him regarding the Black Hand. Bargaining with him in exchange for consideration of clemency."

"Clemency? What clemency?" The idea elicited Constance's clenched fury and her fear.

"A reduced sentence of some sort. A lengthy prison term instead of the death sentence. He knows, actually, that staying in prison would offer him some protection. If he ever escaped, he's a dead man. The Black Hand would see to that. It would spare us an execution."

"Will I be called upon to testify?" She imagined herself in the courtroom, face-to-face with that man, the courtroom filled with spectators, some of them women from the Mardi Gras krewe.

"Possibly. But I believe we can spare you that, ma'am. The evidence we have is clear, though if we could ever locate that young man in the photo, we would need his testimony. We haven't any leads, however, and probably won't spend a great deal of effort to find him, since the evidence we have in the photo is enough for a conviction."

Constance stood very still, staring at Pulgrum in silence. He backed away and gave a curt bow.

"I'm sorry to see you've been so ill, Mrs. Halstead. And to have to leave you with that image of your husband. But it is my duty to deliver this news to you. Perhaps it will bring a bit of solace to your grief to know that murdering bast . . . uh, murderer, has been apprehended and will not only get his due reward but will also aid us in the apprehension of other Black Hand criminals. I do wish you continued recovery, Mrs. Halstead."

Pulgrum donned his cap and nodded to the various occupants of the room. "Good day," he said as he turned and made for the door.

As Pulgrum closed the front entry, the room seemed to empty

of issues that had strained them all, even below their awareness. For Constance, it was empty of any further fear or threat that at the least expected moment she might be arrested, taken from her children, taken from her life. Those gathered remained still, then simply looked back and forth at one another.

"Alice, would you go and bring the children down?" said Constance. "Tell them to bring their dolls. We can all sit together to have a cup of tea. Do we have any sweets, Analee?"

"Yes, ma'am. Indeed, we do."

CHAPTER 47

The atmosphere in the house shifted drastically after Pulgrum's visit, the pall lifting like a dark veil. The closed-in tension evaporated with the opening of windows all over the house, inviting in the fresh air and, with it, the enlivening trills and tweets of chickadees, house wrens, and yellow-throated warblers in their migration. Inside, the house was abuzz with the hectic chores of the spring cleaning. The larger carpets were rolled back, whacked with a broom to give up their hoarded dust, rolled back again over the swept and mopped floor, and all this was followed by several surface runs with the Bissell "Gold Medal" ball-bearing carpet sweeper, which the children loved to help empty and re-empty. Smaller rugs came out into the open, were hung on the clothesline, and pounded with the carpet beater, and the children again were the most enthusiastic helpers, counting up points in an imaginative game at how much dust flew out during a hit. Windows had a vinegar wash, while the clean curtains hung on the line, awaiting the iron and fresh hanging.

In the new room set aside for Alice and the coming baby,

fresh linens covered the bed, their edges embellished with vines and roses stitched by Alice's artistic hands. A small rocking chair covered in woven floral tapestry sat next to the window, ready for nursing, nap times, bedtimes, fussy times, anytime with the eagerly awaited infant. The girls were constantly finding various toys to bring, then deciding this one was too hard for the baby and that one too old, and reappearing with different, softer stuffed bears, which they held squished in their arms, still relishing for themselves the soft give of the plush fabrics. The crib that had been theirs—and David's—stood in one corner, its surface gleaming with a fresh coat of white paint. The girls had tossed so many playthings into it, Alice teased them by asking where on earth the baby would sleep.

"With us, Miss Alice. With us and our baby dolls. We have plenty of room," Delia declared.

Alice laughed, leaned down to straighten and re-pin the oversized hair bow that was forever askew. The love she felt for these children amazed her, these girls who were not hers. Things would change when the baby came. She knew that. They always did. Families reconfigured. Excited adulation turned to jealousy when a child realized that the attention that had been theirs now belonged to another, as her brothers had been jealous of her mother's intimacy with her. Her life here, at best, was uncertain. Over time, Constance might marry again. Alice might become an intrusion on the household. But this island of peace and happiness was all she needed for the present. Everything was in place except the layette, and Constance had assured her that an ample supply of baby gowns remained packed away from her own babies.

The time was approaching swiftly to have all such necessities in place. Alice, with Martin Birdsong's assistance, had calculated the baby's arrival to be in less than four weeks. The baby was lively and, Dr. Birdsong predicted from his examinations, "hefty." Jonathan had been a big boy, over eight pounds, but Alice had birthed him alone, without complications, since Howard had gone to fetch the midwife and failed to return. Her labor had been protracted. By the time Jonathan was born, Alice's exhaustion had made it hard to push. But she had managed to change her position, and then his slick, waxy little body had emerged into the world. There had been no doctor, just as there had been no doctor out on that prairie for her mother. As there had been no doctor for her fevered infant son. Only Howard holding him as he struggled under the cold water of that sink. Until he had stopped struggling. She could not think of that. Howard was gone. She no longer cared to find him. She alone would be responsible now. Howard, whoever he was, who had never existed, could cease to exist. Alice was alive. She existed. And soon this baby, this unforeseen, unhoped-for baby, would be in her arms.

Analee, busy beating rugs, had given Alice a vague description of the small trunk holding the baby things and an equally vague location: "Over to the right a bit, behind a stack of baskets." She would find it. She couldn't stand out here, breathing the dusty air from the rug beatings, however entertaining the girls' game. She was coughing when she opened the back screen and went to get a glass of water. She had been tired these last days of her pregnancy and sat down to rest with her glass of water before she trudged up the stairs to the top floor.

When Constance whirled into the kitchen, Alice looked up in curious surprise.

"There you are." Constance pulled out a chair and sat knee to knee with Alice. "I have the most wonderful idea. No, it's more than an idea. It's a plan."

She took the glass from Alice's hand, set it on the table, and took both of Alice's hands in hers. "Yes, a plan. And here it is.

We've been thinking too small. We've imagined that teaching the girls at the orphanage their basic sewing skills, and then beyond, could equip them for higher-level work. Something beyond the mills. And we've thought they could find work doing alterations and such. And it's true, they can. All that is true." She lifted Alice's hands and brought them down ino her lap for emphasis. "But, Alice, we never thought about creating work for them."

Constance released Alice's hands and sat back, waiting as if her words were somehow self-explanatory. Alice was intrigued, but thoroughly puzzled nonetheless.

"What would that work be, Constance? And how would we provide it?"

"Oh, forgive me! I'm just so excited. And Martin and I have discussed so much, I'm thinking your mind is right in there with ours."

Constance had leaned toward her again, and Alice could see the bright enthusiasm in her eyes. She found herself eager to know.

"Well, here it is. We have the beginnings of a plan, and you are crucial to it. Of course, you are about to have your baby, and you will be quite occupied, but that gives Martin and me the time to organize and raise some funds and find space for a facility and—and I'm running away with myself."

Constance laughed. Alice laughed with her, brightened to hear this new enthusiasm in her friend. True, her veil of sadness and tension had seemed to lift with Officer Pulgrum's news of the arrest of Benton's murderer, but here was an energy and vitality Alice had not encountered before.

"I assume I fit in as the primary instructor?"

"Yes, but for the more advanced skills. You've already prepared several of the orphans and half-orphans well enough that they will be able now to teach new beginners the basics. You see, Alice, we have the makings of a workable system for the advancement of these young women. But we need so much more."

"And where does Martin Birdsong fit into this? Teach them sewing skills for their wounds when they inevitably cut their own fingers with sharp scissors?"

Their mutual laughter melded with the syncopated rhythms of the rug beating outside.

"No, Martin will be helping on the business side. With financing. He's eager to put money of his own into this enterprise, but he's also willing to help raise funding among some of the more charitable businessmen."

"And what enterprise will this funding support exactly?" Alice felt thoroughly puzzled at this point, trying to negotiate a labyrinth of excited words.

"Why, a space and equipment. For a workroom. For dress and costume design. We will turn out to be in high demand among the women of the city. We will support the orphanage in a far more effective way. And we will offer the best design and sewing expertise this Mardi Gras town could ask for."

"Have you thought this out? The logistics seem quite complicated, Constance."

"Yes, too complicated for this one discussion, but here are the basics. While you are busy with the baby, the most highly skilled girls will assume their roles as basic instructors for the younger ones. Martin and I, with Dorothea's help, will locate an affordable space, appropriate and safe, near the orphanage. With additional funding, we will order and install a beginning inventory of sewing machines."

This new plan was coming at her at such a speed that Alice found it difficult to process. Teaching the girls at the orphanage to sew, even to sew with refined skills that might land them more lucrative work, was a long way from setting up their own shop. The management! The marketing! The expense! The whole idea was more than unnerving to Alice. And simultaneously exhilarating.

"That will take such a sum of money, Constance."

"I know. I know. But I believe Martin can raise the initial funding, and as we grow, the work itself will help fund the growth. We will become self-sustaining. With a steady income for the young women."

"Constance, each machine will cost at least two hundred and fifty dollars. That is a fortune. Plus, fabrics and threads and needles and scissors and cutting tables." Alice stopped herself, then continued. "And rent. Or mortgage. And lights and heat in winter."

Alice's mind flew back to Chicago, to her first tiny flat, to the days after Howard's disappearance and her struggle with money, the carefully rationed food, walking to avoid the cost of the city tram. How could they possibly take on these expenses? These financial responsibilities?

She saw Constance's palm come up to quiet her.

"We know, Alice. Truly, we do. But I have to tell you the vision beyond just this. Yes, a basic new machine will cost two hundred and fifty dollars. And it is indeed a fortune. But we would begin with only a few. Perhaps ten. Or maybe only five. We might be able to negotiate with Sears Roebuck on the less expensive machines. They don't need to be like the exotic one from Dorothea. And Dorothea has taken on the responsibility of raising funds from her contacts, and Martin from his business and social contacts. They are both persuasive, believe me. And well positioned for the task."

Alice listened, taking in the hope of such a plan.

Constance clasped her hands and sat back. "Dorothea has contacts, you know, among the powers that be in the city and believes she already has a commitment for a small unused warehouse space only walking distance from the orphanage. She also has someone on the lookout for any used machines. A few seem to be available, as advances have been made in the mechanisms and wealthy women here want the newest innovations."

"That will mean a good bit of maintenance adjustments, probably."

"And you are skilled at that?"

"One has to be if one is to sew. The primary difficulty always is adjusting the tension. It has to be just right for the stitch not to be too loose or too tight. Winding bobbins and threading the needle, of course. These things vary from machine to machine, but not greatly. Now, if the treadle or belts are off, that's a different matter, for which I might need a repairman. However, Analee has been quite adept at helping me with some of my mechanical dilemmas on Dorothea's machine."

"Yes, Analee," Alice continued. "She seems to have an innate talent at a number of things. She could help the girls to learn— not all at once, but as different problems arose."

"Can she help you learn those mechanics, Alice?"

"She has been already. I think I know it, for the most part, from my mother out there on the prairie, where there was no such thing as a repairman. And from working on Dorothea's more complex machine with Analee. I believe, for the most part, we could handle any problems other than the most major and help the girls learn at the same time." Alice almost laughed, imagining herself on hands and knees, working the belts to the treadle.

Constance scratched at her head beneath the relaxed bun. "Of course, in addition, as time passes, these girls will likely fall in love, get married. They will have children and will need to be at home. Our vision is this, Alice. When a girl leaves us, we want her to leave with a basic machine of her own. It will belong to her. She can take in sewing from neighbors, alterations from cleaners, extra sewing from our orders. She will be able to sew at home for her children, her husband. Make school uniforms. The possibilities go on and on, Alice."

"How on earth will each girl have her own machine? Will she buy one used from us?"

The excitement was contagious. This new plan was coming at her at such a speed that Alice found it difficult to process it, yet she sensed a foundation to it, not only for the workshop but also for the lives of these girls, the women they would become, the very lives they would lead. The process could take them into adulthood, could benefit their own daughters and prevent them from becoming half-orphans with mothers laboring away from home. This was a plan that could change the future, give women independence, just with the skills and the means to sew. Alice breathed in the sense of purpose and fulfillment her mother had dreamed of for her—and not through marital dependence on a man.

"Buy one from us? No! We hope to *give* one to her. Now, I see your look, Alice, but it can work. Martin and I have gone over and over the plan. And over! Its success will depend on our fundraising and on your fine-tuned skills and instruction to make this the best workroom in New Orleans. The profits brought in by the girls' work will be used to pay for the machines. It's complicated, I know. And it will be progressive in its fruition. But it can work. I'm sure of it." Constance stopped, then looked around the room as if to orient herself. Alice had a feeling Constance had been in that workroom in her mind.

"But I should let you rest now," Constance added. "I was far too excited after I met with Martin just now to wait any longer to tell you. Go and rest. We've plenty of time for details later."

Constance put her arms around Alice, getting as close as she could get these days, and kissed her cheek. Alice felt the comfort of belonging.

"We are going to do something good, Alice. The three of us can make a difference. Well, the four of us, because Analee will be crucial to our success, as well. It will take time. And the re-working of used donations and things that seem to no longer have value—like the materials for the gown you made for me. We often have donations of things too worn or torn to use for the girls, but with your skills to share, we can put them all to new use. All those leftover materials can be transformed into the making of new lives, Alice. Just think of that."

CHAPTER 48

Constance was off on her explorations now, day after day. Returning home sometimes tired and dejected, but more often full of exciting news about even the smallest discovery. Alice saw her at meals, often shared with Martin Birdsong, who added news of foundational financial support from business associates. At every encounter, he laid his hand over Alice's extended abdomen to feel the baby's activity, or lack thereof.

"Has to sleep sometime," he would assure her. "You've got an active one on your hands, Alice. Or will have soon."

He would take her aside to a private corner, remove the stethoscope from his black bag, and press it to her abdomen where she raised the corner of her skirt. His intent listening always worried her until she saw that smile and nod. He would keep listening, as if to a favorite piece of music, then would ask her if she'd like to hear. Of course, she would. That reassuring rhythmic sound would touch her very heart, then soothe her body into calm reassurance. She would hold one hand over her abdomen, thinking perhaps she could still feel that lulling rhythm, as she handed back the stethoscope, sharing her pleasure, seeing his smile of reassurance.

"Soon," he would say, rolling up the stethoscope and slipping it back into his bag. During his most recent visit, he had begun to ask her pointed questions. "Are you quite ready? Everything prepared?"

"Only the layette to organize."

"Then time to take that on. You don't want to be organizing drawers and arranging blankets between labor pains. Although if anyone could do that, I suspect it would be you."

Alice laughed as he took her arm to return to the drawing room and more talk of the orphanage project. She loved hearing the plans and the vision of a real future for these girls. A change that could be measured in lifetimes rather than second-hand clothes or an extra meal. Now those donated clothes could be transformed and could transform the lives of these young women with them. This century of exciting change in the world could become deeply personal by altering the lives of these girls.

As Martin bid good evening to them, he turned to Alice and actually shook a finger in her direction, like a teacher to a recalcitrant student. "Next time I come may be for a birth. I'm not expecting to help you fold baby clothes."

There was laughter all around.

Alice took his instructions to heart. Indeed, for her own peace of mind, she needed to be done with preparations to welcome this new life she awaited with such hope. She no longer cared about Howard or trying to find him. Chasing after a phantom who might or might not have ever been in New Orleans had kept her on edge, and on edge was not where she needed to be in these last weeks of waiting. The waiting in itself was unnerving enough in the final stages of pregnancy. She no longer required Howard's support. She had hope now for a future on her own, a future of cooperation with men, rather than subservience; a future involved with the creative initiative of women to benefit other women.

Standing by the window, fingers of one hand tracing the smooth edges of the crib, Alice drew back the lace curtain. Below, in the backyard, the girls played an imaginative form of hide-and-seek as Analee retrieved the clean sheets from the line. Back and forth they ran under the hanging sheets, tossing the edges over their heads and over their faces, peeking around the corners, and shrieking with laughter as Analee tagged them. Alice had wanted Analee to go to the attic storage with her, as she would know straightaway where to find the right trunk or the right drawer for various baby items. But Alice needed to get it done and was loathe to interrupt the good times below. Surely there couldn't be too many places to look, and she had her directions from Analee, however vague they might be.

The narrow stairs were more challenging than they had been even recently. Alice held firmly to the railing and took each step cautiously. Everything was becoming more challenging. Alice sensed herself bigger with this baby than she had been with Jonathan. Even sleep had become trying; she could hardly find a way to lie down. Some nights she resorted to sitting up, but her pillow was soft and offered no real protection against the rungs of the hard iron bedstead. Perhaps she might also find some extra pillows stored away, she thought. Now, that would be a welcome find.

As her eyes adjusted to the dim light of the attic space, Alice attempted to orient herself to Analee's vague clues. Somewhere over toward the right, she thought she remembered. Near a stack of baskets? But the only baskets she could see were toward her left. Behind them was a large camel-backed steamer trunk. It was unlocked and opened easily. *What luck!* There were extra pillows, several to choose from, actually. She tested their firmness, pulling them tight in her arms, laying them up to her cheek. One she rejected as being too lumpy, but two others seemed just the right firmness. These two, Alice took and laid on a chest in the hall. She caught her breath a moment before returning to the gloom of the storage. Under the rejected pillow, there were what seemed to be a couple of quilts. Their thinness surprised her, until she remembered that these were made for New Orleans weather, not for the prairie winters. Nothing else seemed to be in the steamer trunk. She clicked the latch shut.

Standing, Alice stretched her back, which now ached when she exerted herself even a bit more than usual. She bent side to side, then wandered about among the chests and odd furniture, scattered in no particular order. She opened a few drawers here and there. In one she found a handful of gowns for a newborn, but that was all. She could quickly mend and personalize them for her infant. There would be time to find those for an older baby, of course. However, infants grew so quickly and required so much attention. Even tired, she shouldn't procrastinate. Now was the time to continue the search and get organized for the coming months. Beyond that chest stood a tall covered basket, perhaps used for diapers? And beyond that a medium-sized lady's trunk. Ah, this must match Analee's instructions.

Alice squeezed between a chest and a ladder-back chair, past the tall basket to the trunk. The clasp was on the far side, near the wall, and she had to tug the trunk round by its leather handles, then use her foot to turn it yet some more before she could manage to open it. When the open top unexpectedly banged against the wall, Alice jumped, then shook her head and laughed at herself. *Everything's so hard these days!* She must sit down. Her roving eyes landed on the ladder-back. It should be easy to lift. She eased it over the trunk and sat down.

Comfortably installed, Alice sat for a minute, regathering herself. Then she examined the top layer of garments in the trunk. As she lifted the tissue paper from the top layer, she had a fleeting memory of her brother wrapping a comb in tissue and playing it tunefully, like a kazoo. White silk spilled into her lap, bits of tulle and lace. The tissue fell to the floor as Alice lifted the yards of delicate fabric. A wedding dress! She covered her mouth with her hand. This had to be Constance's wedding dress. How beautiful it was! The skirt more full than today's styles, the waist a bit higher, the collar beaded to stand high on the neck. It was lovely. Alice could envision how beautiful Constance must have been as a bride. Alice wondered how Benton had felt seeing her walking toward him. Beneath the dress lay a simple veil of not great length, with bouquets of silk roses to poof out at each side, above the ears.

Beneath that, yet more paper. Then a man's suit. This must have been his outfit for the wedding, Alice thought. She lifted the jacket. Hardly dressy enough for a wedding. And what a small man he must have been. She had always imagined him as a medium-sized man. She lifted the trousers. Definitely casual, definitely small. Something fell to the floor. It was an effort for Alice to bend down to retrieve it. *A mustache? A bushy mustache? Wait. And fake eyebrows. Equally bushy.* As she leaned forward, she spotted a man's hat flattened in the trunk.

Alice dropped her hands onto her protruding abdomen, her fingers working the texture of the fake facial hair. Here in her hands were the clothes, the bushy facial hair of the young man in the photo Pulgrum had brought. The unknown witness to Benton Halstead's death. She remembered Constance's fearful reaction when Pulgrum had come to announce the resolution to Benton's murder. Now here were the remnants of that unidentified witness: Constance herself.

Alice sat back. For minutes that seemed timeless, Alice sat. These clothes, this disguise belonged to Constance. What had she been doing on that train? How had she not known that the man who had threatened them, threatened her children, was Benton's murderer? What was Alice doing in this house of unknowns? Unknowns that she had never suspected, never seen hints of. Who was this woman who had taken her in? This woman she trusted? Was Alice safe here in this house as she was about to give birth? The questions piled onto one another, too many to hold. Alice dropped the fake facial hair on the floor.

Leaning into the trunk was difficult, not just from the awkwardness of advanced pregnancy, but from the fear and foreboding that encompassed her. Alice lifted the crushed fedora, felt its smooth texture with her fingers, then threw it onto the floor, beside the eyebrows and mustache, which made even the floor seem sinister.

More paper, somewhat wadded and wrinkled from lying under those unexplainable layers. A fine wedding dress, a sinister disguise, and what else? A stiff envelope with a button closure lay at the bottom of the trunk, its string wrapped tightly back and forth in a figure eight between the two wood buttons. Alice lifted it out and sat back once more. She held the envelope in her hand, flipping it from one anonymous side to the other. There was no label, no handwritten identification, nothing to indicate its contents or its reason for being among this mystifying collection of things. Did she dare open it? Certainly, she was far astray from searching for infant clothing. With a deep breath, she untwined the string. She could not explain the sense of foreboding that took hold of her as she opened the flap and reached inside.

The slick surface and the weight of the contents felt like that of photo paper. Slowly Alice slid the contents from the concealment of the envelope. *Yes, a photo. A wedding photo?* The dim light made it difficult to see. She rose and took two steps toward the louvered light at the end of the attic room. The light through the louvers cast dark bars across the image: Constance, smiling in that beautiful dress, holding a small bouquet of roses. The groom beside her, attired in tails and waistcoat, and smiling full face into the camera, was Howard.

The elusive Howard Butterworth was the murdered Benton Halstead.

Alice's breath came short and fast. Her empty hand wrapped

around the bulge of her abdomen. With the other hand she lifted the photograph again to the barred light. This man was her missing husband, this murdered man buried now above the ground in some New Orleans cemetery, this dead man whose children she adored, whose wife was near to being the sister she had never had. The picture trembled in her hand, and she raised the other to steady it. Her strength was failing. She turned from the light of the window and edged herself onto the seat of a chair nearby. With the back of her hand, she wiped the sudden sweat from her brow, looked again at the image. Though dimly visible away from the light, the image etched itself into her mind, into her very being. As she leaned back in the chair, a box of some sort fell from the seat onto the floor. Startled, Alice stood again, praying that no one had heard, that no one would come to check on the noise.

In silence she stood long enough to still her fright. Disbelief assailed her. She had made a mistake in the dim light. Had mistaken a mere resemblance in the disarray of her emotions. Alice stepped to the window again, held the photo close to her face. Stared at the hard truth.

CHAPTER 49

Here was her husband, her nonexistent husband, the father of the child now kicking vigorously in her womb, the man whose name on her marriage certificate was a lie, the man whose very life had been a lie. Here also was a man who had not deserted her, had not abandoned her to survive on her own. A man, a husband, murdered on his way to her. Murdered in Constance's sight, Constance in disguise as another man. Why had she been there? But she had. Why had she never spoken up, told of this horrid murder of her husband, their husband? But she had been disguised. She had been there in secret. Had Howard—Benton—Howard known who she was? What had she been doing? What *they* had been doing, maybe? Who knew?

Alice's head was whirling with unknowns. With wild possibilities. Doubts. Questions she might never have answers to. Had Constance suspected Benton had another wife? No, who on earth could possibly suspect such a thing as that? Suspected he had another woman somewhere? What if the "young man" Constance had shown up at her door? Alice felt near to collapsing.

She wanted to run. Flee. Escape. But where? And to what?

She could never escape her own mind, her own feelings. There was no escape for that. Not now. Not ever. This was the nail now driven into her life, to hold her very being nailed to her own cross. There would never be a place from which, in which, she would be free of this again.

This stark revelation had become her life. In an instant. She would drag it with her wherever she might be, for as long as she lived.

The sound of Analee opening the door coincided with Alice's gasp of comprehension.

"Sorry, Miss Alice. Didn't mean to scare you so."

Alice turned and stared, overcome by such an excess of thought and emotion that her mind had gone empty, but the urge to flee still impelled her.

"Is you all right, Miss Alice? You ain't took to laboring, now, is you?"

Alice shook her head.

"You don't look so good, honey. You might best sit yourself down in that chair. Maybe you breathing too much dust up here. I should have come with you. Actually, I should have come got those baby clothes for you."

The strength of Analee's support, the firm clasp of her hands on Alice's arms helped settle her back into the chair, brought some semblance of presence back into Alice's shocked reality. As she assisted Alice into the chair, Analee kicked the suit out of the way, reached down to lift the wedding dress and draped it over the side of the trunk. Alice sat, the photo held loosely across her abdomen, where the baby kicked. This baby, fathered by her phantom husband, Howard Butterworth—the murdered Benton Halstead.

"Well, I see you found out the truth," said Analee.

Analee knew the truth? How could Analee know? What did she know? That Benton was also her lost husband? No, she couldn't know that, could she? That Constance had been there on that train?

"She followed him that day," Analee said quietly. "She was desperate to know what he was up to. She didn't kill him. But she hold herself responsible anyhow. She think if she hadn't been there, they wouldn't have killed him. But she's wrong. Them devils would have killed him no matter. Wasn't nobody's fault but his."

Analee knelt before her, slipped the picture from her hand. "I should have come got them baby clothes myself. Don't know what I was thinking."

Alice watched Analee slip the photo back into the envelope, twist the string back and forth around the two buttons to close it. She laid it back at the bottom of the trunk, out of sight. But the image of that impossible double husband had seared itself into Alice's brain.

Did Constance know? Oh God, did the Black Hand know? They seemed to know everything. But maybe only locally. Should she tell Constance? Why had he married both of them, had children with both of them? And, oh God, two infant sons dead.

"You all right, Miss Alice?"

Alice tried to focus, look Analee in the eye, and nod.

"Now you know the truth. That man weren't no good, Miss Alice. She didn't know what he was up to, but he was deviling her for money. And he was gone when he oughtn't be." Analee hesitated. "I'm gone tell you something, Miss Alice. I'm right sure . . . Well, I should say I suspect Mr. Halstead had a hankering after other men, young ones. I heard his stories about where he was, doing what, and sometimes they made sense and sometimes didn't make no sense at all."

The chair felt hard and sharp to Alice. She shifted. *Other men? Men?* Her wedding night flashed before her, and so many subsequent nights, Howard's barely disguised distaste for her body, her small-breasted, small-hipped body, her boy-like body. Why had he married her at all? She was a woman who had fit the shape of his desire. A woman who could legitimize him as a man. One wife had not been enough to prove he was a man?

"She's a good woman, Miss Alice."

Who was Analee talking about? Alice's mind refused to function.

"You seen that yourself," Analee continued. "She just needed to know the truth. They was going to kill him, anyway. He owed them too much money, and she made the mistake to be there. She ain't done nothing wrong."

She just needed to know the truth. *And so, did I*, Alice thought. But the truth was so much more than either one could have known! So much more than Alice could have had any concept of. And more than Constance could yet begin to know. So, Constance must not have even guessed Alice's existence, let alone her marriage to this man, this double husband to them both. In truth, such a thing was not to be guessed. Another woman, perhaps. Another wife? No. Constance could not even now be imagining such a thing, and never would. Alice was the one who knew. The only other one who knew was dead. He had betrayed them both, beyond the wildest scope of betrayal. And for what? To prove he was a man? To whom? Himself? His father? For what?

In the following days, Alice kept to her room. Constance and Analee fretted over her, came and went with food and drink, a book to read, a little vase of fresh flowers from the spring garden. Alice tried to be companionable and decently social. For the most part, she offered fatigue as the excuse for her lethargy. The truth she now held in secret felt heavier than the child she carried, but with no promise of life. Struggle as she might, Alice had no possible concept of what to do with this secret information. Constance had become her friend. The friend of depth she had never had out on the plains. The friend she now loved as she imagined loving the sister she had never had.

There were afternoons when she tried to go outside, drink lemonade with Constance, and watch the girls at play. But that very joy she witnessed between the sisters and in their mother watching their frolic drove Alice back up to her room in unexpected guilt. How could she feel such shame? She was not some mistress, some other woman on the side. She was Howard's wife. She had borne him a son, a son whom she would mourn her whole life, as she knew Constance would mourn baby David. The convolution of it all was terrible to bear.

To further the complexity, Alice now knew that Constance had witnessed Howard-Benton's murder, that she had carried the secret of her presence at his death through every episode that followed: the burden of telling the children, the burial, the visits from the police, the horrifying harassment by the Black Hand, or at least, by the offshoot rogue with the sinister mustache. Alice grieved as much for Constance as for herself. How could either of them find the strength to bear such betrayal? Each of them carried enough.

Now Alice carried this new child, her husband's child, but also the child of Constance's husband. She lay on her bed, hearing Constance outside singing some little ditty with the girls over and over, the accompanying rhythm of clapping hands, and Analee's melodic voice creating a kind of descant over it. She knew this was not carefree. These women were lending their strength to entertain and protect the girls. All while each carried her own burdensome secret. Even the silence between them now was a burden, a weight under which none of them could have the comfort of being who she was. Alice turned her head when she heard one of the girls take a fall and begin to whimper. She could hear the other's consolation and Constance's admonition to "be a big girl now." To be a big girl.

There it was, childhood's primary remedy for every sort of thing that could go wrong. *Be a big girl.* Could she do that now? Draw upon that strength drilled into her all along her journey to womanhood?

Alice let go a deep sigh, rolled from the side of the bed, and drew the window curtain aside. Below, she recognized two women doing all they could to manage the unknown sharing of mutual burdens, doing their best to be big girls. She opened her door and went to join them.

CHAPTER 50

The birth of this child, his child, was almost upon her. She could not imagine how she might manage if she were not here, but how could she birth his child in Constance's house? How dare she commit such a betrayal of this woman she had come not only to love but also admire?

She was lying on the bed one afternoon, struggling with her thoughts, when Constance knocked and peeked around the door.

"Not asleep, are you?"

"No, come in." Alice pulled herself up in the bed, adjusting the pillows behind her as she did. They gave her no ease. She could have no ease now, not only from the pregnancy but also from holding her secret in Constance's presence.

"I brought an afternoon snack, if you'd like."

Constance held out a small fluted bowl of roasted pecans. She knew these were a favorite of Alice's. When Alice took them from her and murmured thanks, Constance sat down on the edge of the bed.

"May I?" she said. "I don't want to bother you."

"No, you're fine, Constance." Alice scooted over slightly to make more room for her.

"Alice, if you feel up to it, I'd like to talk to you. About something quite serious."

Alice's heart began to race. She turned her face to the window. *She knows. How? How could she know?*

"It's about Benton." Constance fiddled with the lace on her jabot. "I need to tell you the whole story."

Alice steadied herself against inevitability, against hearing that somehow Constance had discovered who she was, or perhaps suspected. Was that even possible?

"You will be living with us now. You have become part of our family. Truly. The girls talk about you as their aunt these days. 'Where is Aunt Alice? Is she coming out to play? Is Aunt Alice sick, like you were, Mama?' You should hear them. You have become so very special to them. They even talk about their excitement to have a baby in the house, like a little brother or sister."

Alice shifted, laid her hand over the movements of her unborn baby. She tried to surrender to the thought that Constance knew and had no direct way to tell her. But if this was the roundabout way, it was full of unexpected grace and acceptance. She opened her lips, but nothing came out. No word, no sound.

"In truth, you have become like the sister I never had—more than a friend. So, I owe you the truth."

Alice steeled herself now.

"I've no idea what you may think of me. It may destroy our friendship, but holding this secret means I can never fully be myself with you."

Constance stood, then sat back down. Alice watched with trepidation.

"So here it is, Alice. You saw that photo of Benton's fall from the train. You saw that devil's hand push him. You saw the un-known young man who witnessed all this. What you do not know is that I was that young man."

A confession of her presence. And what more?

"I'm so sorry. I have no idea what you will think of me, knowing this. I was there, Alice. I was there in disguise. So much happened so fast. I have believed I might have killed him."

Constance began to cry. Alice reached for a handkerchief on the side table and handed it to her. She wanted to cry herself—for Constance, for herself. Did she dare tell her own truth? Not now. This was a time for listening, for discovering all she had not known about this man, husband to them both, this man she had never actually known.

"He wasn't ever who he seemed to be."

Certainly not for me, Alice thought. Not his name or his work, not his home, not his family. Nothing more than a mirage.

"I think he tried. I know he tried to be a decent, ordin-ary man."

Married to two wives? *Ordinary* and *decent* seemed ironic.

"He could never be the man his father wanted him to be. Married and settled with a woman." Constance fidgeted. "Well, of course, he was married and settled with a woman. I'm not making myself clear."

Married and not exactly settled with two different women, Alice thought. Her mind was turning bitter.

Constance seemed to hesitate, unsure how much to say. Alice waited. How much more?

"He could never please his father. A man who drank to ex-cess and was often cruel. I have seen it numerous times myself. His father was so afraid that Benton was not the man—not a man—his father could be proud of. I'm beating round the bush. Somehow his father was so afraid that Benton was drawn to other men, especially very young men, boys really. From the time Benton was a boy himself, his father hated him for being different. Beat him for it at times, but mostly with words. Beat him with hateful words. Even after we were married. After we had children. And I saw that Benton was afraid of our own son."

Benton-Howard's father hated his son. Ah, here was a missing piece. If Benton had been a hated son, would that explain his ambivalence toward his own?

"I never saw that difference in him. Not really. I mean, he was different, yes, but I never thought that he was . . . Well, I never thought of that when I got on that train to follow him. I wanted to know what he was up to, why he was hounding me for money, my money from my trust, why he was evading me. It was gambling he was up to on that train. And he lost. Lost a great deal. Then out on that open vestibule, he turned to me. For consolation, I assume. He believed my disguise. He touched me. Only it was that boy he was touching. Until he saw my eyes."

Constance wept in earnest now.

Alice held her breath. Her marriage to this man began to have a different sense to it, her wedding night, his distaste for her body, her body that was so boyish, yet was the body of a woman. She felt suddenly sick. Her breathing quickened. Her husband, two wives to prove to himself that he was a man. Proving he was "normal and ordinary" in desiring women. Too much was making sense. Her head was swirling.

"It happened so fast then, Alice. So fast. I believed I killed him. That I touched him in shock and made him lose his balance. But I couldn't know. That man ran through so fast, and Benton knew who I was, and then he was falling." Constance stopped and raised her head, gazed straight into Alice's face. "All I wanted was to know what awful trouble he was in, why he lied to me and badgered me for money. I had suspected the debts he might be hiding, Alice, so I got my disguise and I followed him. It was true—the gambling and the Black Hand.

You know that already from Pulgrum. But I didn't know when I got on that train. I hadn't any way to know. I couldn't take the lies."

Constance buried her face in her hands. Something shifted in Alice, something tender, something kin.

"And after David died . . ." Constance took a ragged breath. "Oh, Alice, he didn't just die. Benton shook him, shook him, shook the life out of him. Shook him until he stopped crying. I wasn't here, but the children were. They didn't know. They thought the baby was asleep."

Alice's head, her heart, her being filled with the vision of Howard's hands on her fevered infant boy, the cold water closing over his little face, the tiny bubbles rising before she was able to fight Howard's hands away in her own fever. But not in time, not in time. Now this other infant boy dead at his hands. Had she married a monster?

"He didn't mean to do it, Alice. He didn't mean to harm the baby. He meant only to stop the crying. He was a kind and loving father to the girls. It was after David came that he seemed to be less tolerant. I thought he was under stress with his work and travel. Thought he was tired. But then I realized he was still patient with the girls. It was only David's crying he could not tolerate. I had seen him shake the baby, yelling even, to hush him. I would take David from him and soothe his crying in another room. He did not mean to harm him, Alice. That much I know of him. Of that much I am certain."

Alice raised her head. Could she be so certain Howard had not meant to kill their son? He had been trying to get the fever down. The baby crying, thrashing in the water, struggling so fitfully. Howard trying to cool that fever with cold water in a porcelain sink, while she lay sick in the other room. Trying to stop his crying. It was Howard who had cried when the baby stopped breathing, when she snatched the lifeless baby from his trembling hands. Howard choking, mumbling, "Don't, Daddy. Please, please, Daddy, don't."

"I think some deep fear of his father—and of himself—somehow overwhelmed him." Constance's voice shook.

Now Alice was overwhelmed. Her mind, her heart could barely hold so much, barely know where truth might hide itself.

"He wasn't a bad man, Alice. Just a very lost one. Lost from the beginning. I see that now. Now, when it's too late, I see how lost he was."

Constance sat straight, her shoulders heaving, and stared out the window.

"Now you know me, Alice. How lost I may be, too. Now you know the truth of what I am."

Yes, this dear, kind, generous, competent woman, this widow who had carried in her all this time the guilt of a murderer. Alice curled her feet beneath her and slid them over the side of the bed. Now was not the time for even more dire revelation. Perhaps there might never be a time for more. Here was more truth than most lives could hold. Here was trust she could not betray. The quiet in the room felt as if it had physical weight to it. She stood in front of Constance and reached out to take her hands; lifting them toward her heart, its pounding quieted.

"No, not what you are, Constance. But who you are. Come here."

Alice pulled Constance to her feet and put her arms around her.

"Who you are is a treasure to me, Constance. You are indeed more than a friend to me. You have become the sister I have never had. You and I are more closely knit than either of us could have known. We share more than we could have imagined. How did life conspire to bring us together?"

Alice held firmly to this strong woman, and as she did, she knew she was also holding herself. Holding a new strength of which she had not believed herself capable.

CHAPTER 51

Baby Samuel was born at four o'clock in the afternoon on a Tuesday in May. The birth was not easy; the contractions extended far beyond her first labor. A midwife had been brought in to assist Martin with the birth, a small dark woman whose very presence filled the room with comfort, her knowing hands here, then there, adjusting, tilting, raising Alice from the bed to walk, to squat, to breathe. Her face close to Alice with more than instruction—"Breathe now, breathe now. Slow, slow. Now pant shallow, shallow"—breathing with her, panting shallow with her, then slowing, breathing deep between contractions. Martin seemed to turn over charge of the labor to this woman. Because Alice sensed through the pain how he trusted her, Alice trusted her, as well.

Between contractions, he teased her. "You're taking your time, young lady," he said. "Looks like you just want to keep that baby close inside you. You can't just keep that baby to yourself."

She felt his gentle hands holding the area between the small of her back and her abdomen with a steady pressure.

"You want this baby born?"

Want this baby born? More than life itself. This baby was everything for her. She was fighting to bring this baby into life. This was her entirety, her only purpose now to bring this soul to life.

"Good thing you're at home for this," he said.

Yes, at home, she thought. *Yes.*

In another hour, she felt contractions hard and fast, demanding her to push. More unbearably relentless than before. One so sharp she could feel only a narrow point of darkness, a tiny piercing point of light at the center, an escape into nothingness.

And then Martin said, "Ah, here's the head. Push now. Push."

Push she did and felt the pressure ease, the pain slip away.

"Well, Alice, this little boy wants his mama," Martin said. He lay the warm, wet, white, mucus-covered body on her belly as the midwife delivered the afterbirth, cut and tied the cord.

The warmth of that tiny body on her skin overwhelmed Alice with a love she had experienced only with Jonathan. This living reality laid across her belly filled her with light, lifted and expanded her very being. She laid her hands over the slippery little back.

Analee stepped forward and took the infant up in a towel to clean him.

Alice reached up reflexively.

"I'm giving this boy right back to his mama," Analee said. "Don't you fret now, Miss Alice. Just gone get him cleaned up a little bit. Get a diaper on him for you."

Alice watched in awe while Analee went about her ministrations, as if she'd done this all her life. Maybe she had. Beside her, the midwife worked her expert hands into the process, stood beside Analee as she laid him gently into Alice's outstretched arms. She gazed in amazement at his blinking eyes, his sweet baby lips making faint sucking sounds, one tiny hand free of the swaddling waving toward her face. For this moment she had fled Chicago, fled the cold and the treacherous ice and snow. For this moment she had created one magnificent gown of silk and mysterious private symbols. For this moment she had found herself and him a home, unusual as it might be, where he would be the unknown brother to his two half sisters.

"Expect that boy will be spoiled to death in this house full of females!" Martin laughed. "What more could a man hope for? Let's call those girls in here to meet this boy child in their midst."

As the days passed into weeks and the summer heat began to envelop them, Constance and Analee fussed over Samuel—when Alice would relinquish him—changing, powdering, fanning, bathing, cuddling. The girls were ecstatic when one day it was decided they might hold him in their laps, with assistance from one of the women.

"Well, now, ain't that something?" Analee said. "Could be your baby brother. Look at that, Miss Constance. Look like that boy only got the wrong hair. Straight and brown, 'stead of curly and blond. Right near to being a brother."

Right near *is right*, thought Alice. She had recognized the resemblance, the eyes and cheeks, the mouth that bore evidence of a shared fatherhood. She had wondered if she imagined this, if anyone else might notice.

"Yes," she said. "He seems to have my brothers' hair."

CHAPTER 52

Martin Birdsong continued to make regular late afternoon visits, sometimes with the excuse of checking on Constance, sometimes Alice and the baby, sometimes just with news about the success of efforts toward funding the workroom for the girls from the orphanage. On occasion Dorothea would join them.

Their plans became refined and moved toward the complex details: how girls would qualify to work there; how the jobs would be detailed for charges and payment; how much, if any, of the sewing would be done for the orphanage itself or if all of it would come from community commissions, with orphanage work remaining in house with less experienced girls.

Dorothea had put out a plea among the women she knew—there was quite an array and number—for any used machines and had managed so far to have six donations, half of which were practically new and were donated by women who had decided, after a brief try, that sewing was not among their passions. The remaining three machines needed only minor repair, and essentially for related reasons. Something had gone wrong with a machine as a woman attempted to learn to use it, and she had deemed the endeavor too frustrating.

Martin had secured the small warehouse space Dorothea had found, and had negotiated a drastically low rent on the premise that low rent was better than no rent at all. Together the two had already raised three thousand dollars in donations, with a promise of two thousand more within the year.

With the purchase of four new machines and the finalization of logistical details, they should be able to have an official ribbon cutting, with the mayor speaking a few words—though he had never been known to speak a few words, always long winded. The event promised to draw a crowd of New Orleans society, which was perpetually interested in appearing at charity benefits.

On a particularly nice evening, not too hot, and armed with a good supply of Samson's Mosquito Lotion, the whole entourage—Constance, Analee, Martin, Alice, the girls, and Dorothea, who was pushing baby Samuel's pram—set off for a preview of the setup. The new sign, THE POYDRAS INSTITUTE OF DESIGN AND COUTURE, was painted in a combination of white and gleaming gold, outlined in black, and was ready to be installed the day of the ribbon cutting. Constance was beyond excited. Alice was struck silent in hope.

Martin and Dorothea, who were thoroughly familiar with the layout, walked about, chatting and pointing out one feature after another: the wide oak desk and swivel chair for a greeter, who would take initial notes on specific requests; two double-decker paper trays, one side for repairs and one for commissions on new garments. In front of that a three-slotted box to contain design possibilities that Constance, Alice, and now Analee would devise.

The machines stood in two equal rows in back of a new half wall of oak paneling. At the rear, two new dressing rooms waited, with green velvet drapes for privacy. To the side, a triple mirror wrapped around a small podium, on which a client might stand for viewing and for pinning adjustments. Perhaps just to admire herself from all angles. Past the dressing rooms, a restroom to please any lady had been newly installed.

All that was needed now were the girls and the customers.

"Well," said Dorothea, raising her arms for attention. "I have arranged for a round of champagne to celebrate." She leaned down to the girls. "And for you, dear ones, a glass of fresh apple juice."

The girls squealed and clapped their hands!

"Can Samuel have some, too?" Maggie asked.

"Not quite yet. He's still too much a baby," Constance said.

"Aunt Alice?" Maggie pleaded.

"Your mama's right, Maggie. He's too young yet. I don't think he would want any apple juice."

"But how do you know? You could ask him."

"Well, Maggie, he's not quite old enough to tell us."

"Because he can't talk?" said Delia.

"When can he talk, Aunt Alice?" Maggie chimed in.

"Oh, not for a good while yet, Maggie."

"But why? He's making little sounds." Delia leaned over the pram and put her ear to his puckered lips. "Maggie, come and listen." Delia's voice was excited. She patted his tummy. "He's telling secrets. He has a lot of them. Put your ear to him and listen." She raised her face to Alice. "Does he tell you secrets, Aunt Alice?"

Alice nodded. She laid her hands on their blond curls, bent, and kissed them each, her son's sweet sisters, known only to her.

Yes, she thought. *More secrets than anyone else will ever know.*

AUTHOR'S NOTE

Historical fiction by its very nature bridges two realms: that of fiction and of history. The question I encounter often from readers is, "What parts of this are actually true?" I know the question means factual. When I contemplate that question, I always hope to answer that all of it is true, even if not factual. Historical facts are of immense importance and the research for accuracy is demanding and imperative. Without the clarity of extensive research to provide a foundational context, even a gripping story runs the risk of seeming inauthentic. Good research establishes the full extent of place and time, including geography, politics, inventions, methodologies, architecture, food, fashion, and so much more. I find I can hardly write a scene without stopping for some detailed bit of research, usually on daily life, in order to present a world that is as true as possible. Yet the fictional aspect of the story must also ring true for the reader: true in the authenticity, range, and depth of characters and their relationships to each other in the world they inhabit. These characters must be grounded in the reality of human psychology or run the risk of seeming little more than shallow stereotypes, like puppets on a stage.

The research for this novel has been full of excitement for me. I was never an avid student of history as taught in my required classes growing up. Memorizing names and dates and handing them back on a test held little inspiration for me, though I was relatively adept at doing so. Finally in college, I had a professor who sat on his desk and plied us with the stories that make up history. I was mesmerized. Now I find some of my greatest fulfillment in the discovery of exciting details from the past. I am in love with history. It seems that many of us are. Much of that history is surprisingly, sometimes alarmingly, timely to our current world.

The turn of the century in 1900 marked an era of great advancement and innovation. People were inspired, ebullient with expectation of what undreamed-of-new thing might come next. Amid those dreams were a growing desire and commitment among women to gain the right to vote. Though it would take another two decades for that wish to come to fruition, women had already been working for suffrage for years. On the surface, a Mardi Gras ball might seem trivial, yet wherever women could manage to take leadership in the context of patriarchy was significant. The two balls put on by the women of Les Mysterieuses, the first all-female krewe of New Orleans Mardi Gras, were part of that larger effort.

In researching the Leap Year ball, I discovered one very interesting detail. The year 1900 was not, in fact, a Leap Year, because the number cannot be divided by 400. However, all references to this ball refer to it as justified by Leap Year. Perhaps these ladies simply took the license of a normal four-year period between Leap Years to validate their great event without the relevant mathematics. Some of them, like Dorothea, may have known, but proceeded anyway. And none of the New Orleans gentlemen tried to stop them. This is an unusual incident in which historical accuracy conflicts with historical facts.

In another note on timing of the ball, festivities were scheduled in the period between Twelfth Night and the actual Tuesday of Mardi Gras.

Various national monuments added significant symbolism in the design of Constance's ball gown. Of particular interest is her attempt to recall the words of Emma Lazarus's poem, "The New Colossus." Those words are as iconic to us today as the Statue of Liberty itself. Lazarus wrote the poem in 1883 for an auction to raise funds for the pedestal of the statue. Only in 1903 were her words inscribed on a plaque at the base of the pedestal. During those two decades the poem could be found, other than its original, only in catalogs preserved from the auction, one of which Constance's father had guarded carefully.

The research for this book has been extensive. I have made a sincere attempt at factual accuracy for that turn of the century culture between Chicago and New Orleans. The characters and their experiences in this novel are totally fictional. My hope is that this book presents both historical accuracy and human authenticity with an underlying truth that is timeless.

ACKNOWLEDGMENTS

Let me begin by expressing my gratitude to all those un-known people who over the years have contributed to the preservation of a rich trove of historic information pertaining to the New Orleans Mardi Gras. I am especially indebted to the skilled librarians at the Howard-Tilton Memorial Library of Tulane University and at the Williams Research Center of The Historic New Orleans Collection for their enthusiastic contributions to all aspects of my extended research; to The Historical Novel Society, for resource guides on food and weather research; and to Graham Greer, Reference Librarian of the Newberry Library in Chicago for valuable information on the Illinois Central Railroad.

As always I am deeply grateful to Jotham Burello and the faculty and writers of the Yale Writers Workshop for their wise and encouraging support, especially to Kirsten Bakis and Lisa Page. I will always owe a special thanks to Jotham Burello for creating the opportunity for me to meet my outstanding agent, Mark Gottlieb of Trident Media Group. It is because of a simple exchange with Mark that this novel exists as is. In answer to the question, "What next?" I proposed a deep psychological study. When Mark replied, "Sounds like a historical mystery," the sparks were lit for this remarkable adventure into the past. And to my editor, John Scognimiglio, of Kensington Publishing Corporation, for his unfailing kindness and respect for all that I wished to accomplish with this novel. It has been such a pleasure to work with someone who understood the complexities of character I wished to convey and directed his editorial guidance toward fulfilling that goal. I am indebted to Rosemary Silva for her meticulous copyediting of this manuscript and to the graphic designers at Kensington for their stunning cover design; to Vida Engstrand, for her unflagging support and expertise in publicity; and to all the unnamed staff of Kensington Publishing who have worked to bring this book before the reading public.

To my dear friend, Dian Winingder, who introduced me to the city of New Orleans and to the culture of the all-female krewe of Iris, including a memorable ride on her float for Mardi Gras, I am more grateful than I know how to express. I am appreciative also for her keen eye in reading the manuscript and advising me of New Orleans details, from mapping street layouts to instruction on the rituals of Mardi Gras balls. It was Dian who introduced me to Henri Schindler, renown Mardi Gras historian, whose expert guidance and authoritative contribution of visual imagery rounded out my descriptive sense of this historic time and place. Numerous other New Orleans friends, who will recognize themselves without naming, have offered knowledgeable guidance in my research of New Orleans culture and the historic development of Mardi Gras.

I am indebted to friends and family for multiple skills needed in writing this book: to Jody Franco and Maxine Suzman for their generosity in sharing with me their skills in bead embroidery; to Bernice Cox and Mary Margaret Cox for their skill and patience in teaching me to sew, beginning at a very young age on old treadle machines, and to them both for teaching me the fine art of embroidery; to my grandmother, Addie Nelson Dunlap, for the early experiences of sitting at her hearth, working with her as she stitched magical quilts on her quilting frame; and to my father who repaired my mechanical disasters and taught me to drive his old Model T Ford. I am immensely grateful to have had the experience of an overnight train ride from Memphis to Chicago and to my friend, Edna Bacon, for our shared love of the "Windy City." Sandra Fenstermacher, I am not only deeply indebted to you for your dear, steady company, but also most appreciative of your keen eye for birthmarks.

Many thanks to Dr. E. J. Tarbox for meticulous reading of the manuscript with a keen eye for detail and his love of history and research; to Tom Parker, though he doesn't know me, for preserving a very fragile copy of a 1906 Illinois Central Railway Guide and making its treasure of information public; to all those unnamed who made access possible to invaluable information and images from the historic American Railroad Journal. And to Deborah Lieberman, for her expert guidance through this writing process and her constant admonition to "keep it on the page."

Finally I am forever grateful to my family: my husband, Ray, who has supported me and believed in my efforts, and to my children, Brad McPhail, and Melissa Williamson, without whose incisive wisdom this book would not exist.

**Please turn the page for a very special Q&A
with Diane C. McPhail!**

1) **Q:** So much of your debut novel, THE ABOLITION-IST'S DAUGHTER, was based on actual historical characters and events. Is the same true for THE SEAMSTRESS OF NEW ORLEANS?

   A: All historical fiction is anchored in history, but not necessarily on actual people and incidents of a given time. Unlike THE ABOLITIONIST'S DAUGHTER, this novel is grounded in general historical context and events, but specific characters and events of the plot are fictionalized. New Orleans in 1900 was the setting of a grand ball put on by *Les Mysterieuses,* the second all-female krewe of Mardi Gras. Women who aspired to greater freedom and control, pre-Suffragettes if you will, took advantage of the 1900 Leap Year to stage this grand event. In fact, since the year could not be divided by 400, it was not an actual Leap Year. However, the first ball had been in 1896 and the ladies proceeded four years later as if it were a Leap Year.

2) **Q:** The Black Hand and Storyville play such a part in this novel. How much of those two aspects of organized crime are based on history?

   A: The Black Hand and Storyville played an integral part in New Orleans history. Storyville, established by municipal ordinance and named for alderman, Sydney Storey, who wrote the guidelines, was the district of regulated prostitution in the city from 1897 to 1917. Prior to such regulation a family might wake up one morning to find a brothel ensconced next door. Storyville conscribed one strictly defined section of the city, a sanctioned red-light district, thereby confining the approved illegalities and protecting property and culture in the wider areas. The Black Hand, or New Orleans Mafia, was an organization of Italian gangsters engaged in the extortion racket. They

were known for threatening messages demanding delivery
of money, signed with a warning hand imprinted in heavy
black ink.

3) **Q:** The Poydras Asylum for Girls plays a vital role in the
book on several levels. What were the orphanages in the
city like and why were there so many of them?

A: New Orleans was a center of various epidemics—yellow fever, primarily, as well as cholera and typhoid—that
regularly left large numbers of children orphaned, or half-
orphaned, in the terminology used to indicate a child with
only one living parent. Because such parents often were
unable to care for their children, the orphanages provided
shelter and education. The city was full of such institu-
tions of all denominations and color, and were the recipi-
ents of dedicated support from New Orleans citizens. In
general, children of younger ages, especially siblings, might
be housed and schooled together, but as they moved toward adolescence, were always separated by gender. Focus
was generally on religion and trade skills.

4) **Q:** Symbolism is a subtle but important component of
Constance's ball gown. How did that symbolism come
about and did such symbolism play an actual part in
women's move toward greater rights for themselves?

A: Yes, symbolism of various sorts was an important aspect of women's clothing, especially as related to the first
women's krewes and then the Suffragettes. The Mardi
Gras ball encompassed a wide range of symbols in the
choice of themes and *tableaux,* specifically as an unspoken
means of emphasizing the strength and leadership of
women in history and mythology. For the Suffragettes,
proper attire was of vital importance to elicit respect for

women as they marched and protested. The three colors they chose to wear—white, purple, and gold, or sometimes green—symbolized purity, loyalty, and a nod to the sunflowers of Kansas to honor Susan B. Anthony. Later they began to wear diagonal sashes in these symbolic colors over their white clothing. Constance's gown becomes a collaboration in the transformation of defined societal norms. The process awakens the creative energies of both Alice and Constance to find and integrate the symbolic essence of both women, expressing power while remaining subtle and even incognito.

5) **Q:** Dressmaking and skills in stitching and embroidery are crucial to both plot and character. Could you talk a bit about those skills? Did you need to do a lot of research about them or were you already familiar with them to some degree?

A: The dressmaking and stitchery were, in fact, one of the few things in the novel that required very little research. I grew up sewing, beginning with a miniature "toy", but fully functional sewing machine I received when I was about five. In high school, I made most of my own clothes, learning from the women in my family and even from my father, who also sewed.

My embroidery and stitching skills came through the women in my family, as well as the community. In recent years, two close friends have shared their advanced skills in beading and bead embroidery. I love combining these skills to create unique jewelry.

6) **Q:** This era saw the advent of the sewing machine, among other new inventions. Could you talk about some of the history and any experience of your own?

A: For the history of sewing machines, I did need a fair amount of technological research. In its earliest advent, there were multiple efforts to create a mechanism that would lock two separate threads into a single stitch. Ultimately the stitch evolved that even today with our computerized, electric-run machines varies little in its basics from the stitch of those early treadle machines. By 1900 sewing machines had become common household items. I learned and sewed on essentially the same treadle machine as Alice and the girls in the orphanage, with all the maintenance that requires.

7) **Q:** 1900 was a time of great technological innovation. Was there anything in the way of new inventions that took you by surprise?

A: Indeed, there was. If anything needed little or no research, I thought it would be Dorothea's car. My father bought an old Model T Ford when I was about nine or ten. He loved that car and I loved riding in it, standing beside him with my arm around his neck. When I was old enough to learn to drive, my first lessons were in that car. Then I lived in France as a student with a family whose antique cars are now in the museum at Le Mans. I went on rallies across France with them in caravans of antique cars. So I confidently began to write about Dorothea driving, describing the gearshift and clutch, the steering, the accelerator. All I needed at the end of the scene was the make of the car. Imagine my astonishment to learn that all cars at the time were electric, with no clutch, no accelerator, not even a steering wheel, but a throttle and tiller like a boat.

8) **Q:** How did you go about your research for the book?

A: Research of any kind is always an adventure. When New Orleans is the base of your research, it is an even more enjoyable adventure. I rented an apartment in the French Quarter for a couple of years after Katrina, so knew my way around to some extent. I had ridden a float for the Iris parade, an historic all-female krewe, and had attended one of the grand balls of Mardi Gras. When I was invited to speak about THE ABOLITIONIST'S DAUGHTER on a panel at the Faulkner Festival there, I made time for a longer stay, with extensive research in various museums, especially focused on clothing and styles, then long days in the archives at Howard-Tilton Memorial Library of Tulane University and at the Williams Research Center of The Historic New Orleans Collection. Of course, the time arrived when I had to return home and work online, but given the material I was researching, even that was an adventure. One of my greatest challenges for research was to determine the coupling without vestibules between train cars prior to the Panama-Limited.

9) **Q:** In addition to New Orleans, Chicago plays a major role in the novel. Was there anything in your research of that city that surprised you?

A: Chicago is one of my favorite American cities. I took the train with an overnight sleeper from Memphis to Chicago when I was in college. I have returned to Chicago a number of times with a friend to visit the Art Institute. For me, it is such a beautiful and comfortable city to explore. So I was entirely amazed to find in 1900 the unpaved streets, mud deep, icy in winter with plank boardwalks for pedestrians. I had naively expected to find at least cobblestoned streets. I was also intrigued to learn how the streets were named, numbered in one direction, of course, but in the other alphabetized so that according to letter, you would know how far you were from the state line.

10) **Q:** You have talked a good bit about your research for historical accuracy. Are there other underlying goals that inspire your writing?

A: Oh, yes. Perhaps even more so. I want to present my characters not only as fitting appropriately into the era in which they are presented, but as thoroughly human as possible. I endeavor to present them in the full complexity and depth of our psychological and emotional makeup. None of us is "all" of any one thing; the best of us have flaws and the worst of us carry a woundedness that contributes to terrible outcomes. As a therapist myself, I have a deep desire to present the reader with characters who convey that human complexity.

THE SEAMSTRESS OF NEW ORLEANS

ABOUT THIS GUIDE

The suggested questions are included to enhance your group's reading of Diane C. McPhail's *The Seamstress of New Orleans*!

1. Two female protagonists of equal importance do not often appear in novels. In addition, there are other important female characters in this novel. Which of the characters did you like most? And why? Whom did you most closely identify with? And why?

2. Dorothea is a powerful woman in numerous ways. How did you perceive her in the context of the immense change at the turn of the century? What do you think about the efforts of these women to affect change in somewhat "disguised" ways, using the way things were to shift the culture?

3. The Gibson girl look was the fashion of the day. Thanks to Charles Gibson's drawings, we are romantically familiar with this beauty standard today. These trends also gave rise to a sporty spirit for tennis and bicycling, and thus greater freedom for women. Yet the "pigeon breast" distortion of the female body required corsets that thrust the spine forward at the top and backward at the bottom. What are your thoughts about the resulting levels of confinement, containment, limitation and the mixed messages, not just about the body, but also about who women were expected to be?

4. Constance's ball gown has to conceal her identity. Ironically, its design and development foster a process of revelation. How do you see that process working to help bring Constance to a greater authenticity of herself? How does it fall short?

5. Constance's gown is the result of authentic female collaborative efforts. How do you perceive that feminine collaboration in the gown, in the ball, in the orphanages,

in the rise of suffragists? What might other female collaboration look like? What progress has such collaboration achieved?

6. In Alice's skills there is the strong theme of the mother-
daughter relationship through stitching. Do you have
any similar skills that you acquired through a relationship with a mother figure in your life? One aspect of
their stitching is the recycling of used items—torn, discarded, scrap pieces—to create beauty in utilitarian necessities, such as a quilt. The same might be true of
numerous other ordinary skills, such as cooking and sav-
ing seeds, and other creative and community endeavors.
What are your thoughts about using castoffs and leftovers to create beauty and utility?

7. Did you know the tragic history of yellow fever, which
led to the large number of orphanages in New Orleans?
Were you surprised to learn about the half-orphans living in those orphanages? What are your thoughts about
the training those children received? What parallels do
you see today in terms of diverse groups of children in
our educational systems? Can you draw any compar-
isons between the yellow fever epidemics and the unexpected Covid-19 pandemic at present?

8. Napoleonic law in what was the Louisiana Purchase protected women's rights to ownership and property in
ways not available in other parts of the country. Was that
a surprise to you? Are you aware of any instances in
which women's rights continue to be impinged? For example, only a few decades ago, wives could not obtain a
credit card, sometimes a bank account, without a husband's signature.

346 *Discussion Questions*

9. Storyville arose out of a need to deal with the problem of prostitution. Without regulations, one could wake up some morning to find a brothel ensconced next door. Were you surprised to know that New Orleans had a district for regulated prostitution from 1897 to 1917? What are your thoughts on this means of controlling prostitution? And on the rise of the Black Hand? How do you see the power of its corruption connected to politics?

10. In the complexities of this novel runs a deep spiritual theme. Did you find that hidden or apparent? In what aspects of the book did you find it? What was your response to Father Joseph and the idea of "catholic" (with a small *c*) as completely inclusive? What are your thoughts on Benton and Howard as authentically human? What psychological aspects of upbringing and history contribute to that humanity? Is the resulting psychological/spiritual makeup that of a villain or a victim? How do you experience the relationship of Alice and Constance in light of that theme? And Martin Birdsong?

Bonus Question: What do you imagine it would be like for Alice to continue into the future burdened with the secret she carries? Could it possibly not be a burden? How do you imagine that she would be able to manage, and why? Or if you believe it impossible, what do you imagine as the outcome?